SACRAMENTO PUBLIC LIBRARY

1/2014

I0634273

TELL NO LIES
═══ BY ═══
BARBARA RHINE

BRAVURA PRESS • 1440 BROADWAY SUITE 1020 • OAKLAND, CA • 94612
TELLNOLIESNOVEL.COM • 510.451.1180 • COVER DESIGN: RBLACK.ORG

This book is a work of pure fiction. References to real people, events, establish-
ments, organizations or locales are intended only to provide a sense of authenticity
and are used fictitiously. All other characters, and all incidents and dialogue, are
drawn from the author's imagination and are not to be construed as real.
Tell No Lies. Copyright ©2014 by Barbara Rhine. All rights reserved. Printed in the
United States of America. No part of this book may be used or reproduced in any
manner whatsoever without written permission except in the case of brief quota-
tions embodied in critical articles and reviews.
The UFW Eagle and Si Se Puede trademarks are used with permission of the
United Farm Workers of America.
E-book versions of this book are available at Amazon Kindle, Nook, Kobo and
ibooks.

ISBN: 0615998828
ISBN 13: 9780615998824
Library of Congress Control Number: 2014907376
Bravura Press
1440 Broadway, Suite 1020
Oakland, CA 94612
(510) 451-1180

For Demi and Selena

"Tell no lies...claim no easy victories."
Amilcar Cabral
African Independence Leader
1965

CHAPTER ONE

At 7:00 a.m. the doorbell woke her. She pulled on her worn bathrobe and ran down the narrow stairs to the apartment entrance.
A vague shape silhouetted against early light solidified into someone
she knew—Charles.

"Carolyn," he said, and then, "Carolyn Weintraub. I'm in trouble.
I don't know where else to go."

The words came out in a rush, yet after that he just stood there,
a morning paper and a shopping bag full of clothes tucked under
his arm.

Now she was awake. Carolyn ran her fingers through her tangled
curls, hoping she looked all right, and opened the door wide.

"What in the world are you talking about?" she said.

"You don't know what went down at Freeman? This could be dangerous for you, Carolyn."

"So?" she said. "A friend needs you and you turn him into the
street? For God's sake, Charles Brown, too long since I've seen you,
no matter what. Come on in."

Charles stepped into the building, followed her up the stairs two
at a time, and the second they got into her apartment, shut the door.
He sank onto her soft, brown Salvation Army couch, so far down
that his knees almost hid his ears, just the way he used to look in her
parents' living room so long ago.

1

Handsome, always handsome, Carolyn thought. Tall and slender, skin the color of coffee and cream. His soft, mobile lips quivered, and his dark brown eyes held onto a blank spot on her wall. Even his clenched fingers trembled. She sat down beside him.

"Turn on KPFA," he told her. "Yesterday they were doin' that wall-to-wall coverage of theirs, and that way you won't just get the pigs' version."

Elbows braced on his thighs, he buried his face in his hands while she tuned in the radio:

Prison authorities at Freeman Penitentiary are still investigating the cause of yesterday afternoon's explosion, which resulted in the deaths of four prison guards and two prisoners. The blast came while Nyame Jones, political prisoner known throughout the world, was being transferred from the visiting area back to his solitary cell in the Adjustment Center. Authorities have alleged that Jones, after taking the dead guards' keys and releasing others from their cells, made a break for his own freedom across the middle of the heavily guarded yard, where he was shot in the torso and the back of the head from two towers at once. We received word some time ago, and we do not know if this is still the case, that the entire prison is on lockdown, with all inmates stripped naked and lying facedown while officials search for weapons.

Here the announcer cut off to read a new notice, his voice somber:

Nyame Jones, a leader of his people, has just been pronounced dead from gunshot wounds sustained yesterday in the disturbance at Freeman Penitentiary. Nyame Jones is dead.

Charles lifted a ravaged face and emitted a harsh sob.

"Add him to the list," he said. His voice rasped like it was being drawn across sandpaper. "Malcolm, Martin, George Jackson, Fred Hampton, and Li'l Bobby Hutton. So many black men dead and gone." He got up to switch the radio off and sat back down on the sofa, elbows at his knees again, head hung down even farther.

"God, Carolyn," he mumbled. "I must have been about the last one to see the man alive."

"You were in there?" she asked.

He spread the morning paper out on the low coffee table before them. She took In the headline: "Brown Sought for Freeman Murders—Warrant Says He Brought in Bomb." She gazed at the picture underneath, a police mug shot of Charles with a huge head of hair, a patchy beard, and an angry stare.

She swallowed hard and willed herself to stay composed. She read the whole article while his head rested on the sofa back, eyes closed, lids fluttering. The last time she had seen him was October, three months ago, right after her summer in the San Joaquin Valley with the United Farm Workers union. She ran into him, looking good as usual, at a party. A striking black woman hung on his arm, one of many companions he'd had over the years, all of whom, starting with Gwen Washington—especially Gwen Washington—made Carolyn feel plain.

Two days after that encounter—October 5, 1973, Carolyn had found out her mother had pancreatic cancer. By the end of November her mother was dead, just like that. Carolyn hadn't regained her news habit yet. Otherwise she would have known, she told herself; otherwise this wouldn't have caught her so much by surprise.

She touched his knee. He didn't wince or draw away, but he sucked in air like a man who was afraid he would drown. A violent breeze rattled the room's wooden window frames.

What had happened in Freeman? And what did Charles have to do with it? She wanted to ask him up front, but she stopped herself. Ever since the townhouse explosion and the bomb at the University of Wisconsin, the word among those who alluded to these things was "always operate on a need-to-know basis." And for good reason: folks had died. First, three members of the Weather Underground. and then that innocent guy who was working late at his lab. Stupid. Awful. Yet push the people around enough, and sooner or later they'll get angry.

But Charles was a good person, and whatever he had done during that visit with Jones must have made sense. Probably nothing had happened at all; probably he was being framed. She couldn't find out now. When he wanted her to know, he would tell her.

"Have you eaten?" she asked instead. Charles shrugged his shoulders as though he could care less.

"Let's talk it through," she said in a quiet voice. "What are your choices?"

He opened his eyes and looked right at her, so upset that she expected tears. None came.

"I've got to get out of here," he whispered. "I've got to run."

"Oh God, Charles, this is too hard." She wanted to take him in her arms like she would a child, but one look at his closed face told her that was impossible.

"Are you sure you have to leave?" she asked. "What if you turned yourself in?"

"Four pigs died in there, Carolyn. I'll be their revenge." He was still for a long moment. "I'll join the black underground. But it's gonna take time."

If there was a black underground on the West Coast, she thought, and if they didn't hold Charles responsible for Nyame's death. Would they trust him? Would he trust them?

"So we've got to figure out another place for right now," she said in her best practical tone.

He nodded.

For the first time since her mother's death, the crushing depression lifted. She had a reason to be here. She was needed. The trees outside the window, bare branches shifting, rattling in the winter wind, glittering in the chilly morning sun, seemed to have come alive.

"You don't have a single idea of where to go?" she asked.

He was clutching his arms, shivering. The frigid air came right through the cheap window pane. They didn't know how to build for the cold out here in California, she told herself. She had realized this after she got to Chicago for college. After Charles had cut her loose. She got up to turn on the heat.

"My cousin Stanley," he murmured. "In Fresno. I think he's my only choice."

"Family, though," she said as she settled back onto the couch next to him and drew her knees and feet up to the side. He didn't move, but maybe he felt warmer with her close by. "Won't the cops question him?" she asked.

"Pigs won't find this guy. No one in the family but me even knows where Stanley lives."

Carolyn had no idea whether Fresno was the best place. But if he couldn't rely on political allies because the police would head right to them, and he couldn't count on family or known friends for the same reason, where would he go? Where would she go if she had to disappear?

"Should you call Stanley first?" she asked.

"Can't use the telephone here," he told her. "You're political. Might be tapped."

"You could do it from a pay phone."

"I don't want to be out on the street in daylight," he said.

The newspaper lay on the table between them, his picture staring up at them both.

"I could call, then," she said.

"He'll never trust all this coming from someone he doesn't know. I can't think of one single other person or place, Curly." Charles pulled out the nickname he had given her when he was a UCLA man who knew how to tease a girl still stuck in high school.

Now, over a decade later, two years shy of thirty, a wave of old associations washed over her. Seventeen, and could not stop thinking about him. Fascination with the contrast in skin color, hair, facial features, anything and everything that had to do with race. Endless musings, all internal, never uttered, about what was similar—the skin not that much darker, the hair in tighter curls, that was all. And what was not—his nose and lips, so broad, so thick.

Obsession with a certain spot behind his collar bone, traced over and over with her finger whenever they made out, which was whenever they could. First in her mother's living room as soon as the folks were safely upstairs; later in the family's old Plymouth when she disobeyed orders not to see Charles. And in public, too. On the beach, in the park, anywhere he thought was safe enough. When they were alone, she felt unbelievably sexy. Nothing but awkward, though, whenever they were with his brother or friends. And agony if he ever asked her to dance, though it was all she wanted in the world. She was utterly clumsy, while he was unbearably cool.

The hurt when he stopped calling, more hurt when he showed up at the next party with Gwen Washington—white but tanned, tall, slender, and sleek, with bangles on her arms. She would never forget how Gwen looked when she danced. Like all of them back then, long boots and short skirts, but no black tights to cover what lay between. Just snowy white underpants that flashed when Gwen gyrated, with her little up-and-down hop that meant no one could look at anyone else but her. And not just her, but that particular part of her. Carolyn had never seen anything so provocative in public, before or since. One glance at Charles's face as he danced by Gwen's side, slow and subtle, told Carolyn that if she had ever had him at all she had lost him now. After that she suffered for hours, spread across her child-hood bed. She emerged into long, solitary walks through her parents' Baldwin Hills neighborhood, suffused with a vague excitement for what was to come. Charles had hurt her, yes, but he had also freed her to leave all that high school bullshit behind and get herself to the University of Chicago.

What about your elegant date at that party last fall? She suddenly wanted to hurl at Charles Brown. Not worth much if you can't count on her in a pinch, is she? Face it, though, she told herself. This man she cared for was in her living room, on her couch, in despair.

She got up from the sofa and stood where Charles would have to look up at her, then took a deep breath.

"I'll drive you to Fresno."

For a second she thought he hadn't heard, so she cleared her throat, prepared to say it again.

"You'd do that for me?" He gave out the soft exclamation and lifted his face. Next he was on his feet and hugging her, his lanki-ness awkward over her compact form. They stepped back from one another at once.

"But don't use the phone, okay?" Carolyn said. "And let me cut your hair."

"Hey girl, don't you be takin' no scissor to me. This is black folks' hair."

He bounded down the hall to the bathroom, and her heart soared in an absurd excitement.

"I'm gonna shave, that's for sure," he called back at her. "Quincy brought me a razor, but how about scissors and a hand mirror? I think I can clip this bush myself." His voice was muffled; he must have found the shaving cream and lathered up already.

"The drawer to the right of the sink. You sure you don't want help?"

"Naw, I can do it. Get your stuff together, Curly; let's get on the road."

She looked at her watch. Eight fifteen. By ten they should leave, eleven at the latest, during that lull after the commute when the mothers and toddlers were on the streets. A glance in her bedroom mirror revealed adrenaline-pumped blue eyes staring out from under the loose mat of wild dark curls that had inspired the nickname. Fresno was less than two hundred miles from the Bay Area, but it hadn't changed one bit since the fifties. Her friend at the UFW had told her that, so she would understand how to dress when they went to court to get the strikers out of jail. Now she would have to put on something more conservative than her usual flannel shirt and faded jeans.

She stripped off her clothes while a list formed in her mind.

"Do we need more money?" she yelled down the hall.

"Always," he replied, and she smiled. This exchange was familiar.

Go to the bank, squeeze in a load at the Laundromat. Better not stop for gas with Charles in the car. She could fill the tank while the clothes dried. God, though, all this would take time.

She pulled on stockings and shifted her body into a hardly worn gray wool skirt, white jersey, black jacket, and black low-heeled shoes. She stepped in front of her full-length mirror, smoothing the jacket that ought to be ironed and crisp. Thinner than usual: the one benefit of being miserable about her mother. Her office clothes, which she hadn't worn for two years, fit better than before.

If she hadn't done anything illegal yet by having him in her house, she would the minute they walked out the door. Motherless child with a fugitive on board.

She brushed at her hair to tame it, stuffed laundry into her duffel bag, called down the hall to tell Charles where she was going, and headed out.

When she returned two hours later, he was at the door. He looked so different from the wild man who stared out from every newsstand that relief swept over her.

"You've done it, Charles, truly." She gave a soft whistle. "Straight as a ruler. Ready for that other world."

Clean-shaven and close-clipped, dressed in creased tan slacks, white starched shirt, sports jacket of a chestnut and ocher weave, dark brown polished shoes, he appeared as respectable as he had seemed eleven years ago when she first met him.

"You too, girl. Lookin' good, lookin' fine." He waved a brown and yellow striped tie at her and lifted a wiry eyebrow to inquire whether he needed it. She shook her head, so he rolled it up and put it in a pocket.

"But what if we go into a restaurant or you have to talk to your cousin in a public place?" she asked. "You don't want someone who's seen the mug shot to hear your first name."

"Good point, Curly. I've always been partial to James myself."

She was amazed at how quick he was, how eager to slip out of his identity. But then again, Charles had never been easy to pin down.

"Okay, so James it is. How about James Sweet?"

Sweet now, and he had always been sweet to her, even as he moved on. She had told her college roommate that Charles was the first boy she ever loved. Had he loved her back? Over the years, off and on, he kept in touch, so he must have cared for her in some way.

"James Sweet, not so bad," he mused. "Not bad at all. I found me a satchel in the hall closet. Okay to take it?" She nodded. "Then let's move, girl, before the *po*lice charge in your door."

She ran to her bedroom, smoothed down her striped afghan as though it mattered to make her bed, grabbed some last things, and wrapped a small silver-framed picture of her mother in a sweater. She zipped the duffel bag tight and scribbled a note for her neighbor: "Rick, out of town for a while. Do you mind taking in my paper and the mail?"

That ought to do it; she didn't owe him an explanation. When she left town, whatever friends she still had after dropping out of sight since her mother's death would assume she had disappeared to continue grieving.

She bade a silent farewell to her room, shouldered her bag, and met James in the front hall. Small suitcase in hand, bathed in sun from the high window that faced south, he still looked as though he would never get warm again.

The point of no return. Yet you had to help a friend in trouble, didn't you? It wouldn't be right to stop now. They started to tape the paper on Rick's door, decided it ought to be in an envelope which Carolyn ran back to get, then clattered down the narrow staircase at last.

Keys in hand, Carolyn pretended to be confident while James blinked in the bright light. As she strode forward to unlock the back of her Volvo station wagon, a woman walked toward them. If the lady recognized him from the picture, Carolyn told herself, she would get him in the car and still speed straight out of town. But the stranger went by with a friendly nod. Her knees weak, she watched James put their luggage into the back.

A cloud bank massed in the west. She had her raincoat over her arm, but what about James? Not safe to chase one down now; they could buy things later if they had to.

She got in, reached over to open James's door, and started the engine. She knew her '67 automobile needed warming up in the winter, but now that they were out here she couldn't stand to wait. The motor coughed and the car jerked forward as she pulled away from the curb and headed for the freeway.

CHAPTER TWO

James put on his dark glasses. Their familiar weight felt right. Should've done that first thing, fool, he told himself. He flipped down the visor to check himself in the mirror. The shades covered everything from cheekbone to eyebrow.

He tried to calm his thudding heart. On the move. Better than sitting around trying to decide. But the new James Sweet was one scared motherfucker. He swallowed hard and shivered.

They drove past the Claremont Hotel and up into the hills where the rich lived. Never had been in a single one of these houses. Damn, this cold, windy weather made him shake all over.

The heater kicked in around the time the road straightened out and became Highway 13. Warm enough at last to try and settle back, he closed his eyes. James Sweet, from here on in. Not so much to give up a name, slave name at that, come right down to it. Slave on the run, so frightened his heart might burst, his eyeballs might pop out of his head.

He twisted around in his seat to make sure no one was following them. To his relief, cars were passing on both sides. He shut his eyes again and managed to be still.

"James," Carolyn was saying, as if she was talking to herself. "Jimmy. Jimmy Sweet." Jimmy Sweet, did it have a black sound?

"Like Jimmy Cliff," he muttered. "You know, *The Harder They Come?*"

"'You can get it if you really want it,' she sang in a low voice. Not bad on the tune. "'But you must try, try, and try, you'll succeed at last.'"

Nyame Jones—now that was one brother who had tried.

Only, the trouble was in the title of the song. "'The harder they come, the harder they fall.'"

Nyame Jones, shot down, just like Jimmy Cliff at the end of the flick.

"Come to find out," he told her, "my auntie couldn't have spoke more true. She told me I'd be in a mess of trouble if I hung around the leader types."

Carolyn had no reply, unusual for her.

Black men, always run to ground, like dogs. And now Nyame. Worst thing was, the new James Sweet himself had been the very bullet to Nyame Jones.

Damn, don't think about it. Can't afford to fix on what you cannot change.

He checked the dashboard and, sure enough, Carolyn had the dial right at fifty-five. It was conspicuous to go this slow, yet anything was better than a stop for speeding. He wanted to turn on the radio, but after the warrant and the picture in the paper there was nothing to listen for except how many pigs were gonna be lookin' for him, which he did not exactly want to know. Silence was better; silence was okay. Thank the Lord Carolyn didn't rap on like she could. Not that he'd mind the sound of her voice, but then again she might expect him to chime in. There was so much she could ask him that he didn't want to answer.

He leaned back, the line from another song playing over and over in his head. "'Got me runnin', got me hidin', run, hide, hide, run, anyway you want me . . .'" Now who the hell was it wrote that, anyway? Marvin Gaye was too sweet for that line, more like Lou Rawls, but it wasn't him either.

Try and compose himself. He ran over the events that led to this point.

At 12:45 p.m. on Thursday, January 23, 1974, Charles Brown had parked his old blue sedan in Freeman Penitentiary's outer lot. He loaded Mars Bars, JuJu Beans, Juicy Fruit, and Pall Malls into his briefcase alongside files, yellow pads, pens and pencils, envelopes, and stamps, and hurried over to the meeting place. He'd hoped to be there first, but Kwesi was already in place, lounging against the granite wall by the iron gates that guarded the prison's main entrance.

They shook hands, clasped wrists, and ended with quick, clenched fists. To his relief Charles accomplished the motions with ease; he'd been known to screw up the order.

"Here's what it is." Kwesi talked so low it was barely above a whisper. "I see you have your own shit and all, but you also got to take this in. Nyame wants to type up the notes for his book."

He handed Charles a green metal case with a leather handle. It was little but solid from the weight of the portable typewriter inside.

"You think they'll let him have it?" Charles asked.

"The pigs'll always give you a hard time," Kwesi answered. "But that's exactly why you got to try every little thing you can think of."

He fixed Charles with a hard stare.

"Nyame wants this," he repeated. "You go on in there and make sure he gets it. Report back to the office when you get through. I'll be expecting you, hear?"

He glided away without waiting for a reply.

Charles hitched the typewriter case under his right arm and used his left to pull open the heavy gate. What did the man's attitude matter, so long as he got to meet Nyame Jones? Jones's *Not For Sale*, a book of letters to his lawyer had hit the best sellers list, and now he was supposedly at work on *Blood on Their Hands*, a blueprint for the revolution. Not everyone who worked for the Prison Rights Project got to meet Jones, and Charles was excited. And nervous. He trudged up the long road lined by Mexican palms to the high walls, guarded by gun towers every forty feet.

Once inside, he gave his name to the uniformed deputy behind the window and settled in with his other files for what Kwesi had told him would be a wait. Ten minutes while the heavyset cop found a folder that must have contained Nyame's visitor list. He ran a stubby, thick finger down the page, then lumbered over to ask Charles his name again. After that it was a long hour and a half while Charles tried to read his other files, and the cop thumbed through papers on his desk. Finally the officer ambled over to the window and called him up there again.

"Well, son, you ready for your visit now?" he asked, as though Charles was responsible for the delay. Why exactly was it that way out here in California? The cops still reminded him of ones he'd seen in Florida as a kid. This one, for example, was the type who dragged out every action, every word, every syllable. A pig. Not that he'd been raised to call names, but when people acted like animals, he felt they deserved it.

"Been ready since I got here, sir. How about you?" Charles moved toward the door by the window.

"Okay, then. You just do what I tell you and we'll all be fine."

Still in slow motion, the pig pressed a button, and Charles pushed with his shoulder at the wood door, heard a muted click, and went through. Three steps took him across a square room to the next door, where he tried the knob. It was locked. He willed himself to stay calm. This was the pigs' way, he told himself. A long moment later another click sounded, and the second door opened.

He found himself facing the first officer and two more: all whiter, taller, broader, and fatter than he was. A metal detector, a table, and yet another door flanked them.

"Well now, young man," said Slow Pig. "We're gonna have to search you. So take everything out of those pockets and put it all on the table."

Charles obeyed, walked through the detector, then stood quietly while the second officer patted him down. Slow Pig emptied his briefcase, opened each cigarette packet, pen, piece of chewing gum, and candy wrapper, and leafed through the other files Charles had brought, page by page. The third cop just stood there.

"You'll have to leave these files out here with us," drawled Slow Pig.

"They're confidential," objected Charles. "Lawyer-client communication."

"Well I don't see no lawyer standing here right now, do you?" Slow Pig asked the others. "Anyhow, nothing goes in there unless it pertains to the case of your particular prisoner. That's the rules."

They would read everything in those folders and copy what they wanted, but what could he do?

Charles shrugged.

"Your jacket now," Slow Pig demanded. When Charles removed it, the one who had done the pat-down turned it inside out, searched each pocket, and moved his fingers up every seam and over all the lining.

"What's that other item you've got with you, son?" Slow Pig gestured at the typewriter case, alone on the table now and untouched.

"A typewriter," Charles answered.

"What's that for?"

"To type."

"Just what are you tryin' to tell me here, son?"

"Mr. Jones needs that typewriter. To type up the notes for his next book."

All three guards smirked. The nearest deputy ran his fingers over the outside of the soft cover and placed the case on the floor with the rest of Charles's things. Then they watched while he turned his jacket right side out, replaced the items for Nyame into the briefcase, loaded up with the typewriter, and stood there.

He didn't let the second double door take him by surprise, and after he was through it, a fourth deputy, this one a smaller guy who looked Mexican, led him without a word into a visiting room about twelve feet square. The deputy left him alone.

Charles sat in the one chair available and glanced around. He was at one end of a table, maybe four feet long, that ran under an iron screen, with another straight-backed chair directly opposite. The screen, which bisected the entire room, was in two parts that came up from the floor and down from the ceiling. The top and bottom latched by sections, and the one over the table had been locked into a position that left two or three inches of space underneath.

They hadn't given back his watch, money, or keys, so he had no idea how long he sat there. The tables were gray metal and brand new. No scratches, no writing, no marks. And nothing on the walls, not even a picture of the warden. Despite the winter weather, a conditioner hummed from somewhere, and the air was stale and cold.

Finally the door on the far side of the room opened, and the prisoner, held at each elbow by two deputies—one black and one white—entered the room.

His wrists were handcuffed to a two-foot chain in front of his waist; his legs were shackled to a longer manacle. Yet Jones, his muscled biceps rippling out from under the sleeves of his green jailhouse issue, looked more powerful than his guards and chains put together. Charles had read in his book that his chosen name, Nyame, was from the Ashanti tribe in Ghana, and referred to the highest God among lesser ones. The authorities had tried to break this man's spirit every which way they knew how, but here in the flesh, with his size and his grace, it appeared that the threat to his enemies would be eternal.

"Power to the people." Jones raised two clenched fists in greeting, as far as the short chain would allow. "Welcome, my man, to my humble abode. And how are you on this very fine day?"

"Very happy to meet you, sir," Charles said. "And I am truly fine, from this moment on."

Charles fell into the rhythm of Nyame's formal speech at once. He couldn't take his eyes off the man's face. High cheeks and wide nose that could have been carved from teak, chestnut eyes and a grin that split the black of his skin like white lightning. His expression managed to exude the magic dignity of an African mask, but one with human warmth. Charles felt privileged to be in his presence.

Nyame sat down, and his guards left through the door they had entered. So much the better: now they would be alone.

"Since I am a man in prison, I have one primary request." Nyame's voice was low and sonorous. "Have you, by any chance, brought cigarettes?"

Charles got the treats out of the briefcase and passed them under the grill. Nyame, adept despite his fettered wrists, pocketed all but one pack of Pall Malls in his coveralls.

"You have made me a happy man, sir," he pronounced, beaming as he tamped two cigarettes out and slid one under the screen to his visitor. "I hope you will see fit to join me in this small gratification of mine."

"Indeed I shall," answered Charles. He hadn't smoked for two years, but he would have shared anything with this man.

Nyame lit his own cigarette, then scrutinized the art-lesson ad on the back of the matchbook as though he might enroll tomorrow. On closer examination Jones looked older than his forty-two years. Deep vertical lines scored both cheeks, and his luxurious Afro was gray at the temples, receding at the top. The wrinkle between his brows could have been an inch deep. Then again, he had lived more than most. He tapped the matches under the screen to Charles, who lit up. Both men inhaled with deep satisfaction.

"So, my new friend," Nyame intoned. "I am always interested in a fresh view. Tell me, how would you describe this great movement our American black nation is building? What factors must yet be brought to bear for the moment of revolution to come about?"

"We need education," answered Charles. "And jobs."

"And where does pick up the gun enter the picture?"

"That time may come."

"Perhaps it's in the here and now."

As the two talked politics, Nyame tossed in references to W.E.B. DuBois, Frantz Fanon, and Regis Debray, and Charles realized the man had read everything he had and more. Eventually, though, Jones must have feared the visit was about to end, because all at once he crushed a half-smoked cigarette under his foot and turned to business.

"What have you brought besides trifles?" he asked. "What do you have that I can *use?*"

Charles emptied the briefcase at once, passing along yellow pads and writing and postal supplies, but after Nyame had examined all this, still he did not seem satisfied.

"Nothing else?" he demanded.

"The typewriter, of course," said Charles. "I almost forgot."

He lifted the slim case from the floor under his chair. Then Nyame, eyes bright, did a strange thing. He tore a sheet off one of the legal pads, wrote a note, and slid it to Charles.

"Open the case and show it to me," it said in a slanting childish hand. James was startled, but he obeyed at once. He unzipped the cover and took out a tiny Olivetti typewriter of metallic blue, so small and light it almost seemed a toy.

"Pass it under the gril!" came the next message, written in such a hurry that the final word was misspelled.

Charles tried to comply, but, slim though the typewriter was, the space at the bottom of the screen was not quite wide enough for it to slip through. Damn the guards; they probably knew this all along. Both men spent a moment trying to push or pull it past, but the screen, locked into place, would not budge.

"Open the cover," scribbled Nyame, desperate in his haste.

The lid of the well-crafted machine rose smoothly under the pressure of Charles's thumbs, and then he began to understand.

Beneath that lid, molded into the circular well that should have housed only the aligned shafts of typewriter keys, was a substance the color of pea soup, which looked like modeling clay. A metal cylinder, about an inch and a quarter long, stuck through the middle of it. This odd item, the diameter of one of the cigarettes they had smoked, was dull like an old dime. From it protruded two rubber-covered copper wires, their stripped ends turned away from each other, gleaming.

"Remember Algeria?" wrote Nyame. Charles nodded, his mouth dry, his fingers shaking alongside the deadly typewriter.

Was it Frantz Fanon or that movie, *Battle of Algiers*, that had described it? Plastique. The weapon that had driven out the French. Easily hidden under women's robes to pass it through the *gendarmes'* checkpoints. And embedded in its center was an electric fuse, which meant that if those wires touched . . .

"Lift out the bomb," Jones wrote, "and slide it under the screen."

Charles's mind, floodlit by the prisoner's insistent stare, lined up his alternatives. He could tell Nyame no, turn over the evidence to the pigs, insure that his hero would be at their mercy for life. Then he'd face Kwesi on the outside.

He could say no to Nyame, shove the plastique right back into the typewriter, and try to get the hell out of there without giving anything away. And *then* face Kwesi on the outside.

Or, he could—

"Now!" Jones murmured. He was still, like a slow-moving flood, exuding all the power of his majestic voice into the one lone word.

Charles obeyed and dug his fingers, oh Lord Jesus keep me safe, into the typewriter's well to pry out the plastique. It gave way from the keys smooth as could be, holding their imprint as though it was kids' clay. He held the soft shape at arm's length before him, like a child with an offering to his made-up God.

Nyame positioned his hands on top of each other and nodded. Charles flattened the mass between his palms to make it thin enough. Careful, so careful not to disturb the small sinister cylinder. The plastique felt cold and stiff to the touch, then smooth and warm at once.

He pushed it under the screen. At first it stuck to the table's surface, but then moved easily toward Jones's broad eager fingers. A quick flick of the palm and the lethal object disappeared into the same large pocket that held the candy and chewing gum. Nyame tore the notes he had written off their pad and slid them under the grill toward Charles. In that instant the door behind the chained man opened, and the two deputies who had brought him in reappeared to take him out.

"Dare to struggle, man," said Jones as he stood, fists clenched at his waist. "Dare to win." He flashed his pearly smile and was gone.

Charles made his fingers work to close the typewriter back into its holder. He had just slipped the damning notes into his briefcase when his own escort entered from behind. He felt like he couldn't breathe, like he might pass out, but he managed to walk back through the first set of double-locked doors. Out by the table the same three deputies as before waited for him.

They would bust him right there, he was certain of it. But instead they took his things, motioned him through the metal detector, handed everything back—his watch, keys, pocket change, and the extra files—and escorted him through the second set with no delay.

Once again, he found himself on the outside, facing the palm-lined avenue. The landscape looked the same, but Charles understood one thing very well: his life—he himself—had changed.

He willed himself to stroll, not run, down the road between the palms. His mind still raced between the alternatives, back at the cell, back when he still had a choice.

Should he have turned Nyame over to the pigs? Impossible. A betrayal of everything he believed in.

If he'd said no and walked right out of there, every black militant from the Panthers on would've been after him once word got out, and if the police caught wind, they'd want him too.

He hadn't quite decided, though, and then came that one word—issued with the magnetic force of a spell cast by a shaman. Charles had obeyed. Now he was more scared than he ever thought he could be.

He swung the familiar Ford onto the highway back toward the Bay Area, and for a couple of minutes he felt a little better.

Damned car had chosen this day to run right for once, wouldn't you know; otherwise, he never would have made it out here. He'd slid into a precious parking place on Ellsworth first thing this morning, two doors down from the PRP office. He'd gotten out whistling "I Got Sunshine—on a Cloudy Day," even found himself thanking the Provider, as his auntie always referred to her God, for the Temptations. Then he'd seen Kwesi, leaning on the cracked yellow stucco right beside the office door, waiting.

He had strolled along the sidewalk, meaning for Charles to stay with him. Secretive little guy, the type who liked to brag about his black belt. Never would say a thing inside the office, which was bugged for sure. Charles fell in step and walked straight on into the setup, just the sucker Kwesi had needed.

Charles shuddered now as he drove, the freeway almost clear of traffic. He wanted to speed but willed himself to stay just under the limit. He became aware of a buzzing in his ears. Anger—and fear.

Nyame was an intelligent man. He'd use this power with wisdom, wouldn't he? Oh Provider, let that be true. Child, you ain't seen danger like this before. Maybe the pigs would never know. Sure as hell Nyame wasn't gonna be the one to tell them. Only a half-hour had gone by; nothing could have happened by now.

He flipped on the radio, set at the all-day news station. The announcer's voice was frantic:

"There is a dire situation unfolding at Freeman Penitentiary—there's been an explosion! Two officers down, maybe more! And prisoners killed; no way to know how many. It's chaos out there, and no press has been allowed anywhere near the scene, so there's not much more to say right now. Except that it's serious—very serious indeed!"

At this Charles began to shake so hard his teeth chattered. Every other second he looked in his rearview mirror, but there was nothing unusual there. His eyes swept each access road for the wave of patrol cars that would have to be hurrying out to that godforsaken prison, but they must be coming from another direction. He snapped the radio off then on again and all around the dial, but no station had any more detail than the first. All he could do was drive.

He headed home, the sun setting to his right in a wash of orange and vermilion that filled him with dread.

By the time he got back to Oakland it was dark. He wanted nothing more than to go to his apartment at Telegraph and 32nd Street and climb into the bed where he'd opened his eyes that morning in such a good mood. Free, black, and more than twenty-one had danced through his head as he'd dressed for work, enjoying the feel of his chambray shirt, his jacket with the leather elbows, even adding a tie when he'd remembered he had to go to the lawyer's office to report on what was in those files. He'd just about stoked up the Meerschaum pipe he'd bought himself the day he got into UCLA, but he had told himself in his father's voice to wait on that, wait until he went back there and earned the BA he'd run out on. This very morning, less than twelve hours earlier, Charles had even dared to imagine himself in law school one day.

Now it would never happen. The pigs had to know he was the last person who saw Nyame Jones before all motherfuckin' hell broke loose—they'd be all over his place. Now he couldn't even go home. He drove aimlessly through the streets of North Oakland, trying to decide what to do.

He stopped at a pay phone and called Quincy, his main man, his friend who he'd planned on meeting after he got the case ready for the parole board, kick back, and take a toke or two of Q's amazing dope, find out what was goin' down over at the Panthers office where Q spent his days.

"Hey, bro, how's my man?" came Quincy's rock-deep voice. Charles was so glad to hear it he just about cried.

"I need to see you," he said.

"Whassup? Hey, you hear about the shit came down at Freeman today?"

"Yeah, I heard. And I was out there right before it happened."

"Don't you be tellin' me any such thing! We got to be gettin' off this telephone then, right now. Where are you?"

"Broadway and MacArthur."

"Too close. I'm a meet you over at Eli's, you know where that is?"

Eli's Mile High Club. Hadn't he been there with Quincy more than once? At least no one had to give the location over the phone. Too bad the name had even been mentioned.

"All right, man," he muttered. "I'll be there."

He hung up the telephone, drove the five minutes over to Grove and 36th Street, and sank into the dark and quiet place that became a blues club later on at night, packed with writhing bodies.

He ordered a beer, waited until the bartender was safely occupied on the telephone, then dug the crumpled notes out from the briefcase he still carried as if it might save his life.

He wished it could have turned out to be his imagination, but there was Nyame's childish handwriting scrawled all over two sheets of a yellow pad. Charles ducked inside the deserted bathroom where he crumpled them up and burned them over the toilet bowl. In this place everyone smoked. No one asked what it was you were puffing on.

He held the burning paper as long as he could, then dropped it with a little yelp when his finger caught the flame. The blackened mess sizzled when it hit the water, then lay there, right on top. He flushed, but the sluggish thing regurgitated black fragments, once, twice, three times, and then he couldn't get any response from the handle at all. The ash floated on the water, and his fingers shook worse than ever.

He walked back to his table okay, but the next time he glanced down, one finger oozed bright red blood where he'd used his teeth to tear a hangnail to the quick without even knowing it. He wrapped a napkin around it hard, pulled hard at his beer, and went back over again how he'd gotten into this mess.

"How'd you like to meet the man hisself?" Kwesi had whispered to him as they sauntered to the corner of Ellsworth and Haste streets. "Nyame Jones, just you and him?"

And Charles, fool that he was, had said yes right off, no questions asked. They'd reached the corner of Haste Street, where all the churches were, near the University. Kwesi had told him he'd see him at Freeman, showed him a quick clenched fist, and headed off toward his car.

Charles had called him back, agitated.

"Hey, man, I just thought of something. Damn! I'm never gonna get into Freeman."

"Why the hell not?" The little guy was getting impatient now.

"'Cause of my record."

"What'd they get on you, man?"

"Well it was just civil rights and all that. Me and Marlon Brando even got hauled in together with a hundred other people once. A Torrance real estate office where they didn't want no bloods in their fancy new suburbs. My last charge was a felony, battery on a police officer. Free Huey in downtown LA, you know,

Darryl Gates's turf? First they kick your ass, then they lie in court and send you away?"

Kwesi looked bored and Charles felt foolish. Of course, he'd heard and lived things a thousand times worse. A horn honked and some blonde girls leaned out of their car, laughing like crazy.

"Where'd you land up?" Kwesi asked him.

"Got knocked down to a misdemeanor, so I spent six months in LA County. Nothin' like Soledad or Freeman, none of that shit."

He sure had been glad to get his middle-class ass out of there though, and he made certain that would happen as quick as it could by obeying every one of their chicken-shit rules. And that's exactly why he admired Nyame, who just would not take mistreatment from the white man, no matter how many times they threw him in the hole.

They stood on the corner for a second while Kwesi thought about it. Long enough for three or four long-haired college kids to whiz by on their bicycles.

"Hey, don't you be worryin' yourself none," he said. "We've already arranged it. We put your name on Nyame's visiting list, just like the rules said, so they could check everything out. That was a month ago, and ain't nobody said a thing. You just be ready to meet the man, all right?"

Then Kwesi left him there like a fool.

He never had fit in with Kwesi and the others, not really, given the protective shell he'd been raised in. Still and all, though, he'd learned a couple of things, even before he left home. Class, for one. He might have come up in a neighborhood where everyone had a fit if you didn't mow your front lawn, but Carolyn Weintraub, first white girl he'd ever touched, or rather Carolyn's spreading house in Baldwin Hills, behind all its diachondra and ferns and shit, had taught him how middle class for whites in the middle class would have meant rich if they'd been black.

Next came the riots, or the Watts Rebellion as his brother Ronnie would say. Whatever you called it, after all those looters risked being burned alive for their canned food and TV sets, he understood just how bad off his own people were. So he'd decided to shed his privilege, thrown over an academic scholarship to UCLA in the middle of his first year, and joined the Movement.

Of course his mother and auntie had just about died. School nurse and school librarian, no child of theirs was gonna run wild in the streets. Even though neither one of them had seen his father in ten years, they called the man up where he taught at Bethune-jive-ass-Negro-College in Florida to try and change Charles's mind. But he never had gotten on with his dad, and he wasn't that surprised when after jail time the old man said he wasn't any son of his no more. So he'd paid his dues, but still, as it turned out, he was simply the perfect patsy.

"We've already arranged it." Those were Kwesi's exact words. Arranged a month ago to send his motherfuckin' ass to jail.

The Mile High Club's front door heaved open, icy air rushed in, and by the time Quincy was halfway over to the table, Charles was on his feet, moving toward the only man who could help him.

"Calm down, man," were Quincy's first words. He set a large brown shopping bag down on the floor and shoved it under the table with his foot. "Be cool. Let's not attract any notice, bro. That ain't gonna help nothin' now, is it?"

They sat again, and Quincy ordered two more beers.

"You been back to your own place?" he asked Charles as soon as the waiter left them alone.

"Naw, not yet."

"Well don't. I brought you clothes and a toothbrush. Don't you even think about showing your face there. And don't send anyone, either. They'll just be followed straight back to you."

Charles sat back to digest this advice. Next Quincy asked him what happened at Freeman, and listened without a word to the whole story.

"What'd the pigs say when you first came in the door?" he asked when his friend stopped talking.

"Nothing. Just told me to wait."

Another blast of cold air, and two foxy ladies came in with a white guy who carried a guitar case. Charles turned his face down to the table. The place was starting to fill up.

"And how long did it take after that?" Quincy asked.

"An hour and a half," Charles said. "At least."

"Time enough to check every damned criminal register in the country," Quincy murmured.

"But the pig just sat there at his own desk," Charles said. "I watched him."

"Did he ask if you had a record?"

"No."

"Social security number?"

"Nope. Nothing but what I've told you."

The cold air destroyed his shred of warmth all over again. White girls this time, with their guys from Cal. They glanced through him and Quincy as if they weren't even there.

"So, just like that, they let a recently charged felon into their maximum security prison," said Quincy.

"Yeah. After looking through everything I had with me except the typewriter case. Then I'm in a room with a screen that could've been up for me to pass Nyame the typewriter itself, yet it was pulled down so it wouldn't fit. It doesn't make sense."

"Yes it does. They were in on it."

"The whole damned force?"

"Just takes a guard or two."

"What I'm gonna do? Should I turn myself in?"

"You'll die if you do that."

The words lay flat on the red Formica table between them. Charles picked up his beer, ran a finger around the wet rim it had left, and drank it down, before he could come up with a feeble reply.

"Just life in prison." He laughed in a nervous squeak. "No capital punishment in California anymore. Caryl Chessman was the last one executed, remember?"

"You'll die in jail. Pigs will get you. They don't take kindly to it when some of their own go down. You gotta split, man."

"Where?"

"Cuba. They're taking political refugees from the US these days."

"Cuba. Damn. Seems far away."

"Only ninety miles, man, just your basic ninety miles. Plus they got a lot of bloods down there, and Spanish ain't that hard to learn."

"I'm gonna have to think about all this."

"That's cool, but in the meantime we shouldn't even be together. Pigs know me and all the other Panthers' front men like we're their left hand. Who you got to go to?"

Everyone so far had passed through into the other room where the music would be, but now two black men came in and settled nearby, their pea coats radiating the cold.

"No one up here in the Bay Area but you, Q. Most of my friends are in LA."

"That's where your family is too, right? Can't go there. And you shouldn't be here, either. Think of somewhere else."

"I have this cousin in Fresno."

Stanley, on his father's side, his uncle's half-brother's son. His mother and auntie didn't even know where Stanley lived by now, so the pigs wouldn't be able to find out. Stanley, the family fuck-up, which was why Charles had liked him so much once upon a time. He'd be reliable in a situation like this. Wouldn't he?

"Better get somewhere fast," said Quincy. "I'll collect money, bro. I can promise you that much." Quincy was on his feet, ready to move away from there.

"Hey now, when I'm gonna see you again?" Charles's voice betrayed his panic.

"When you get a safe telephone number. You call me at home." Quincy emptied his pockets and pushed the crushed bills and loose change across the table.

"Better yet, have someone else to make the call. Give the number in code, every number but the first goes up one. Can't do the first, 'cause ain't no phone number that starts with zero."

"Then what?"

The piano in the other room sounded a note; the guitar started to tune up. The bartender lifted an eyebrow—did they want more drinks? Charles shook his head no. Then they better be ready to go, the man's glance said. The door opened every other minute now.

"After I have the number I'll get right out to a pay phone, I promise you that," Quincy said. "I'll call you back, and we'll figure out how I'm a get some more money to you. And I'll contact some brothers in the underground, too."

"How long you think that's gonna take?"

A string of blues chords sounded from the other room. Music written for him, along with every other pathetic brother around the place, thought Charles.

"Hard to say," said Quincy. "You got to lay low until then, though, you hear? Don't think I'm deserting you, man. I'm a person that does what I promise, but I got to go. Won't help either one of us if they catch us together. Don't go back home, and don't use your car no more, either."

With that, Quincy was out the door.

In his wake of cold air, Charles counted the money. Twenty-three dollars and forty cents, plus the five of his own he had in his pocket. Maybe enough for a Greyhound ticket to Fresno, but the police would watch the station.

He looked in the bag, a whole outfit of brand new clothes. There hadn't been time for Quincy to shop; must've been something he had got for his own self. Wasn't it just the other night they'd commented on how they were the same size? Suddenly he felt like crying.

He drained his beer instead and made himself go out into the cold street, now deserted as the music started up. He looked in both directions. Maybe Q had waited for him after all, or maybe someone else he'd rather not find: the pigs, Kwesi, someone sent by Kwesi. All he saw was asphalt, yellow in the glow in front of the club, dark as sin underneath the freeway to his right.

He turned left and walked past his own automobile as if he didn't even know it, and on up Grove Street toward Berkeley.

Hunched against the brutal wind, he knew at once he'd never been so alone. He wanted his brother. Ronnie and him, always together at Dorsey High, people used to call them twins. But the worst thing he could do was call. If the pigs weren't listening to Ronnie's phone along with his mother's, they weren't doing their job.

He went by a house with purple flowers on the side that stuck out an angle like spears, shifting in the wind. He glanced up at a thin sickle moon that curved in an evil smile.

Okay, then, a woman. Surely there must be a woman he could call. But the important ones, like Rosetta, were long gone. Since the divorce two years ago she'd be even further into her *Better Homes and Gardens* trip by now. For all he knew, if he called and told her, she might even turn him in. There'd been others since her, but he'd been trying to wean himself off that. Quick and easy at the time, but it always seemed to lead to trouble later. Now he didn't even have a woman's bed to call his own.

There'd been the ones who'd meant a lot but hadn't lasted. Like Carolyn, from way back when she was still in high school and he was on his way to UCLA. Smartest woman he ever had known, and maybe that had been exactly what couldn't quite work. They'd kept in touch off and on. Last time must have been more than six months ago, though, and she'd seemed a little stiff. Lived in Berkeley, on Stuart Street if he remembered right, yet for all he knew she could be long gone by now. Damned if he was gonna turn up on her doorstep at midnight out of the blue asking for help.

A car shot by, wheels squealing, and he stood there, frozen in fear, waiting for the cop car sure to follow. When none came he turned his collar against the wind, jammed his hands in his pockets and, head down and eyes averted from the street, he forced himself to walk on. One of the countless anonymous black men strolling down a sidewalk in the dead of night with no car, no home, no job, the exact type the pigs would pull over to spread eagle and interrogate for no reason at all. If that happened, he would be at their mercy, in the dark of night, without a soul around.

All he could do was walk, jump out of his skin just about every time a car went past, then realize he was still standing there, pull himself together, and walk a little more. Walk that endless night, and hope he lived to see the morning.

Quincy had left him out there all alone, but he'd brought what James needed in that paper bag. He'd even included a little killer marijuana with Zig-Zags in the new jacket's inside pocket with a note: "This pleasure is worth the risk, bro. If you get busted, this will be the least of your problems." And he'd said he'd raise money, promised to be in touch.

Q had just said it like it was, hard to hear but accurate. And he'd kept him from stupid mistakes, like going home or calling family. Then the man left him all alone, true, but you couldn't hardly blame Q. Too well-known on the streets, too easy to track.

Well, all it had taken was one night out on the street for him to change his mind about Carolyn. He glanced over at her profile as she drove without a sound. She must be enjoying the peace and quiet. A true friend.

The car heater warmed his body at last.

He snapped awake. Must've dozed a while. He looked out the window. They were past East Oakland. The station wagon glided along the freeway between undeveloped land still used for ranching. Horses grazed in bright sun that cast shadows from high clouds onto the steep green hills. Cow paths traveled over the slopes, past salt licks and feed bins, into vertical ravines made muddy with winter runoff. Acacia trees looked like a mass of gaudy yellow feathers.

A sudden joy swept through him. He wanted to tell Carolyn to stop and let him out here; he could survive on land like this. The fences were easy to get over; he would hide in the gullies. Earth and trees would shelter him, streams and animals sustain him. The Volvo slipped down onto the flat, past the long, low buildings of the county jail, past signs for the town of Livermore. That's where they kept the nuclear weapons, he thought. He shuddered. An illusion to think he would ever be safe again.

He could just see his mama. Ramrod straight in her pleated-back chair, she'd finger the crisp white doily off its arm, fold it, flatten it, worry, call and talk to his brother Ronnie for the tenth time that day, wait on the bad news. She'd mourned that way for years, but this was the worst yet.

"How do you feel about stopping?" Carolyn asked. "I could use coffee."

He jumped at the unexpected sound of her voice. Just the thought of a restaurant made him start trembling again. If he wasn't moving, people could see him, look up from their morning papers and check him out.

"I'll bet not that many people read the *Chronicle* out here," she said. She had the same fear, of course. "These things aren't covered in the Valley as much as the Bay Area."

"You crazy? Freeman's only about a hundred miles north of here."

She didn't answer, but he disliked the way he sounded. He didn't want to be sharp with her. He was just scared.

"Not yet," he mumbled. Not ever. How in the hell was he gonna get the nerve to walk around out there?

They drove over the Altamont Pass and south on Highway Five. The countryside spread out. On the right, green pastures gave way to low hills, and on the left a reddish blur of bare-branched apple trees rolled off to a smudgy grey horizon. When cars passed, the Volvo seemed like it was standing still.

"What do you think?" she asked. "Other drivers get mad at you out here if you stay at the limit."

"Maybe try sixty. Should be safer."

He liked these efficient blocks of conversation about the business at hand. The two of them resolved each small thing as it came along. A canal with cement lips and calm, colorless water angled off into a vast and empty space. The landscape looked unreal, like an architect's drawing.

They drove on through the huge deserted Valley, half-plowed, half-layered over with new green grass. The monotony of the ride soothed him, and he dozed again.

He awoke from the motion of the car as it turned off the highway onto a two-lane road.

"Don't worry, everything's fine," Carolyn was quick to reassure him. "I'm taking Jl instead of 152. My friend Mary Lou taught me this way last summer. It's a little longer, but there aren't as many cars."

"Okay," he ventured after he got his bearings. "That's cool."

The clouds lowered and expanded; their dark, urgent shadows moved over the landscape. For a moment each shifting patch offered a comfortable place to hide from the light of day. Then the sun was gone, replaced by an ominous gray. Large drops splattered one by one against the windshield.

"James, see that coffee shop up there on the left? I've got to go to the bathroom."

Truth was, even if the rain got thick he'd still rather pull over to the fields on the side, but they were gonna have to stop sometime. He nodded yes, and she turned into the gravel parking lot of the cafe.

"Want to come in? I think it's safe, I honestly do. Or, I can get takeout."

"Good idea. I'll just wait on you here." Did he look anonymous; were the sunglasses doing their job? Isolated raindrops gave way to a slow but steady drizzle.

"You want coffee?" He nodded yes. "Cream? Sugar? How about a sweet roll or donut?"

"Yeah. Everything."

She promised to be back at once and he tried to smile, but fear stiffened his lips. Her door banged closed, and she was gone.

He pulled the rearview mirror down at an angle so he could see behind the car, then slouched into his seat. She'd taken the keys, so the damned heater was off. Cold rain pecked at the top of the Volvo. He hugged himself to stay warm.

At least this place way out here wasn't like the Emeryville Denny's where all the pigs came in for their coffee. He glanced in the mirror once more, and there it was, as if he'd conjured it up. The black and white highway patrol car nosed its quiet way into the wet lot like a shark. He slid down further to be sure the back of his head couldn't be seen from behind. He held his breath and heard his heart pound.

Wheels squashed onto the gravel. The beat of the rain intensified. Car doors opened; footsteps crunched toward the restaurant. He shivered violently, his teeth chattering out of control. He forced himself to be still. Sweat rolled down the sides of his chest under the new white shirt. He strained for any sound, but the downpour was all he heard.

After an eternity, the Volvo door popped open and there was Carolyn. Shaken and nervous, her raincoat dotted with water, she reached in to hand him two large styrofoam containers.

"Did you see them?" she asked.

"Hard to miss. Be cool, but let's split."

She started the car, fumbled at the wiper switch, and pulled back into the road, slow and cautious. James stayed down.

"They're still in the restaurant," she said. "They're eating breakfast. No one's following us."

The sound of the two-lane country highway was different, more intimate. Row after endless row of wet trunks swept by in moving fans from the car to the horizon. He couldn't bring himself to straighten out. He clutched the coffee cups against his chest and clung to their warmth.

"It's okay, James. We've gone two miles, and no one's behind us."

She gave a clumsy pat on his shoulder. He had to trust the woman; he had to come up sometime. He tried to look casual as he stretched out his long body and rubbed at the parts that tingled. The trees had been replaced by huge, bare fields that went on as far as he could see.

"I swear, Curls, this must be how it felt under a cartload of straw headed north." He smoothed out his clothing.

"What's up with all this empty space, though?" he asked. "I expected swamps and hound dogs." He managed a weak smile.

"This is agribus, James. Out here the growers get paid *not* to grow anything. See how it's not even plowed? It was probably cotton before."

"I did not like to see the *police* like that," he stated, emphatic.

"God, I nearly died when I came out of the bathroom, and there they were." Carolyn would talk on now, he knew.

"I had already ordered the coffee, and I was ready to pay for it, but they sat down at the counter right next to the cash register."

She reached to take one of the cups out of his hand and managed to flip the lid off without his help.

"I forgot to even look for sweet rolls. And I was going to see if there was a phone so we could call Stanley. Damn."

She took a sip of her coffee, though it was still so hot it must've burnt her tongue. He couldn't begin to get that brew down yet. And food was out of the question, even though he hadn't eaten a thing since yesterday lunch. Sure did wish he had a cigarette, though. Stanley would have some. He wanted to be at his cousin's tumble-down place in West Fresno's ghetto right now; he'd be a whole lot more comfortable with some brothers around.

"I hope the cops didn't realize I got two coffees and there wasn't anyone else in the car. Well, one person could get two coffees for herself, couldn't she? Anyhow, they acted like they were into their breakfast. Although they did look up. One of them even smiled. The other was reading the *Fresno Bee*. No picture of you on the front page, you'll be glad to know."

James sat still, listening to Carolyn's voice against the steady rhythm of the windshield wipers and watching the large wet land pass by. Now there were furrows, but nothing planted yet. Just strips of dark foliage at some edges, muddy unpaved roads at others, and the occasional large warehouse. He'd last visited Stanley two years ago, but he didn't remember that it looked like this. Flat. Empty. Desolate. The storm settled over the land.

She drove exactly at whatever limit was posted on the curves, reaching out her hand to get her coffee on the straight parts. Finally he managed a taste. His body came back to something like its normal state, but his fingers and feet stayed cold. Every once in a while, he took a tiny sip from his own cup, but mostly he just held it there between his knees.

At last they went by a couple of houses tucked up under tall, bare trees, drove through a town so small and wet it looked as though no one even lived there, and found themselves in sudden traffic on a larger road. Carolyn fiddled with the radio, listened to the boring twang of country music, then one of those stations where they shout the ads in Spanish, then snapped it off, thank God. The rain was so thick they could hardly see.

Then there were muddy lanes and tiny, rundown houses every which way, and after that came actual paved streets but no sidewalks. That was one thing he remembered about Stanley's entire neighborhood. Not one sidewalk anywhere. A poor little backwater type of a place. Everyone called it West Fresno, like it didn't even belong to a real Fresno.

"Starting to look familiar," he told Carolyn. "Where's Highway 99?"

She pointed ahead, and they bumped over about ten railroad tracks, then found themselves in a place that was about to be an entrance to the highway.

"Naw, we've passed it now," he said. "Turn around. Stanley's house is right here somewhere." He strained to look back as she did the U-turn, and realized with relief that this was exactly where he'd gotten off 99 when he'd driven north from LA. Now he almost knew where he was.

He directed her left, then right, on instinct. Two guys, bundled up in heavy clothes, tromped along in work shoes through the mud at the side of the road. He looked closely at their wet shapes as Carolyn slowed so she wouldn't splash them, and felt better when he saw they were black. If the pigs came, he could run here. Black people would understand. They'd let him in if he asked, feed him, save him. In a neighborhood like this, everyone knew you had to stay away from the police.

He squinted at houses, not even looking for numbers, hoping he'd know the place from that little messed-up shack he remembered being stuck out in the front yard, like an old chicken coop but set up with a mattress. Stanley used to sleep in it when he was a teenager and hated every single adult in his life.

One broken-down shanty after another out here. Everyone so poor it was pitiful. Now he remembered why he'd lost touch. He liked Stanley, but his cousin had been a man without a future in this godforsaken place. Who was he kidding? The police would have the run of the whole entire neighborhood. Still, Stanley would take him in. He was sure of that.

"There it is!" he said, excited. "Someone painted that chicken shack in the front since I was here, but I'm sure of it." Carolyn pulled the Volvo over carefully onto the mud shoulder and stopped. They squinted at the house and its sagging porch but saw no sign that it was occupied.

He hopped out into the slanting rain, his head down and his jacket collar up. He jumped a little roadside ditch filled with runoff, opened the waist-high gate of the low chain-link fence, ran up the two steps, and rapped at the door.

He waited. He watched Carolyn wipe the condensation from the inside of the passenger window. He knocked again and pressed a button that might have been attached to a bell. Waited. He rattled the door knob and peered in through a window to try to see around the edge of a pulled-down shade. He knocked once more. Waited. The rain slid down his neck and behind his jacket; his cold, wet shirt began to stick against his back.

Eventually, reluctantly, he retraced his steps. Carolyn opened the door from the inside and he lowered his body back into the car.

"No one home." He hated to admit the obvious.

She nodded and started the motor for the heater's warmth. Together they watched the water slide down the front windshield.

"What now?" she asked. "You think we should come back later?"

"Naw," he said. "The man might be gone forever for all I know. Truth be told, I haven't even heard about him for the last year or so. We kinda lost touch."

He could see that look, like she was thinking *now* you tell me. He felt like a fool.

She wanted him to come up with the next move. He didn't have one, but he had to say something.

"How about a motel?" he offered. "You drop me off, and I wait there 'til Quincy . . ."

His voice trailed into the drum of rain on the car roof.

"God, James, I can't just leave you out here alone. You don't even have identification with your new name."

He settled back with nothing more to say. The rain was so thick it was starting to get dark, though it was only three thirty in the afternoon. The ramshackle houses seemed as though they might melt right into the wet and the mud. There was no one in sight. Anyone in their right mind would have to be inside right now, even with all the leaks.

"Damn, I know!" All at once the girl just about bounced off her seat, she was that excited. "God, why didn't I think of this before? We can go to Allen, where I worked on the strike. Mary Lou might even appreciate the company. Although . . ."

Although Mary Lou, whoever she was, would not like his situation one bit. He'd talked to these farmworker types before, always in front of the Berkeley Co-op with their petitions. Here it was 1974, people gettin' killed every day at home and abroad, long past time for that shit to change, and those folks were still collecting signatures, patient as Job.

He waited to hear what Carolyn decided. But she just sat there and looked at him. He realized he still had the sunglasses on. With it so dark and rainy, he couldn't hardly see a thing. He folded them into his pocket and lifted his eyes to meet her gaze. He hoped she wouldn't make him say it: Yes. Please. Take me to your friend. I don't know what else to do.

His nod was almost imperceptible. She released the brake and turned the wheel. Two minutes later they were on Highway 99, going north.

CHAPTER THREE

"**Y**ou can't always get what you want . . ." Mary Lou found herself humming while she waited for Jerry Jensen, head of Colonia Winery's labor relations, to come to the telephone. She didn't even like the Rolling Stones, let alone hippies, free sex, any of that stuff. "*You can't always get what you waa-nt . . .*" That part was more than true. "*But if you try sometimes, you just might find . . .*"

Not her, not Mary Lou Gilman in January 1974, stuck here all by herself in this huge, cold office on Highway 99 halfway between Fresno and Stockton with the rain banging on the tin roof. She tried all the time, and she never had gotten one single thing she needed.

She brushed aside a strand of hair and set her jaw against a sudden threat of tears. She cradled the phone on her shoulder, tapped a cigarette out of its packet and lit it. She sucked in deep, drummed her fingers on her battered gray desk top, and glared out at the storm. Through the dripping window, past bare poplars and silvery wet railroad tracks, the neon sign for Jovita's Cafe flashed red and blue at the semis that ground down to a halt for the first stoplight north of the Mexican border.

The only other window in the large, gloomy room gave on to the vineyards. Dark, gnarled trunks draped over dripping metal wires that marched off to the horizon. The scene's bleak beauty did nothing to temper the taste of anger at the back of her throat.

She was going to choke on this rage if she couldn't get it out. When Jensen finally got on this phone, she would just let him have it. How would he like to live out there at the labor camp when it rained like this? By now the drains would be clogged, so that whole families, women and children, were wading through three inches of *caca* floating on water, just to get from their pathetic one-room cinder block rows into those God-awful communal bathrooms where the doors to the stalls either hung off one hinge or weren't there at all. A sour bile rose to the root of her tongue.

"Miss Gilman?" She did not like this secretary's sickly sweet voice. "I'm so sorry for my previous mistake, but Mr. Jensen is otherwise engaged after all."

"Well, please relay this message to your boss," Mary Lou aimed for a polite tone, but failed. "If he doesn't fix those drains by tomorrow, we'll send out a press release to boycott every single wine label that has the town of Empire on it. The Eastern liberals can get the list straight from the *New York Times*. It may be 1974, but Colonia Winery still treats its workers like goddamned slaves!"

She slammed the phone down and felt worse, like she wanted to throw up. She took a final drag on the cigarette to still the sense that her stomach was rising, then stubbed out the butt in the dented aluminum ashtray that matched her desk. She seldom swore at all, but how in the world could that woman even keep up the charade of politeness in a world as cruel as this?

And Jensen? He wouldn't call back. To talk about this with Mary Lou would imply a relationship with the Union, which was exactly what Colonia didn't want. But he'd send equipment over, maybe even this afternoon, and drain the filthy mess. *Get what you need?* Hardly.

They wouldn't make things sanitary, of course, but life would go on out there like it always had. The United Farm Workers Union would've helped the workers and their families through another day, but gotten none of the credit. And nothing basic would change, except she'd have lung cancer before this was through.

She lit another cigarette and watched the match's flash of warm color 'til she had to shake it out.

Her gaze swept the cavernous office. Last summer both desks were piled high; people fought over who could use typewriters and phones. Even the corners were filled with the sleeping bags of volunteers from the city. Everyone and their brother, from the Nebraska minister to the skinny ex-junkie out of the Haight-Ashbury, had bunked down here at night.

Change the workers' lives? She couldn't even change her own, for God's sake; she'd already let it all slip away.

If only Rojelio were still here. They may have looked funny together, his stocky frame up to her nose—dark, *muy indio* as he liked to say with pride—and her skin so fair it would burn to a crisp by the end of a day in the fields. But the farmworkers hadn't minded. Everyone, from Amelia Martinez, modern Mexican revolutionary, to Lupe Muñoz, prude of the year, loved Rojelio Aguilar.

On a brilliant fall day after the harvest was over and the strike still not won, only two months ago, with the dust settled from the room-sized gondolas where the pickers threw all the wine grapes and the heat down from 104 degrees to a cool eighty at last, Rojelio had asked her over to Jovita's Cafe for a Coke.

She'd already had a bad feeling by the time they reached the shimmering yellow poplars, and as the two of them picked their way across the railroad tracks in the clear, bright sunshine, he told her what the Union's president had said to him on the phone.

"'*Mira*, listen to me.'" Rojelio swung into the soft accented cadence of Cesar Chavez's voice. "'The strike will never work by itself. Too many *mojados*—illegal, dirt poor, and willing to scab. You know the only way to win this thing? Put a big dent in Colonia's sales. The boycott is the key. We'll have to place our people in every major city. We need a good organizer in Detroit. Will you go, Rojelio?'"

"Once Cesar calls you a good organizer, you do what he asks," Rojelio told Mary Lou, eyes gleaming. He was still excited by the compliment.

He swung the café door open for her, and they settled into the red Naugahyde booths. They were the only ones there. Even Jovita was missing in the back somewhere.

"When do you leave?" she whispered into the hush. Even those four words had been hard. To utter any more, to say she would miss him, was unthinkable.

"Tomorrow morning."

She waited for Rojelio to tell her to come, and he waited for her to ask. Both knew that Cesar tried his best to keep couples together, married or not. Rojelio wasn't the type to refuse her much, but he needed to know she wanted him. Which was exactly what she couldn't say.

Her throat constricted, but she wouldn't let him see that she was upset. In the total silence of midafternoon in a deserted restaurant she could say it to herself, but never to anyone else, and least of all to him. It just didn't work between them in bed. Her cheeks flushed. When he made his moves it was like he was asking for her permission, and all she'd want was to sleep.

Of course, every day during the strike she and Rojelio had been up since five a.m. to reach the picket line before the scabs showed, worked the whole day long, met with strikers out at the camp in the evening, and fallen out late, bone-tired. But there was more to it than that.

Maybe she just didn't like sex. Not the worst thing in the world, not if she had had a baby to cuddle. If she'd gotten pregnant she would have gone with him. But she never had used a thing, and still it hadn't happened.

Jovita had appeared to save them from the unbearable silence. She bustled around them and, relieved, they had ordered their Cokes, pretending everything was the same as before that awful gap in the conversation. His eyes searched hers out to plead his case, but all she could do was look down. She didn't want to be alone again; that was what she feared the most. Yet she couldn't lie, and she watched his face settle into the conclusion that she didn't care, that she would do just fine on her own, that he could find someone else.

When they left the restaurant the high, white clouds, the bright sky, and the joyous leaves mocked her heavy heart.

Now it was three months later, on this winter day with the rain coming down in sheets of impenetrable mist like a shroud thrown over the fields. It was as if she was one of those grapevines outside the window. Cold and bare. Shut down, as though spring would never come.

Her plumbing must be wrong, the way it was out at the camp. Wouldn't that be just like her? Go all through this lifetime and not even get to have kids.

She went across the room to get her coat, the one she'd picked out from the donation box last summer. Rojelio had given a wolf whistle when she'd first put it on. Now she huddled into its satin-lined warmth.

She surveyed the pile of papers on her desk: unemployment applications with which the workers needed help; an official letter that denied Rebecca Flores her disability, which only Mary Lou knew how to appeal; a note in Basilio de la Cruz's childish writing asking could she get him "a ride *en caro* to doctor *mañana*"; and her own scribbled reminder to talk to Enrique Vargas, who wanted a promise that if he stayed with the strike he'd be promoted to irrigator after they won, since he'd worked for Colonia for thirteen years.

Her thin lips compressed into a line; her chin trembled. Being busy might work when the weather's bad or you're lonely, but not when both poured down.

She put her head down in her hands and actually wept out loud. It lasted she didn't know how long, and ended with hiccups, like a baby. She made herself go into the tiny bathroom, where the toilet ran even if you jiggled its handle. She pulled off a wad of toilet paper and blew her nose, went back to her hard wooden chair, and reached in her purse for a mirror.

She grimaced at her skinny face, red and splotchy from the tears. Usually at least she liked her hazel eyes, the kind that changed colors with the light, but today they just looked muddy. Down to 115 pounds, this was what always happened to her when things got bad.

Not enough meat for her bones was what her mother would say, and then the argument would start about why Mary Lou wanted to hang around with all those Mexicans in that Union of hers anyhow.

She bent over to plug in the tiny old heater that stood next to her desk. Too bad if the Union always bugged her about the electric bills. Next to the glow and faint whir of the motor, she hugged her arms close to her sides.

She thought about when she was a kid. The blackberries were the worst. You got all dirty and scratched while you picked, and then the danged things shook down in the box at least three times before they added up to anything you got paid for.

They may have had their own speck of land, but the labor camps were still full of Okies just like her own family. Her father put in so many hours between his place and everyone else's that he hardly said a word at home. That never changed before he died. Okie, Mexican, Portuguese, whatever, none of that mattered. She understood just how hard these farmworkers' lives were.

The phone rang and there was that unmistakable voice. Not like Rojelio's or any other Mexican man she had ever known, despite the hint of the original Spanish. Not even a tinge of bravado, just a little dance of lightness in the tone. And even though he was important, known throughout the country—no secretary, no pretense—the total opposite of Jerry Jensen, with his little cartoon name and flunky job.

"*Mira*, Mary Lou," came that sweet and determined imperative. "Isn't it time to have some fun?"

She could just see the small smile, the mischief in his eyes, the charismatic seduction that got people to do what he said. When Cesar Chavez was on the line you had no choice but to listen.

"You had a good idea at the Executive Committee meeting." She didn't know what other union presidents were like, but this one never forgot a thing. She had suggested a one-day march two weeks ago. The fact that he remembered thrilled her.

"But why not make it bigger, turn it into a giant pilgrimage, like the original *Peregrinación* in '66? Start in Delano and go all the way up to Empire. You, the Colonia workers, and a hundred thousand other people. Walk right into Colonia's headquarters, through that glassed-in aviary with the tropical birds. Knock on Jensen's door and take over their company town. Show them who has the balls, the *cojones*, the numbers."

She had to laugh, and the mere fact that this happened made her want to cry again, this time with gratitude at the tiny moment of joy.

"Sure," she answered, relieved she hadn't dawdled at Jovita's, over the one cup of coffee she allowed herself in the afternoon, or left early. Cesar didn't like it if no one answered the phone. "Sure, Cesar. I'll do it."

The same as when Cesar had pulled her aside at La Paz, the creepy old tuberculosis sanatorium near Tehachapi that was UFW headquarters, and asked would she be the one to keep the Allen office open while the boycott took hold? Sure, she'd told him, surprised he had even thought of her. Tickled pink, and with absolutely no idea of what she was getting into, sure, she'd said.

Now it was dark, and the rain just poured down, clattering on the tin roof like stones. Her heart fell again at the thought of the lonely night ahead, but it was time to close. May as well sit and feel sorry for herself at home on Joseph Street. Tomorrow morning, if the office hadn't sunk into the winter mud, she'd call Basilio and set a meeting to tell the workers about the march, then start in on the pile on her desk. When she had something to show for her effort, she'd ask Cesar to send Rojelio back to help her.

She'd learned something from all this, and she promised herself she'd remember it forever. It's a lot easier to be sure you're not in love with someone before he leaves than after you make him go. Maybe she could get him to take her back. Happiness was too much to ask apparently, but she sure could use some company.

Five minutes later she was home, dashing through the dark wetness without umbrella or boots to let herself into the side door. Funny little place she had rented, she thought, as she reached for the light and then the heater. It had a sidewalk by the front door that she never used because there was no sidewalk on Fourth Avenue, which left room to park right by the kitchen door. So that was the door she and everyone else used. Address on Joseph Street; entrance on Fourth. But that was the way this Valley was in these small towns—sidewalks here and there, and then the fields, right outside these tiny places for rent. Except on the other side of town, of course, with the housing tracts. That was where the white people lived. Sidewalks everywhere, brand new streets, nothing but cement as a matter of fact. She was white, but she'd rather be here. And at least she had a house, not just a cinderblock room in a desolate labor camp.

CHAPTER FOUR

Carolyn turned right at the highway's stoplight and looked for the funny little backyard filled with cactus, plaster statues, and green cement paths. That was where to turn left onto Fourth Avenue. Of course there wasn't any street sign until three blocks down, at the corner of Joseph Street where Mary Lou's house was. The Valley was so weird the way everyone described how to get somewhere by the look of the turns, and not street signs and address numbers. Anyhow, once she saw that cactus yard, even in the dark and the rain, she knew exactly where she was.

She pulled up in the muddy space between the house and the asphalt single-lane road, right behind the battered VW.

"She's home," said Carolyn to James, who let out a sigh. "That's her car. And the light's on in the kitchen." She cut off the motor, and they offered each other small uncomfortable smiles.

Could this house be bugged? She had never thought of it this way, but the UFW office certainly ought to be—why not here? She would have to get Mary Lou outside to explain things. Yet if Carolyn said she was worried Joseph Street was wired and it was, wouldn't she have given it all away right there?

"Hey, girl, we gonna sit out here all night long or what?" James spoke with forced cheer.

"How am I going to explain this?" she asked.

"Why not just start with how you and I are old friends?" James said. "And this morning we thought it might be a nice day—"

"—and I was telling you about working for the Union last summer," Carolyn broke in. "We had some spare time, so we decided why not take a drive, visit Mary Lou, and now with this storm we need to spend the night?"

How easy it was to lie, Carolyn realized.

She clenched her jaw, opened the car door, and got out. At first she had to struggle against the force of a gale that blew sheets of rain at her at a sharp angle, needles against her skin. Gusts of wet air tore at the corners of her clothes, and then the wind dropped, all at once.

The rain fell softly. She joined James on his side of the car and they walked through mud, then up wet steps to the small overhang at the kitchen door. Both of them scraped their shoes on a bristly welcome mat. Carolyn gave a sharp knock. She would never have thought it got this wintry in the San Joaquin Valley. It had been so hot last summer that by five thirty p.m. like this they were lucky if even a hint of a breeze whispered through the baked screen door.

And now that very door opened: Mary Lou was there in an instant.

"Carolyn, what a surprise! Jeez, I was right here at the stove. You scared me half to death. No one comes around now that it's so cold. I must have missed your call."

Mary Lou hugged her friend quickly, then backed off from her cold, wet coat, laughing.

So relieved to step inside the kitchen that promised a magic circle of safety, Carolyn just about burst into tears at the sight of the chipped blue enamel teapot over its high flame. Mary Lou looked at her, glad and concerned.

"And your friend?" Mary Lou asked. James was still on the porch, waiting. "Let's let him in, too," she said. "What do you say?"

Carolyn jumped aside.

"Oh. This is James—" For an awful second she could not remember his last name.

"Well, James." Mary Lou stuck out a hand. "Come on in and get dry."

"Sweet." Carolyn pounced on the word. "James Sweet, Mary Louise Gilman."

Was Mary Lou's polite glance a bit of a stare? Carolyn tried to remember even one black person out here during the whole time she had worked on the strike, but she couldn't. She looked at James, but he was staring at Mary Lou's curtains, lime green with crisp snow-white frills that she worried over whenever grease flew.

"Now get on out of those wet things of yours," Mary Lou beckoned. "Before you catch your death, as my mother would say. God, your mother, Carolyn. She passed so soon ago. Must still be hard."

Carolyn managed a constricted nod, shed her wet coat with a series of wooden gestures, and stood there. Eventually she remembered where things belonged, and went to hang the coat in the living room closet.

Back in the kitchen James sat in a straight-backed chair next to the kitchen table; its green top seemed fresh. New contact paper. He leaned over to warm his hands at a furnace vent, still in his wet sports jacket.

"What can I get you?" Mary Lou asked him. "Coffee? Beer?"

"A beer would be great," he answered.

"All I've got is Tecate."

"Can't say I'm familiar with that kind, but I know I'll like it fine."

"We sure drank our share of Tecate last summer, didn't we Carolyn?" Mary Lou chattered.

"Tecate beer, at the end of each and every fifteen-hour day." Carolyn liked how her own voice sounded, almost normal.

"Can't drink this without lime and salt," Mary Lou announced. She plunked the cold cans and a saucer with a green wedge and a mound of Morton's down in front of her guests. "Hamburger tacos okay for dinner?"

Carolyn nodded quickly. James assented with a slow smile. Both looked down at the floor.

"God, Carolyn, you know what Cesar laid on me?" Mary Lou was dicing onions as if she would never stop. "On top of everything else he wants me to organize this huge march for the Colonia workers to go on up there to Empire and demand their rights."

She put on the rice and browned up the hamburger.

"Now how on earth am I gonna find time to do that? But I called Rojelio, and he said after I got things going they might let him come back to help."

Carolyn and James watched her work with a respect that bordered on awe. They had forgotten all about the commonplace world where food was prepared.

"How is Rojelio?" Carolyn remembered to ask.

"Cold. He's in Detroit, you know. Says brown skin isn't made for snow and ice."

Carolyn glanced at James. She had never known how to talk to him about race. Would this offhand allusion bother him?

"I've had the exact same thought," he chuckled. "Far as I can tell, black skin doesn't do so good anywhere north of LA."

This made their hostess laugh out loud. James salted the rim of his beer can, popped the top, squeezed lime in, and took a long draught, then bent over to catch the warm air from the vent again. Carolyn slid her back down the wall into a crouch and held her hands out too. Like birds that had just found their branch, they shifted their weight together, then settled.

CHAPTER FIVE

After dinner, the two women, used to being in the kitchen together, moved around each other in efficient circles to clean up.

Who is he? Mary Lou wondered. Must be Carolyn's boyfriend. Jeez, all it took was her and Rojelio in an Okie place like Lyle's to raise eyebrows; just imagine how much harder it'd be to walk in with a black guy. Tell the truth, though, she was sick to death of the pasty-faced white people out here in the San Joaquin Valley, even if she was one herself. So mean to the Mexicans. Maybe it was because they sort of realized that some things were better on the dark side of town. The people were more polite, nicer. More like family.

She glanced at James, who gave her a slick smile that showed the gap between his front teeth. Just when you thought this man looked kind of nice there was that ugly space right there in the front of his mouth that meant you changed your mind.

"Food was downright delicious," he said to her. "Makes a person feel almost alive again. Now why don't you ladies let me wash the dishes while you catch up on each other?"

So he had to be nice, after all. Any man who offered to wash the dishes had to be nice. Still, though, she knew her way around her own kitchen. She wasn't about to turn it over to a stranger.

"Want to take a walk, Mary Lou?" Carolyn asked.

"Go outside? Look, Carolyn, I was raised on a farm. I know better than to leave my own warm house on a night like this."

"But the rain's stopped. It would be nice to get some exercise."

"You're the only friend I have who would insist on this kind of crazy idea." Mary Lou laughed. "It's freezing out there!"

"No, really. I need to talk to you."

Oh Lordy. The last thing in the world Mary Lou wanted to do was go back into that cold, dark night, and especially not for one of Carolyn's long, complicated discourses.

"Later, maybe. You two are tired. Why don't you sit back and digest your food for a while."

She bustled around wiping down the counters, scrubbing at the grease on the tabletop, polishing up the salt and pepper shakers. Honestly, to watch these two eat dinner she could have sworn this was the first decent meal they'd had in days. Then after he was finally through, James had sat for the longest time, twisting his third beer around in his hand with scarcely one word. He wasn't the sort she'd have expected for Carolyn's boyfriend—not talkative enough.

Then again, Carolyn wasn't saying much either, which was really unusual. Plus, she had a different look since her mother died. Skinny, which was not her style. She'd always been the type who ate well, then worried about her weight. And dressed up, in a skirt no less. Yet her hair was longer and wilder, curls in all directions. She didn't know why they had come here, may they'd just had a fight in the car. Whatever, having them in her kitchen, whatever shape they were in, beat another evening all alone.

Just as the dishes were stacked and ready to wash, someone knocked. More company in one night than she'd had in the last six weeks put together. She opened the door right off.

"It's the Martinezes," she announced back over her shoulder. "They're bringing me eggs."

And they all came in, Amelia, Jose, and their four kids, earnest and polite down to the two-year old. She found her jar of hard candy, pressed one into each little hand, then lifted the blue and white crocheted blanket that covered the newest bundle asleep on his mother's chest, just enough so she could see the little scrunched-up flower face.

"You remember Carolyn," she said in Spanish. "And this is her friend, James." But when she turned from the baby, he was nowhere to be seen, and Carolyn, flushed beet red, was trying to cover up for his sudden exit.

"*Buenos días*, I mean *buenas noches*," Carolyn stammered, embarrassed by her pathetic Spanish. "*Dispénseme*, or *el*. He had to go, God, how do you say it? ¿*Tenia que ir al excusado*? He needed to use the restroom."

Mary Lou held the bundled baby against her body with her right arm and strode about to get the kids soft drinks, the adults beers. That done, she offered to heat up leftovers, which the Martinezes declined.

"Carolyn, how are you?" Amelia slowed down her Spanish for the neophyte. "It's been so much time since we saw you. Your friend, is he all right?"

"*Si*, I mean *no*." Carolyn's face colored again. "He hasn't been feeling well. *Esta enfermo y no quiere que los niños* . . ." She had no idea how to say James was worried the kids would catch his cold.

"*Este niño, o bebita*—she remembered a blue blanket meant it was a boy—*bebito*. I mean, *es nuevo, verdad?*"

"His mother says he's four months old today. He's called Gerardo. He's the sweetest thing, isn't he?" Mary Lou's adroit Spanish got everyone's attention riveted back on the baby. "Wake up, Gerardo, this is me, *Tia* Mary Lou, and I'm talking with you. Do you know how to smile?"

CHAPTER SIX

Carolyn murmured something about checking on James and managed to leave the room. She went down the hall and tried the handle on the bathroom door. No James. She stepped through to open the door to Mary Lou's bedroom. Only the smooth expanse of lavender chenille bedspread. She crept back to the hallway and opened the other door that led to the living room.

He sat by the couch in the matching chair, which held his long, slender frame with space to spare. This couch and chair, matching in their raised green velvet pattern but different in their arms—the couch's curved, the chair's broad and flat—were Mary Lou's pride and joy. She always said how she bought them at Goodwill, the best purchase she had ever made. And James looked at home, elbows bent and face hidden behind the latest edition of *El Malcriado*, the Union newspaper. He peeked out at her and lifted an eyebrow, trying to make light of the situation.

"What's up, Curly?" he whispered.

"You must have freaked out when they all came in here! And Amelia Martinez is just the type who likes to gossip. Damn! Are you okay?"

He shrugged, and she remembered she had to be calm, for both their sakes.

"How long will they stay?" he asked.

"Who knows? I'm sure they wonder who you are."

"I'm sure they do."

There was nothing to be done about that, so they left it. Carolyn sank onto the couch and rubbed her palms over the shape of its arms, up and down the dark polished wood that ran their length.

Laughter and rapid-fire conversation filtered in from the kitchen, just like last summer, when the tiny house was always jam-packed and you never could get your head straight.

"Didn't you tell me your friend spent a lot of time alone?" said James.

"Every time she calls up she complains about it, so I thought she did." Carolyn paused. "God, this is so complicated. Maybe we should just leave."

"How could we do that?"

"Go in there and tell them we decided to drive back tonight."

"It's late and it's cold. Wouldn't that make Mary Lou wonder?"

"She's wondering right now, believe me. She's not dumb."

"Where would we go?"

The same question as before, with no better answer.

"Okay, we'll stay here if she'll let us. As soon as they leave I'll make her come outside so I can explain who you are."

"Now why would you want to do a thing like that?"

Carolyn stared at him in surprise. All of a sudden she felt she was talking to someone she didn't know at all.

"You mean we should ask her if we can stay here and not tell her?"

"Isn't it better for her that way?" The newspaper was in his lap now; his broad hands and long fingers splayed in the chair's flat arms.

"I can't do that, James."

"Why not?"

"It wouldn't be fair. It puts her in jeopardy."

"Less than if she knows who I am."

"I can't lie to her about something this important. Maybe it's stupid of me, but we've been friends too long. Besides, we wouldn't get away with it. Sooner or later she'll trip us up."

"Tell you what, girl." He was smiling his sweet smile that used to freak her out totally when she was in high school.

"We might not even have to figure all this out," he said. "Say they know who I am, and they're calling the police right now."

She wasn't sure if he was serious or not.

"So why don't you go on in there and see what's happening," he suggested. He put his newspaper up again, rustling it as if there was nothing he would rather do than read it. "If things are cool, make my excuses for me so they don't think we're even weirder. Tell them I'm sick."

"I've already done that," Carolyn told him.

"Good. Just be yourself. The people have got to leave sometime."

There didn't seem to be anything else to do, and she had been gone too long already, so Carolyn crept back to the bathroom, flushed the toilet, ran water in the sink, and returned to the kitchen. Only then did she remember she had said James had to go to the bathroom, not herself.

Amelia and Mary Lou were chattering on. Jose nursed his beer and laughed at their jokes, the kids sipped their drinks, lively eyes fixated on the adults, and the baby continued its peaceful sleep. A wave of fatigue washed through Carolyn. She put out a new filter for coffee, stood by the stove, and waited for the water to boil. No matter what happened, a long night still lay ahead.

She tried to calm her frazzled nerves and concentrate on the Spanish. Something about Patricia Muñoz, Lupe's younger sister, being pregnant. She knew the sisters because they had helped in the office during the strike. So Patsy was pregnant; that was usually good news in these circles. Then what were the women so agitated about? A problem, some argument with her dad. Unmarried maybe, and now she was ruined so she never would get married? Her boyfriend wasn't going to do anything about it? Carolyn wasn't sure, but Jose, who hadn't said a word, stood up suddenly and took his beer can across the room to the trash.

His wife knew the signal. He was ready to go. Mary Lou gave Geraldo one last kiss on the cheek, and the pickup's motor roared into the quiet night. It was over as quickly as it had begun.

"Please, Mary Lou," said Carolyn the instant they were gone. "Come out with me for that walk."

"All right, Carolyn," she said, still smiling at the sweetness of the encounter with the baby. "We'll act like we're in the Bay Area and get our exercise. Why not?"

She went into the living room to get their coats. Carolyn followed her down the hall and watched from the doorway, saw her squint at the curtains, now pulled closed. James was still buried in his paper.

"I'm sure you don't want to go outside," she said to him.

"You got that right." His voice was weak; he was trying to sound sick.

"It's only Carolyn, your friend and mine, who's that crazy."

"Got that right, too. Crazy from way back."

That's true, thought Carolyn. Crazy for James. From way back. And under these circumstances, that was crazy indeed.

The two women went out the kitchen door into the chilly night air, then turned the corner onto Joseph Street, where the sidewalk gave way to a dirt track two blocks down. The storm had passed, and a fresh wind blew light clouds across the face of a crescent moon. Although it was not yet nine o'clock the streets were still. Windows of the dilapidated pastel houses were lit by the gray-white flicker of television or already dark. Farmworkers got up before dawn during the growing season, Carolyn mused. They probably went to bed early all year round.

Her fingers were already frozen; she wished she had thought to bring gloves. She wished especially that she didn't have to talk about why she was here with James. A small short-haired dog yapped at them from its chain behind a tree, and she jumped at the sudden sound.

"So who in the world is this new boyfriend of yours?" asked Mary Lou.

No choice but to begin. She sucked in the cold, sharp air and expelled it in a rush of words.

"James isn't my boyfriend. I've known him forever, though, about as long as I've known anyone."

"I never heard you mention him last summer."

"I guess he's from a whole different part of my life."

Carolyn stepped carefully around puddles in the muddy path. "Anyway, he's in trouble and he needs a place to stay for a while, just until he works out his next step."

"What kind of trouble?" The question came sharp.

"The police say he was involved in that event out at Freeman Penitentiary last week."

Mary Lou stopped to look at her friend. The steam from their breath hung in the cold air between them.

"You mean that riot?"

"Yeah." Riot. Carolyn found she couldn't say the word. "You know, when they killed Nyame Jones?"

"Carolyn, you can't be serious!" Mary Lou's eyes, wide with horror, looked flat as plates in the cold light of the moon.

"Oh yes, I am serious. And the situation is serious, too." Yet in an attempt to be ordinary, Carolyn turned to walk on.

"Not that riot where all the guards were killed!" Mary Lou hurried to keep up.

"Yeah, that 'riot.' The one where they made all the inmates lie naked on the ground while they strip-searched them, one by one."

"Well, what in the world did your friend James have to do with it?"

There was total quiet while Carolyn tried to decide how to answer. Even their footsteps made no sound in the soft, wet dirt.

"I said they *say* James was involved. They *say* he got enough plastique in for a bomb. Past a computer check, past a metal detector, past a search, through a screen, handed it to Nyame, who was supposed to have hidden it under his arm or something, and that was how the whole thing started."

"What do you mean, computer check?" Mary Lou zeroed in.

"I mean James has a criminal record." Of course, she realized, this was the absolute wrong thing to say. "You know, he was arrested during the civil rights days."

Carolyn stopped this time and faced Mary Lou.

"He's my friend, Mary Lou. He's a good guy. I want you to take my word on that."

Mary Lou walked on, and now it was Carolyn who had to scramble to keep up.

"James did visit Nyame that day," she explained, a little out of breath. "They let him in as part of the legal team."

"But if the bomb hadn't got in there," said Mary Lou, "then the whole thing wouldn't have happened. No one would have died."

"It was just yesterday afternoon and already they've put out at least three inconsistent stories. James had it in the briefcase, he had it in the typewriter, he had it in his coat. Well, where did he have it? Nyame set off the bomb by accident. He did it on purpose. He did it in the corridor. He did it on the yard. How could he have even hidden this bomb at all when his wrists were in chains? Damn it, Mary Lou, you know better than to believe everything the police say!"

They had come to the edge of the town where houses trailed off into the fields, so they turned to pace their way back. The wind blew cold and steady in their faces.

Mary Lou folded her arms, shivering, and studied her moving feet. She looked like she was trying to remember something.

"My God, Carolyn," she said suddenly. "Was it his picture in the paper, with the long hair and that mean look? Is he the one who's been charged with all those murders?"

"Conspiracy to commit all those murders."

"You're ignoring the main point. What's the truth? Did he have anything to do with it?"

"I haven't asked him."

Suddenly it was so still that the vapor of her breath hung in the air.

"Why in the world not?"

Mary Lou sounded shocked and surprised.

"He would tell me if he wanted to."

"You're risking your life to help this so-called friend of yours, and you don't even want to know what he did?"

"I know James, Mary Lou. I trust him."

"Well, you're a fool then." Mary Lou's words tumbled at her like rocks in a churning stream.

"If he brought that bomb in, Carolyn, then he's responsible for those deaths. That makes him just like the one who did the killing, doesn't it? You're running around with someone who might be a murderer, and as a matter of fact that makes you an accessory to the murder, doesn't it?"

"But Mary Louise," Carolyn interrupted, "you don't want to hear what happened in there. It's safer that way." How could Mary Lou not understand something so obvious?

"Look," Mary Lou answered. "Either I know whether this guy is a murderer or he can't stay here, even tonight. Which is what my answer should be anyhow, and surely would be if you weren't a friend who knew me well enough to call me Mary Louise. You know what the most amazing thing is, Carolyn? You don't really care. You don't care about the guards who got killed!"

The women were almost back to the house. The same little dog yammered and snapped at their feet through a chain-link fence. The moon was gone, the stars clouded over again.

It was true, Carolyn realized. Maybe it was wrong, but she hadn't thought about the guards yet. She had been too busy worrying about whether James lived or died and whether she was going to end up in prison herself. But now Mary Lou wanted to examine the actual facts. Carolyn had no idea how James would react.

"I'll lend you money for a motel in Emerald while you figure out what to do," her friend was saying. "I'll take it out of savings. But I'm not gonna get involved in some hare-brained militant scheme that's already killed people and is liable to kill more for all I know."

It was time to give in. Too late, maybe. Mary Lou was holding tough. Maybe James could tell her his side, whatever it was, explain it forever and she still wouldn't let him stay.

"When we get back, I'll ask James to talk to us," Carolyn said. "Then you decide what we should do."

Now that she had put herself into Mary Lou's hands, she was exhausted, thinking only of the yellow light that waited behind those starched kitchen curtains. But as they came around the final corner, one of Allen's small fleet of black and white police cars cruised by on its silent patrol, and she jolted awake. The officer behind the wheel stared at the unexpected pedestrians, then tipped his hat and grinned as he passed. By the time her body had geared up to full fear, he was gone.

"Friendly, huh? Just too friendly like," said Mary Lou as they watched the red taillights fade. "Remember how they did whatever Colonia wanted on the picket line last summer? It's a small town. It's not like they don't know who I am, Carolyn. In their own way, the police are after me too."

"We're just two women," Carolyn replied. "He flirted with us. He wasn't serious. It's not the same at all."

"You think they don't notice what we do out here?"

"I think James has no safe place to go. I think for him it's a matter of life and death."

They went up the three stairs onto the cement stoop and into the bright-lit kitchen.

CHAPTER SEVEN

He could tell Carolyn was nervous the minute she came back in the living room, but he had to know.

"What did she say?" he asked before she could even sit down. He couldn't help it. He was tired. He just wanted a place to lay his head.

"She's pissed," Carolyn said. She sank back onto the couch again. "She wants to know what came down at Freeman."

"Why would she ask that? It's dangerous for her."

"She says she won't take risks for a person who got those guards killed."

Oh yes. The guards. He'd seen their pictures—family shots with wives and kids—when he switched on Mary Lou's old black and white TV the minute the ladies left the house. There'd been the whole sorry story with his very own face all over the place, big as life. Same photograph as they had in the paper. Made him look like one of those raggedy-ass niggers who ran out on his family, the ones his mama and auntie always made a point of hating. Nothing in the story he didn't already know. Just a reminder of what deep shit he really was in.

"I told you it was worse to tell her," he told Carolyn. "Does she mean it?"

"She couldn't be more serious."

"So if I don't tell her, we're back to square one."

"That's right."

"And if I do, we may well be in the same exact place."

"Depends on what you say, I guess." But Carolyn nodded. "She's already offered to lend us money."

"How much?"

Carolyn looked shocked at his question. Sure, she'd gone to the bank and come up with $700 to add to Quincy's change, which was more than generous, but how long would that last if he had to leave here, between paying for places to sleep and buying food?

"Mary Louise is the type who'll give you the shirt off her back, but she's not rich," was her answer. "Not rich at all."

"Can she keep a secret?"

"She'll keep quiet if she says she will. If she can't promise that, don't tell her."

"This is one motherfuckin' risk, Carolyn."

"Mary Lou has fought for the underdog all her life." Carolyn had her head back now, her eyes closed. "She might not want to be involved, but she wouldn't turn you in."

He raced through his few alternatives. He hadn't even met the woman a few hours ago, and now he was supposed to tell her about Freeman? And Carolyn too? They were both going to wish they never knew what went down that day.

Carolyn needed to hear it, though, just in case she was thinking of bailing out. He knew Carolyn, loyal Carolyn. She'd always felt sorry for him, just on account of his being black. He liked the fact that she tried to understand, but her obvious pity made it hard to be a person like anyone else. Just wait until she got a load of this.

No. Get out of here. Get rid of everyone. Sit around in some dipshit motel, read all the papers, watch the hunt on TV every day. His judgment would go bad, he'd be bound to act crazy. Move around then, stay busy. Worry about the dozens of people who would see his face every day.

If he told the story? These women were bound to understand how frightened he really was. Of the pigs, of Kwesi. Of his own thoughts. Always keep your dignity, no matter what the circumstance, his father used to say. Useless advice. Circumstance could rob your dignity in an instant.

He hated making decisions since Freeman. So important, every single choice, and no idea, none whatsoever, of whether what he came up with would work out or lead him to his death.

"I'll tell you both about it." James stood up and paced the room, agitated.

"You're sure, then?" she had the nerve to ask him.

"Oh yeah." He gave out a hollow laugh. "Real sure." He moved toward the door.

"What about security?" Carolyn whispered all of a sudden, as though that would make a difference.

"Fuck security. If the place is bugged and they arrest me, at least I'll know where I'm sleeping in from now on."

Since that brave statement did not ease his mind one bit, he turned right around and put the needle on the Joan Baez record that was already in Mary Lou's player and turned the volume as loud as it would go. Background noise, to cover up the conversation they were about to have.

"*Gracias a la vida, que me ha dado tanto . . .*" came the folk singer's voice. Damn. Was it all anyone did out here, speak Spanish?

He marched down the short hall to the kitchen, sat again at the chrome and green table pushed up against the kitchen wall, in the same place he had held for dinner. He tipped his straight-backed chair against the wall, took a deep breath, and told them. Everything. Down to the last click of the last door when he finally got out of Freeman. Down to his fear that they would find the typewriter he'd thrown into the water near the mothball fleet by the Carquinez bridge. Down to what he'd remembered while they were gone, that he'd left the yellow legal pad in his own car on the street, whose next page would be indented from the page with the notes he'd burned at Eli's Mile High Club, that the pigs would've found it for sure by now.

At last he stopped. Carolyn was staring at him with her mouth open. Shocked and dismayed, as he'd expected. After a moment of total silence, she blew her nose into a crumpled Kleenex.

"God, James. You were betrayed!"

"You got that right." Motherfuckin' Kwesi. Shame for these white girls to see into a Movement brother so bad.

"Did the plan include the police?" she asked.

"Their fine hand does seem to be in there, doesn't it?"

"But why would it be in their interest for all that to happen?"

"Gave them a good excuse to kill Nyame."

He switched his attention to Mary Lou, who was harder to read. Both of them got real quiet, waiting for him to say more, something that would tell them all what to do now. Well, damn. He didn't know that any better than they did. He brought the legs of his chair to the floor with a smart crack.

"Hey Mary Lou, can I smoke one of them?"

He gestured to her Parliaments on the counter. He'd already smoked two back to back while the ladies were on their stroll. May as well get one more off the woman before she put him out in the night.

She jumped up, grabbed the pack, shook out cigarettes, handed him the matches, and waited while he lit up for both of them. His fingers trembled, and it showed in the flame. Lord, how he hated to be up against the wall in front of a stranger.

"So why'd you go to Carolyn's house?" asked Mary Lou. She probably did not believe a single word he'd said.

"An old friend. Hadn't seen her in a while. Figured the pigs—" he noticed her wince at that—"the cops wouldn't check her out too fast."

"The police searched everything on the way in?" She seemed to be trying to work something out in her mind.

"Everything but the typewriter. They even read my other files. I remember, because they moved their lips."

"Your story doesn't hang together. It just doesn't make sense."

"You got to understand the police mentality," he told her. Might take this woman years to get what Carolyn grasped from the get-go. "They were in on it. They set Nyame up to be killed."

"Along with four of their own guards?"

"Then it went wrong," said Carolyn. "Maybe they expected a knife, or a gun. Turned out to be a bomb. A strong one, I guess . . ." her voice trailed off into uncertainty.

"You can go crazy thinking about it," James admitted.

"Seems like there are pieces missing," said Mary Lou.

"Maybe a hundred," he agreed, and he caught at her eyes with his own. "But I don't have them, and I'm not sure I ever will."

"This Nyame Jones, whoever he was—" she began slowly.

What was he doing here with a lady didn't even recognize the name of the finest brother that walked the face of the earth until two days ago, and he had to depend on her?

"Nyame Jones," she repeated. "He's probably the one who set you up."

No! Not Nyame. Kwesi, yes, who knew exactly what was in that typewriter, and also knew James didn't have the slightest idea. But Nyame must have believed James was in on the plan; he wouldn't have used him like that.

"Look, Mary Lou," he answered. "I've given you everything I know."

"Why'd you pick Carolyn?"

"I told you that."

"Why'd you come here?"

"My cousin in Fresno wasn't home. It was Carolyn's idea."

Carolyn nodded to confirm this.

"I'll give you what money I have. You can go somewhere else."

"Like where? Black people don't exactly have their choice of country homes, you know."

That shut her up for a minute. It might have offended her, but damn. This woman was going to understand at least one thing about him. He did not know where else to go.

CHAPTER EIGHT

Mary Lou stubbed out her cigarette. With that stare of his he looked just like the ugly picture in the morning paper. Carolyn wouldn't bring someone dangerous here, would she? Someone who might actually hurt them?

If he was telling the truth, though, this surely was one sad story. She stood up to clear the cups and wash out the coffee pot.

"So what's your decision, Mary Lou?" Carolyn asked.

For the life of her, Mary Lou didn't know why, but her friend trusted this man.

Her decision? She couldn't have him here. The town of Allen was at the center of the fight against Colonia. James would stick out like a sore thumb. Too much was at stake.

She glanced at the clock on the wall, quietly ticking its way through the silence as they waited for her reply. One-thirty a.m. Where would they go? That place on the highway, by the stoplight, the one everyone called the Punjabi Motel since it'd been bought by those Indians? Someone would still be up to let them in, probably the son-in-law. These people had even tighter families than the Mexicans, and they weren't about to pass up a paying customer either. Jeez, though, anyone there could easily recognize Carolyn from last summer. No, it'd be safer back down 99 to Emerald, or on up to Empire; there'd be bigger motels there.

She stood still and ran water at the sink for nothing. Cold outside, wintertime. James and Carolyn together. Unusual combo here in the San Joaquin Valley. She'd send them out of the house, and they'd get themselves caught. How was she gonna feel when that happened?

"What about the Martinezes?" she asked Carolyn.

"They didn't get too good a look. Tell them he's sick, like we already said. So sick he can't be bothered. No one can come to the house."

"They'll expect to see you at the office, Carolyn. You can't be around and not show up. The people know you."

"I'll be there. You can give me work to do."

She could turn over the pile on her desk to Carolyn and get started on the march. But just imagine if James got caught here. They would all three of them end up in jail, and the boycott against Colonia, maybe the whole entire Union for that matter, would be ruined by the publicity. No.

She shut the water off with a snap and turned around. She opened her mouth to tell them to leave. Their faces tilted up at her, like chicks that wanted to be fed again.

"He can stay the night, Carolyn. The night and a couple of days maybe, at the outside. Then he'll have to move on."

These people were here in her kitchen. She just didn't have it in her to turn them out.

CHAPTER NINE

Carolyn woke up earlier than she wanted the next morning, shoulders and upper arms so tense there was no chance to sleep again. The wrinkled sheets beside her were empty. Mary Lou would be up and gone; Saturday was just another work day in the Union. She rubbed at her stiff neck. A low throb had begun its pattern in the back of her head. Of course. Her body demanded back what had become its normal state. The ache of sadness. The strain of grief.

She reached into her duffel bag for the photograph of her mother. Mona of the black and white picture in the silver frame. Carolyn turned the memento over and over in her palm. The young Mona, dark eyes flashing from under a commanding brow as she delivered her fiery speech to the annual banquet of the Committee to Protect the Foreign Born. Activist Mona, vibrant Mona, tireless defender of the people Joe McCarthy tore to pieces. Exhausted Mona, who mixed more than one drink whenever she finally got home and proceeded to repeat over and over the stories that bothered her most, the friends who lost their government jobs, who would not play with the symphony again, who instructed their kids on what to say when the FBI came to the door.

And then there was Phil, who listened until he could bear it no more, then shut the book on his lap with a exasperated snap and went upstairs to bed. Phil wanted a wife to come home to, instead of a dinner plate covered with tin foil. He filed for divorce and pursued it with a determination that was as efficient as it was fair. He agreed to alimony without a fuss, and of course generous child support, but he never once reconsidered his decision, whether Mona begged him to when she was drunk or sober. Her father was much happier now, launched into his new domestic round. Carolyn understood him well, even sympathized with him, but couldn't quite forgive him. Phil, still among the living. Mona, who was dead.

The familiar lump rose, then settled into the usual place in the back of her throat. Why so much grief, given the Monas her daughter hadn't even liked? Listless Mona after Phil left, the one who drank too much, then shed her maudlin tears. Cowardly Mona, with all her high and mighty principles, who yet and still managed to forbid her high school senior self to go out with Char—no, James. James, James—get the new name inside her head. Mona the hypocrite, yelled down by the teenager's bold certainty about right and wrong, when all she had been was frightened for her daughter's safety in good old Inglewood, California, whose inhabitants bragged that a black man better not get caught outside after sunset.

Inglewood. Black now, she'd heard. She never went back there anymore. Apparently everyone really did leave when the blacks came, like they always said they would. Carolyn could have understood her mother's fear if only she had been able to admit it, if only her bluster had included a little honesty.

She was relieved to get away for college, if the truth be known, and after that she hadn't even been that close to her mother. So why the overwrought sentimentality now, for God's sake, when it did no one any good?

She set the picture on the bedside table with a gesture so violent it fell facedown. She grabbed it back, to make sure the glass hadn't cracked. Next she made herself get up and put on Mary Lou's flowered lavender robe over the purple nylon nightgown she had cadged from her friend the night before. She shuffled in socks across the room to look out the window. A translucent cold mist, so thick it blurred the outlines of the rusty junk pile in the neighbor's back yard, lay close to the ground. Each winter she read in the newspaper about the tule fog that caused car accidents out here, where whole families died. It looked as though it might hang around for days.

A flock of gray birds chattered in bare branches so close to the tiny house that they must have scraped it during yesterday's storm. Would these birds be the same ones whose sound attacked her too early every morning last summer, when she slept on the living room foldout couch? That clatter would force her out of bed to meet the sun, already furnace-like. The house would be hot and still except for those birds, Mary Lou and Rojelio long gone to the picket line. Chitter, chitter. Get to the office. Don't be lazy. Such a short time ago, and she hadn't understood yet what a privilege it was to have a healthy mother. Gobbled up by the Union and its interminable tasks during the last days that Mona had been a whole person on earth.

She went back to sit on the unmade bed, to shred the wad of damp Kleenex clutched in her hand. Those last high school years she had lived with Mona. That would have been the time to get to know her. But Carolyn had been busy. Her studies; her school friends; her friends from Anytown, USA; the interracial camp run by the National Conference of Christians and Jews; and friends who lived in parts of town her school friends didn't even know about. Her Anytown love who was now James. His crazy laugh that came from way deep in his throat, that sweet creamy brown that covered his long limbs, that made him so much more sensitive than the white boys in her high school, with their horrible jokes about niggers and jungle bunnies. The awful racist humor every single day. Mona had taught her it was wrong, wrong, wrong, but she never told her daughter exactly what to do about it.

James was her escape from it all, until that last summer before college. She hardly heard from him anymore. She spent her days in the typing pool of the Southern California Automobile Association with women whose pleasure in life was an old-fashioned donut at morning break and a thick sugar cookie in the afternoon. Her evenings were taken up with walks in the waning summer sun, full of adolescent dreams, until at last it came time to leave home. She didn't have so much to do then; she was just waiting. Why hadn't she talked to her mother more?

There was at least one significant conversation, though. Due to James's self-control, or whatever it was, in August her mother's pre-college lecture on birth control was still in time. Sensible Mona had cautioned against promiscuity but said Carolyn didn't have to marry the first man she slept with as long as, but only if, she was "careful." And Mona told her exactly how to be careful. Nothing common about that advice in 1962. Carolyn had listened well and had never gotten pregnant. For which she was grateful then, and grateful now to remember something that went right between her and her mother, even if it was too late to give her the credit she deserved.

James was always nice about Mona. Carolyn remembered Mona's ancient '47 Plymouth, inching through the winter rain, James at the wheel and her sopping up the water that came through the floor boards with every puddle.

"Does your mama know where you are right now, Curls?" he asked.

"You kidding? I told you what she said. 'It's just not safe.' And here she's full of lectures on how principle should never yield and all that crap!"

"So where does she think you are?"

"She didn't ask."

"Let you have the car, though."

"She always does."

"Just scared for her baby, Curls," James would say. "Go easy on your mama. She's paid her dues."

And so she had.

Sudden tears slipped down Carolyn's cheeks. With an effort she made herself move, this time into the bathroom to find something for her headache. Even Mary Lou's tidiness could not bring order to the tiny, cluttered space. She located an aspirin bottle so old it was coated with white powder on the inside, got out two, and swallowed them with a grimace at the alkaline taste of the tap water. Then she padded to the kitchen where she found starched curtains drawn against the fog, ashtrays cleared, cups rinsed, counters wiped clean and brewed coffee still hot on its Chemex over the burner flame. Mary Louise never was one to leave a mess, even on four hours' sleep.

She poured herself coffee, went back to the bedroom, dressed in her own jeans and sweater, and felt a little better. Tonight it was back to sleeping in T-shirt and underpants, even if that was not Mary Lou's style.

She heard his tentative rap at the bathroom door, then the sound of the shower. She dabbed at her face with a wad of tissue. James shouldn't have to see that she had been crying; God knew he had problems of his own.

She finished her coffee, combed her fingers through her hair, and returned to the kitchen for a second cup. This time she saw the note right away. Mary Lou's squarish hand was easy to read:

> *Carolyn. Have to find out if plumbing's o.k. at the camp and start calls for the march. Will tell anyone who asks you're here to help, but your friend is sick. With what? Hepatitis maybe? It's catching, so people might stay away. You folks decide, but let me know. Back around five. Help yourself to what you need. What's going to happen next?? ML*

She wished she knew. They might have a place to sleep for a while, but how long would Mary Lou let them stay?

Mary Lou would already be telling everyone that Carolyn had come to work in the office, so work she would. She grimaced. She'd have to go in there today; there was no other way to be in Mary Lou's world. Helping James was only right, though, and the same went for the UFW for that matter. Mona would have approved—enough of this moping around.

By the time he appeared she had set the table, mixed a can of frozen orange juice, put bacon on, and was ready to cook eggs. On tiptoes, her cheek on his unshaven one, her untamed curls next to his new damp haircut, she hugged him.

CHAPTER TEN

He had woken up a little calmer, he thought, but he flinched at her touch. It was as if they'd put him in the joint already; in fact, jail was where he had learned to surround himself with a safety zone. That zone had to be empty right now, maybe forever, for all he knew.

"Mm, you smell good," Carolyn said as he extricated himself from her embrace. "What did you put on your skin?"

"Hey now, that's my man Quincy bought it for me. He don't mess around." James held her at arm's length, and tried out his smile. If only Quincy could be right here, right now. A brother would understand.

"What kind of eggs do you want?" She got the signal and backed off.

"Sunny side up," he said. "That'd be mighty fine."

"Did you sleep well?" she asked.

"Might have been a couple hours where I was actually unconscious there."

"Well that's progress." Eggs sizzled as she cracked more of them into a frying pan. "How are you feeling?"

"I'm alive," he answered. He emptied his juice glass and glanced out the window. Still nothing but steamy white ground fog. What kind of place was this, anyhow?

"Your friend Mary Lou scared me," he said. "For a while there I thought she was gonna turn us out."

"She still might."

Carolyn flipped the eggs and turned off the fire, then showed him Mary Lou's note. He read it through three times while she eased the food onto a plate in front of him.

"She's as much as promised she'll keep her friends away," he said. "The girl's cool, but what if we need to be here for a while?"

"We've got to have a long-term plan," Carolyn answered.

Even if Quincy came up with the money and identification tomorrow, it was hard enough just to stay on top of the panic that lay around the corner.

He should leave the country. But go off by himself to a strange place where they didn't even speak English? Scared him to death. There was always the underground. Kwesi had been one to talk on how cool the underground was.

There must be other choices, but he couldn't think of one. And he had meditated on it ever since the instant he saw that gray-green clay like lump inside the damned typewriter. Whatever. At least on this one day he was relatively safe. And there were eggs that were getting cold.

He began on his breakfast. A red sedan slid by the kitchen window, and just the shape emerging from the white air was enough to get his heart to pound. As the car passed onto the next block, the fog closed behind it and all was quiet again.

Carolyn said nothing more, mercifully, until he finished eating. He knew she would start in again, though, when she went into the living room to turn on the TV as loud as it would go. First she worried some about how much they were imposing on her friend, and then she worried some more about how soon Mary Lou was likely to make them leave. Then before he had time to react to all that, she was on to something else.

"I don't ever want Kwesi to know who I am," she said.

"I don't exactly mean to introduce the dude to all my friends," he muttered under his breath. But the girl was right. Kwesi was dangerous. He wished he'd understood that a whole lot sooner himself.

"I can't quite hear you, James." Dramatic organ music of a Spanish soap opera offered the perfect backdrop. It almost made him laugh out loud.

"I said he won't know you, Carolyn," he almost shouted. "You won't meet the man. Not in this lifetime."

"What about Quincy? They're both with the Panthers, aren't they? Is he a friend of Kwesi's?"

"Naw. Kwesi works in Richmond. Quincy's in the Oakland office."

"But they probably know each other, right?"

"Maybe, maybe not. Quincy's different, Curls, he's loyal. He's the one that's helping me, remember?"

She rose to clear the table. He jumped up, took the plate out of her hand, and managed a reassuring pat on her shoulder. Funny. He used to fancy himself Carolyn's protector as she drove their young selves through segregated LA, but now he was the one who needed protection, who counted on her to provide it. A rush of gratitude swept through him.

"Carolyn." His old self for a second, the one who never minded being next to a woman, he even touched her cheek. "Thanks. For everything."

He'd meant to say it before, but now was never too late. She flushed, and he could see she was pleased. She moved forward and there she was, bright blue eyes a foot from his face.

"Now sit yourself down, Curls," he said, stepping back. "Let me clean up. All this thinking about jail reminds me how much I like doing dishes."

She leaned on the kitchen table and fingered the note.

"Well, what's the sickness going to be?" she asked.

"Your friend suggested hepatitis," he said.

"What do you think?" she said. "You're the one who's going to have to fake this illness."

"It means you've got to rest a lot." He'd seen the disease when he was orderly once in the county jail's sick ward. He filled the sink with hot water. "Gives a good excuse to stay inside all the time."

Now this was what he liked, when they got down to business and solved the little problems, one by one. That and the fact that he still had another cup of coffee to drink. Might be like this for him from now on. If he was lucky.

"Plus, hepatitis is so contagious no one will want to come near you," Carolyn said. "Once I knew this girl? She told me when she got it, her own boyfriend wouldn't even be in the same room with her." She found Mary Lou's dish towel and began to dry.

"Well, it sounds all right," he said. "Good idea. Your friend Mary Lou is smart. Do I look yellow enough around the eyes, though?" He widened them at her, which made her laugh; then he bent to scrub out the frying pan. "Probably all you can see is red," he told her.

Another car went by the window, and this time he managed not even to look up.

"Sometimes you have jaundice, sometimes you don't," Carolyn said. "It didn't show on my friend. She couldn't drink, though."

"Couldn't drink? Well, then, better stock up ahead of time." He went straight for the refrigerator and got out a beer.

"Come on, James," Carolyn said. "This early in the morning?"

Yes, goddamn it, this early. He took a big swallow and she had the sense to let it go.

"So it's decided then?" she asked.

"Yep," he said. "Hepatitis it is."

Done. Good. Now he could slow down; he had to, to convince people. Suddenly he really did feel tired. He sat in the hard chair and tipped it against the wall. The fog was beginning to lift. The curtains were sheer. Was he hidden enough? He didn't have the energy to think it through.

The kitchen back to its spotless state, it reminded James of his mama and aunt. They always had told him and his brother they didn't want helpless males around, so one thing was, he knew how to keep a house. He clacked the chair down and went into the living room where there were real curtains, drawn. He clutched his can of Tecate like a lifeline. He'd give anything to have a normal day. Drink some beer. Smoke some dope. Rap things down with Quincy and some other brothers. But normality wasn't going to happen. Not today. Not ever.

He sat on his unmade sofa bed and stared at the TV. A guy was giving a news broadcast in Spanish. He caught a word or two. Should've paid more attention to that old hag who'd tried to drill high school Spanish into his head. Nothing here about himself or Freeman, though.

"I'm going to the store," Carolyn called in from the kitchen. "It's just a couple blocks down Joseph Street. Want anything?"

"Yeah. Cigarettes."

"I thought you stopped smoking."

"I thought so, too," he said.

"It's unhealthy."

Now tell me, Lord, he asked himself, just how was it possible to feel so grateful and then two minutes later equally irritated at the very same person? He would take help, he probably even would take advice, much as he hated it, but he needed not to be questioned.

"So's life, unhealthy as shit," he answered. That ought to shut her up, but no.

"Something else to thank Kwesi for," she had to add, standing in the doorway. "God, James, think of what he did to you."

James grunted. It wasn't going to do any good getting into all this right now.

"Sometimes I believe these people on the left fringe are just as dangerous as the ones all the way to the right, don't you?" asked Carolyn.

Girl always was the type to analyze, blur the lines he felt were clear.

"Nope," he answered. "It matters whether you're on the side of the people with the money or those without."

For a moment it was so quiet he could hear the ticking of Mary Lou's clock on the kitchen wall.

"What kind of cigarettes?" Carolyn asked.

"Marlboros," he answered. His old brand. He could hardly wait.

A moment later the kitchen door slammed, and he was alone for the first time since he'd knocked on Carolyn's door.

He sat totally still until she was around the corner and past the house. Then he snapped off the TV and began to examine everything. He didn't have much time. She'd be back before long. He didn't even understand what he was looking for, but he knew he had to do it.

Two of the living room windows opened, the third was stuck. He worked the lock on the front door to make sure he understood it. He looked through the coat closet, which had an old sweater on a wire hanger and not much else. He went into the bathroom and checked the medicine cabinet and linen closet. Acne medicine, a new toothbrush still in its box, a jumble of things white women use to fix their hair. Two extra sets of sheets, an old cotton sleeping bag, an old blue electric blanket. Not much and nothing unusual. The bathroom window was high, narrow, and louvered. He went down the hall and started in on Mary Lou's room.

The near window, by her bed, was painted shut, but the one on the opposite wall opened easily. He put down the Venetian blinds on both of them, then stood there, looking out of the crack on the side, to calculate. Here was the way out if they came to get him at both doors at once. Sprint across the two back yards and between those houses and you'd be right on the next block, real quick.

He felt in Mary Lou's dresser drawers, one by one, trying not to notice her cotton underpants and sensible bras, surprised by her collection of short, gauzy pastel nightgowns. Not his style, to look through a woman's things, but it was hopeless to want to be the way he was before.

Finding it made him realize what he was looking for. In the farthest corner of her bedroom closet was an old rifle, a .22, with ammunition on the shelf above. A gun he actually knew how to use. All that hunting with his daddy in the woods come in handy at last. He checked all the parts to make sure it would work, then put it right back where it was.

He liked that it was there.

Carolyn would be back any minute. Time to rest easy now.

A knock came at the kitchen door, and he jumped sky high. Damn, did people come through this house whenever the fuck they felt like it?

He did not want to answer that door, but whoever it was might've already heard him moving around. He opened it, his blood surging with a fear so intense it resembled excitement, his face averted to avoid the head-on view. A small dapper man with flowing white hair and a clipped silver mustache smiled up at him.

"*On'ta* Mary Lou?" he demanded in friendly fashion. When he saw the confused look on James's face, he switched into an accented but fluent English.

"Where is she, Mary Lou?"

"She's not here," answered James.

He could see curiosity written on the man's face, the more so once he realized James wasn't Mexican. The stranger worked his way into the kitchen as though he had been here before. Carolyn had to be back soon. She'd know how to handle this.

"Not at the office, either. Maybe Jovita's for lunch? But I brought food here, for Mary Lou."

The man gave an expression of exaggerated sorrow and plunked down a brown paper bag redolent with a spicy smell. He unpacked foil-wrapped burritos, then a six-pack of Budweiser beer. He sat at the kitchen table. James didn't want to tower over him in the small room, so he sat too.

"My name is Rafael Ramirez. And who do I have the pleasure of meeting?" Mr. Ramirez was amiable enough as he squinted up at James, but definite with his question.

"James. James Sweet." He tried to sound weak and confused, as though he had a fever. Where the hell was Carolyn?

"I came through town, and of course I must see Mary Lou," said Ramirez. "But since she is not here, I will open one of these instead."

He popped the tab off the can closest to him, wiped the top with a shirt sleeve, and took a long pull. He looked as though he planned to settle in for the afternoon.

"Would you like one?" He snapped open a second one and proffered it. James couldn't think of how to extricate himself, so he gripped the cold can and swallowed half its foamy liquid, the Budweiser bland after the Tecate he'd already had. He felt small beads of sweat form on his forehead and wondered if the man could see it from his side of the small table.

"Against the rules to drink during the work day," said Ramirez. He threw out a little boy's mischievous smile. "Mary Lou wouldn't like it. But since she's not here, I'll pretend I don't hear her tell me to stop. Would you like food?"

James managed to shake his head no. Ramirez unwrapped a huge paper plate of rice and beans and shredded meat that looked like it could be either beef or pork. He started in on it at once, then talked on between bites and swigs of beer.

"I'm going to Stockton, to talk to the judge," he said. "To tell him how poor I am, so the lady lawyer for the Union can argue the jury should include people as poor as I."

Ramirez shrugged and lifted his eyebrows in disbelief. James watched, mesmerized by the man's constantly moving mouth.

"I come all the way from Mexico, and there's not even work here, not in the grape, not in the tomatoes, *nada*. It's winter, *¿como no?* I should be home, in Michoacán. Still, Mary Lou says I must come. And why should I mind? The judge sent money to pay my way."

Ramirez took out a bundle of bills and waved it in James's face. This was crazy. Ramirez. The Martinez family. Even if they didn't see or read the news in English, even if he did look different from that mug shot the police had spread around, already out here in this godforsaken place he was no longer a secret. He glanced outside. The street lay empty, cold in the thin winter sun.

"Can you believe it?" Ramirez continued. "They want to hear I have no money. So they give me twenty dollars a day for food and a place to stay. Now I am richer than I have ever been."

James couldn't help but laugh. He liked the old man's company. Small bits of meat had flown in all directions during the discourse.

Ramirez finished the first beer, opened two more, and again shoved a can across the table to James, who quickly downed the one he had begun and started in on the next. For the first time since Freeman, he was beginning to relax.

"Well, so? I'll tell them," Ramirez rambled on. "I'll tell them I have two houses, one room each, one for the family here, one for the family in Mexico. Not enough money for either place. Then I'll tell them the ways the *pinché* Colonia cheats you, every time. The way they don't pay you overtime, slice money from your check, hand it to you, then look at you like what're you going to do about that, you little *mojado*, you wetback? After that I'll come back here and take Mary Lou dancing."

With this he stood and waltzed in circles around the small kitchen, bumping gently into the table, then into James himself. James was proud that he didn't flinch. This beer wasn't a bad idea at all; it meant he could act natural.

"Ay, how I would like to dance with the lady lawyer the Union sent for that case," Ramirez crooned in a dreamy voice as he whirled. He returned to sit before his half-eaten food, then emptied the can before him.

"What was your case about?" James asked. He had to say something. This man, after all, was still only about two feet away, just the table separating them. The birds outside clattered suddenly, and he jumped. Ramirez didn't seem to notice.

"Who knows?" he answered. "They say I hit an *esquirol* when I was on the picket line." He saw James's mystified expression and explained.

"One who breaks the strike. In English a scab. Now do I look like a man who is capable of a thing like that?" He leaned halfway across the table and held up a face carved with injured innocence. James found himself grinning again. He should memorize that exact expression, in case he got caught. The street was so near it would take the pigs exactly one second to get in. And those gauzy curtains really were too easy to see through. Again he resolved to stay in the living room more.

"You plan to stay for how long?" Ramirez asked, still leaning toward him. Suddenly he seemed quite sober, and James could still feel liquor in his veins. Careful here. Ramirez was way too curious.

"I don't know," he said. He got to his feet and retreated toward the door to the living room. "I've been sick." He should have said this to begin with. His mind was fuzzy. How many more questions? What if he had to make up new facts? Would they be the right ones? Would he even remember them?

The door opened and Carolyn flew in, arms loaded with groceries.

"*Buenas días,*" she said, eyebrows raised in surprise. She put the two bags down on the table right in front of Ramirez, as if that would keep him away from James.

"*Buenas. Rafael Ramirez. Me recuerde de la huelga el verano pasado?*"

"*Cierto. Mucho gusto de verle otra vez.*"

Girl's Spanish sounded pretty damned fine, something about how they knew each other from the strike and how happy she was to see him again. Easier to understand Spanish after a few beers. Next she turned to James.

"I'm surprised you're up," she told him. "That doctor said to rest during the day, remember?"

She herded him into the living room and made a show of getting him to lie down on the sofa, even finding an extra blanket and tucking it around him. He did have a headache, in fact, and he felt drowsy. It felt good to be fussed over.

She went back to the kitchen and closed the door. James could hear her chatter as she put the groceries away.

"Mary Lou went to the camp to see about that drainage problem. You didn't give James a beer, did you? If there's one thing that doctor was clear on, it's that people with hepatitis shouldn't drink. I'm surprised he did that, he really shouldn't. And hepatitis is contagious. Did you know that?"

Ramirez, tipsy and embarrassed, was gone as soon as he could manage to say goodbye. She waited until the sound of his car faded, then came back into the living room.

"For God's sake, James," she said, looming over his low bed. "Hepatitis gives you the perfect excuse for that not to happen. You say you can't talk, you can't drink, you have to rest."

"I'll do it from now on," he promised. Couldn't blame Carolyn for scolding him, but events unrolled before you could stop them.

"If anyone else comes, just be quiet," she said. "Don't even open the door. Under any circumstances."

For about a minute he had actually felt ordinary there, but apparently one of the new rules was that ordinary was dangerous. Motherfuckin' little town of Allen was clearly not the place to be. Yet he couldn't even think of going back on the road, strangers in every car, cops in the restaurants, afraid to stop for the night.

"No one else will come," Carolyn reassured him. "Mary Lou said things are real quiet over the winter. This has been unusual."

She sounded as though she wanted to convince herself, he thought. Then he turned over and sleep descended upon him.

CHAPTER ELEVEN

On Saturday Mary Lou was in the UFW office by nine a.m., and by ten she had her service cases in a pile, a stack of thumbed folders a foot high, all ready for Carolyn to take over. Juana Andrade's workers compensation case was on top. Juana had hurt her back lifting crates right on the job, but of course Colonia's company doctor denied the injury was work related. It had to be appealed by Wednesday.

Finally, at two in the afternoon Carolyn dragged herself into the door and over to her desk. How could it be this late and her friend managed to look like she had just gotten out of bed? Had Carolyn even run a brush over those tangled curls of hers?

"If you can do these, I'll start on the march," Mary Lou announced at once. Carolyn shrugged.

"Read the files," Mary Lou continued. "Then we'll go over them together."

They both got to work. Mary Lou made preliminary calls to the guys in charge of the UFW offices in Selma, Delano, and Arvin-Lamont. She told them that Cesar had decided he wanted the march. They talked about what date it should begin, how long it would take to get from one town to the next, the type of program when it ended in Empire, and how many marchers each office could produce. The whole danged buildup needed to start in March when the workers were drifting back from Mexico, but the march had to be done by April when the work in the fields picked up and everyone had to get in there to feed their families. Above all, the planners worried about the weather. Would the winter rains be over? Would it still be so cold the women wouldn't come with their babies? Well, what could they do about any of that? They began to plan the route.

The men talked endlessly. Mary Lou listened to everything and agreed when she could. She watched Carolyn out of the corner of her eye.

Her friend sat and flipped through the files, twirling a curl of her hair, biting at her fingernail cuticles, frowning. Not only had she lost a lot of weight, she looked like she couldn't even concentrate. Unusual for Carolyn, who digested files at her desk every single day last summer, even when all hell was breaking loose.

"Hey," Mary Lou called. "You over there. Across the room. Know why I'm looking forward to this march so much?"

Carolyn glanced up.

"And just why is that, Ms. Mary Lou?" she asked, a smile teasing at the corner of her lips. "'Cause you just love it up there in Empire, right? You like hanging out with the hotshots from Colonia?"

"Because I hate Colonia so much. They are such pigs!"

"No kidding," Carolyn laughed. "You hated them last summer too, but I thought it was just the heat." They both studied the low gray sky outside Mary Lou's window for a second.

"You know why I hate them so much?" Mary Lou asked Carolyn.

"Because in the olden days, which were about ten years ago, as you have told me many times, Colonia foremen still made the workers ride in the back of the pickups while the dogs were in the front?"

Mary Lou smiled with relief. This was the Carolyn she knew so well. She walked the length of the drafty room to look out the window at the front of the building. Railroad tracks, the stoplight, Jovita's red and green neon, all quiet in the January gloom.

"That's part of it," she said as Carolyn joined her there. "They like the animals better than the humans. Reminds me of some of your Berkeley groups. Vegetarianism ranks way higher than the working class half the time."

"Hey now," said Carolyn. "Berkeley's my town and don't you forget it."

"So, keep guessing," Mary Lou teased her friend.

"'Cause Colonia would divide the workers by setting the Mexicans and Portuguese men in different rows next to each other's women so they'd get jealous and fight all the time instead of organizing against the boss?" Carolyn asked.

"That too," Mary Lou said. "You remember all my stories, Carolyn. I was worried city life would make you forget us out here."

Both women chuckled. Now Carolyn was looking in the other direction, out the side toward the fields. Mary Lou followed her gaze. The vineyards, with their dark, dripping limbs draped on wires. Yesterday they just seemed like death and destruction, but today they held a bleak beauty.

"Okay, well wanna hear the latest story?" Mary Lou asked. "You've read that Juana Andrade comp claim? What it doesn't say is that Colonia made her keep coming to work, even though she'd injured her back so much hauling crates of grapes around that she had to hold onto the wall just to walk. So *finally* they let her see the company doctor."

"And he says she's faking, right?"

"Nooo." Mary Lou had to drag it out. Carolyn finally looked like her old self. Her friend's blue eyes radiated interest. Her black curly hair just about stood on end. "It wasn't that simple."

They both watched a hawk circle low. Hunting, that was all the big birds did. Mary Lou had been watching them as long as she could remember, but she'd never seen one actually dive down and get its prey. She shuddered. What if James got caught, right there in her very own house?

"So what did the doctor say, then?" Carolyn asked. She stood there with her arms folded, still staring where the hawk had been, even though now it was over the horizon.

"That doctor poked at Juana's back for a second and then he looked her right in the face and had the nerve to tell her that she ate too many beans!"

"You have got to be kidding!"

"Nope," said Mary Lou. She paced along the window and back. "That's the way those Colonia pigs really are. Doesn't matter if they're in those fancy offices in Empire or down here in plain little old Allen. Vicious anti-Mexican, anti-farmworker creeps!"

"So how did Juana respond to that?" Carolyn asked.

"Well, she's sort of shy, you know, but she managed to say it wasn't true, that she didn't eat that many beans, that she didn't even like beans," Mary Lou said. "By the time she got to me she had it straight, though, and she told me that she may be Mexican but that did *not* mean that all she ate was beans. Of course the doctor wrote in his report that the injury wasn't work related."

Mary Lou picked the file up off Carolyn's desk and dropped it back down with a smack.

"We'll win this one on the appeal," she added. "But that's 'cause Juana knows to come to us and we know how to do these things. What about the ones who don't? They just go away and don't cost Colonia any of their little precious blood money, that's what."

"And then they feel bad about their own food, no doubt," Carolyn added. "Frantz Fanon, internalized oppression, and all that. But you know what Frances Moore Lappe says in *Diet for a Small Planet*, don't you? Turns out that beans and rice combined make a complete protein. So people aren't going to have to eat so much meat, so the rain forests will stay around. Mexican food turns out to be the perfect combo. Don't you think that's interesting?"

"That is just like you, Carolyn." Mary Lou laughed. "You think of this totally other thing, you claim it's connected, and then you ask if it's 'interesting.' Well how could it be anything else but interesting by the time you've done all that?"

"I'll take that as a compliment," Carolyn said. She smiled wide enough for her dimples to show.

"Still, though," Carolyn stood there musing like she always did, like she'd never get back to work. "It's hard to believe they consciously come up with these tactics. Someone sits at a desk or they have a meeting and actually figure this shit out?"

"Well, believe it," said Mary Lou. "'Cause that's exactly what they do. I'm tellin' you the only thing that's gonna bring Colonia down is organizing these people who work for them, to the point where they'll never let up."

Carolyn took the hint and got back to the file. This time she did it with purpose, as if she had the energy to make something out of Juana's case after all. By the time they closed the office at six they both had gotten a lot done.

The evening at Joseph Street was quiet, all three of them feeling their way around all the subjects they didn't want to talk about, being careful not to take up much room in the small space they shared. Mary Lou fried up some hamburgers eventually. Carolyn tossed a green salad. James trailed the two of them, wiping down counters and doing dishes as they went, then popped three beers. Then they sat to eat.

"Cesar phoned the office today," Mary Lou said after the first few moments of contented chewing. "Just before you got there."

"The Great Man himself called you up, just like that? What did he want?" Carolyn asked. She wiped her mouth, then began to construct her second hamburger on the bun. Tomatoes, lettuce, mustard, no onions. She hated onions.

"He says we have to make sure we get all the Colonia strikers out for the march." Mary Lou frowned, her lips in a thin, straight line. James had finished his food already, she noticed, and tipped back his chair to watch the two of them. The man didn't hardly eat at all.

"Well, of course," Carolyn said. "It won't be that hard, will it?" Her words were muffled as she bit into her creation.

"Are you kidding?" Mary Lou answered. "Maybe half are still around here, the rest are scattered all over. Mexico for the winter, out on the coast looking for work, everywhere. We're gonna have to track every single one of them down."

At least none of her people were scabbing that she knew of, not yet.

"So, you call them up," Carolyn, still eating, waved her left hand for emphasis, as if she knew what she was talking about. "Or write a letter, and tell them when the march will be. What's the big deal?"

"The big deal is a bunch of 'em won't wanna come."

"Why not?"

"First off, the ones they know as leaders, like Rojelio, are out on the boycott so they won't be able to help. Second, the big day, when the march ends? It's a Saturday, and people'll have to take off work, which means they lose money. That'll make it hard, especially to get the Portuguese, 'cause they're such tightwads. But the thing they're really gonna worry about is they'll be seen, and then they'll lose their jobs."

"Oh come on," Carolyn said. "The blacklist went out with the fifties."

"This is the fifties here, Carolyn." Mary Lou felt James nod his head to agree with her, more than she saw it. Here was someone who understood how hard it was for things to change.

"But there will be thousands of people by the time it gets to Empire, right?" Carolyn asked. "Now how is Colonia going to pick these workers out?"

"Don't be naive." Mary Lou stood her ground. "Colonia knows what goes on with its workers, especially the ones who have the nerve to go out on strike. And they know how to pressure the other growers around here, too."

"So what's to do about it?"

"We'll have to find every single striker, Carolyn. Talk to 'em, convince 'em this is what they have to do, for the Union. I thought maybe you'd find it an interesting project to work on."

James, of course, would be long gone before the march occurred, but even if Carolyn just got started on this, it'd be a help. And who knew, maybe she'd even stick around.

"Just what I need. More interesting things to do with my time." Carolyn rolled her eyes and reached for a fresh paper napkin to work the juice from the meat off her fingers.

At least she didn't say no, Mary Lou thought as she watched her friend and James rise at once, as if on a hidden signal, to do the final cleanup so they could closet themselves in the living room to talk under the sound of her clock radio turned up loud. As for her, she had the night to read in bed. Old *El Malcriados*, the UFW newspaper they printed up in La Paz, put her right to sleep. She didn't even hear Carolyn crawl into her bed.

On Sunday Mary Lou always closed the office unless there was something urgent. It was the one day none of the honchos in La Paz would call. She slept so late that James and Carolyn were both up and dressed before she appeared in the kitchen, still in her bathrobe at ten thirty a.m. She cooked again—scrambled eggs with chorizo, flour tortillas, orange juice, and coffee. James wolfed the meal down for once and told her it was delicious, but otherwise he was completely quiet. He didn't even seem surprised that her white Okie self knew how to make Mexican food, which she discovered she loved during her time with Rojelio.

As for Carolyn, she talked through the whole meal about anything that came to mind, from the fact that the fog was socked in even more than usual to asking about every single person she could remember from the summer before. It was as if she knew that if she stopped chattering, even for a minute, Mary Lou would start asking the hard questions. How long were they going to stay? Where would they go from here?

But the minute James had finished with the dishes, and the man certainly did know how to clean up a kitchen, she had to give him that, Carolyn was off and gone. To Fresno she said, to pick up some things for James. As for him, he disappeared into the living room. She didn't hear a thing from in there until Carolyn got back, and by that time it was almost dark.

Carolyn came through the door loaded down with what must have been every newspaper she could find, which was a lot being as how Fresno was the largest city in the San Joaquin Valley. Plus her own transistor radio and books, which as usual she seemed totally proud of.

"Look at what I found," she exclaimed. "*Another Country* by James Baldwin. I was surprised it was out here. I got it for James, but I wonder if he already read it. But check it out, I also found this."

She held up something called *Small Changes* by Marge Piercy as if Mary Lou should know what she was talking about, which she certainly did not. She picked up the book and thumbed through it while her friend chattered on.

"And I also got these Nero Wolfe mysteries," said Carolyn. "I am so excited! My mother used to love these. 'Don't you flummox me,' she told the House Un-American Activities Committee when she was called. 'I know flummery when I see it!' The fat man with the orchids who solves all the crimes? That's the way he talks in these mysteries."

What in the world was Carolyn talking on and on about, wondered Mary Lou. But this Marge Piercy book looked interesting, she had to admit. Nothing like having Carolyn around to keep your mind occupied. She looked up to laugh at her friend but found that tears were sliding down Carolyn's cheeks.

"Oh, your mom. I am so sorry about your mom, Carolyn," said Mary Lou. Carolyn even walked toward her like she wanted physical contact, a hug or something, which Mary Lou dodged by turning to the dishes in the rack, drying cloth in hand. She wasn't one of these Berkeley touchy-feely types and she never would be, but she snapped open two Tecate beers for the two of them, complete with a saucer of lime and salt. It was still her day off, dang it. Maybe this would make them both feel better.

James chose that moment to get out to the kitchen at last, rubbing at his eyes as though he had just woken, curious maybe about the women's chatter? He had on his jeans and a white T-shirt that didn't look so clean, with a hole worn a third of the way around the neck. His feet were stuck into his street shoes without any socks, and he hadn't shaved since they'd gotten here. What in the world had he been doing with himself? Not a single sound from that living room all day. Carolyn perked up, though, when she saw him, and she watched his every move as he ambled over to the sink to rinse his hands and face.

"Want a Tecate?" Mary Lou offered hers, still untouched, trying to be friendly.

"No thanks," he said, glancing at Carolyn. "Got any coffee?"

"I'll make you some," said Carolyn, and she went into action as though there hadn't been a tear on her face. James buried his head in the newspapers, sitting there at the kitchen table, taking up a whole lot of room and not even saying another thing. Mary Lou took a tug at the beer. Of course he was in a bind and all, but the least he could do was be friendly to Carolyn. After all, she was helping him; even Mary Lou was helping him. Who did he think he was to sit around like this and do nothing?

Carolyn disappeared into the bathroom to put herself back together, and Mary Lou began to cook. Chicken enchiladas, made from scratch, rice and beans. It was going to be good.

"That food is smelling mighty fine," said James, lifting his head from the papers at last.

"No green salad, though," she said, her back to him as she searched the crisper and handed out tomatoes and a cucumber, which he had to take because he was sitting between her and the kitchen table.

"Why not? No lettuce?" he asked, lining them up neatly on the table behind him. "You got something to cut on? I can slice these things."

She bent in another direction and got a worn wooden board back to him, still not turning around.

"No iceberg lettuce, that's for sure. And you can't find any other kind in the stores out here. You haven't heard about the boycott?"

He shook his head.

"Where's your friend been?" she asked Carolyn, who emerged with her face scrubbed red and her eyes dry. "Timbuktu?"

She tried to tease them, but they both looked serious so she just kept talking.

"Grapes and iceberg lettuce," she said to James. "After the harvest Cesar sent most everyone out to the cities. They're sleeping in churches, working with union organizers. Grapes are over now, but iceberg lettuce is year-round, and they want everyone to boycott it 'til the Salinas growers sign on with the UFW."

"Must be some organizing job," observed James. "This country's a big place."

"Yeah, like tell it to those waitresses at Lyle's," Carolyn said.

"Where's Lyle's?" James asked.

"It's this place in Visalia," Mary Lou said. "Where all the white people go. I don't even like it there; it's like the Mexican world out here disappears completely when you're in Lyle's. But Carolyn stopped there every time she drove to Delano last summer. The girl just had to have her hamburger and french fries."

"The amazing thing was," Carolyn said to James, "every single time we would ask for a salad with no iceberg lettuce the waitress would look at us like we were crazy. First of all she wouldn't know what iceberg lettuce was, I guess because she didn't have a clue that there was any other type. But mainly she acted like she'd never heard of the UFW. 'United Farm Workers Union? What's that?' Only the union that was on the front page of the paper and in the TV news every day, that's all."

Mary Lou glanced at James. He was just taking it in, listening to Carolyn talk. And the tomatoes and cucumber were all cut up, she noticed. Arranged on the plate in a circle, real nice.

"I don't even like iceberg lettuce that much," Carolyn continued. "Romaine is better. And healthier. More vitamin B."

"Count on Curls here to know the important stuff," said James with a grin. Carolyn flushed red with pleasure.

Mary Lou served up apple crisp for dessert, with coffee made fresh. They both ate like they weren't sure where the next meal would come from.

The newspapers. Mary Lou read them herself that night after the other two were asleep, James in the living room and Carolyn in her own bed, snoring softly right next to her while she leafed through the stories. "*Jones' Last Visitor at Folsom Disappears.*" The *Modesto Bee*, lead story. "*Where is Charles Brown? Did He Bring in the Gun?*" The *Fresno Bee*, same thing.

She really did have a fugitive hiding out here. She just could not have this going on in her house for long at all. No one had come by since Raul Ramirez, but that was only because it was winter and they hadn't gotten going on this march yet. When they did, her house would be full. He had to be gone way before then.

Monday, Tuesday, and Wednesday it seemed like all she did was work her butt off at the office and slink around at home, trying not to hear them talk in her own danged living room. Carolyn knew the terms of the bargain. She put in her hours at the office, and she got Juana Andrade's appeal filed on time too. But when Juana showed up to thank her for the work, Carolyn had this look on her face that said she wasn't even trying to understand what Mary Lou and Juana were saying. Pathetic Spanish to be sure—half the time Mary Lou was embarrassed for her friend— but still, all last summer at least Carolyn had tried to keep up. Now she just sat there staring at what had become endless rain again during the week, like she was trying to figure some whole other thing out.

Which she was, Mary Lou knew that. She felt bad for the both of them. James looked like a doe caught in the headlights whenever she caught a glimpse of him, his soft brown eyes injured, his skinny legs about to be knocked right out from under him. As for Carolyn, all she did was worry about him, her eyes following him everywhere he moved. Mary Lou hoped her friend's feelings didn't get hurt by this man on top of everything else. Not only did he seem indifferent to the deaths out there at Freeman, he didn't seem nearly as tuned into Carolyn as she wanted him to be.

By Thursday morning it was raining, and Mary Lou was still at home after nine. What if Cesar called? James, up and dressed and silent as always, poured her a cup of coffee.

His look had changed. His shirt was tucked in, and he had shaved. He watched as she took her first sip. Good, she had to admit. Dark, strong, and delicious. He had made it; he did that every morning now. And he had cooked the breakfast. She helped herself to scrambled eggs with salsa straight off her very own Thanksgiving platter with the red-wattle turkey design, added two warm Bisquick biscuits slathered with butter and honey, and when she finished that cup, he got up right away to pour her a second. She saw what he was doing; he was making it nice for her. The circumstances were nuts but still, they had settled in, like a little family.

She sat back at the kitchen table. James as always had his head in the *Modesto Bee*. Mary Lou glanced at the headline—*Charles Brown Disappears Without a Trace*. How long would this thing be on the front page? 'Without a Trace'—that was one good thing, right? Except that here he was, long brown limbs taking up half the room as always, and putting everything at risk.

"Things would be lazy if they weren't so crazy, and I wasn't following you . . ." Carolyn was actually singing under her breath as she moved around the two of them to get her own food. "Dave Mason," she informed both Mary Lou and James. "And that's the only line I know." She couldn't carry the tune at all, but James was underscoring it with a soft thump of his palm on his chair. Everything was getting way too cozy in here.

"What happens next?" Mary Lou asked. She found she couldn't meet their stare, either of them.

Carolyn went immediately toward the living room to put on the TV or the phonograph.

"Honestly, Carolyn," Mary Lou said. "That is part of the problem!"

Mary Lou's annoyance stopped her friend cold.

"I don't like secrets," Mary Lou continued. "And I don't like all the noise it takes to cover them up. It's ridiculous to think this place is bugged. And I don't even care if it is! Drag one of them Colonia brothers in here for me and I'd tell him everything, I swear, 'til he was sick to death of listening. I'd love that chance."

Carolyn sat down, chastened, but James still knew what was important. Wearing his calm expression and without asking permission from anyone, he simply switched on the transistor the two of them had in the kitchen. He turned up the volume with a don't-you-dare-stop-me look Mary Lou had never seen before. A Mexican *cumbia* blared out. "Where are you two going to go after this?" Mary Lou asked them.

The rain dribbled over the eaves and plinked steadily into the furrowed lines directly beneath. Things were soaking out there. James got up to pour coffee around yet again.

"You remember Quincy, don't you? He's that friend of James we told you about?" Carolyn asked. The question sounded rehearsed, as if they had already discussed what should happen when this moment came.

"Yeah, you mentioned him before," said Mary Lou. She couldn't help but glance at her watch. She had to get to the office; she had a call coming in from Porterville at ten.

"Well I've talked to him. I called from a pay phone in Fresno. Safer for me than James." She saw that Mary Lou was worried about getting out of here, so of course Carolyn decided to talk on at length.

"Like everything that has to do with James," Carolyn said, "it took time. Quincy told me to call back at a public phone, but he said he couldn't get there for an hour. Then when I tried it the number wasn't even good. Though *finally*," and here she stopped to laugh at herself, "I remembered the code."

"What code?" Mary Lou asked, against her better judgment.

"We decided all numbers should be said in code, in case the call at his house was picked up," Carolyn said.

Mary Lou waited to hear what the code was, but it didn't happen. Like cops and robbers, she realized, and she wasn't in on the game yet. And she didn't want to be, she reminded herself.

"So did this code thing work?" she asked. "What did you figure out?"

"It did work. I was *so* relieved. But after all that this bald middle-aged guy right out of straight America was there by *my* phone, tapping his foot, wanting us to be done with it. And it was a long conversation. So we had to put it off again. We picked a time to really talk. Today."

Carolyn stopped and looked at her, to see if this would fly.

"Today?" Mary Lou repeated. "You're just going to get going on this today?"

"Yeah, today at three," said Carolyn. "Of course I'm going to have to get out of the office."

Not eager to give her permission if she was even being asked, Mary Lou said nothing. Five days already, and no plan. No plan at all. The drips off the roof were slow and distinct now, because the rain had finally stopped. A weak sunlight infused the street. A car drove by, and James shifted in his seat.

"Three o'clock or two?" he asked quietly.

"Three," said Carolyn. "That is, if he's using the code."

"God, the code," she went on. "We agreed to all that three days ago, but I swear, it seems like a lifetime. Do you think he'll remember that it applies to times as well as numbers?"

"So you should be there at two, in case he forgets," said James. "Where?"

"The phone by Jovita's," said Carolyn.

"That's awfully close," said James.

"It's the only place where I can run in and out of the office." Carolyn stole a glance at Mary Lou.

The music had stopped, and for an instant it was so quiet all they could hear were small birds chirring as the meager sun warmed them a little.

"So you had some time to talk before the guy scared you off, you must have," said Mary Lou. "What'd this Quincy say?"

"That I should tell him where to come, once he got the plan together. Where James is, so he can take him to the next place."

"So he hasn't got the plan together yet, whatever that means," said Mary Lou. "When's that gonna happen?"

"It all takes so much time, Mary Lou," pleaded Carolyn. "Every single detail is like pulling teeth to have it fall into place. He has to get a place, get the money together, figure out who . . ."

"You gave him my address?" It took her a minute for it to sink in, but once it did Mary Lou's voice rose so loud that James used both his hands for a downward gesture, begging for a quiet that would come in under the announcer's rapid tones.

"What else can I do? James needs money and an ID. Then he can move on. Though where, we're not sure yet. People are trying to contact the Cubans."

"You told him the actual street number? Or do you plan to?"

A joyful clatter started up outside. The sun was out from behind the clouds, and all the birds seemed to have discovered it at the same time. Mary Lou looked at her watch, 9:51 now. She had to get out of here. She jumped up, but James began pacing side to side in the narrow kitchen, taking up even more space.

"I'll use the code," Carolyn said without answering her question. "I use it all the time." If this hadn't been so serious Mary Lou could have laughed out loud at the absurdity of believing the code made it okay for this Quincy guy to come here to her house.

"How do I know Quincy's safe?" Mary Lou asked. "Who is he, anyhow?"

"He works for the Black Panthers," said Carolyn, as though that would soothe her.

"Hey, Mary Lou," James broke in. "Q is my best friend. I hope you trust him, 'cause I do. But he's got a huge Afro and he always has on his black leather jacket, and the minute he leaves his place to drive out of town he'll be tailed. He knows that."

She stood stock still, hands on her hips. She couldn't believe this. Did he mean for this to reassure her? Jays shrilled at each other outside, as if they were down to their last breath.

"I'm sure he'll send someone else," said James, and he put his large hands on her shoulders, gently. "Whoever it is won't stand out. We're not dumb. We know black folks aren't that common out here. He'll find someone white, and they'll just stop by. Probably during the day when you're not even here."

"What if whoever Quincy picks just happens to bring the police right along with him?" Mary Lou asked, turning back to Carolyn.

"He won't," Carolyn said. "These people know what they're doing."

Carolyn and James had no choice but to believe this litany. Just like James believed this guy Kwesi.

"And after that?" she challenged them. "After whoever it is gets out here?"

"Once James has ID," Carolyn repeated, "he can go to wherever he plans for his next step."

"Well, I don't want people to know my address."

"We'll get a post office box," James said. "We'll use that from now on."

So they had given out her address. He'd as much as said so, unlike Carolyn who couldn't get her past and present tenses straightened out. She stared at him, and he stared right back. Well at least he didn't lie to her.

"This is how it is," Carolyn was saying. "Each detail, every single little fucking thing..." she paused, remembering that Mary Lou didn't like that kind of language.

"Every tiny decision takes the longest time to analyze," she went on. "And then you have to make it, whether it's right or wrong. And then you think of something you should have thought of before, like a PO box. Of course! But it's not as if we've ever had to figure this type of thing out. It's not as if we've done it before."

Yet she claimed that some mysterious "they" knew what they were doing, thought Mary Lou, but she didn't quite have the heart to say it out loud.

"The trouble is," said Carolyn, going on and on, "that it took us until yesterday to get to the part of what type of identification. If it's a driver's license, James could buy a car and move right on. That is, when he gets the money. But if he's going to leave the country, he'll need a passport. That would be best, of course. We don't know if anyone's started on that yet. That's the first thing I'm going to ask when Quincy calls today."

Mary Lou stared at James. He was bouncing on the balls of his feet now, as if he couldn't stand the women tossing words back and forth between them as though he weren't even here.

"Listen, Mary Lou." He kept his voice down low. "I don't want to be here one more minute than I have to. Once I have money and identification, I'm gone. I swear it! I promise that to you."

He looked at her like he hated to have to beg this skinny white girl for what he needed. Still, he held her gaze with his own. And there were those doe eyes of his, liquid and even beautiful, staring into hers, pleading for more space than he already had, pleading for his life.

Maybe he was even more desperate than he sounded. Maybe she needed Carolyn to keep working in the office. Maybe she didn't like it here alone. The longer they stayed, the more difficult it was for her to make them leave. Which she hadn't quite had the nerve to do in the first place.

"Jeez, I have to get going," she said, breaking eye contact to look down at her watch. "I've got that call from Porterville. I might have missed it already. Plus I told Basilio I'd meet him out at the camp. He says he has family in Emerald who'll help with the march."

"I want to hear more about the march," James said to her. "I want to understand better why it's so important."

Could it be the man actually had some working class politics and didn't just believe in picking up the gun?

"Why? Because Colonia is a bunch of pigs," she answered him. "A bunch of motherfuckin' pigs, that's all."

She said it to make him laugh, and it worked. Carolyn looked at them both like they were crazy, but she was smiling too. And the sun was out; despite it all the sun had actually come out and steam was rising from the road and all the bushes.

"Two weeks, Carolyn," Mary Lou said. She didn't dare look at James. "And that's all. Two weeks total, and that's it."

She picked up her purse, ready to leave the house.

"I have to be able to get into the living room when I want," she added. "I've got files in there."

He nodded, and she charged into his space, expecting to find it a mess. Instead the bed was folded all the way up and everything was tidy. He must have put his stuff into the coat closet. The only sign of his presence was a neatened up pile of newspapers, unusual only in how many were there, and the Baldwin book, with the store's bookmark indicating he'd almost finished it.

"Are you ready?" Mary Lou asked Carolyn.

She headed out to the car, aware that Carolyn was struggling into her coat to keep up.

"Never give anyone my address out here, ever again," she called behind to both of them as she swept out the front door.

"We won't," they chorused, like the birds on the telephone wire outside.

CHAPTER TWELVE

Carolyn hurried into the passenger side of Mary Lou's car, glad now to do her stint at the office. She opened her window to let in the yellow sunshine and fresh air. She was struck with the tumult and beauty of the white clouds skidding giddily across a blue sky, but almost at once her mood changed to an unexpected melancholy.

The weather had been exactly like this when she took her mother to lunch for the last time. She had been sure Mona would like the outing, especially because the crazy autumn day was so thrilling. Carolyn had driven Mona from San Francisco to Berkeley at a moderate pace, on the far right just next to the side of the Bay Bridge.

"Don't you remember?" her mother had asked her.

Carolyn, annoyed immediately by the question's querulous tone, had had no idea what she was talking about.

"Once before you were old enough to drive you told me that when we were on the side like this you were scared, with all the metal rushing toward you."

"I was just a kid then. That was a long time ago."

"Well that's how it feels to me now. We swerve one bit and we're cut in half. I don't like it."

She had moved over two lanes and slowed down to a crawl, but already they had been unsettled, blown off course by the tricky wind.

The minute they had cruised by the Mediterranean on Telegraph Avenue, Carolyn's favorite coffee shop and cheap too, she had known her choice of place was all wrong, but she was unable to change course. It had taken ten minutes to find a parking place, and then they had had to walk three blocks through ragged gusts that threw trash and dust at their faces. Mona, small and gaunt from the last round of treatment, had hunched down into her coat and forged ahead, but nothing had been easy for her by this time. Inside at last, the restaurant had turned out to be too noisy, too dirty, too many young people, too much her kind of place instead of her mother's.

They had both gotten moussaka, cafeteria style, and sat down.

Carolyn, though miserable between bites, had been starving.

"What should I do?" she had asked her mother, her mouth half full. "About my social life?"

"Enjoy it." A flat answer, delivered without humor.

"But I keep ending up unhappy. This guy I was going out with? After two months"—of sleeping together, of course, but she had the sense not to go into that—"he said he didn't want to see me anymore."

"Did he give a reason?" her mother had asked.

"Yeah. He said I argued too much."

This made Mona laugh, which had seemed unkind to Carolyn.

"It's how we raised you," Mona had said to her daughter.

How *you* raised me, not my father, Carolyn had thought. He was never angry. Then again he had been the one to leave, so that didn't quite square up, did it?

"Well I'm unhappy a lot," she had announced to her mother. "What should I do about that?"

"Stop thinking about yourself," Mona had snapped. "Focus on other people for a change."

Then she had asked for coffee in a voice that sounded as if she hadn't rested in months. It was only after Carolyn had delivered her mother back into her city apartment, and had left with the relief that always marked their separation those days, that she realized that Mona had taken only one or two bites of her food. Her mother was right—she thought only of herself.

"Whatever happened between the two of you, anyway?" Mary Lou had turned the car around and backed out in a spatter of mud. Now they were headed toward the intersection with Highway 99. "Why didn't you and James end up together?"

"For God's sake, Mary Lou." Carolyn snapped out of her reverie. "How many people do you know who are still with their high school sweethearts?"

The exchange annoyed her; the weather annoyed her. The memory of being so bothered with her mother when she was dying annoyed her a lot.

They bumped over the potholes that came just before the highway crossing, throwing splashes of brown water in all directions.

"It's you city folks who are lucky enough for these casual affairs and all," Mary Lou said. "Out here we still take it real serious."

"Lucky enough." Carolyn caught the wistful words. Could it be that her straight-laced friend was just a little bit jealous of the so-called sexual revolution? Rojelio was one thing; everyone knew those two were serious about one another. But Mary Lou and casual sex? Nothing would surprise her more. It was the jagged wind, tearing even this conversation in crazy directions.

"All we did was make out," Carolyn said. "Everywhere we could. Being as how it was 1965 and we were an interracial couple, we were scared out in public. So it was a challenge."

She found herself smiling at the memory. James and her, doing it wherever they could find a place. Her mother upstairs, pacing and worrying no doubt, or maybe asleep after a few drinks, but still alive. Mary Lou was still waiting for an answer to the question.

"And then we grew apart, what can I say? Right before I went away to college."

Carolyn had been sure he liked another girl better. Gwen Washington. She had been such a cool dancer, not constantly awkward.

"Maybe he was sad you were leaving," Mary Lou said.

"Maybe he can't be trusted."

With horror Carolyn realized she couldn't have put it worse.

"In that way, I mean," she added, her eye trained on Mary Lou, who didn't react. "There's stuff he doesn't tell you," she murmured. "He's honest and he keeps his word, but he doesn't always say what's going on inside."

At the highway stoplight, the huge trucks' grinding motors made further conversation impossible. Even as she spoke of its being long over, sitting there dwarfed by the semis and drowned out by their gears, the desire to make love with James smacked into Carolyn like a sharp gust of the flying wind. She bit her lip so hard it gave her a salty, metallic taste. Out there in the open, on that hillside of tawny grass right over the next rise, just the two of them, under the tumultuous sky.

The fantasy softened her so much that it hurt, just like back then, kissing and touching and grinding, as James had called it, turned on without end. Mona still here, but Carolyn long gone from her mother's grasp. It was James who had stopped it from happening, who had kept them from going all the way, as they called it those days. Well, now she wanted that whole entire complete thing. She wanted him with his clothes off, wanted to be underneath his slender, long-limbed body, kissing that special spot she loved right under his collar bone. She wanted him inside her, she wanted to be groaning under his weight. Then she would feel safe from her mother's death.

Safe. She almost laughed out loud. There was not one thing about this whole entire situation that was safe, so why not add something good? She could make it happen between the two of them. He was lonely too, after all. She saw it on his face at the end of every long day before he cheered himself up to make a good impression on Mary Lou. It would be crazy, but so what? This situation was already insane. As for parting, they had done that before, hadn't they? They would deal with that when the time came.

"Well, I'll tell you what," Mary Lou was saying once they were past the intersection. "If it was me, by now I'd be wishing I'd turned the gun in and gotten Kwesi arrested."

"If he became a stool pigeon it wouldn't exactly make him popular with his old friends, you know," Carolyn answered.

"James shouldn't hang out with those types in the first place," Mary Lou went on. "Those guys shoot off their mouths about guns and you know what happens? Other people get killed, and it's always innocent ones, caught in the middle. It makes me so mad."

Carolyn wished just for once Mary Lou wouldn't sound so damned sure of herself. And now, of course, she had to swing into the speech that her friend had heard a thousand times before.

"All those Berkeley radicals sit on their behinds in their fancy restaurants talking like the Revolution's coming tomorrow, and they don't even think about the farmworkers who put the food on the table. Everyone knows more about Vietnam five thousand miles away than they do about the San Joaquin Valley right over the coastal range."

"Nyame Jones probably didn't eat in a fancy restaurant once in his whole life," Carolyn said. She hated the way Mary Lou always claimed the high moral ground. Things were just not simple, and this situation least of all. "And those guards in places like Freeman? They're hardly innocent unarmed victims. They play their role in it all."

"Well now, that may even be true, but does it help when they die?"

"Maybe it does help. Maybe that's the only way change will happen."

Carolyn could not believe they were in this conversation. This was not the time to argue with Mary Lou. Thank God, though, they were pulling into the muddy UFW parking lot. A small group was by the door waiting, huddled against the sharp wind.

"How in the world can you say it's better for people to die, Carolyn?" Mary Lou asked.

"You tell me how you expect the people on the bottom to get up if they don't bring down some of the ones that are right on top of them," Carolyn answered.

"Through nonviolent leadership. Like Cesar's."

"Did I miss something? Have the growers recognized his moral superiority and declared a truce? Are the farmworkers any less dirt poor now than they were before Cesar came along?"

"This glamour about violence is exactly what Cesar hates about the left. He'll fire me if he finds anything out."

Mary Lou settled on a rutted space some distance away from the people. She snapped off the motor and turned to face her friend.

"It took Gandhi a long time, Carolyn; same with Martin Luther King. And anyway, it depends on people like us just as much as it does on the leaders, maybe more. If we get our butts in that office and work, farmworkers will be better off some day."

Mary Lou opened the door and got out. She had to let the workers in. Carolyn knew she was meant to follow and greet the folks, but she just was not ready to do that. She sat in the car and watched the others file into the office, furious tears sliding down her cheeks.

Nonviolence, my ass, she thought. Just how was all this fucking service work she had stacked up on her desk going to change things? She needed time to herself. She needed to get over her mother's death. She needed James.

But what she was going to do this minute, she told herself as she rustled in her purse, found some crumpled tissue, and blew her nose, was exactly what Mona had said to her that day at the Med. Stop thinking about herself. Stop arguing with Mary Lou. Get in there and work so her friend wouldn't change her mind about letting them stay.

She went inside, preparing an excuse for her delay. She would tell them she wasn't feeling well, something like that. Or maybe her friend would have the sense to remind them that her mother had recently died.

Mary Lou was already on the telephone and the others were in a cluster at her own desk, bent over charts Mary Lou had given them about the march's route and what had to be done each step of the way. No one looked up as she hung her coat and walked across the empty space to join them. Fine, she told herself, so as usual she didn't even matter that much. But she did matter to James, she knew that.

CHAPTER THIRTEEN

He hadn't been outside these four walls for days. One more quiz show, one more used car commercial, and he'd go crazy. He was about out of cigarettes, and Carolyn wasn't around to go to the store for him. It should be safe enough at three in the afternoon. Small town. The people who read the paper and watched the news ought to be at work. Scared him to death, but he had to go on the street again sometime in his life. Otherwise he was already in prison.

He wanted to make sure he'd look right, *clean* as Miles or Dizzy might say, like a black man had to be in order not to draw the *police*. He changed into the same jacket and white shirt he'd worn the day he left the city, smoothed his collar and hair enough times for it to feel silly, put on his shades, breathed deep, and stepped through the kitchen door.

Right away a little yellow dog strained at its rope from across the street and yapped at him. But the sky, broken only by a few bright white clouds, was a brand new baby blue, and he could see so far over the flat land, all the way to the horizon. The temperature was warm enough to promise that there would be a spring someday as long as he stayed in the sun. The wind tossed bare branches against each other with enough force to scare off all the birds. There wasn't a piece of trash around. The storm seemed to have scoured everything clean. He could smell fresh, wet earth.

By habit he reached for a cigarette and realized he hadn't even brought the pack outside. He'd rather just take in the fresh breeze anyhow. This being California the air here was dry, more like LA where he lived most of his life than like Florida where he was born. Good air, he thought. He turned the corner onto Joseph Street and swung into a rhythmic stride.

The two long blocks to the store were just fine. Different look but still, these little places, some with no sidewalks in front that appeared as though they hadn't been painted in a hundred years, reminded him of the South. He'd hated the South. People so constricted they had to go hat in hand just to find a place to eat or piss, or even a simple drinking fountain. And in the middle of it all his daddy, who read every book around and pretended respectability in his fancy suit with the gold watch chain over his belly. But he had to take his hat off when he talked to the Man, didn't he, just like all the rest?

Here in Allen, though, it was like those small places in Florida where his daddy's family lived. The people's places were far enough apart that the town was at least as much country as city, and that was one thing down there he never had minded one little bit. The houses he was passing were one story and jerry-built, crazy angles of blackened planks surrounded by a sea of mud, even a couple of chickens pecking around here and there. The ramshackle quality of it all reassured him. Poor people couldn't care less about the Freeman guards. Maybe.

He hoped to see black faces, but there wasn't anyone out at all. He could breathe out here. It all felt fine.

Until he got to the store. Four men wearing soiled jeans and work shirts open at the neck, cowboy boots and hats lounged at the corner, suddenly sidewalk, right by the front door. Their faces were darker than his, weathered and tough, but he was the one who was black. Not a brother or sister in sight. How he hated that. Odd person out, everywhere and all the time, ever since Freeman had happened.

What a fool to dress for a city street; isolation must have affected his brain. Allen was a farm town. Just like the beers with Ramirez. By the time he thought things through, it was too late. He couldn't turn around now. He'd buy another pack of Marlboros. It wouldn't take but a second.

His legs carried him like a robot through a door so low he had to duck, and then he was in the cramped aisles of the small grocery, baskets filled with sponges and cheap copper pan scrubbers, narrow shelves stacked with cans of beans and cellophane bags of rice. The women inside, faces averted under long black hair, were half his size, and even the men came only to his shoulder. No one stared, but they had to notice him, towering in his city clothes. Just to postpone the inevitable face-to-face contact when he paid, he walked to the back of the store.

He hovered in the corner by the canned soups, then forced himself to go back to the front. The neat stacks of cigarette packs—green for Kools, blue for Parliaments, and red for Marlboros—beckoned at him from behind the cashier's head. Had to wait in line behind two large women whose wire baskets were full with napkins and paper towels and fruit and—wouldn't you know it —iceberg lettuce. One lady even had two heads of it in there with her toilet paper! So where was this boycott Mary Lou was so fond of?

Soft Spanish swirled around him like a subtle threat. He could be recognized and turned in without understanding a word.

Money in hand long since, he paid without a word when it came his turn. He wanted fresh matches but he didn't ask, for fear that they'd figure out he wasn't Mexican. But of course they knew that anyhow. The clerk said nothing, and she'd spoken to every other person who'd passed her by.

Outside again at last, part of him wanted to scurry to the safety, or at least the familiarity, of the Joseph Street house. But the vast windy space drew him on, and in a split second he decided he shouldn't go back right away, in case a neighbor was curious and had watched to see where he went. He'd double back another way, he told himself. He took a deep breath and continued east. The small houses became even farther apart, separated by huge bare trees with nests near the top and occasional tire swings at the bottom. The road stayed paved, but any trace of sidewalk disappeared for real now.

After the first long block his breath evened out to where he could taste the fresh air again, and after the second he got up the nerve to look behind him. He could see no one. He stopped and lit a cigarette, took that first deep drag, and felt great. Outside. The only wall a line of narrow yew trees that shot up like arrows all the way to the horizon. Smell of the soil, turned over in fields that alternated with dinky backyards tucked behind little houses, both ready for planting.

Cars passed every once in a while, but no one else was walking. He'd gone about half a mile feeling good, maybe even the calmest since he'd left the city, when, with that suddenness that always caught him by surprise, everything changed. At first it was just the sound of another motor, but then it didn't pass him on by. He didn't want to turn and look so the pig inside could see his face, but he knew it had to be a black and white, just by the way it loitered to follow him. Neck hunched into his shoulders, he plodded on for three long blocks, praying the crazy fashion in which his breath was coming ragged with panic didn't show up in the way he held his body. Tall, black, and dressed like he was headed for some office. Couldn't be more conspicuous if he tried. So scared he could smell his own fear; all he knew to do was walk right on.

Only one last half-block before Allen totally gave way to the countryside. Vineyards on one side, the flat earth of an almond orchard on the other, not a fence in sight. If he got that far he could cut and run across the fields. He'd take the orchard, with that ground swept level and clear as a floor. His body primed on adrenaline for the hundredth time since Freeman, he knew he could go fast. Might even have a chance. On the other hand, a bullet could always catch up. What would he do if the pigs yelled at him to stop? He'd keep running, that's what. Take his chances.

Instead, at the town's edge, the purring motor changed its smooth course, and the vehicle that had been sliding along right behind him veered left, onto the last street of the town.

When he thought it was far enough off, he turned to see who had followed him. White man, of course. Ofay, as they called him in LA, wearing a baseball hat or some shit like that, bright red, and driving his large pickup, light green and tan, with a thick antenna that stuck straight up from the middle of the cab. The vehicle accelerated into the nearest turn, its wheels screeching mildly with the effort, then disappeared. The quiet that settled back around him was such a relief it brought tears to his eyes.

What was that all about? Not a pig at least, or not one in uniform. But the engine had a souped-up sound, and the antenna definitely had that security look. Utility truck, maybe? He'd heard that was what they used when they wanted to follow you or stake you out, some common-looking PG&E vehicle, or a telephone repair van. But why track him? Why not just arrest him if they knew who he was? Probably just a crazy kid practicing to join the Klu Klux Klan. Or maybe he'd dreamed the whole damned thing.

This time, he realized, he'd have chosen to die rather than get caught, but when he was slouched down in that restaurant parking lot he'd felt just the opposite. And in the store? Or if Ramirez had recognized him? Damn, who knew? His life had become just a frayed string between these incidents. Anytime it might snap.

His ears were still twitching, listening for sirens in case the dude in his fancy pickup had recognized him and gone for help. Nothing but the lonely hollow sound of a woodpecker drumming out in the orchard.

He kept on walking, and in the deeper silence that settled with no buildings at all around him, he finally calmed down.

Fuck it. If he was already caught, so be it. He almost wanted it to happen; at least everything would be clear. In the store his body's panic had told him there was danger. But it was afterward, just when he let his guard down, that the real threat arrived. If he couldn't tell reality from paranoia here, how in the hell would he figure it out in some other damned country?

Quincy had talked about Cuba. Socialist, of course, and lots of black people there. All he'd have to do is brush up on his high school Spanish. So far out here, though, it sounded like Greek, and he couldn't make himself say one damned thing.

Would prison be so much worse? He'd been there before—well, not exactly. County jail and state prison were two different things. Anyhow, he'd memorized Nyame Jones's books like they were gospel, then rapped it all down with the brothers. The Professor, they called him. His dad would've got a kick out of that if he'd bothered. Yeah, he'd been in jail, though not in the joint, and not for life. He'd hated every minute of it.

The strange, green, claylike object molded onto those typewriter keys came into his mind, each feature as clear as if he had memorized it at school. Nyame would say go for the Underground, do his part to build the Black Revolutionary Army that would free his people at last. And the weasel Kwesi would agree with that too.

The orchard had changed to plum trees that were busy declaring a very early spring. Pink blossoms swung in the breeze like ballet dancers among the bare branches, and a sweet scent lifted into the cool, sunny air. Damn. Outside, and right this moment not one single human being in sight. Get it while you can. With an effort he pushed the deadly bomb to the periphery of his mental field, almost off the screen.

A time with Carolyn, years ago, in her mama's old Plymouth parked at a UCLA lot, him behind the wheel, the smell of flowers heavy in the summer air. Both of them so excited behind those steamed-up windows. She'd been a virgin for sure, and himself not that far along either, if truth be told. She was a serious lady. Maybe he'd liked her too much to mess her up with his black ass before she went to college. Or maybe he'd liked the Washington girl better. She turned out to be a lot of fun. Whatever, all that with Carolyn was long past and done with, even if he was trouble for her again right now.

Here he was, though, throbbing like an animal in heat, and this was not the first time since he had been out here in the Valley waiting for what came next, not the first time at all. Yet he was so damned scared back there at Joseph Street that he jumped if Carolyn so much as came close to him. He couldn't even strip down past his underwear without wondering what would happen if the police came roaring in with him buck naked. Was it the fear, the intermittent adrenaline rush that made his body trick him with hard-ons? Like a teenager when there wasn't the least likelihood of getting it into anyone, at any time, in the foreseeable future. As for Ms. Mary Lou, with the scuttling walk as if she never had spread those long, slender white legs very far apart, she kept as far away from him as possible. She was beautiful, though, all angular and folded up like the egrets settled in the fields he had seen on the drive out from the city.

If only he and Rosetta were still married, he'd have someone in this mess. They both knew when it was done, her on her whole bourgeois trip, him more and more into his street thing, but that didn't make the divorce any damned easier. Now Rosetta did not like it one bit to even think of the black man and the white woman, spoke all the time about it, how a white girl put up with any shit the black man ran down. Yet he'd give anything for real acceptance from a woman he liked, didn't matter if she was green as long as she'd take him for who and what he was. Never had found it before, though, and now it was about the least likely thing to happen.

Orchard had given over to vineyard, sloping hills lined with row after row of clipped branch and wire on both sides of the road. A flock of starlings rose, then settled, the only sign of life. Every tenth row held a sign stapled onto a solid stake and printed in both Spanish and English: "No Trespassing—Violations Subject to Prosecution under Sec. 602, California Penal Code."

This must be Colonia's land, definitely the Man around these parts. The biggest grower by far, from what Mary Lou said. The signs might mean the fields were watched, but damn it, he had to piss. He cut in on a dirt road that went off at a right angle, aimed right at the bottom of one of their goddamned plants, took his sweet time, then shook himself off and zipped up his pants.

Down the slope was one huge-ass field the pruners must not have gotten to yet. Last year's branches shot off the vines in all directions. Whole rows were torn out, gnarled trunks upended, twisted roots in the air. Colonia playing God, replanting the whole damned place. Farther along, the road led to a cluster of enormous, round metal tanks surrounded by a chain-link fence topped with barbed wire.

Even a guard house at the gate. It actually smelled like wine around here; that had to be where the grapes fermented.

Past the tanks the dirt road became a gravel driveway lined with palms that led the way to a spacious white house, one story spread out all over the place, with wooden shutters painted a fresh bright green, nestled in a landscape of well-placed trees and shrubbery. The place was so fancy it looked like a Colonia brother himself could live there, but no, Mary Lou had said they were in Empire. Must be one of the foremen she was always talking about, but this was pretty fancy. Some grown kid in the Colonia family? Jensen, that labor relations guy Mary Lou hated so much? Whoever it was, this would not be a friendly house.

He kicked at one of the trespass signs and broke it off. Damn Colonia. Damn this desolate place he was stuck in. He booted the base of a vine so hard that he hurt his foot. And damn Kwesi, the betrayer. Who was the hard little guy anyhow, a pig or just a prick who had to prove himself, show how cold he was? And why in the world hadn't James asked questions like that before he'd gone to Freeman? Now he couldn't see how he'd ever understand exactly who all and what all was behind what had happened to him.

One thing he knew all at once, out in this space where the chill wind had cleared his head. No underground here in the belly of the beast that was America, filled up with FBI provocateurs and men like Kwesi, was gonna win out over anything as big as Colonia, not in this lifetime. These sad-ass groups that made all the noise about how they were gonna off the pigs were not enough.

Got to get out of the whole damned country. Cuba, wherever, but go! The minute he had his papers and the contact was made, he would just fly on out of here. Leave this place. Never see an American police officer again. Never run into Kwesi on the street.

He felt as though a huge rock had just rolled into place to cover up a gaping hole. Never mind if he was shivering in the late afternoon cold, with charcoal clouds suddenly stacked on the western horizon. Never mind if he missed his little Joseph Street sofa bed, his living room with the drawn shades that had been such a confinement two hours ago. And never mind if he wouldn't see his mama and brother and auntie for who knew how long, and if he dreaded being all alone out there in some whole other country about as much as he dreaded being caught right here. At least it would be a new place. He was young; he'd learn the language and he'd find his woman too. At least now, for the first time since Freeman, he had the beginnings of a plan.

CHAPTER FOURTEEN

It was five at last, and Carolyn was filling out an insurance claim form for Amelia Martinez as fast as she could. She wanted to go home.

"Ready soon?" Carolyn asked Mary Lou, who was at the other desk working on her timetable of tasks to be done before the march.

"Yeah," she replied without looking up. "Jeez, it's cold."

The wind rattled the old windows in their frames. Outside the west window the sun had fallen behind a shelf of purple bruised-looking clouds. The vineyard, with its mass of dark crosses that held up bare branches, was dark and foreboding.

"Let's have heat, for God's sake." Carolyn plugged in the space heater. She should have done it hours ago.

"Cesar sees all the bills, you know," came Mary Lou's dutiful remonstration. "You get in trouble if the electric runs too high." She made no move to change things.

Car tires crunched the gravel in the parking lot; whoever this was would delay their departure.

Lupe Muñoz entered, her sister Patricia in tow. What a contrast they were. Lupe, dressed in pressed jeans and a prim white blouse with a round collar, thin lips stretched around a polite smile, struck Carolyn as so virginal she had to be younger than her twenty-six years. Patricia, on the other hand, blowsy, plump, and overly made-up, looked much older than she was at seventeen. Carolyn, at the desk nearer to the door, rose to greet them.

"Lupe," she shook her hand. "*Cómo estás?* How are you doing?"

"*Bien, bien,*" came the instant reply, but it didn't sound as if she was doing well at all.

"And Patsy." There were streaks through the powder she wore to hide her teenage acne. She looked so forlorn that Carolyn wanted to hug her, but she didn't.

"How are you, Carolyn?" Patsy sniffled. "We heard you came back. Nice to see you." She spoke an unaccented English that had surprised Carolyn before she knew that their father was a year-round foreman at Colonia. They had lived here all their lives.

Lupe and Mary Lou had a rapid exchange in Spanish that Carolyn couldn't understand.

"Do you mind if we talk?" Lupe asked Carolyn when it was done. "Patricia needs Mary Lou's advice."

"No, of course not."

No place to go except the drafty bathroom, or outdoors, to give them their privacy. Surely they didn't expect her to leave the room. She went back to her insurance form, trying not to listen, but the three other women, standing between her desk and Mary Lou's, spoke in English so there was no way to ignore what was being said. Even with the heater it was getting colder. How long was this going to take?

"Patricia is in trouble," Lupe said. "She really is."

"I know," said Mary Lou calmly. "They say the man is Jesus Vargas."

"And Chuey tells me it was my fault," wailed Patsy. "He wants to know how he can be sure it's his. How could it not be his? The only person I've ever been with is him!"

Chuey was the nickname for Jesus, Carolyn remembered.

"Calm down, Patsy." Mary Lou rooted in her purse for a tissue, offered it, and gathered the younger woman in her arms. "*Cálmate, m'hija.* It's going to be all right."

Calm down my daughter. Carolyn was pleased she could understand, as long as the phrase was short and she watched the speaker's lips. What sweet endearments the Spanish allowed. Mary Lou stroked Patsy's smooth, dark hair. Jealous in a flash, Carolyn wished for nothing more or less than what Patricia, standing about two feet to her left, had this minute. Fat chance. Mary Lou never treated her like that.

"So Chuey Vargas is a coward," Mary Lou said, putting Patricia at arms' length the minute she quieted. "I'm not surprised."

"You should never have gone around with that boy." Lupe spoke from pursed lips.

"Why didn't you say that then, Lupe? You used to laugh with Chuey; you thought he was funny." Patricia started to sniffle again.

"I didn't say it was all right to do *that* with him."

Lupe would make a good nun, thought Carolyn.

"All right, Lupe, you calm down too." Mary Lou was firm. "Anyone can make a mistake."

"Yes, but what is she going to do? She's ruined. Now she'll never get married."

"You still work at the drugstore, don't you?" Mary Lou asked Patricia, who nodded, wiping at her eyes. "So that's fine. You can save money for the baby."

"But she'll get fired when they find out," said Lupe.

"They can have their suspicions, but it's awhile before they'll know it for a fact, isn't it? And you never do understand what those old birds who run that place will do anyhow. Last time I was in there Mr. Wright went out of his way to tell me what a good worker your sister was."

"He did?" Patricia managed a weak smile.

"She can't just be out in public like that," said Lupe in a firm voice. "Not once it shows."

"Why not? In fact, Patsy, what I'm gonna do is take you to this cheapo jewelry place in Empire and get you a plain gold wedding ring. Then you'll look like everyone else."

Patricia grinned like a kid.

"I mean, what in the world are the Wrights gonna do about it? Ask if you're really married? Then toward the end, you take time off to have the baby and come back to work directly. You're still living at home, right?"

"That's exactly it." Lupe sounded triumphant. "Our father found out about this, and now he's kicked her out." Her sister's face clouded over again.

"Well that's just for now, I'm sure. Why don't you just go over to Maria's, Patsy. Stay there until things calm down, help her with the kids."

Maria was the other sister, with a kinder heart. Mary Lou had an answer for every hard part.

"I hoped I could be with you for a while," Patricia said in her little girl's voice.

"That would have been fine, but Carolyn's here."

"And that man. What's his name?"

Carolyn's ears cocked. How did the Muñoz sisters know about James? From the Martinezes? Rafael Ramirez?

"That's Carolyn's friend, and he's got hepatitis. For absolute certain you can't be around him. It'd be bad for the baby." Mary Lou's voice didn't change at all.

"How long will he stay, anyhow?" The chance at gossip seemed to perk Patsy right up, Carolyn noticed with dread. People were like that; they would all be talking.

"Until he's well, I guess," said Mary Lou. "Otherwise Carolyn can't help us on the march."

"*Porque están aquí juntos? Es su novio?*" Patricia giggled at the naughty thought.

"Not her fiance." Mary Lou refused to be drawn into the Spanish. "Just her friend." She stuffed her list into a folder with other work and gathered up her purse.

"*Es mayate, ¿verdad?*" This from Lupe, her lips pursed in disapproval again.

"*No es importante*, Lupe;" Mary Lou said. "Look, I've got to get home." Mary Lou stood to put on her coat.

"I've heard he's cute," Patricia said. "You should go see him Lupe, he's about your age." She tittered again, pleased to shift the focus to her unmarried sister's search for a husband.

"Oh no, not me," Lupe replied. "I wouldn't look at a man like that." She shuddered, pulling at her hair and straightening her blouse.

"Well, no one can see him anyhow. He's got to rest all the time. And what he has is catching."

Mary Lou delivered the three short sentences with the firmness of a party edict, walked the Muñoz sisters to the door, and gave Patricia's upper arm one last squeeze of comfort.

"Don't worry, Patsy. Your dad will change his mind, you'll see. Your mother will want the baby around."

"What does '*mayate*' mean?" Carolyn asked as they crunched over the mud and gravel parking lot a minute later. The sun was down and the dark clouds now covered the whole sky. The rain had begun in earnest. They moved fast.

"Nigger." The word hung between them with its ugly sound.

Mary Lou started the car and dug in her purse for a tissue to wipe off the inside of the windshield.

"How do you think they found out he was there?" Carolyn asked.

"People talk. Everyone knows each other." Mary Lou sounded worried. She leaned forward to squint through the glass as she turned out of the wet parking lot. Already the mud was giving way to puddles.

"Well you handled it just right, I thought," Carolyn said calmly.

"Don't take me literally, Carolyn. About your staying long enough for James to get well. Two weeks at the outside."

The trucks at the intersection cut them off, and when Carolyn could be heard again, she made sure to change the subject.

"You really think Patricia should have this baby?"

"What else can she do?"

"Well, uh, she's so young." Carolyn found the word "abortion," which came so easy back home, hard to say. "With this big deal about virginity, won't it wreck her life?"

"People in these parts aren't like they are in the Bay Area, Carolyn. They don't get rid of their babies."

"Oh, Mary Lou, come on. It's been a year since *Roe v. Wade*. Women need some choice, for God's sake. What if it happened from a one-night stand?"

"Ugh. What a thought."

"Why so terrible? Because it's immoral?"

"Forget about morality. What's appealing about getting into bed with a stranger?"

"Getting laid." The disgusted look on Mary Lou's face told her this wasn't the right choice of words. Carolyn tried again.

"Having a good time?"

"Doesn't sound like fun to me." But Mary Lou was smiling.

"You'd be surprised," said Carolyn, as if she did this all the time.

"I would," said Mary Lou, laughing. "I surely would."

For the second time today Carolyn realized that she did not want to fight with Mary Lou. This was her friend's territory, and along with it came her friend's point of view. She and James were lucky to be allowed here at all.

"I'm sorry I got mad this morning," Carolyn said.

"When was that?" Mary Lou asked.

"Oh, you know. About nonviolence, all that stuff."

"Nah, don't be silly. You worry too much."

Stung again, even by this, Carolyn wished she could be like Mary Lou. Say what you mean, and don't look back.

"So the march has got me thinking," Mary Lou rattled on. She wiped at the steamed-up windshield again and leaned forward even farther to see through the driving rain. "Do you have any idea what it takes to put together a huge thing like this? Cesar's gonna have to send me some help. I hope he realizes that."

Exhausted, Carolyn leaned back and closed her eyes while she listened for the rest of the short ride to Joseph Street. But her heart lurched the minute she saw the darkened house. It was night already. This was winter. Why didn't James have any lights on?

To keep from getting wet they ran up the steps, and she pushed open the unlocked door. Everything looked normal, except he was nowhere in the home. No note. His things were still in the living room, so he hadn't packed up and gone. If there'd been trouble, they'd know it, wouldn't they?

Carolyn's stomach clenched in anxiety, all too familiar since James had landed on her doorstep six long days ago. But this was worse, this was the first time he was gone. She wandered from the kitchen through Mary Lou's bedroom, into the bathroom, out its other door to the living room where he should have been, pausing only to pull the curtains apart and stare out the living room window at the rain before she started back again, while Mary Lou, who must not have known what else she could do, began making dinner.

Fifteen minutes later, James showed up at the Joseph Street entrance that led straight to his living room. Carolyn appeared in the warm yellow doorway at once, so relieved she was smiling. Mary Lou was right at her shoulder, and even she seemed glad to see him. Both women clucked over his muddy shoes and his wet pant legs, which were soaked up to the knees. He grinned, foolish in his happiness to be home.

CHAPTER FIFTEEN

Now nine days had passed. Mary Lou headed home from the office. Seven o'clock on Saturday night, way past when she had meant to leave. She was not going back into that place to work again until Monday morning, no matter what. The logistics of the march were falling into place, slow but sure. Tonight it was whether people would come that bothered her the most. The small staffs left in the California offices couldn't get enough workers to come; the best activists were out on the boycott in the cities. Cesar would have to call them in. But he hadn't promised to do that yet, and she had heard that unnamed people on the Executive Committee thought the march was a waste of time compared to what had to be kept going on the two coasts. It was all this that had kept her talking to the Fresno, Delano, and Stockton offices into the evening.

She was tired and it was winter time, dead dark outside. No moon, no stars, no fog. She felt as though she was driving through outer space. All she wanted to do was get home.

She rumbled across the railroad tracks and the highway intersection, bounced through the potholes without slowing down, and pulled up to the Joseph Street kitchen door. She was here. And there was warm yellow light behind her kitchen curtains. Then right away just the rasp as she pulled up the emergency brake grated on her nerves.

James, of course. His presence was so quiet she always had to remind herself how dangerous it was. Nothing much had changed. Carolyn worked at the office all day, as promised, then turned on the radio and huddled with James all night. Soon he had to be gone. She meant to stick to the two-week limit. She promised herself that for the thousandth time.

She banged open the kitchen door to find Woody Guthrie singing "Deportees" from her Pete Seeger album that blared in loud from the living room. Carolyn was setting the table as James stirred a large pot.

"Hey, girl," James murmured without looking up. "What you know good?"

"I don't have to work tomorrow." Mary Lou couldn't help but smile.

"That qualifies." He tasted the contents and flashed a sweet grin of satisfaction so different from the times she had distrusted him that it was hard to believe he was the same person.

"What in the world is going on here?" she asked him, happy at last to be home.

"Your kitchen has been taken over by the People's Army Brigade for the Creation of Saturday Night."

"We decided it was time for a special event." Carolyn's explanation was simpler, her eyes so excited it seemed they might make her curls jump right off her head.

"So where's the mint juleps?" asked James.

"Oh yes," said Carolyn. "Mint juleps. How could I have forgotten?"

She pulled three Tecates out of the refrigerator, plunked them down near a saucer of salt that already had rings in it, and cut up a lime. She upended the beer cans in the salt like she was punching out biscuits, came out with three white-coated rims, popped the tops, and put a wedge of the fruit on each.

"Sir James?" asked Carolyn, managing a curtsy so clumsy as she handed him one that Mary Lou gave out a loud chortle that startled her as it came rolling off her lips.

"Lady Mary Louise?" Carolyn proffered hers with a click of the heels and a formal bow.

The first swig of beer tasted so good that Mary Lou took another one right off, which she never did. For the life of her, she couldn't remember when she'd last had fun.

Carolyn held her beer up for a toast.

"To Saturday night."

"To a good time," said James. "Yeah."

He sounded frightened that this was the only one he might ever have, which Mary Lou could understand. Every time she was unhappy, like after Rojelio left, she wondered if there'd ever be another good time again, and that was without being afraid of going to prison.

"Saturday night and Sunday," she found herself chanting. "Sleep late, wash my hair, maybe even get my laundry done."

They clicked their three beer cans together in a quiet toast and drank.

"And the menu for the evening is—" pronounced Carolyn with a sweeping gesture toward James that said he should take the stage. Mary Lou's mouth watered in anticipation of his answer.

"Let me see now." He counted on his fingers. "Hog maws, chitlins, pigs' feet."

Her face must have crumpled, because the other two broke into guffaws.

"Barbecued spare ribs, you dope," said Carolyn. "James has planned this for a while."

"*And* worked my fingers to the bone, I might add. Plus a mess of collard greens, which Carolyn had to go to three stores to find. I'm not letting you off the hook here, you are going to eat soul food, my dear Mary Louise."

He emptied half his beer and with a flourish pulled the chairs out for the ladies. Mary Lou collapsed into hers like she'd been waiting for this all day.

"You look like you been working too hard, Mary Lou," he commented.

"That's what it's like with this Union," she said.

"But this is worse than usual," offered Carolyn. "It's the march."

"So when exactly is this here gigantic event gonna occur?" James asked Mary Lou.

"It begins March sixteenth," she answered. Five weeks away. Not that much time when you think of all that has to be done. Which was exactly what she did not want to think about, not tonight. She took another swallow of beer, then set the can down on the table. She never drank more than one or she would get a headache.

"What's the march supposed to accomplish, exactly?" James asked Mary Lou with an intensity that suggested he was truly interested in her answer.

"Get Colonia on the front page of the *New York Times*," she answered. "Embarrass them. Make the boycott truly take off all over the country. Get those SOBs worried that they'll never shake off the image, even after the boycott's over." Despite the beer's sweet buzz she could feel her lips settling into that thin line of discontent that always happened when she thought about how much she hated Colonia.

"Is there an example where that's happened?" he asked. "Where a boycott got what the workers wanted?"

"How about Coors?" answered Carolyn. "The unions started boycotting Coors Beer—let's see, when was it? Back in the thirties, maybe. I've never drank a bottle of Coors in my whole entire life."

"But Coors is still in business, right?" said James. Carolyn didn't answer; Mary Lou wasn't even sure she had heard him. As for Mary Lou, she didn't have an easy comeback to that one.

Carolyn squeezed the lime into the hole at the top of the can, shook salt on her wrist, licked it off, sucked the lime, and swilled the beer.

"If there's a right order to this Tecate ritual, I certainly do not know what it is," she said, laughing. "But Cesar's gonna send you help, right?"

"Yeah, Ramón's gonna show up. Cesar okayed that much today, even if he wouldn't promise hardly any boycotters. And Rojelio too, probably."

If there was one thing clear, it was that James had to be gone before Rojelio came. He'd pick up on the strangeness of the situation in a second. Well, so James would be gone in five more days. That was when the two weeks ran out. No need to get into all that now and spoil the evening.

James got up for his Marlboros and her Parliaments, took hers out, lit it, used it to light his own, and then handed it over to Mary Lou.

"That's just how you used to light my cigarette, James," said Carolyn with a tipsy giggle. "I'd be all worried Mona would smell it upstairs. Remember?"

"Want one?" he asked her. "You look like you do."

"You know I stopped smoking two years ago. No thanks," she said reluctantly. As for Mary Lou, she took a grateful drag.

"Well, this is only the eighth of February," James was saying. "You've still got more than one whole month to get the entire thing together."

He drew the sentence out like he was talking about eternity instead of just thirty days. Mary Lou watched his face. It was dreamy, as if he was thinking about what it would be like to have the luxury of time.

Carolyn must have worried this line of conversation could lead to more talk of deadlines, because she changed the subject real fast.

"What do you guys think about this Patti Hearst kidnapping?" She drained her beer and got up to get another.

"Jeez, that is so terrible," said Mary Lou. "Cesar sent a sympathy telegram to her parents today."

"Such pigs," said James, back at his pots and pans. "William Randolph Hearst, master of yellow journalism. Wealthy, reactionary, the perfect target."

"You think if you have money you don't feel grief when you lose a child?" asked Mary Lou.

"Doesn't happen to the rich nearly as often as it does in the ghetto," he muttered. "That's all I know."

Mary Lou studied his back and wondered for the thousandth time if she even liked this man. He kept the kitchen as spotless as she would on the one hand, and cooked up this great meal. Then in the next minute he could sound so mean, dangerous.

"Symbionese Liberation Army," mused Carolyn. "Wonder where they got that name."

"You wouldn't happen to know any of these SLA people, would you?" Mary Lou asked James.

"Naw, they're from back East somewhere, aren't they?" he answered.

"They're crazy," pronounced Mary Lou with the certainty of one beer gone. James plunked another down in front of her, salted and ready. Right away she broke her own rule and took a sip.

"Crazy and violent," she said again, as if they hadn't already heard her.

"You see that part on TV where Hearst had to set up the distribution center in East Oakland to meet their demands?" asked James. "Truckloads of food. Shows what the Man can do when he wants to, doesn't it?"

"Can't you feed the poor without kidnapping an innocent girl?" asked Mary Lou. "This Union does it all the time. We'll feed hundreds on the march. Thousands on the big day at the end."

If those thousands showed up they would get fed. But would they come in the first place?

"I can't quite make up my mind about the SLA," said Carolyn. "They are extreme—"

"Common crooks," said Mary Lou.

"No, I don't think that," said Carolyn. "After all, they aren't in it for their own gain."

"And the folks that run this country are clean, I suppose," said James. "Nixon and the rest. They really set a good example."

"No call to stoop to their level," said Mary Lou.

"'No easy victories,'" Carolyn pronounced.

The other two stopped short and waited for her to explain.

"'Tell no lies; claim no easy victories.' Amilcar Cabral."

"Who in the world is that?" asked Mary Lou, laughing. Trust her good friend Carolyn to come up with something obscure. But interesting.

"Leader of Guinea-Bissau, at and after independence," said James. "Cape Verde too. Good quote, Curls. I'm impressed."

"What does it mean?" asked Mary Lou.

"Damned if I know." James laughed.

"Everything's complicated." After the beer Carolyn's words rolled loosely off her tongue. "Nothing's simple, that's what it means. And we've got to tell the truth about all of it." She stopped and thought for a second. "Even while we're telling lies every day about James, I suppose."

"Hey now," he remonstrated. "Fibs is more like it. Temporary untruths, shall we say."

"You're gonna go back and correct all of them someday?" asked Mary Lou. She almost wished they'd lied to her about James. Then she wouldn't know who he was, and they could fill up her house as long as they liked. They were good company.

"Anyhow, the man is dead," said James. "Cabral was assassinated last year by one of the guys he trusted most in his own party. I'm sure the CIA was involved, too. Just like Lumumba."

"'No easy victories,'" said Carolyn again. "I rest my case."

"And he certainly will rest his," said Mary Lou. "For a long, long time."

All three of them chuckled at her stupid joke, the tipsy response to a notion that was actually too close to home, given the various people out there who wanted to get their hands on James.

"Well, I'll tell you something good about the SLA," said James. "Between them and the House of Representatives calling for Nixon's impeachment on Watergate? Not one word about Freeman Penitentiary in the newspapers or on TV since Wednesday, and I am so relieved. Thank you, revolutionary brothers."

He swallowed some beer and bowed in one direction. "And thank you, Richard Millhouse Nixon, for having turned out to be one lying fool."

He bowed in the other, and they all laughed again.

"Did I ever describe how Mary Lou looked when she fell in the canal during the strike?" asked Carolyn.

"Naw, you never did tell me that story." James stirred the pot of greens, then opened the broiler to turn the ribs.

"It was on the picket line," said Carolyn. "Eight in the morning and already 104 degrees in the shade. Town cops, county cops, highway patrol, they were all there. Amelia Martinez, who knows her history, was arguing with them through a bullhorn. She had finished with the Bill of Rights in English and was just starting in on the 1910 Mexican Revolution in Spanish.

"So the growers had this injunction that made each picketer be a whole hundred and fifty yards from the next one. Of course it meant the scabs could walk right into the fields without a confrontation, right? Just what the *pinché cabrón* growers wanted, right?"

Mary Lou had to smile. Carolyn's Spanish might be limited but she sure got the swear words, didn't she? *Pinche cabrón.* Hard to translate. Fucking goat-like growers? She must be getting drunk. It felt good.

"Anyhow," Carolyn continued, "Amelia's goal was to distract the police so they wouldn't see Mary Lou and Rojelio run into the vineyard and pressure the scabs to leave. And it worked. They got in there from the other side, yelled at the pickers that their relatives would hate them forever, and some of those *esquiroles* actually tailed it right on out of there."

There it was again, Carolyn remembering her Spanish for strikebreaker. This was her pal, thought Mary Lou, revving up on her very favorite kind of story. This was the girlfriend she knew and loved.

"The cops saw what was happening and started chasing Mary Lou and Rojelio. They trapped them over by this irrigation canal, and just to let them know who was boss, they pushed them in!" Carolyn ended this statement with her hands out and her mouth in an O of mock astonishment, then looked at James for his reaction.

"Did you know how to swim?" James sounded genuinely alarmed. "I would've drowned if they did that to me."

"No, I don't know how to swim," stated Mary Lou. "And let me tell you, I was terrified."

She had panicked when that water closed over her head, but Rojelio managed to pull her over to the side, and then the cops laughed at them as they struggled up the steep cement incline, clothes clinging, arms and legs scratched and bleeding. Just like Rojelio, sweet as sugar on the outside, and then he comes up with a crazy scheme that just about got them both killed. But it worked.

"While all that went on," continued Carolyn, "the rest of the scabs got so scared—or pissed off at the cops, who knew which—that they *all* ran out of the field. When we saw it from the picket line, we went crazy, it made us so happy!"

James gave out a soft whistle. "Then what, Mary Lou? They bust you?"

"Nah, they hustled us out on the side farthest away from the line and left us there. What I think was, if they'd arrested us, even more people would've found out how we tricked them."

Everyone chuckled, and James brought the food over.

"Okay, enough of this talk. Let's get ourselves down to this here scrumptious meal."

He hummed to himself as he put out three plates piled high. Ribs that ran with thick barbecue sauce; dark, moist greens that smelled of spice and sweet at once; and crusty corn bread fresh from the oven. He'd gotten Carolyn to shop for him and cooked all afternoon just so he could surprise Mary Lou when she got home from work. His way of saying thank you.

He got out three fresh beers but put one back right away when she waved it off. Then he sat to survey his handiwork. At home her mother would have said grace, thought Mary Lou, which was definitely not her style. But something was needed. She raised her glass.

"To the poor getting richer," she said. "Something we can all agree on."

"And the rich—" Carolyn began.

"Getting poorer!"

All three of them finished together. And then they ate.

James took a bite or two, but mostly he sat and smiled while the two women oohed and aahed about how good everything was. After a spell of eating sounds, the talk started up again.

"Well, now, you should've seen this one." James gestured with a rib toward Carolyn. "Toolin' around during our young days with my black ass in her mama's old car."

"That was a '47 Plymouth," Carolyn said. "Water used to come up through the floorboard when it rained." She smiled at James. "I always let you drive, and we always stayed out late. Mona must have spent her time wondering when and if her only daughter would get home."

"Once we were up in Griffith Park and we laid ourselves right on down, behind the bushes, you know," James shifted into a rolling preacher cadence, "to engage in various activities that the young are wont to do upon occasion," then took up his previous tone, "and anyhow, I see these white boys go by. Must have been at least four of them. Then I see them come back again, which I know is not a good sign. But Carolyn's not even thinking about it. She's too into what we're doing.

"So I pull her off the ground and make her run with me down this steep hill behind us, full of eucalyptus trees that shed those buttons that make you slide every which way. By the time we get to the bottom, huffin' and puffin', no one's behind us, though, for which I am very grateful indeed.

"'Ain't nothing runs faster than a scared nigger,' was what I said to her, and it shocked her. I'd forgotten—you couldn't use that word around the good white people. Might give them a heart attack.

"So then," he continued. "Check this out. This girl has the all-out nerve to be upset, and not with the paddy boys, mind you, but with me! Oo-ee, I'm tellin' you, she lit *into* me. I shouldn't have run away!

We should've stood up for our rights! How were things ever gonna change if we didn't confront the enemy? You remember that?"

Carolyn nodded, laughing so hard she couldn't talk.

"I told her we'd be layin' down for our rights the minute after we stood up for them, and we might not even get back up again. This was back in '61, you know what I'm talkin' about? And she lived in Inglewood, where this particular black boy knew he better not even be caught out alone after sunset, much less with a white girl on his arm.

"I am sitting between two very brave ladies." James reached over the table corner to dab at a spot of red sauce on Mary Lou's cheek.

"Either brave or foolish, hard to know which," Mary Lou said.

"I hear you." He tipped his beer to empty it. "They're very close together sometimes."

"I was scared to death," said Carolyn. "That's just the way I cover it up, by getting angry. And you were right that day. Running was the best choice."

Carolyn sticks her neck out with a serious statement right in the middle of the fun, thought Mary Lou, and no one knows how in the world to answer her. Then she's disappointed. Mary Lou could tell by the look on her friend's face as she reached for a fresh paper napkin to work the sticky sauce off her fingers.

"You want more food, James?" asked Mary Lou. He was just sitting there, not eating or smoking, not even drinking beer.

"Naw, being here together reminds me of when I got out of jail. I'd sit in the kitchen with my mother and my auntie and there was not a single thing I wanted more than to listen to those ladies jawbone. I just want to hear the two of you talk. Doesn't matter what it's about."

A soft knock sounded at the front of the house, and all three of them jumped at the unexpected sound. Mary Lou hurried through the living room to answer it, traded hushed words in Spanish, and came back to the other two whose faces turned up to her, frozen in concern. Their relaxed evening together shattered, everyone shifted back to emergency mode.

"It's Lalo. Don't worry, he'll stay outside. He lives at the camp, and he says that scab Silveira is out there with a gun. Apparently he even shot into one of the houses."

"Jesus." Carolyn was on her feet. "Nothing that bad ever happened last summer."

"It's worse out here with everyone gone. Silveira's drunk, I'm sure, but he could hurt someone. I've got to go out there."

"You'll need help," said James. But they all knew it couldn't be him.

"I'll come," said Carolyn, yet she didn't move. "The old Matthews County Sheriffs Department is bound to show up, though, isn't it?"

"At least them," said Mary Lou.

"That's all we'd need," muttered James to Carolyn. "For you to get arrested."

"I've got to go with her," Carolyn said again. "It could be dangerous."

"I'll go alone," said Mary Lou. Carolyn wouldn't be much help anyhow if all she did out there was worry about James.

"That doesn't seem right—" Carolyn began.

"You shouldn't have to—" James was trying to say the same thing at the same time. Mary Lou should not go out there alone.

"Don't exaggerate, you two," Mary Lou said. "You know how it is in these parts, Carolyn. They don't shoot you, they just keep you real poor." Mary Lou tried to sound certain, but the fact was Rojelio had always been with her when emergencies came up before.

"They're not gonna follow you back here, are they?" James asked.

"Who?"

"The pigs."

"Nah, they already know where I live," Mary Lou said. She began to scurry around to gather her things. "Whatever happens out there, it'll all be over by then."

"Anyone else?" James was tense and focused. He had to be.

"I'm just gonna quiet things down and send everyone back to bed," Mary Lou told him. She felt so sorry for him; he looked lost and afraid. "I'll come back alone. I promise."

"You gonna take your .22?"

"Of course not. How'd you know?" Now, just as this guy got her sympathy, the next thing she had to believe was he really had his nerve. If he knew where the gun was, he must have searched her bedroom.

"I had to look around, Mary Lou," he told her. "I had to know what was here. You can understand that."

She said nothing, so he asked her again.

"You gonna leave it here?" Apparently he didn't believe her the first time.

"It's Rojelio's," she said.

"You know how to use it?"

"Of course. But it's for burglars. Don't you know the main reason this Union's nonviolent is so we can keep ourselves from getting killed?"

She scrambled into her blue winter coat, ran to her bedroom to grab a legal pad and a pen, and then she was out of there, careening around curves on the two-lane road out toward the camp, scared to death she'd have an accident just from trying to keep the red spot of Lalo's one taillight in sight. That taillight, she kept thinking, he's got to get it fixed or he'll be stopped like every other Mexican in this Valley. The distance that should have required at least twenty minutes in this tule fog took them only ten.

In front of the camp, across from the low stucco building where Colonia assigned out workers before the strike, the people converged out of small uneasy knots toward Mary Lou's car. A teenage boy who held a flashlight stepped forward to open her door.

"He's gone," the kid said in Spanish. "He ran that way."

"But there's blood," someone yelled. "Show her the blood!"

"He shot someone?" Mary Lou asked.

"No, *gracias a Dios*." A woman's voice rose in near hysteria.

"He must have cut himself," the teenager explained. "He broke a window, over there on the shed."

"He went back home," a man growled. "*Ándale, pues.* Let's get the *esquirol.*" The crowd surged around them.

"*Más despacio*," Mary Lou said. "Slow down here. How do you know where he went?"

"The blood goes in that direction." The teenager gestured with the flashlight along a line of sporadic blotches in the dirt. It trailed off in the direction of Silveira's shack down by the slough.

"Look, Mary Lou. Where the bullets hit!" A woman waved wildly toward the line of shacks where the people lived.

"*¡Pinche cabrón!*"

"*¡Cálmate, cálmate!*" Mary Lou had to shout to be heard. "We need a plan. The police will come. We need to be ready."

The teenager tapped her shoulder and pointed. Three cars were pulling into one end of the circular driveway—two green, with the emblem of the Matthew County Sheriff's Department, and one black and white, with Allen's logo on its side. Behind them came Jerry Jensen with his driver in his Colonia pickup, which blocked the other end. Between the pickup and the cop cars, no one could leave the camp. A wave of anger washed through the crowd.

The sheriff in the middle car hauled out his bulk and stood upright. He took out a clipboard, braced it against his paunch, then clicked on his flash. The beam revealed red cheeks and a chin too big for the face.

"Okay folks, now who speaks English here?" His voice was a study in affability. The police stepped out of the other two cars, hands resting on sticks.

"Look, Deputy Sage." Mary Lou stepped right up to him. "We know exactly what happened and who it was. I want you to go arrest him."

"Well, well, looky who we've got here." Sage grunted with surprise that she had arrived there before him. "Now let's just hold on a spell, Mary Lou. Maybe you'll tell me what happened first. That is, if you don't mind?" His tight smile showed teeth so pointed and white they could have been an animal's.

She gave a quick explanation and pointed in the direction Silveira had taken. "He's probably at his house by now, but he won't be there much longer if we don't go get him."

"Now just one gol-darned minute here," Sage drawled. "You got to let us determine the facts, don't you? How'd you like it if we arrested one of your people, just 'cause Jerry Jensen here told us what he wanted us to know?"

"So why not send one of your guys to question Silveira while you talk to witnesses here?" Mary Lou asked.

"Well, young lady, I believe I'll be the one to decide how to run this operation."

"Why is Jensen blocking that driveway?"

"Man can do what he wants to on his own property, now can't he?"

A murmur ran through the crowd. It was all in English, thought Mary Lou, so Sage was sure they couldn't understand him. But the people weren't dumb. They knew disrespect when they saw it.

"So let's just you and me go on over there," Sage added, "and see this place he supposedly shot at."

Rojelio or Cesar might have known how to make something happen at this point, effective and nonviolent at once, but all she could think of was to translate what the deputy wanted. The crowd led the two of them to the Cuevos', at the end of the nearest row.

Sage and Mary Lou squeezed into the middle of the family's one room, spotless with its elaborate arrangement of curtains and partitions. One small table held a cluster of portraits: the wedding, the children, Cesar as he gave a speech, Robert Kennedy at Cesar's Delano fast, all presided over by a painted wood statue of the Virgin of Guadalupe, mounted on the wall above. Beds were everywhere. Six somber children, two on each bed along the far walls, the littlest ones with their mother, watched. Newspaper already covered the shattered window.

Cold air surged in behind the crowd. A tiny gas stove, both burners on and the oven door open, provided the only heat. A beaded film of water covered bare cinder-block walls. Señor Cuevo stood silently, pointing out the bullet holes. Everyone crowded forward to see them. The bullets had missed the patron saint of the poor, but barely.

Sage proceeded to conduct his investigation. First he interviewed Cuevo, with Mary Lou as translator. Next, everyone trooped along as he led the crowd back to the one outside light. This was where the teenager who first talked to Mary Lou had seen Silveira, arched in silhouette, lift a bottle, yell a challenge, and raise his gun to fire. Together they followed the trail left by dots of his blood until it disappeared into the vineyard. Finally, an hour after he had arrived, Sage summed up.

"Now listen to me, Mary Lou," he told her, with everyone listening to each word. "Tomorrow we'll go on over and hear what Silveira has to say about it. There's at least two sides to every story with you people out here. Just stay calm, all of you. Get a good night's sleep. Here's a card that's got the district attorney's number on it. You call him up on Monday for his decision."

"We all know you'll take your time, Sage. But I want you to understand one thing." Mary Lou drew her words out as though she had a credible threat to deliver, and for all she knew maybe she did. "If Silveira's not arrested, Cesar Chavez won't let it drop. The boycott will take this on. Churches, labor unions, community groups, everyone. We'll put Allen on the map, right up there with Delano where Cesar fasted until the growers signed, remember that? And Selma, Alabama. The cops didn't come out of that one so good, did they?"

Without waiting for a reaction, she turned her back and motioned everyone together in front of the Cuevos'. Sage and the Allen police left right off, but a sheriff's car and Jensen's pickup still blocked the road.

"Let's go inside after this and they'll all leave, including '*rata blanca*' over there," she said in Spanish. Children giggled at the nickname.

"Silveira won't come back. He was drunk as always, now he's gone to sleep it off." A thin laugh swept through the crowd.

"Cesar will know about this. People in all the parts of the country will send telegrams. And it is necessary to come to the march next month. That's where we'll show Colonia our force, our power. Questions?"

There were none, so to end it she got the people in a circle to sing *De Colores*. A song about colors in the springtime, she thought as they went through the verses. Was that the best they could come up with in their helplessness? Rojelio would've done more with that quiet, macho way of his. He was definite; he always had a plan. Might not work so well in bed, but it sure as heck did out here. Oh well. At least no one had gotten shot.

She walked back to her car wondering when and how she'd be able to leave. Jensen's flunky kicked the pickup's motor into life and idled up from behind her. Oh God, and now this jerk. Static crackled from the two-way radio on the dash, and the sound of it made her flesh crawl.

"Can I go now, Mr. Jensen?" She hoped her sarcasm was clear.

"Of course, Mary Lou," he said in a benign tone. "You haven't committed a crime, have you?"

"No, but Silveira has," she answered.

"You must understand, that's up to the district attorney," Jensen said. Mary Lou kept right on walking. He couldn't drive next to her forever; he'd crash right into her car.

"Sure it is," she said between gritted teeth. "Colonia has nothing to do with it. Of course."

"But I did want to say one thing to you, Mary Lou. Watch out about this march. Your people might suffer for it, more than it's worth."

"Is that a threat?" She took a deep breath, ready to argue. "I thought we had free speech—"

"I'm just warning you, that's all."

Jensen nodded to his driver, and the pickup backed out of the driveway and took off in the direction away from Allen.

She waved away the people that had started to come over and climbed into her car. What in the world was all that supposed to mean?

Aware that a sheriff's car was still behind her somewhere, she drove way under the limit. Just as well, since the tule fog hung around the car like wads of cotton batting. She was glad for the steering wheel to steady her shaking hands, and she was soaked with sweat. This Colonia situation was too much for her; she couldn't handle it all by herself. All she knew how to do was work hard, and that wasn't gonna be enough. She'd tell Cesar. She'd call him tomorrow, and if he didn't send someone to help, she'd up and quit this danged Union, she really would. She was in way over her head. 'No easy victories?' No victories at all was more like it.

CHAPTER SIXTEEN

"Damn. Can't just relax since Freeman," said James to Carolyn after the sound of Mary Lou's car died down.

"Ain't that the truth?"

The house was dead still once Mary Lou and Lalo had gone. Too quiet.

"Hope she'll be all right," Carolyn replied. The concern on her face mirrored all his own, so he pushed back his chair with a sudden scrape and rose to work on the cleanup.

"Girl seems to know how to take care of herself." He knew he sounded clipped, but he was scared for Mary Lou. For himself. For all of them.

"We can't stay here forever, James." Carolyn's voice was almost a whisper. Outside one lonely bird call echoed through the dark night.

"Tell me something I don't already know," he replied, wishing Carolyn would stop talking right now. But that rarely happened. Not with Carolyn.

"When do you think we'll hear from Quincy?" she asked.

"Next time you go to Fresno, buy me a crystal ball." He just could not go through all this again, not right now. The evening had been so damned nice. Made him want to cry, but he wasn't gonna do that either. Not in this lifetime.

He was scrubbing dishes at the sink, and through the starched green curtain he could see the Allen black and white, sliding around the corner between Joseph Street and Third Avenue, like it did every evening just around now. And every evening it scared him about half to death. Tonight was no exception. It turned the corner and disappeared. No problem, except he could feel the usual beads of sweat on his forehead. Carolyn noticed nothing.

"Let me help," she said. Dish towel in one hand, she slung the other arm up and over his shoulder in a friendly hug, which left him further on edge.

"Naw, Curls." He kept his voice even. "Go on and read your book for once. I don't mind." Why couldn't she understand? Cornered like this, he needed to be the one to make the choice of physical contact.

"I'd rather have company," she insisted, and began to dry what he put in the drainer. They worked together for a moment in silence.

"What's it like out at that labor camp?" he asked after awhile. "Mary Louise gonna be okay?"

"I'm pretty sure," Carolyn answered. "The cops will be all over the place, though."

"That can be the biggest problem."

"Yeah, but around here they don't shoot at people."

"Unlike in Oakland," he said. "Remember L'il Bobby Hutton?"

"Black Panther," she murmured. "Pigs shot him dead. First Fred Hampton in Chicago, then L'il Bobby Hutton in Oakland. I wonder that doesn't happen more out here." Carolyn had that inquiring tone that meant she wanted to theorize.

"Seems clear as black and white to me," he commented. He smiled. The familiar politics meant they were on safer ground.

"It's not as though no one ever died in labor disputes in this Valley," she said. "They killed strikers in Muscle Slough and in front of the general store in Pixley, down near Delano. Back in the thirties, though."

"Damn. Sounds dangerous." He scrubbed at the sink as though he would wear the enamel through.

"It's the goons the growers hire, as much as the cops themselves."

"You get shot, you get shot. Makes no never mind who pulls the trigger."

She leaned on the counter, using the dishtowel to dry her hands. "There ought to be plaques in those places so people will remember history."

"The Revolution in our lifetime, Curly. Then you could be the one to put them up."

She laughed at that, put her arms around his waist, and leaned her cheek against his back. Seemed like she was trying to make it the most natural gesture in the world, but he felt nothing but awkward.

"This reminds me of us being back in Baldwin Hills," she said in a dreamy voice. "Mona still alive, her and Phil still together."

Gently he disentangled himself, turned around, and damned if there weren't those blue eyes of hers drilling right up into his face, asking couldn't things between them begin all over again.

"Things weren't so easy then," he hedged. "You gotta remember that." He sidestepped her, went over by the door, got the mop, wet it down, and started in on the floor.

"We didn't know what the 'us' was," he said as he mopped. "We couldn't talk about it 'cause we had to be cool, and your parents were so worried, they didn't even like me. No matter how hard I tried, it scared them."

"We had fun, though," she said. "Until Mona freaked out and said I couldn't see you anymore."

"Mona. How come you never call her your mama? Mom, like all you white girls say? Or Mommy? How come you never called her Mommy?" He laughed gently. Mona hadn't exactly been the mommy type, even he knew that.

"She didn't really want me to," said Carolyn. "She thought in an ideal world mothers would be like anyone else to their children. Phil was the same way. It was part of their belief system. Weird, huh?"

Her voice broke as she said this, and when he looked up from his careful work, now there were real tears sliding down the girl's cheeks. Being as how she was the one crying, it was safe, so he put his arms around her and patted her back to help her try and collect herself.

"And what did you think?" he asked her quietly. "What would your ideal have been?"

"I guess I wanted a mommy." Her voice was muffled against his shirt. "Like I bet you came home from school for lunch, didn't you?"

"My mama worked. You know that." He was looking over her shoulder while he comforted her, checking the corner through the gauze curtains like he always did. No cop car, no car at all, and no one walking either. Still dead quiet out there. You always had to operate on at least two levels at once. That way you could stay safe. Maybe.

"Yeah, but didn't she work at your school?" Carolyn asked.

"That was my auntie. My mama worked at a law office, remember? And my auntie being at me and Ronnie's elementary school every day meant we always had to act perfect. Plus she had to ignore us so the other kids wouldn't think she was playing favorites. Later she claimed she made sure the cafeteria cook gave me and Ronnie special treats, though."

"Your mother was always around, James, and your aunt was too. But not Mona. She had to save the world."

Carolyn lifted a tear-stained face to state this, and James backed her off to arm's length.

"How about your father?" James asked. He hoped his voice sounded gentle, but to be honest he got kind of sick of it when white folks found ways to tell him how unhappy their lives were.

"Phil didn't say much," Carolyn answered. "I hardly know him, even now." Her tone of voice indicated she was not through feeling sorry for herself, but she did back off and sit down on the kitchen chair that faced the window. He stayed standing. He wasn't about to have his back to that pane.

"At least your daddy was there, wasn't he?" he reminded her. "Didn't he come home every single night?"

"I guess that's right," she said. "You must not have known yours at all."

"Knowing's not the same as liking." He gave a bitter little laugh. "After Freeman, now he really will never speak to me again, I'll tell you that."

"Oh God, James, I'm sorry. Your problems are so much worse than mine."

He felt even more annoyed once she turned the topic to him.

"Who's to compare pain in this world, Carolyn?"

She always had been sorry for him, the Negro boy in her life, and now she had way too much justification. Was it gonna be this way for the rest of his life? Putting up with the pity of white people who helped him? If he stayed out of prison, that is.

"I must have drunk too much." Carolyn grabbed a dishtowel off the rack and dabbed at her face.

"You don't have to apologize," said James, remembering all at once that she was his friend. "Drinking beer. God, it already seems like that was hours ago."

"I don't want to put you in this position," she added, voice muffled by the cloth. "Where you have to be the one to comfort me."

"Compared to all the other positions I'm in, this one is easy," he assured her.

"It's just that—" Carolyn gulped in air to get her emotions under control but failed and started to cry again.

"It's just that your mama died," he said softly. She buried her face in her hands and let him lead her into the bedroom.

"I'm so tired," she sobbed. "And I feel so silly."

"Get into your PJ's, Curls. I'll be back to tuck you in."

His auntie did used to bring him warm milk the times he was little and missed his mama, when she had to transcribe extra tapes late at night for some damned downtown lawyer who never would have colored in his front office, as she used to put it. He heated a little saucepan of it until the top skimmed, then brought it back in Carolyn's favorite coffee cup. In a clean T-shirt with her face washed, she looked better.

She took a sip at once, grimaced when it burned her mouth, and set it down on the bedside table. She took a deep breath, then started in.

"James, I was wondering—"

"Tell you what, Carolyn. Let's not talk anymore tonight. I'm tired, too. Let's figure things out in the morning."

"All right." She gave out a wan smile.

"Didn't you say you liked this here mystery about the fat man?" He got her Nero Wolfe book off the bedside table, handed it to her, and tucked in her sheet.

"Take your mind off things," he told her. "Drink your milk." He pecked her on the cheek, then left in a hurry. He'd seen the way she looked at him before the upset began. Any conversation about how now was the time to finish up what they had started so many years ago should be postponed, forever if possible.

He scrubbed out the pan where the milk had left a crust, and then scrubbed a whole lot more until the entire kitchen was white-glove clean. The last thing he did was finish up the floor for once and for all and let himself out onto the kitchen step. He'd taken to smoking a nightly cigarette there, about as far out of the house as he allowed himself after that one walk, and only late like this, when the pig on his rounds was long gone.

Outside and all at once, he wanted it, just a toke or two. Once upon a time it'd been Saturday night, after all, even if this Lalo guy— damned if these Mexicans didn't have some strange names—had fucked it up.

He tiptoed back inside across the wet floor, dug out Quincy's green velvet bag and Zig-Zags from his suitcase pocket, and rolled a joint so slim it mighta passed for a toothpick. Had to make the stuff last; who knew when he'd ever get more? Fidel Castro was tough on drugs, from what he'd heard.

He slipped back out onto the stoop, hunkered down on the steps, and lit up. He held it in his lungs, and damn, did this taste good! He coughed it out and sucked at the joint again and again until it was all smoked up.

He stared into the tule fog that lay quiet all around him, and the night became luminous, as though he could see right through it. He squinted up at a pale, misshapen moon that hung straight overhead, watched the mist blow over its face, then off it again. A brushing sound made him jump, ears cocked like a mule deer's, to hear if he was someone's prey. But the street was silent, except for the sound of the highway half a mile away. Night animals, must be. He didn't care. He would enjoy this high even if it was the last one ever.

He dragged out a kitchen chair, tilted the straight back against the door frame, and let his mind float into a Mary Jane dream.

Mary Jane—now this was a woman he loved for sure. Mary. Mary. Mary Louise sure had enjoyed the food he'd fixed up. She'd laughed so hard there a few times that her long hair just about got tangled up in the barbecue sauce. And Carolyn had herself a good time, too. The three of them felt like their own little family for a while. It wasn't the first time. Their little trio—like a family when things were going good.

Too bad Mary Lou had to go out to that camp alone. A man should want to help her, but the fact that he couldn't was a relief. He never had known what to do about people like this crazy fool with a gun. Not to mention the pigs. Just avoid the pigs altogether, slink around a corner. Made things simpler. Maybe not the most courageous, but no fool either. The way to survive. Claim some easy victories after all. He laughed to himself.

Carolyn wanted him back. Clear as day in that look she'd given him, and just as clear again that he couldn't do it. Every time she touched him he freaked; he was in no shape to get it on with a woman. And, as she would be the first to say if she was her usual self, it wouldn't be right. To get involved with someone at this time certainly would not be the correct thing to do. He produced this sentence in his mind with her cadence, and had to laugh again.

At some point he realized Carolyn's light had gone off. Not too long after that Mary Lou pulled up to the curb in her battered old green sedan. When he got through jumping out of his skin yet again, 'cause for a second there he had absolutely no idea who she was, he worried about whether he smelled of marijuana. He reached in his pocket for the mints he used to solve this problem in the old days before Freeman, but of course they weren't there.

She climbed out of the car, ghostly in the fog and the pale moonlight.

"What are you doing awake?" she asked.

"Saturday night's not over yet, Ms. Mary Louise."

Up on the porch with him now, she didn't seem to notice, 'cause she surely would get mad if she thought he was smoking dope anywhere around here, and what's more, she'd be right. Instead she actually sounded pleased that someone was still up.

"Where's Carolyn?" she asked. Two questions in a row. She loomed over him, and her face looked like the moon made right, pale and full.

"Gone to bed," he said.

"What in the world are you doing out here in the cold?" Question number three. Was she happy to see him? Or mad?

Either way he was chilled, now that she mentioned it, so he got up and followed her right away, hauling his chair back into the kitchen's warm light.

"So what'd you do with yourself after our dinner was so rudely interrupted?" she asked. Nothing but questions, this girl. Well, he had all the time in the world; he'd just answer anything she asked.

"Mopped up your floor," he told her.

"I've got to say one thing about you, James. You do know how to clean a house."

"That's something we both understand."

That got the two of them to smiling. He found his cigarettes and lit one for her first, then himself. They stood next to each other for a moment, smoking. Then Mary Lou sank into her usual chair at the table, right under the window. A quick check showed it dark and quiet in the night behind her.

"What happened out there?" he asked her. "Nobody got shot, I assume."

"Nah. Nothing ever gets better at that camp, though. Where all the families live…" Her voice trailed off.

"Well, think of it this way. When things stay the same, at least they don't get worse."

He turned and got out two beers from the fridge.

"Come on, Ms. Mary Louise. Let's go sit in your living room for a change, where there's music."

In there before she was, he saw it all register in her eyes. The sofa bed was made up and real neat; she liked that. The coffee table was pushed off against the far wall, and it had his clothes on it, but at least they were folded. There wasn't any other place to put them, he wanted to tell her. Only the small light was on, the one on the tiny table at the far end of the couch; he hated the harsh glare from the overhead fixture. The curtains were drawn shut; here they were hidden away from this endless dark night.

Mary Lou settled into the one oversize easy chair and plunked her beer down on its flat, wide arm. He paced quietly behind her, enjoying the feel of the icy can in his hand.

"God," she sighed. "It's all so serious. The camp, your situation, nothing's like it should be."

"Hey now, girl, don't you worry about one thing. If I just get the clothes up onto that high closet shelf and fold up your couch, your living room would be set right in an instant."

That made her smile, and she took a long draught of her beer. Not like her; she usually drank slow, if at all. Then she told him how Deputy Sage had ignored what happened out at the housing camp.

"Too danged serious for me," she concluded, repeating the words she had been saying to herself throughout the long drive home. "I was so inadequate out there. I couldn't make anything happen."

"Your job was exactly that, don't you think? To make sure nothing happened?" He stopped behind her to pat at her shoulder. Second woman who needed comforting tonight. Well that was okay. Least he could do. "Sounds to me like you did it just right."

She drained her can and set it carefully on the floor as though it would be the first in a long line.

"Have you ever been afraid?" she asked him, turning in her chair to search out his eyes.

"Are you kidding me?" He held her gaze, smiling but with his jaw set, hands open in front of him. "When am I not afraid?" Nervous at how truthful he was being, he had to laugh.

"But I mean really frightened. And alone."

"Are you kidding?" This time he didn't have to say more. She laughed too.

"Well, you seemed pretty brave in Freeman," she said. He stared at her, wanting to hear more.

"You could have just crumbled," she added. "Let things take their course. Instead you thought about it, made up your mind, and did what you had to do."

He paused before he could think of a single thing to say to this. It was a surprise to hear her say she respected him.

"And you know what, Mary Louise?" Now he just had to grin, mouth open wide. The whole thing seemed funny. "Ever since then? I've been scared. All the time, every single minute of the day."

He set the needle carefully on her Otis Redding record, the one he had listened to over and over while the ladies were gone during the day, dropped down onto the far side of the sofa bed, and bent over to take off his shoes.

"Take this cut, for example. 'Sittin' on the Dock of the Bay.' Otis. My man."

"I love this song," she agreed.

"But have you ever listened to the words? White folks think he's just hanging out, laid back, so cool. But actually the man checkin' out the waters is depressed. And afraid. One lonely motherfucker, I'm tellin' you."

Now how could he be so dumb as to use that word, when he knew very well how she felt about bad language. He glanced over; she hadn't moved. With a soft sigh he swung his long legs onto the thin mattress and rested his spine on the cushions stuffed between the metal frame and the back of the couch. Damn. This was exactly the place to be.

"You know," she said, "that creep Jensen just ran the show out there. I can't handle this stuff by myself anymore."

"Doesn't sound like anyone else would've done much better." He'd already said this once before, just about word for word, but she didn't seem to mind.

"He's not gonna fire every single person who goes to that march, is he?" She asked as if he would know how to put together this whole damned event she thought was so important. "That's illegal, right?"

"Who says they're into following the law?" His voice was lazy, his eyes were closed, but he knew it when she slid her feet up onto the bed, carefully away from his.

Second time this evening he was close to a woman, but this round he wanted nothing more all at once than to jump the gap. She'd stop him for sure, but he found that he had to try.

He touched her ankle with his sock-covered toe. She flinched, but she didn't move. He lay there, eyes closed, sliding the ball of his foot up and down her calf. His body stirred and hardened up, and an eternity later he heard her sigh. He loved being stoned. It made him understand the way everything was interwoven with everything else, cause and effect, as it all unfolded through time.

He glanced at her from under his eyelids. She hadn't moved the leg he touched, not one inch closer or farther away. Honey hair fanned out, eyes closed, he could tell by her mouth that she was permitting herself to like this. But she'd never take it further, not in this lifetime. He'd have to be the one to do that.

And so he did. Smooth as fine liquor, he got back up, flowed across the small space to her chair, kissed her on those thin, scared lips, took her by the hand, and led her back to lie down beside him. The contact, through their clothes and along the length of their bodies, flowed like the blood that circulated in his very own veins, one and the same.

He took off his own shirt first, and then helped her out of various articles of clothing, one by one, each phase long and languid.

Complete in itself. Even if she stopped it right this instant, Lord Jesus, it was already motherfuckin' complete and whole.

Relax. Concentrate on the music. The touch, above all, the touch. Didn't matter how long it took, not at all, 'cause he would be happy to go on like this forever. Her eyes were still closed. She never had opened them this entire time, he was certain of that, and then they began to make love.

The silky feel of her, first all the long way up and down the outside of her pale, naked body, was beyond his comprehension. How had he ever found his way to this place? All he knew was to keep moving. Maybe the drug, maybe a hallucination, whatever this was, however this miracle had come about, he would just take it.

Then in, and in, and all the way in. So hungry for closeness, for a long, long time, for what was surely forever, all he could do was move up into her, back down, then up again, as far inside her as he could reach and go and merge and far, far up into her, seeking that place and finding it, where he could leave his sorrow behind.

She said nothing and made no sound, and though she didn't stop him, all he could manage was this one motion, this on and on through a sea of touch and kiss, caress and stroke, that threatened to overwhelm him. Not at all certain he was making her happy, not at all certain he would even come, ever, into her endless space, now he too, afraid to see her disappointment and certainly afraid to show his own need, had his own eyes shut tight.

Did she wonder what was in it for her? Well she'd get a lot out of him if she'd just give it a chance; the way he felt right now she'd damned well get whatever he had. He wanted this with her as much as he'd ever wanted anything in his whole life. He'd turn himself inside out for her, if that was what it took.

He felt her clutch at him, shudder, and grip again. Her legs clenched his, then shook like leaves trembling in the wind. She is moving was all he could think, caught up in her tide. His fingers grabbed at her straight hair, tangled it in their haste. His knees felt rubbed raw by his pressure against the sheets, his toes were cramped, everything about him ached all at once, and he had no way to stop.

Her motion took him so far off he could never have guessed how he got there or even where he went, 'til Jesus, she was all at once a thousand women, all opening to him, all letting him inside, all rocking him to keep him safe. His sound began deep behind his throat, and when it started he couldn't stop, moan after groaning moan emanating from his stomach through his chest, even though he knew he shouldn't. He sensed her reaction to the noise, he knew it scared her and stilled her at once, but by then he was broken, irrevocably, upon her shore. Finally it was quiet again.

His sounds had changed her. He had lost her along with his own self, and he understood that now he must thank this woman. He must let her know that she had saved him, saved his life. He managed to disengage limbs and pull off her, turn on his side, prop his chin on his hand and get his eyes open to stare at her face, but she still wouldn't even glance at him. She was embarrassed, he realized, so embarrassed she might never look straight into his face again. He pulled the sheet and blanket over them both. All that, the whole thing, made him smile so wide his cheeks ached, and still he couldn't stop. Her lips curved upward in response, which was what he needed to know.

"Sweetness," he was able to murmur, "sweetness and light." With that he fell off, he couldn't help it, the sleep would be that precious, the sleep would be that deep. It would be a sleep he had not known since he got here and maybe way before that, a sleep he never thought to find again. Like everything else since Freeman, he had to take this when it came. The last thing he felt was his cheek on her breast, her hand stroking his close-cut head. In wonderment, maybe. Probably she'd never felt a black man's hair before in her life.

—m—

You have got to be crazy, Mary Louise, was what she was saying to herself as it began. Yes, nothing tonight has come out the way you intended. Yes we did have fun at dinner, but this makes no sense, however you look at it. No sense at all. He rubbed at her leg with his foot and gave her a lazy version of his gap-toothed grin. She shut her eyes to ward it off, but that only made her realize that what she wanted to do was hold that foreign-looking face of his in her hands, kiss those wide puffy lips, run her tongue over that gap between his teeth once, just once. Why couldn't she? That would be as far as it would go and no harm done.

Then his lips played with hers and covered them in just the way she'd imagined. Next thing she knew he was rolling his tongue all down inside her mouth and she couldn't stop it at all; she was reaching with her own, first to touch that gap between his teeth, then, to her complete and utter surprise, to reach as far back in his mouth as she could find. Her eyes were closed so tight she would never let him see that she knew she was doing this.

Later she couldn't even remember the moment she sank down onto that sofa bed with him, the decision to let him take off both their clothes. So this was what Carolyn meant by a one-night stand, she thought, as she allowed herself to be folded into his light brown limbs, enclosed in his long, smooth world.

And when he entered her, she wanted him. She expanded with it, swelled at it, just about grabbed for it, which amazed and chagrined her at once. She was so ready she could grow to any size, and she knew her body had never understood this way to be with a man before. He slipped inside her, simple as that, and he stayed there. So long, so gentle, so patient that she actually relaxed. Shivers began along the backs of her thighs, flushed all the way up the length of her. The sensation ebbed and she thought sure that was all, but then there it was, and the elusive energy radiated up from deep inside again. She felt as if the bottom might fall right out of her body, but then his voice welled up.

A soft moan, and she found she loved that sound, but she couldn't help worrying about Carolyn. She stiffened up, he let out groan after groan, low but massive, and she froze in place, listening for Carolyn's reaction. He lay absolutely still on top of her until he slipped out.

Then he gently moved them both onto their sides and held her, combed through her hair with his fingers, traced out her lips and eyes. Not a sound from Carolyn's end of the house, thank God. He mumbled something and slipped away, limbs twitching as sleep settled over him. She listened to him breathe for the longest time, and eventually she slept too.

CHAPTER SEVENTEEN

Carolyn drove through Chinatown with James huddled in the back of the Volvo. A scuffle broke out in a crowd. Someone drew a huge curved knife. Police sirens drew closer. The street dipped underground and widened into a boulevard lined with luxury shops. An occasional cell fronted onto the thoroughfare; in each, a prisoner grasped the bars. The police net drew tighter.

She looked down from an upstairs room. James, covered with coat and muffler, was riding an old, slow, one-gear bicycle down her dark, deserted Berkeley street. She could do nothing. He's caught, she thought. He began a soft lament and then accelerated into a desperate wail.

Carolyn woke with an awful sense of fighting something off, of being trapped, unable to move. Her ears strained to hear the cry again, which would tell her the dream was real. Slowly the shapes in Mary Lou's bedroom took form. She turned her head to the alarm clock's green fluorescent dial. Twenty after two. A tentative pat on the empty side of the mattress corroborated her sudden understanding that Mary Lou had not yet come to bed.

She switched on the lamp. Unwrinkled sheets. At once she knew the meaning of the sound that had formed the boundary of her dream, and she hated it.

She curled into an angry fetal ball, then had to unwind to get into the bathroom. Determined not to be intimidated, she tiptoed through the dark and knocked her shin against a desk leg. The sharp pain brought tears. Mortified, she clicked on the hall light.

To her immense relief, a careful quiet had descended over the other half of the house. She used the toilet but didn't flush, and crept back into bed. Sleep was impossible.

How could they? Mary Lou would never—but she had. And James, nursing her with warm milk earlier instead of wanting the physical intimacy she had all but offered him. Her cheeks burned at the memory of her arms encircled around his waist, her cheek laid along his back, the coarseness of the new blue work shirt she had bought for him in Fresno. How could they do this to her? She didn't cry. She wouldn't do that again. But she stayed wide awake, stiff and unyielding, until the tule fog that lay around the bedroom window lightened with the winter dawn.

She sat up at last, miserable in her mangled sheets. All that ever helped was to be alone, and she'd be damned if she would share this room for even one more night. By the time Mary Lou emerged, sleepy and rumpled, wearing James's one clean shirt, the only other one he had, Carolyn, already drinking warmed-over coffee made chalky with skim milk, was waiting for her at the kitchen table.

"I'll stay in the living room tonight," Carolyn said.

She saw goose bumps on Mary Lou's legs and she knew her tone was sharp, but she was not going to mince words when this had happened.

"Freezing in here," muttered Mary Lou, embarrassed, as well she should be. Well, too damned bad. "I have to get some clothes on."

Carolyn wanted to scream, to plunge a kitchen knife between Mary Lou's shoulder blades as she disappeared down the hall. The toilet flushed, and she returned, tying her lavender bathrobe around her.

"I'm serious, Mary Lou," said Carolyn the second she reappeared. "I will not be lying in there one more night wondering where you are. At least give me the space I need."

"Okay, okay, I heard you." Mary Lou spoke just above a whisper. "But don't get on your high horse here, Carolyn. Just remember, he wasn't any boyfriend of yours. I didn't take him from you."

Yes you did, Carolyn wanted to say. He was going to be mine. I was going to get him back.

"You could at least have had some respect for my privacy," she told Mary Lou.

"Well, I'm sorry about that, I truly am. But it's been lonely out here."

"And James is going to help that, right?"

Carolyn got up to put more of the awful brew into her thick, white porcelain cup. For the first time she noticed a hairline crack along its rim. Disgusted, she left it on the counter without drinking it or rinsing it out. Ugly old cup, and anyhow, they didn't even have any decent coffee out here in this godforsaken Valley. How she had hated the coffee last summer, and she hated it even worse right now.

"I don't know what James will do," Mary Lou was saying. "I have no idea, Carolyn. Don't tell me you're the one saying I have to get it all figured out before I even start."

"You're a fool," Carolyn told her. "You'll suffer for it."

"Probably so. When have things been different?"

When you were so goddamned sure of yourself about the purity of your views, Carolyn wanted to tell her. When you just about had us convinced James endangered everything you believed in simply by being here. What a convenient time to change your mind. And now you even sounded like him all of a sudden, with that dry fatalistic streak that ran through everything he said.

Even in the midst of her fury, though, Carolyn knew she wasn't totally right. Hadn't she wanted James for herself only hours before? What had she thought, that she would hide with him in Cuba the rest of their lives? Unbelievably stupid. And she had let him do it to her again, goddamn it. Mary Lou this time, instead of Gwen Washington. She would take a walk, a drive somewhere to get another lousy cup of coffee, anything to be gone. She slammed the kitchen door without another word.

—⚭—

Once she heard the sound of Carolyn's motor cut through the quiet Sunday morning, Mary Lou went into her own bedroom. The bed was made and smooth, as though no one had slept in it for days. Carolyn had already packed and left her suitcase by the door to the hall. For a minute she thought her friend was leaving altogether, dropping James in her lap. But she had claimed the living room and roared off without her clothes.

Mary Lou couldn't have James in here with her under her very own lavender chenille bedspread just like that. She felt her heart beating under her breath. Could she? Anyway, would he want to leave his little cave in the living room? Yes. He would. Still and all, this was way too fast.

No matter how she thought about it, though, the green and black plaid canvas suitcase just sat there, saying that this very evening James would be right here, in this bed with her, all night long. Suffused by the rush of her own attraction, she knew that insane though all this was, she surely did look forward to it.

She showered and dressed, and by the time she got back out to the kitchen he was up. He had made fresh coffee in fact, and was sitting at her table like all the other mornings, only he didn't have a shirt on yet.

He caught at her hand as she tried to pass and get to the stove.

"Where'd Carolyn go?" he asked.

"Out somewhere. I don't know."

"She was mad, wasn't she?"

Mary Lou nodded. She scrambled eggs in a bowl, got bacon out of the fridge, and turned on a burner, all the time aware of his eyes on her back.

"She's already packed her clothes," she told him. She motioned to the hall where the suitcase stood and watched his eyes widen.

"Does that mean she's gonna leave?" he asked, panic in his voice.

"She told me she wants to sleep in the living room."

"Well, now." He dragged the two words out, relieved. "That's okay with me."

He got up to stand behind her, dropped his hand to her waist, and placed his lips at the nape of her neck. "And how about you? Is that okay with you, Mary Louise?"

She meant to turn and face him, to make a joke and push him off, to fix their breakfast and pretend it was a normal day. But all she could do was nod, head down. He reached around the stove to turn it off with one hand, gently lifting the hair off the side of her cheek with the other. He turned her, covered her lips with his, slid his tongue deep into her mouth, and she was back in that new place with him all over again. He led her by the hand to her bed, folded back her lavender spread, and lay them down together. By the time he was inside her, she was so excited she came right away. It was just like a girlfriend had told her once, a long time ago. You knew when it finally happened to you; you couldn't mistake it for anything else.

CHAPTER EIGHTEEN

Four weeks tomorrow since Freeman, thought Carolyn, and still no word from Quincy. She was sitting at her desk at the UFW office, chewing on her index finger cuticle and staring out the window at the grapevines that had sprouted new shoots that stuck straight up, brown with no trace of green. If she didn't know better she would have thought it was warm outside, all cloaked with a crystalline sunshine. But at eight thirty a.m. the radio news announcer had declared that it was thirty-eight degrees, and by noon, when she had trotted over the tracks to Jovita's for coffee to go with the food from Mary Lou's kitchen, maybe the temperature had gotten as high as forty-five. Now it was after three and getting colder again.

Carolyn wanted the Bay Area, where a sunny February day would be up in the sixties, with yellow sour grass lining the sidewalks and the tulip trees blooming. She pulled at her blue wool sweater to get it further down her chilled, jean-clad thighs, glad she had her black turtleneck under it instead of a T-shirt.

"Iglesias," Mary Lou was droning through her endless list of names with Lupe and Patricia, writing down what they knew about each and every one. "Pedro Iglesias."

This morning Mary Lou had said she could have a complete list of Colonia strikers ready for Carolyn in a couple of hours, but first it took most of the day for the sisters to arrive and everyone to get working on it, and now there was no end in sight. Carolyn's job was to answer phones and handle whoever came in the door, but the office was deserted except for the four of them.

"He's in Michoacan with his wife this time of year, isn't he?" Mary Lou asked the other two.

"Which wife?" Patricia giggled.

"What do you mean, which wife?" Lupe sounded annoyed, as always. What a prig she was, thought Carolyn.

"Pilar, of course." Lupe answered her own question. "There's only one wife. She and the kids, they all live out by the Colonia tanks."

"Then why did she tell me in the drugstore yesterday?" Patsy asked. "'Pedro is gone,' Pilar said. She wants Mary Lou to help her get on welfare."

"So is he in Mexico or isn't he?" asked Mary Lou.

"Chuey told me he was." Patsy slid fast over the mention of her baby's father. "Pedro Iglesias has a whole other family down there."

"Chuey!" Lupe snorted in disgust. "Well, he's probably right. That's the type he spends his time with, I'm sure."

"Lucky for the Union Chuey knew these people, Lupe—" Patsy sprang to her lover's defense.

"Sure it was," Lupe answered. "Meant he had all sorts of places to go when he wanted to run out on you."

"I'll put him on the page of people we have to find." Mary Lou put an end to the bickering and went on. "Knight. Isn't he that Okie tractor driver who walked off with the Mexicans the first day?"

"He's moved over to the coast," Lupe said. "He'll never come back for this march."

"Well now, you never do know about that," Mary Lou replied. "I'm gonna put him on the 'to find' list."

At this rate she would never get back to Berkeley, thought Carolyn. Twice more she had driven all the way to Fresno to try to call this Quincy, but never any answer. Another afternoon she had gone to Emerald and rented a post office box under a false name. Sally Jones or Janice Quigley? For a second she couldn't remember which of her high school friends' names she had chosen for that PO box, and of course you couldn't write anything down, you had to keep it all in your head.

Sally Quigley—they had decided to mix and match the names. Anyhow, now Quincy could write a letter instead of showing up— scaring Mary Lou half to death, as she would have put it—but no way to tell Quincy about it. It was hard to believe her life would ever get back to normal again.

It was time to go home, she told herself. James had found comfort in his time of need, and Mary Lou was no longer lonely. They were more and more of a couple. Not that they showed it so much in front of her, but they didn't have to. They slept together every night. Carolyn was superfluous.

"Lopez." Mary Lou sounded more energetic as she swung into the middle of the alphabet.

"Don't forget Lopes," Lupe said, pointing to the name above. "'Course he's Portuguese."

"Yeah, but his wife's Mexican," Mary Lou replied. "I heard she had cousins with the *huelga* in Delano."

"It'll be hard to get the Portuguese to come," Lupe said. "But the Punjabis are the worst."

"You know how Colonia used to put a Portuguese guy in a row next to a Mexican guy's wife?" Patsy asked. "Well, once the Punjabis showed up, they stopped doing it that way. Mexican guy wouldn't even bother being jealous of a Punjabi." All three women laughed.

Carolyn was disgusted. They reminded her of the kids in her high school, only one step away from calling blacks jungle bunnies. She didn't believe in talking about people in groups; she didn't belong here.

She wondered how Mary Lou felt about James being black. Why couldn't he see what dangerous ground he was on with Mary Lou? Could he be going through the motions, just to make sure she wouldn't turn him in? The James she knew was nowhere near that calculating, but then again, his life hadn't required sheer survival measures before now. Should she ask him? She would never have the nerve.

"Now here's Lopez," Mary Lou said. She stood to stretch her arms, her whole body long and slender and taut. Why wasn't she cold dressed like that, with only a bright red T-shirt stenciled with the UFW black eagle flag on above her jeans? How could she look so thin and fit? This was a woman who never walked anywhere if she could drive in a car.

Patsy and Lupe both had on skirts and tights. Patsy's was short and plaid, with her ample black-clad legs crossed, the top foot swinging back and forth. Lupe's skirt was a wool weave, blue and white, draped down to her calves above the neatly crossed ankles, the whole ensemble set off by a crisp white blouse, ironed with razor-straight creases down the long cuffed sleeves. Neither of the Muñoz girls' looks appealed to her at all, but Carolyn felt dumpy compared to all three of them.

She was sick of living out of her suitcase; the next time she was in Fresno she would spend some of the money she was running out of on new clothes, though where she would find anything out here that looked at all cool was unknown.

"There are three Lopezes," said Lupe, plugging on. "The first is Eriberto; he's the one who lives with the illegals. I know right where to find him. The other two are his brothers. Eriberto's the oldest, so he'll have a big influence on whether any of them will come to the march. I don't know what he'll do; he's always on the fence."

"Count on Lupe to know every name," said Mary Lou with relief as she scribbled in the information.

"I gotta get to Maria's, Lupe." Patsy got up to put her canvas jacket on. Sure enough, her stomach was pooched out from under that loose white smock she was wearing on top. Puff sleeves; she looked about twelve. But she was all of seventeen, and maybe her skirt even had the elastic pouch in the front; maybe she was already wearing maternity clothes. On her left hand gleamed the cheap shiny gold band Mary Lou had recommended.

"I told her I'd watch the kids 'cause the chicken farm put her on swing shift this week. You're the one with the car." Patsy kept talking, apparently unaware of Carolyn's scrutiny. God if it were me, thought Carolyn, I'd feel embarrassed every single minute of the day.

"I'll take you there." Lupe turned to Mary Lou to get her permission to leave with her sister. "Then I have to go cook my father's dinner. Our mom's on that shift, too."

"Can you go out with Carolyn and Ramón tonight, if he gets here in time?" Mary Lou asked. "You three would be good together."

Don't allow volunteers to escape your clutches until they promise to come back, marveled Carolyn. Now for the persuasion.

"You know the strikers," Mary Lou continued. "Ramón's from Union headquarters in La Paz, so he can tell people what Cesar wants, and Carolyn's the *gabacha* who came all the way from the city 'cause the march is so important. Don't you think the combination will impress them, Lupe?"

Mary Lou would say it was the only way to get the job done, Carolyn supposed, but she never let up. People had to resent it, the way she was always hectoring them to do more.

"What time?" asked Lupe, willing enough. She rubbed the small of her back, stretching her spine, and pulled on a shapeless grey coat. Suddenly Carolyn felt ashamed of her comparisons; these girls' outfits might be ironed and matched, but everything had to be secondhand. No one had had a paycheck in months. She remembered the grab-bags always here last summer, filled with clothes donated by city UFW supporters.

"Ramón's supposed to be here already," Mary Lou was saying. "I'll have him call when he shows. And will you come back tomorrow afternoon so we can get further on the list?"

"Okay, okay." Lupe held up her hands to stave off more requests, but she was smiling. "I'll be here after work. Same time as today, all right?"

"Me too. I'll come straight from the drugstore." Patsy said it without even being asked.

Carolyn realized that she was the one who resisted Mary Lou's pressure. And resented James's demands. And was afraid of the emptiness of her life back home. What would she do there, go back to crying about Mona? Whose money, by the way, would soon run out and then her daughter would have to get a job, go back to school maybe. Both at once was what she ought to do, but would she have the energy for all that? Overwhelming. She wanted to cry, but she was sick of that too.

Well cut the crap, is what her mother would have said. If you just sit around and contemplate your own navel, you'll be hoist by your own petard. Why not "hoisted?" But no, it was always "hoist." Shit or get off the pot, even if what you have to do scares the bejesus out of you. Carolyn had loved the way Mona talked as a child, hated it as a teenager, and right now at this minute all she could come up with was how unusual it had been for the Los Angeles suburbs of the fifties. A grown woman, and she couldn't even figure out how she felt about her own damned mother.

Fresh air and a glimpse of sunny blue sky stirred her for an instant when Patsy opened the door against unexpected wind, and then it banged shut and the sisters were gone. The office seemed bleak without them.

"So I'm the white girl of the team, huh?" she said to Mary Lou.

Maybe if she brought things up more. What she thought about the way everyone threw ethnic categories around out here, for example. Or how much it hurt, Mary Lou being with James. Just get it all out in the open. Maybe that would make her feel better.

"Yep, that's you," Mary Lou answered. "Can you stay late tonight, go out with Lupe and Ramón?"

"I guess so. But I need to come in later in the mornings if I've got to go out at night. I feel like I'm about to get sick." Carolyn got tissue from her jeans pocket and blew her nose.

"You do what you have to, Carolyn."

"So how's Patsy doing?" Carolyn asked. Maybe she could get Mary Lou to close the office for ten minutes and go to Jovita's for a Coke. Then they could actually talk.

"Patsy?" Mary Lou used her pencil tip to count the strikers they had located. "Seemed like she was fine today, didn't it?"

"Do you think Chuey Vargas will show back up before the baby's born?"

"Nah, he's long gone." Mary Lou didn't raise her head. "Patsy should not count on that man for one single thing."

"Did her dad say she could come home?"

"Not yet, but he'll change his mind. Right now she stays with her sister Maria and her husband and kids."

Mary Lou started back at the top, checking every possible name for the march once again, making new pencil marks here and there.

"Did you ask Cesar to heat up the boycott on Silveira yet? Seems like the sheriffs need pressure about that scene out at the camp."

"Sure, I asked him." Mary Lou straightened up at last. "You know what he said?"

"What?"

"He said I already had my hands full with this march. He said by the time it got here, there'd be at least five hundred people who'd need food and places to sleep. He said the whole thing would be a flop if we didn't get the strikers involved. He said Colonia—"

"All right, all right," Carolyn said. "You have to work. I get it, I get it." She grabbed her purse and coat. "I'm thirsty. I'm going over to Jovita's."

Couldn't there ever be one fucking minute free of somebody else's fucking priorities? When did she get to tell her two so-called friends that it wasn't just farmworkers, black people, Mary Lou exhausted with work, James afraid for his life? When did she get to have her own emergency?

"Ramón ought to be here any minute, Carolyn," Mary Lou said. "You'll be back soon, right?"

"I'll be back, Mary Lou. I'll be back in time to meet Ramón and do the visits. I'll be back when I've had my Coke!"

She slammed out of the office and found herself in light so bright it hurt her eyes. She stood for a moment, adjusting to the immense cloudless sky blown clean by the last rain. The poplars by the railroad tracks were still bare as bones. This damned winter was endless.

Mary Lou and all her self-righteousness. James and his endless need. She traipsed across the railroad tracks, willing her own anger to last, but it seemed tiny in the still, cold space under that huge sky.

At the entrance to Jovita's Café she noticed the purple shelf, majestic in the east. The afternoon was so clear you could actually see the Sierra. She had heard about this last summer, but today was the first time she believed it. Had she missed this before, just staring down at the ground? The mountains, so far off she could make out no detail, were absolutely beautiful. How ridiculous to have to fight just to get out of the office.

She stopped long enough to take in a few deep breaths of the freezing air, then pushed open the heavy glass door. Warmth rushed to surround her, and as she settled into the nearest red Naugahyde booth and took the menu from its tarnished silver clip, for an instant she was almost happy.

She hadn't even had lunch, for chrissakes, and it was four in the goddamned afternoon. "For chrissakes." "Goddamned." She was her mother's daughter. Her stomach growled suddenly, and irritation flooded back in with the small sound. If Mary Lou were a grower, the UFW would take her ass in front of the labor commissioner for insisting on hours like this. Instead, she and everyone else in this outfit worked all the time, and you felt like a lazy fool if you weren't just dying to do the same thing.

She ordered a hamburger and french fries, and on impulse added a vanilla shake. This thinner self was about to go by the way-side, but it was the product of misery anyhow, so what the hell? Mary Lou was the one who drank Coke; she didn't even like the stuff. It was better to be here without her. Carolyn was sick of Union talk.

So why did she stay?

"Maybe I should go home," she had said to James yesterday while they worked together on the dishes. It was pitch dark outside, the stars glittering in the cold outside the kitchen window where he always had his eye. Mary Lou was late for dinner as usual, and he was carefully wrapping her portion in tin foil, saving it for her right at her table place as if it could make up for her not being there. Despite the attention to his lover's each and every need, his reply had been quick.

"Please. No." He turned from her task to look Carolyn straight in the face, big brown eyes pleading right along with his voice

"Why not?" she asked. "I must have a life back there somewhere."

"I need your help," he said. Just 'til the next phase."

"You've got Mary Lou." Her voice quavered, which she hated.

"She's not the one Quincy's gonna contact, Curls. She's not the one who understands the Movement, who can help me to get underground long enough to leave this damned country. You're irreplaceable. You know that."

And like an idiot Carolyn had been complimented, pleased that James thought highly of her, trusted her. Maybe he would ask her to come to Cuba with him. If he asked, would she go? She supposed she would, even now, even after Mary Lou. What a pushover. What a needy, lonely fool she was.

So she was still here. Nowhere close to leaving, actually. She supposed she stayed at this point for the same reason she had come in the first place. Because if she worked hard at being a good person, then everything might just come out right. Because Mona had taught her to be tenacious, especially if it was on behalf of a principle. Mary Lou and her mother would have liked each other, would have gotten along just fine.

And just what was the principle? Helping a friend in need? Carolyn had already saved James's life, hadn't she? But not really, not until he was safe. When he got to Cuba he could speak out again, he could tell the truth of how Nyame had died, he could be a leader and people would listen to him. And that would be because of her.

Maybe it was just sex James wanted from Mary Lou, but even that, especially that, twisted at her insides. There were, she supposed, things more important than sex, like loyalty and follow-through. Ugh. How could the two of them be so insensitive to her? The house was so small. She never heard any sounds, but she was aware of every minute they were in that bedroom together.

The food came, and she attacked it like the enemy, but with precision. First the burger, next the fries. When only the shake was left, she felt a little better. She slowed down to take tiny sips, to make it last.

What on earth could take Quincy this long? They had to believe he was sincere, otherwise they were at a total dead end. But if another week went by with no word, she would go to the city and talk to him. At his house or at the Black Panther office? Both were bound to be under surveillance. She would have to call him with the code, every hour of the day and night, different pay phone each time. Not like here in Allen, where there was exactly one public telephone, which she certainly would not ever use in front of everyone, outside that little grocery store up the street from Mary Lou's. Plus one phone only; it pinpointed the location so exactly if anyone happened to tap into the call.

She'd find Quincy all right, and then she'd get him to meet with her at a public place. One o'clock would mean noon; he would remember that. Both of them needed to stay safe. Each would be motivated to do it right.

Of course, sure as anything, someone she knew would stop by her own place while she was in Berkeley or see her on the street. But what she would say when that happened was simple, so simple it meant she didn't have any real intimacy with anyone. On postcards to her father, her friends, her neighbor, she had told them all she was out here to work with the Union. She would just talk on and on about the march, like Mary Lou always did.

Easy. She would tell the truth to everyone, except for everything she wanted to conceal. She had gotten good enough at it that it felt all too natural. "Tell no lies," or at least as few as possible. Amilcar Cabral couldn't mean it literally. He'd been in danger every minute of the day, until his enemies got to him anyhow. With the help of the CIA, of course. "Claim no easy victories." He was reaching for a deeper level when he said that.

Did Mona have to lie like this, she wondered, to protect her left-wing friends? Had she lied to Phil, to her own husband? In any event, her mother had stuck by her McCarthy victims even though it cost the marriage, so Carolyn could get through this until James made it to the next stage.

James would be her own special contribution to the revolution, even if no one knew it but her and him. He would be grateful. He would recognize her worth. This thing with Mary Lou hurt right now, but it would be long over by then.

Through with the food, she sighed and patted her stomach. All she needed to keep her priorities straight was what you should get on any job: breaks every two hours plus lunch. Through the window she saw that a red and white pickup had pulled into the Union parking lot next to her Volvo. The fabled Ramón.

She made her way down the long narrow restaurant to the cash register where Jovita herself, portly and resplendent with lavender eye makeup and cherry-bright lips, waited to take the money.

"So how's everything going, Carolyn?" The drawer clanged as it flew open, and Carolyn handed her ten dollars, which disappeared at once.

"Good," she answered. "We're all working on the march."

"What march?" Jovita counted out three dollars plus change and handed it to her. Carolyn was stunned. This was like when people pretended they had never heard of the lettuce or Colonia boycotts. Union people were a mainstay of her business; surely her sympathies were with Chavez.

"Come on, Jovita, with all the UFW people who eat here you haven't heard about the march against Colonia? You'll walk with us, at least on the last day, won't you? That's when it has to be big."

"I can't close the restaurant." She shut the cash register with a bang.

"How would you face Mary Lou afterwards?" Carolyn asked. "Think about it."

She meant to joke at the expense of the organizer's doggedness, but Jovita didn't laugh.

"I have to get along with everyone, Carolyn. I love the Union, but they're not the only ones around."

She turned to the next in line. The conversation was over.

Back at the office a small man with a thin face leaned on the front of Mary Lou's desk and listened to her plans for the march. He wore a clean white Western shirt with mother-of-pearl buttons, boots that looked brand new like his pickup, and a cowboy hat that held its shape. *Muy macho*, thought Carolyn; the peacock type. He stood before she got to him and stepped forward.

"You must be Carolyn. *Mucho gusto.* I have heard of you, and of your help for us last summer."

He accompanied the fluent accented English with a small bow from the waist. Afraid he was mocking her, Carolyn stuck out her hand, concentrated on a firm grip, then turned to Mary Lou.

"So, I'm always grouchy when I get that hungry."

That was as close to an apology as she would offer, but Mary Lou didn't even seem to notice.

"What's the plan?" Carolyn asked her, hurt once again but resolute. "We still go out tonight?"

"Yeah, you'll take the list," said Mary Lou. "Ramón, you wanna call Lupe? See how soon she'll be ready."

While he was on the phone, Mary Lou delivered her instructions. Apparently the *gabacha* was the only one who had to hear all this.

"Now look, Carolyn. You gotta talk 'em into it, hear me? They're all gonna say they have to work, they have to go to the Mexico, to the Azores, *p'y p'aca*, everywhere but here. The Portuguese won't give you any promises, but if you get one to say he'll be there, he will be. The Mexicans will tell you anything, but that morning you'll just have to see who shows up."

Ramón finished the arrangements, hung up, and rejoined them.

"Tell them if the strikers aren't there, the press will pick up on it, and the whole thing will look like a fake," Mary Lou continued. "If they need a ride, we'll find one; if they have to take food to their sick grandmother that day, we'll do it for 'em. But they gotta be there. Cesar wants it, tell them. No excuses. Okay?"

They both nodded heads, couriers standing side by side in front of her, taking their orders.

"So, Lupe's ready?"

"She says come get her, and she will help us for the evening," he answered.

"Where are you staying, Ramón?"

Carolyn winced at Mary Lou's question. Didn't it encourage him to say he needed a place, and then what? Mary Lou certainly couldn't offer hers. To conceal her discomfort she straightened the undone work on her desk into neat piles for the morning.

"There, the hotel of the Punjabis." He jerked his head toward the Country Inn across the highway.

Mary Lou gave a low whistle. "I'm impressed. Cesar never pays for anyone to use a motel."

He shrugged, as if to say a man had his ways.

"How's Catalina?" Mary Lou couldn't stop asking questions.

"Better," Ramón said. "Resting after the baby."

"And how old are the other two now?"

"Four and two. It seems they come each two years."

To Carolyn, Ramón, slender and hardly taller than she was, barely looked substantial enough to be a father at all. He sounded pleased with his ability to people the earth, though. We get many more of these babies every two years and there won't be any room left. Didn't these Catholics ever think about that? She chided herself. Talk about putting people in categories. Apparently she was catching the habit.

"Will she be able to come to the march?" Mary Lou asked. "We'll help with the kids if that's what she needs."

My my, Mary Lou had actually sounded like she was just asking about Ramón's wife, thought Carolyn. But no, there was always the ulterior motive. Her friend, if they were still friends, was nothing if not single-minded.

"I hope so," he said. "She says yes, if she's healthy."

Ramón, Patsy, Lupe, none of them seemed to consider the Union an imposition on their lives. Apparently Carolyn was the only one who did. No, James minded. She had seen it show when Mary Lou went on and on about every detail at home at night. They were the two who wanted more of Mary Lou than they got.

Carolyn grabbed her purse, a yellow legal pad and extra pen, and nodded at Ramón that she was ready. They started toward the door.

"Here's the list." Mary Lou came after them to thrust an untidy folder into Carolyn's hands.

"See, it says after each name whether they're Mexican or Portuguese. If they promise to come and you believe it, put 'yes.' If they won't even talk to you, put 'no.' If you're not sure, put that there too, and we'll try to revisit as many as we can. But I don't know if there'll be time, so make the first one good."

She couldn't stop the instructions, now from the doorway as they crunched across the gravel lot. When they got to the vehicles, though, Mary Lou was finally far behind them. The entrance to the office closed and she was gone. What a relief. Just like when she finally got out of her mother's house, long before Mona was sick. It was a relief to be away from the lectures, the bravado, the unending strong personality.

Ramón opened the passenger door to his pickup as if there were no question about which vehicle to take. God forbid he should be the one driven around by her, thought Carolyn. It wouldn't fit his image. Nonetheless she accepted his unspoken offer with relief. He guided her elbow to help her up the high step to the cab, and she settled onto the clean, wide seat.

He picked a route out of town she wasn't familiar with. Soon the smooth pavement with the center line gave way to a country lane, with naked plowed fields right up against the road, biting small bits out of its paved edge. Then suddenly they were in a flowering orchard.

"Those incredible white blossoms," Carolyn said. If she didn't make the conversation happen, this man wouldn't say a word. "Almonds, right?"

"Yes. *Almendras.* See the flat earth through the whole orchard? That permits the machines to shake the nuts down onto the ground."

He glanced at her. She expected him to be amused at her ignorance, but his poker face hadn't changed. A razor ridge down

Ramón's high, thin nose separated ink-black eyes, each embedded at its own angle. The two halves were distinct enough to belong to brothers. An unusual face. Strong for such a small, compact person.

"So are the almonds the first trees to bloom?" she asked.

"No, first come the plums, like those." He pointed to the left, where smaller trees, mostly leafed out, still had a few pink blooms that bobbed like tiny ballerinas in the evening breeze.

"And next?"

"Then the almonds, then the peaches."

"What about the grapes? Do they even have flowers?"

"Yes, of course. They are green and small; they come after the leaves. Easy to miss."

Carolyn could think of nothing more, and silence descended. Mesmerized by the fresh landscape that rolled by under the setting sun, she forgot to be uncomfortable in the absence of words.

Ten minutes later they drew up to a cozy house tucked into a corner by a vineyard that rolled up a small hill surrounded by oaks and sycamores so bare of their summer canopy that every bird's nest showed. Ramón turned the truck into the circular drive and stopped at a front door framed by the spires of two small yew trees. Lupe ran out at once and climbed into the cab next to Carolyn, who could smell a light, fresh scent and see the dark wetness of her black hair, which had been scooped back into a fresh ponytail. Lupe reached across to shake Ramón's hand, more animated than Carolyn had known her to be before. The two exchanged greetings in a rapid Spanish Carolyn lost track of immediately.

Carolyn glanced at Ramón's angular profile, etched like stone against the twilight. After all that clucking at her sister's conduct, surely Lupe would never have the nerve to set her sights on a married man. Some things were still wrong, even in this women's liberation day and age.

"Where do we go first?" Lupe switched to English.

"Maybe we should start with the hardest ones," said Carolyn. "Mary Lou mentioned we might have to visit some twice."

"She's crazy. It'll take months just to get through the list once."
Lupe gave off a lighthearted laugh not particularly consistent with
what she had just said.

Carolyn couldn't see how that would be true. They had four weeks
to contact two hundred strikers. Say they visited seven families in an
evening; that would come out about right. Of course they might not
make it out every single night between now and the march, but then
again a bunch of the strikers were all together at the camp, where
everything would go fast.

"Why don't we start with the Lopezes?" Lupe decided. "They live
close to here."

"So, *en que dirección?*" Ramón started up the motor.

"*Izquierda,*" Lupe directed. He swung out of the driveway and
turned left.

"Then after that almond orchard you passed, we'll go left again,
up by the tanks." Directions were one of the few things Carolyn
could usually understand, but again, presumably for her sake, Lupe
switched to English.

"What's the name of the street?" asked Carolyn. She liked to visualize things on a map.

"I don't know," Lupe said. "I never noticed."

Just like everyone else out here. No one could tell a street
name, or how many blocks away you were, even if they'd lived
here all their lives. It was like you got places by osmosis, landmarks
maybe.

They picked up speed.

"You have a nice house," she said to Lupe. "That's the first time
I've seen it."

"Thank you. That's what Colonia gives you to live in when you're
a foreman."

"And now your father's out on strike?" Carolyn asked.

"*Cierto,*" Lupe replied. "He's been with Cesar from the first, of
course."

Mr. Muñoz had a lot to lose. Carolyn wasn't sure what she would
do under the circumstances.

They approached the huge cluster of vats that dominated this part of the landscape behind their tall fence topped with barbed wire, and a guard in the outside shack watched them impassively. After that Carolyn was soon lost, as Lupe directed Ramón through a series of intricate turns. At last the pickup pulled onto a driveway that led toward a dirty row of stucco rooms hidden from the road. A group of men lounged in front, beer bottles in hand, but by the time Ramón stopped the truck, everyone had disappeared.

"What happened?" Carolyn asked. "Where'd they go?"

"Illegals," he responded. "If someone you don't know drives up, maybe it's better to be inside, or even out in the orchard where no one can find you."

He turned dark asymmetrical eyes onto her to see if she understood. Oh good, she thought sourly. Someone else besides Mary Lou to explain things as if she were a child. Of course she had asked him; she was being irrational.

City Chicanos made this big point anyhow, she wanted to lecture back, that since these people were in what used to be their own country, there was nothing illegal about them. But she didn't think she should question his label. This was his scene, after all. At least he hadn't said *mojado*, wetback, which was what everyone yelled at the scabs all last summer.

"There's a Colonia foreman, DeSilva," Lupe was saying. "My father hates him. He's an *esquirol*. He rents to Lopez, who lives here." She pointed to the biggest unit, at the end of the row.

"DeSilva pays Lopez for each room he can fill. So Lopez talks to his cousin, who's a *coyote* in Tijuana. The *coyote* smuggles the *mojados* across the border. They're here in time for Colonia's pruning. No questions asked."

"You mean this Lopez we're about to visit helps Colonia get its scabs?" Carolyn asked.

It was true, but neither Ramón nor Lupe seemed all that bothered.

The three clambered down from the truck. The wind had fallen, and a thin crescent moon sliced a small corner of the darkening sky.

Carolyn felt large and out of place as they went up the tiny concrete stoop that was the entrance to the Lopez family's home.

Lupe knocked quietly. No answer. She knocked again, the door cracked, and a woman's timid face peered out.

"Señora Lopez, ¿*verdad?*" said Lupe. The woman nodded.

"Lupe Muñoz, remember me?" Lupe spoke in Spanish. "Daughter of Arnulfo Muñoz? Last summer we talked on the picket line."

The door opened wide to reveal a small, plump matron who smiled with relief.

"Ah, Lupe, come in! And your friends too. You must excuse me. We are so alone out here we don't know who comes to visit us."

They crowded into one of two small rooms. A toddler with tiny gold earrings peered from behind her mother's skirt; a larger boy with serious eyes stood by to see what would happen next.

"This is Ramón, who works with Cesar, and Carolyn, who came here all the way from San Francisco to help the Union with the march."

Carolyn stepped forward to shake the woman's hand. She thought she had met Señora Lopez before.

"Sit down, please," said Sra. Lopez. "Would you like coffee?"

"No, thank you," Lupe replied for all three of them. "It's not worth the trouble. We've come to speak with you and your husband about the march. Is he here, Mr. Lopez?"

"He's out back," Sra. Lopez answered. She gestured toward the fields that spread behind the stucco row. "Manuelito, go find Demetrio. Tell him to get your father." The solemn child nodded and was off, calling out his brother's name in a shrill voice.

Señora Lopez insisted on coffee and brought out part of a white store-bought sponge cake. It wasn't Carolyn's favorite dessert, but she couldn't refuse. So she sat with Lupe and Ramón to eat a small piece, drink the weak brew, and listen to them talk in Spanish about the strike. It was hard to stay awake in the overheated room. A half-hour after they had knocked, work boots clumped up the cement steps and a stocky, thickset man entered.

Ramón sprang up to shake Mr. Lopez's hand, and then they waited while he took off his jacket. His wife served him coffee and cake. At last the conversation could begin.

"We hope you and your family are well this winter of the strike," Lupe started off. Señor Lopez gave a noncommittal nod.

"We know it is difficult when you can't work for Colonia, the biggest employer in these parts."

To her surprise Carolyn understood every word. Every once in a while this language revealed itself for a minute, like the pebbles at the bottom of a clear stream before the rapids came.

"There is no work that Colonia doesn't know about," Sr. Lopez replied. "They make sure the scabs have more choices than we do."

"Cesar has sent me to tell the Colonia strikers that the boycott is strong in the East," said Ramón, taking the lead. "Colonia's profits are down."

"When will Colonia sign with the Union?" Sr. Lopez asked.

"Soon," Ramón replied. "It will be soon."

"Before the harvest?" Sr. Lopez pressed.

"We hope so," Ramón said.

"It will be difficult to strike again in the harvest," Sr. Lopez said. "The *mojados* come up and take all the jobs. The grapes get picked, but it is our families who go hungry."

But not you, you get your money by bringing in the wetbacks, thought Carolyn, slipping all too easily into the forbidden terminology. Indeed Señor Lopez, with his big paunch, did not look hungry. But no one could say his family was rich, either, in this tiny, crowded place. Immediately she was ashamed of her critical attitude. How far would her principles take her if she had a large family to feed?

"That is why the boycott is so important," countered Ramón.

"The boycott is important, yes," Sr. Lopez agreed. "But I can't go there."

"We did not come to ask you to do that. We came to make sure you plan to attend the march."

"What march?"

The same question Jovita had asked. Suddenly Carolyn remembered where she had seen Sra. Lopez. She had come in the office last week to ask about food stamps. Mary Lou explained the march at length to everyone who set foot in the place.

"Carolyn can tell you." Ramón gestured that now it was her turn.

Everyone listened as Carolyn related when the march would begin, what date it would come through Allen, how it would end up in Empire on Saturday afternoon where San Joaquin Valley and Bay Area groups were to converge at Colonia's offices to hear Cesar speak. She didn't quite dare do it in Spanish, so after each sentence Ramón translated, which meant it took twice as long.

"I worked on the strike last summer. This march is so important that I came back from the city to work here again," she concluded. Ramón said it in Spanish, and silence fell.

"So we want to know if you will come." He filled the void with a direct appeal.

Carolyn prayed Mr. Lopez would just promise to attend so they could go on to the next family. It was already late. You couldn't visit farmworkers' houses past eight-thirty; they had to get up too early. At this rate they would never finish the list. She shifted in her seat. Everyone else was still.

"I must go to work on Saturday." Sr. Lopez looked at his boots.

"It is important that the strikers come, at least on the last day," repeated Ramón. "Otherwise there will not be proper publicity for the boycott."

"My employer will want me to work," said Sr. Lopez.

Sra. Lopez pinched the plastic tablecloth between her fingers.

"You know, it is not legal for Colonia to punish you by bringing pressure on anyone who hires you," continued Ramón. "You have the right to march. The Union's legal department in La Paz will make sure of it."

Lopez did not look convinced.

"My father sent me to speak to you about this," Lupe tried another tack. "He said to remind you. He knows what it means to suffer for *la causa*."

Lopez nodded. She had his attention.

"He also is worried. He has lived in his house for the past eighteen years, only because of Colonia. He knows we will have to move if the strike goes on much longer. He takes this terrible risk of his free choice. But that is exactly why he wants to march. The strike is here, but in the winter there is no harvest to picket. Colonia knows who the strikers are. If the company isn't forced to sign with the UFW and we have to go back to work without a victory, Colonia will get rid of us all, sooner or later. This march will put pressure on Colonia to sign a contract right away."

This speech had more impact on Lopez than the rest of the visit put together. Sr. Lopez stood up and paced to the other side of the room and back. Now at least he was undecided. He leaned over the table and spoke to Lupe.

"I will think about what you have said. And I will talk to my brothers about it."

"Can I mark your name as one who will come?" Carolyn was embarrassed to push him one more time, but as keeper of the list this was her job. Ramón translated.

"You can mark as you wish. I will speak with my brothers."

Lopez still stood. The visit must be over. Handshakes followed murmured thanks to his wife for the refreshments, and the three of them were out in front of the silent building again. As they jounced back down the driveway, Carolyn imagined doors opening behind them, the people reemerging, laughter and talk starting up.

"Will he come?" She looked at her watch by the light of the dashboard. Fifteen after eight.

"Who knows?" Ramón said.

"I think so," Lupe answered at the same time.

"What shall I put by his name?" she asked.

"A question mark," suggested Ramón.

"And the same for the two brothers right below him." Lupe pointed to the names. "We'll visit one of them next time; they're not too far from here. Maybe then we'll get the answer."

This made Carolyn feel better, as though they had fit in three visits instead of one, though even at that rate it would take way too long. None of this seemed to concern the other two.

"I think we have time for one more near here." Ramón switched on the overhead light so Lupe could flip through the list.

"How about Hernandez? He's close by, and he's with Chavez for sure."

Carolyn felt an absurd eagerness at the hope of a quick visit followed by a "Yes" next to a name. But when Lupe directed Ramón to a shack under the last spreading tree of a walnut orchard, no lights showed. An old pickup was outside, which might belong to Hernandez, she said, but it also might be the one he junked last year. They sat with the motor on for a couple minutes, in the hope that the porch light would come on. Nothing happened. So either no one was home or everyone was asleep. Or no one wanted to talk, but that seemed unlikely if Hernandez was so strong for the Union.

Twenty to nine. They had to stop. At Lupe's house, Ramón went with her to the door and stood talking for a while.

When he pulled the pickup into the office lot, he jumped out and crunched over the gravel to Carolyn's side, opened the door, and helped her down off the high seat. Without a single word. It made her feel clumsy and dumb. She said good night. If he replied, she didn't hear him.

The tiny smile of a moon had risen in the sky, and with no street lights on this side of the railroad tracks it was totally dark. She noticed that he watched her as if she were a kid he had to protect, until her Volvo started, and she began her way to Joseph Street.

CHAPTER NINETEEN

James and the march. Mary Lou's mind wrestled with both, back and forth, when she woke up on Sunday morning. It had been that way for a while now. Worlds so far apart she couldn't begin to connect them. Whenever the march gave her a spare moment, it was all James, asleep next to her this minute. Broad lips, cushions for her own when they kissed. Flared nostrils, curved like perfect sea shells; symmetrical curls, twined in a springy mat like moss. His brow furrowed as if he was working at something serious, a worried crease that seemed like it'd lengthened right up his forehead, and deepened, too, in the short time she'd known him. She wanted to take her finger and smooth it for him. Then he'd be perfect. Coffee and cream. Sweetness and light.

One-night stand, my eye. She was falling for him, if it hadn't already happened. You've got to be crazy, Mary Louise, she told herself every time she tried to think it through. The very same sentence that ran through her head the instant he'd touched her foot with his while he sat on her own living room sofa bed. You've got to be crazy, Mary Louise, don't let this happen. But she'd let him get up, come over to her chair, and drag him in there with him anyway.

And now she lay here next to him in the real bed, waiting for him to wake up. She shivered with desire just thinking about that first night. And now she was waiting for him to pull her toward him again, put her on top of him like he did, where it was easy for her to come. Waiting for them to make love, which she couldn't get enough of. She was in deeper and deeper, and no matter what she knew she should do, she was doing nothing to climb back out again.

The kitchen door banged shut, and Carolyn's car started up. She'd be going to visit strikers. Fine, that meant they didn't have to worry as much. Though over the last two weeks they'd proved they could do it with no noise at all, late at night after Carolyn slept, early in the morning before she woke up, over and over, happy each and every time. Physical thing, that's what Carolyn would probably call it. Well, if this was what she and all the women's libbers wanted their freedom for, Mary Lou could understand why. Physical thing. The most basic of all.

He stirred, then stared at her, first with some kind of haunted look on his face, but after that he started in on his slow smile. She shut her eyes, embarrassed still when he looked at her like this.

"Hey now, Mary Louise," he slurred. "Why y'all pretendin' to be asleep?"

Sometimes he slipped back into the long-gone South when he spoke to her. She liked that.

"I've been awake," she told him. "You're the one who's snored halfway to noon already."

"Well I'm up now, girl, and I'm gonna stay wide awake and just look at you."

"You can do what you like."

"You mean that? Do what I like?" He reached for her and started to run his hands all over her body in that way he had that made her hope this just might go on forever.

"Feel you everywhere at once?" He teased as he touched her. "Disappear inside you, leave no trace? Drag it on out, all morning long? Too good."

This time they even came together and with as much noise as they wanted, as if the whole thing was a dance they learned better each time.

They were still lying there as if it might start all over again when the danged telephone rang. Annoyed, she stretched her arm toward the bedside table.

"What if you don't answer?" he asked.

"I can't do that," she said. "It might be important. It could always be Cesar."

Her back turned to him, she propped herself up on one elbow, brought the receiver to her ear, and said hello in a voice she knew sounded lazy.

"What the hell's goin' on up there? Why aren't you at the office?"

She sat up straight and held the sheet over her chest as if the man on the line could see right into the bedroom. Jack Marsh. Now here was one fellow Okie she could not abide.

"It's Sunday, Jack, in case you hadn't noticed. You've got no call to bother me here on my one day off." She reached for her robe, lying on the floor beside the bed.

"Sheeit," James muttered softly. "Motherfuckin' Union never does let go." And to hell with your ban on swearing, his face seemed to say when he saw her look of disapproval.

He lit two cigarettes, left hers in the ashtray, grabbed up his clothes, and headed for the bathroom. She got into her lavender chenille and yanked the belt tight around her waist. There. Private now, protected from Jack's intrusion.

"Cesar called me yesterday," Jack was saying. "There's still a lot to do on the march, you know."

"I understand that, Jack." She pulled at her cigarette, grateful to James for leaving it for her. He was always thoughtful on the small things. One of the reasons to love him.

"Cesar told me the march is the goddamned most important thing for the boycott right now," Jack continued.

"Is that why you called?" she asked. "I think I could've figured it out on my own, thanks."

The words these men used. Didn't she deserve more respect? She took another drag, deep and impatient, and glared out her bedroom window. Through the strip above the starched curtains she could see that it was a gray day. No rain, just a total, complete uniform gray.

"I called to tell you, Mary Lou," Jack said, "that I'm gonna get the march to Allen by Thursday night. Here's the plan. I start my people from Delano on the twelfth."

"Delano? I thought it started out of Fresno." Her brain shifted into work mode. The work. That was what always saved her when things were confused.

"Cesar changed his mind," Jack said. "We won't get too far the first couple of days, and me and Aurelio are gonna cover that stretch. So we come out of Fresno on the sixteenth—"

"Wait a minute," Mary Lou interrupted. "Aurelio was gonna do the part from Fresno through Emerald."

"Well that was before the plan changed. Then we walk twelve miles on Tuesday, maybe fifteen on Wednesday, and hit Emerald Wednesday night. Fresno will handle food and housing Tuesday and Wednesday. You handle Emerald."

"But that's a whole other city."

"So? You don't have contacts there?"

"Of course I have contacts, Jack. But Aurelio—"

"Then we come through Allen on Thursday, and we make it to Carleton. We get to Empire Friday night, and headquarters in La Paz will pick up the big shebang on Saturday. You have to cover your stretch of the road."

He paused. Two separate offices to work on the bottom part of the march, and the resources of the whole Union at the very end. But she'd be the only one responsible for the middle, and her section had just gotten considerably longer. Just tickled him to death to think she'd have to scramble to make sure it came out all right, didn't it now? The creep.

She heard one labored breath, then another, the sounds of a heavy smoker as he waited for her reply. She stubbed out her half-smoked butt. The water that had been running in the bathroom sink stopped suddenly. James must be lathering up to shave.

"How many people, do you think?" she asked.

"Maybe two hundred from here. Then Teófilo and Aurelio say they'll have 250 more out of Fresno and Visalia. How many you figure to add?"

Best ignore that question, since she had no idea what the answer was yet.

"Did Cesar say he's gonna send help? All I've got here is Ramón."

"Heard it through the grapevine that Carolyn's there. What about her?"

She hadn't told Cesar that Carolyn was here, yet Jack knew. Well, that was no surprise. Cesar was legendary for knowing everything that went on in the offices up and down the Valley.

Now the faucet was on again. Rinsing his razor? Brushing his teeth? She wanted to take a shower with James; they hadn't had a chance to do that yet, what with Carolyn being around the house and Mary Lou always running off to the office. But today was Sunday, dang it. She wanted to be in there, under that fine, warm spray. With James.

"Carolyn's helping find the strikers," she said to Jack. She hoped she sounded normal. "But just that is gonna take up most of her time. She's out on it with Ramón this minute, if you must know. I still need more people."

"And that friend of hers?"

The water stopped again, as if James could hear this question by osmosis. But no. The shower started right away. Without her. It was not going to happen today.

James needed to know that Jack was asking about him, though. It was serious. Carolyn had been in the office, so it made sense that she'd part of the gossip circuit. But who in the world had told Jack that James was here? And did Cesar know?

James could get caught this way, right here, right now. As quick as she had found him, she was gonna lose him. Panic just about closed her throat.

And Cesar would never forgive her. He wouldn't be mad just because James being there put the Union in jeopardy, which was surely true. But also because he would think what James had done was wrong. Just like she had thought. Until she understood the kind of person James was. She found tears in her eyes. Lose James, and lose the Union too. Everything that was important to her.

James absolutely had to be gone by the time the march came through town. She tried to imagine him in jail. Wherever they sent him, she could go there to visit, right? And if James made it to Cuba? It was illegal even to travel to Cuba. She'd probably never see him again. She felt like she couldn't breathe.

"What's his name?" prodded Jack, impatient.

"Who, James?" Her voice sounded squeaky. "He's sick. He can't work."

Jack said nothing to this, waiting.

"He's got hepatitis, and the doctor told him to rest. As soon as he's well there's a job in the city waiting for him. He plans to go right on back."

Jack Marsh would surely know this sounded weird. She wasn't used to lies. Not to mention the three of them hadn't even agreed to the part about the job. It was said now, though, and it couldn't be taken back.

Now the shower was off, and the bathroom was dead quiet. To her total relief, Jack passed on to the next subject.

"You heard from Rojelio yet?" he asked.

"Naw," she answered. "He hasn't called."

"Well, he ought to roll in there about any time now. Left here early this morning."

"Rojelio's coming?" Mary Lou got that much out, then lost her voice, coughing.

"Too much smoking," she croaked. "Cesar said it was okay? Cesar's sending Rojelio?"

Rojelio. The whole reason she loved this Union as much as she did. She'd been a maverick before Rojelio, sure, as her mother would be the first to tell her, but he was the one who had showed her a whole different world. And he was going to walk into this house, any second now.

The receiver slipped from her shoulder as she reached for her cigarettes, and she barely caught the phone.

"Yeah, he's on his way," Jack was saying. "How come you don't know what's up on your own turf?"

Interesting question, she thought, reaching wildly for that detached part of the brain that would focus on the work.

Why had Cesar told Jack Marsh that he was sending Rojelio to Allen, but not even called her and she was in charge of the area? She lit up, her fingers trembling.

She heard James rustling in the kitchen, her ears standing out from her head like an animal's. He'd be dressed, right? 'Cause he'd taken his clothes into the bathroom. Probably making coffee, like he always did. But she was going to have to act like they weren't close, starting right now. That door from Joseph Street into the kitchen could open at any time. Rojelio might even feel like he still belonged in this house.

"Good," she told Jack as she expelled the smoke. Her mouth was so dry she had to run her tongue over her teeth to keep on talking. "I'm glad he's finally sending Rojelio."

"Great, in fact," she rattled on. "I'll put him on fund-raising. Or have him start in on housing and food."

Of course, saying this meant she'd managed to let Jack know exactly how far she hadn't gotten on the work that needed to be done. Oh well. That was the least of her problems.

"But what about the march that's supposed to come down from the Bay Area?" she asked, determined to sound normal. "Who's gonna coordinate that?"

"Cesar said he'd send Hank to work with the press when it was time. And he threw out that pretty soon Carmen gets spring break from that law school of hers."

Rojelio, Ramón, Hank, Carmen. Decent crew, especially if Carolyn stayed on and finished with the strikers. Together they could get the work done. Time was short and the task had just grown, but together they could build the march.

James. She would have to push him away. A drag on the cigarette turned into a silent sob. How in the world was she going to do that?

"This thing has got to be big, Mary Lou." Jack continued his lecture. "Cesar's counting on it."

"I understand that, Jack. But listen." She'd meant to tell someone higher up about this for a while; it'd nagged at her.

"You know that night with Silveira out at the camp?" Mary Lou asked Jack.

"Yeah, what about it?"

"Well, Jensen was out there, and just as I left, he made this big point. He told us if we did the march, something serious was gonna happen. To the workers."

"Look, Mary Lou, don't you let that Colonia asshole scare you." Mary Lou winced, but she had to admit that this time the swear word did fit.

"Think about it," Jack continued. "What do the workers have to lose? They're already on strike."

"They're worried about their other jobs."

"Yeah, well, you can't let that change things. If they lose the strike, Colonia's gonna grind their asses in the ground for the rest of their lives. We gotta up the ante, get the goddamned boycott to hit Colonia in the pocketbook, that's the only thing they'll listen to. And it's the publicity from this march that's gonna do it."

He was right, of course. Why did she even give the man a chance to tell her what she already knew?

"So what about today? Are you gonna lay around on your butt or get work done on this thing?"

"I'm gonna do my laundry, that's what, Jack Marsh." Suddenly Mary Lou was furious. "Then I'm gonna mop the kitchen floor. You want me to report in after that for further instructions?"

"Nope. It's up to you. But you better have it all together by the sixteenth."

It was only after she hung up that she realized the fool had answered like her question was serious. What a jerk. He'd get a crowd out for this march, though. He knew how to organize.

—⁂—

James came in from the hall, drying his head with one of Mary Lou's soft purple towels, wearing another around his waist, and he was singing: "'Though it's cold outside, I've got the month of May . . .'"

"Oh my God, what are you doing?" Mary Lou asked.

The girl looked panicked, but then again she often did. Like she'd told him more than once, she wasn't used to this much contact. All gray and still out there; no one walking by, no cars, nothing going on. A quiet Sunday. For once they had some time.

"You don't even have your clothes on," she said to him like something was his fault. Well, she couldn't be feeling that; they had just been so close in bed. When she tried to get around him to the closet, he grabbed her at the waist and moved her into a slow dance.

"I guess you'll say, 'what could make me feel that way? My girl, my girl, my girl, talkin' 'bout my girl . . .'"

He laughed at his own falsetto that didn't quite make it up to where it should be.

"Smokey Robinson. Man knew how to lay it on the line." He leaned his whole body into her and loosened her robe.

"James, be serious," she said. "I gotta get things done."

"What's the hurry?" he asked her. "I thought we were gonna slow ourselves down for today."

"Well, we were," she answered. "I mean, I am. I did it already. It's late. I gotta take my shower, and then I'll fix us some breakfast. After that I should head over to the office."

"The office? Hey, I thought Sunday was this Union's big day off. I thought I'd have some company for a change, not just the TV."

"We do have Sundays off, but not when there's a huge march I'm responsible for."

"Didn't I hear you say last night that you wanted to lay up in the bed all day long today?"

He hated to beg. She could probably hear it in his voice. Beg a woman for her company? He was the one who always needed his space. But he had been counting on her.

"That was yesterday," she said briskly. "Today I realize there's a whole lot still to do."

"That's what the man on the phone convinced you of, huh?"

How could this woman be so different from one minute to the next? He could not stand how this was going, but yet and still he couldn't stop. He moved close again, to try and put his arms around her one more time.

"James, I told you. I've got to get dressed." She stepped back, re-tying that belt of hers as tight as she could, determined in that way that only Mary Lou could be.

"Who's this cat can just call you up on the phone and you jump?" A crazy anger that he couldn't even recognize sounded in his own voice. He could see the shock on Mary Lou's face.

"That was Jack Marsh, head of Delano. He orders me around, and he's rude, but I certainly do not jump when he calls."

"You jump for Cesar Chavez and this candy-ass Union all the time, Mary Louise. You let it take you over!"

"Well, let me tell you," she answered. Her face was red and blotchy. "I'd a whole lot rather do this for Cesar and nonviolence than for Nyame Jones. Talk big, call yourselves revolutionaries, run around with guns, get people killed! Little boys do play their games, don't they?"

She had the nerve to talk this way about Nyame? Damn this woman, she had no right. He scrambled into his trousers as he answered her.

"At least Nyame Jones is a man and not some nonviolent Uncle Tomas," James said, his voice rising. "Shufflin' up to whitey to prove how good he is."

Was a man. Until James helped get him killed. He wanted to stop it right here and think all this through for the thousandth time, but she kept on, and she was just about yelling now.

"When've you ever seen Cesar shuffle?" Mary Lou asked. Her eyes were so green in this gray daylight that they took on a life of their own. What happened to that sweet brown-eyed look, in their morning bed?

"How're people ever gonna get anywhere if they don't pick up the gun?" he asked her.

"At least they'll be alive to see the change when it comes—"

"How about Allende, in Chile? Motherfucker gets himself elected democratically just like American money says he's supposed to, and guess what? The CIA comes up with Pinochet, who takes the whole damned country over militarily, and no one around here among the powers that be says boo. Now that happened because the revolution couldn't defend itself!"

"Well, this is not Chile," she told him, her face flushed with anger. "It's America, and if Cesar'd gotten people all armed like you say, it'd be over by now. And the farmworkers would've lost everything. Instead Cesar's admired. Even Bobby Kennedy came out here to see him—"

"Kennedy!" James snorted with derision. "Ruling class motherfucker. Don't you know his whole family hated unions anyhow? Where'd that get your Cesar Chavez?"

"And where has picking up the gun gotten you?"

The woman looked like she wanted to hit him and he just about ducked, but before he knew it she was past him with her armful of her own clothes, headed down the hall to the bathroom.

"How about South Africa?" He yelled at her back. "They may not have shit down there, but at least with a gun in their hand they die with dignity! Take a few torturers down with them, while they're at it!"

"Cesar's got more dignity in his little finger than your Nyame Jones had in his whole entire body." She turned around to say the next thing, right up under his face again.

"Maybe Nyame was the one who ordered Kwesi to set you up, did you ever think of that?" She swept into the bathroom and slammed the door. The shower went on right away.

Goddamn this woman. Nyame Jones suffered for his people, every day of every long year in that solitary cell in the white man's damned penitentiary. He may have died in a stupid plan, but he didn't use people for himself. He wasn't the type. Everything was for the higher goal. She had no right to talk about Nyame like that. There was such a thing as too far, and she'd gone there.

James stood at the bedroom window and banged his fist into the frame until his knuckles were sore. The worst thing was, and he knew this too, he needed her company more than he'd ever needed any other motherfuckin' single thing in his whole life.

He strained to hear anything besides the sound of the water, any movement of her body. That long, skinny body of hers. The woman had him, in every way that mattered. And he had nothing to bring to her except the whole sorry mess of his life. So typical. Exactly the place he'd sworn his black ass would never be in.

Claim not one single victory, not now, not ever, was how this situation felt. And the worst thing was, no matter how many times he thought it all through, he couldn't find any choices other than the ones he was already making.

By the time she emerged into the kitchen, dressed and fresh, he had done his best to collect himself.

"How would you like your eggs this morning, Ms. Mary Louise?" He tried to make it light like he always did in the kitchen, insisting that he could be useful in some small way, but it sounded flat.

"Scrambled, please," she answered. Subdued, she seemed worried. The next thing he knew, she actually came up behind where he stood at the stove and leaned up against him, her arms around his waist, her cheek flat against his bare back. She never did that sort of thing. She always left it up to him. Her touch made him rigid; he dared not move.

"I'm sorry, James," she said, peeking around his tall frame to look up at him.

"For what?" His face felt folded so tight it might could never unbend again.

"For what I said about Nyame. And for the change in plans."

To his horror, a lake of tears rose in his eyes. He wanted to run and hide, throw himself in a hole and cover it up, but she was right there, turning him around so she could kiss him. Helpless in his shame, he buried his face in the rough wool of her sweater, and she held him like she would a child, stroking the back of his head.

"Hey, James Sweet," she whispered. "Everything's gonna be all right."

This had to stop. He wiped his cheeks with the back of a palm and straightened out.

"Well, I guess I'm sorry, too," he managed to get out.

"For what?" Her face turned up toward his, smiling as she repeated his words, her eyes a green-flecked brown again, and sensible. She wanted something, anything, as long as it came from him.

"For needing you like this." What a line. He felt like a fool. But she seemed to like it.

She kissed him, and even as he swore to himself that he would never let his sadness or fear show that way again, the argument was over.

After their breakfast was over and the kitchen was clean, they sat down to drink their coffee and smoke, fingers of their free hands twined together on the table.

"Jack Marsh knew you were here." She rushed her words, like there was still more to tell him.

"Jack? The sucker on the phone? What'd he say?"

"He wondered why Carolyn's friend wasn't working on the march."

"That's how he put it? 'Carolyn's friend?' Did he ask what I was doing here?"

She answered his questions one by one, still playing with his fingers, looking down, not meeting his eye. Now was the time he could get her to go back to bed with him. Not that he could break her determination to work, but it wouldn't take all that long, and it'd comfort them both for the afternoon apart. Just the thought of it got his body ready, in an instant.

Someone knocked at the kitchen door. Startled at the unexpected noise, they separated at once. They stood, James caught between fleeing and not wanting to look scared. He lifted a brow as if to ask who. Her face got all red again, and the door opened before either of them could move any further.

"¿*Cómo estás*, Mary Lou? I wanted to see you right away, you know, and since it's Sunday . . ."

His words tumbling out before him, one hand pushing back tousled black hair, the other holding onto a single rose wrapped in cellophane, a short, stocky good-looking Mexican guy rolled on into their kitchen like he owned the place.

James's eyes swept around in panic. The door that led down the hall to Mary Lou's bedroom was closed, thank the Lord, and the remains of breakfast for two could be explained by Carolyn's early departure. But he was terribly conscious of his naked chest.

"Hey, how you doin' man?" Rojelio laid the rose on the table and advanced toward him, hand outstretched. "I'm Rojelio. You must be the one who came down with Carolyn from Berkeley. You're sick or something, right?"

Did everyone in this damned Union know about him, or what? And Mary Lou's motherfuckin' boyfriend, of all people! Hard to believe how the Sunday he'd looked forward to could turn so very bad.

"Nice to meet you. James." He shook hands with what he hoped was a firm grip. "Just got out of the shower, man, excuse me. Got to get a shirt on."

He took up the towel he'd left draped on a kitchen chair and exited to the living room where he waited to calm down. He'd have to go back down the hall and through the bathroom to the bedroom, where his clothes were. He paused, though, to listen through the door he'd left a little ajar.

"James is a friend of Carolyn's," Mary Lou was saying automatically. Rojelio had just said that. She sounded foolish. There was a shuffling sound, like Rojelio was shifting his feet.

"So how are you?" he asked Mary Lou.

"He's been sick," she went on. "Hepatitis. He rests here while Carolyn helps with the march." It was as if she hadn't heard the man's question at all. Rojelio was going to know there was something off.

Mary Lou traipsed over to the sink; he could hear water running. Probably putting the motherfucking rose into a vase, tidying everything up like she always did. Thank goodness she'd had her shower; otherwise Rojelio would smell James all over her.

"I'm all right," she answered finally. "Except for this march. Carolyn and Ramón are out to round up strikers, but it's slow as molasses. So much to do you wouldn't believe it. Every time I start in one direction, I've got to turn around in the middle and get some whole other thing done. It's driving me crazy."

She was talking fast, going over the kind of detail they'd probably always shared before.

"Jack just gave me a whole huge section to do by myself, but he says Cesar told him Hank's coming," she continued. "And Carmen too. I need a lotta help to put this thing together. I'm glad you came, Rojelio, I really am."

They were both quiet. What was happening now? Was she kissing him? James wanted to throw up.

Now she was on the move again, walking around the table, then back at the sink, scrubbing at the cast-iron pan the eggs were cooked in.

"You want breakfast, Rojelio? I could make more coffee." She must have cooked for him a thousand times. Why wouldn't she insist that they head straight to the office? Because she wanted to cook for him again, that was why.

"Sure," Rojelio answered, and James heard the chair scrape as he moved it—James's chair, the one he'd just vacated, and sat down in it. "I'd like that, *m'hija*. I really would."

"Hey, James," Mary Lou called, making a show of being polite. He moved back from the door as if it were hot. "I'm gonna make a fresh pot. And breakfast too. Want some?"

She'd already made breakfast once, of course. What a liar she was. She probably lied to him, too, all the time.

"No thanks," he called back. "Time for me to get my rest."

He tiptoed back to the bedroom, got his shirt, tidied up. In the meantime, he supposed, Rojelio ate, and maybe she did too, to keep up the show. Then they sat and talked, their voices a murmur from where he sat in the living room, afraid to listen at the door anymore. Catching up on each other, no doubt. He shivered.

After forever, Mary Lou and Rojelio left together for the office.

James's day began its stretch into the long afternoon. He got out a beer from the refrigerator, lit a cigarette, switched on the TV. When Carolyn came home at five she found him on her living room couch, head slouched down at an uncomfortable angle, asleep to the drone of a used car commercial.

She shook James's shoulder and gently prodded him awake, then tiptoed across the small room to turn off the fat man with his endless patter.

"I know it's almost night now, but it's still too early to give up on the day like this," she chided.

"Why?" he asked. "What's wrong with sleeping? It's a way to fill time."

She had no answer to that, so instead she started in on tales of strikers who wouldn't commit or couldn't be found while he rubbed his face and eyes as if he wished he could erase them. When he was awake enough to go with her into the kitchen, she rummaged through the fridge for leftover rice and beans, plus salad fixings, for the evening meal. He was sick of the march along with everything else, including this tired old Mexican food, but he tried to listen to her monologue and even show interest. Yet before he knew it, as soon as they were through with the meal she had to go out again, to continue the endless search for everyone on Mary Lou's list.

"I'll just leave these dishes, James," she told him while she gathered up her stuff. "Plus I brought a stack of miscellaneous papers home. If you wanted to alphabetize them, they would be easier to file. I thought you might not mind a little job to fill up time. No need to hurry on it."

Without waiting for a reaction, she slammed the kitchen door and was gone.

"Get your rear end out of this hard-assed kitchen chair and *move*, boy," he told himself in his auntie's tone, trying not to get caught in how much he missed them. His mother and his aunt. The two women in his life who had held him together. And now Mary Lou. He got a beer out of the refrigerator.

He managed to wash the dishes and get the papers in order for the Union. The tasks complete, he popped open his beer, put another match to another cigarette, and went back to his couch to turn on the news.

He and Nyame had disappeared from it, as if they were both dead and gone. And indeed they were. Nyame dead, and him gone, out here to this godforsaken town no one had ever even heard of. He crushed the empty aluminum can with his shoe and sent it flying across the room where it pinged off the record player and skittered to a stop in front of the TV. And the trash on that thing, he was sick of it. He snapped off the set and sat in the silence of the unlit room, which by now was totally dark.

He thought of just about the only thing he could want and have. Not much weed left, and absolutely no idea where any more would come from, but why save up? Trick was to get through this day, this night. A little toke wouldn't hurt. He got the purple velvet pouch from his suitcase's inner pocket, rolled a thin joint, and headed back to the living room.

The small glow at the reefer's tip was warmth and comfort itself. He inhaled deeply, held his breath, and exhaled in a whoosh, eager to be saved from despair. Three more times of this and then he just sat where he was and grinned for a while. When he looked down, the small roach was still there, pinched between thumb and forefinger.

With care he preserved it back in its soft bag, put the bag in his pocket, leaned back on the couch, and folded his hands over his stomach. Next he found himself fingering a roll of fat he was certain had not been there before Freeman.

Hadn't Nyame Jones pounded his hands into cinder block walls and concrete floors every single day in solitary to keep in shape and fill his time? James claimed to admire the man, but he hadn't paid attention, not really. Exercise. He began the series he used to do with his wife, lifetimes ago. Toe-touches, right, left, right, left. Knee-pulls for the hamstrings, then beyond where Rosetta would go, to sit-ups, push-ups. His body stretched and sweated. This was right; he should've thought of it long before now.

Panting, he moved into kicks and punches from the six-week karate class he'd taken years ago, taught by that crazy little cat in Oakland. Tiny guy, hard as a brick all over. Wrote poetry, mimeographed it off and hawked the copies himself, on the Avenue. James bought a volume once. Long shit, hard to make sense out of it. Anyone else would've been laughed out of town, but this dude was respected. 'Cause he had his physical act together, that was why. Thrust, push, kick, pound at the imaginary enemy. His grunts and the rustle of his clothes ate into the silence of the black and empty room.

When he sat again he was tired, but better, much better. Next he'd put music on, take up with Mary Lou's books where he'd left off. Already he knew more than he wanted about growers and the slaves they called farmworkers out here, but study sure as shit beat the TV. He sighed and laid himself back down again, knees over the edge of the couch, legs dangling, chin on his chest, to listen to the slowing of his heart.

So now this Rojelio shows up, and with a rose no less. The ex, if he was an ex, would see inside Mary Lou right off, wonder who the hell was this black man took up his place in bed. Maybe he had already remembered why this very same Afro-American looked familiar, where he had seen his picture before.

That is, if Rojelio even thought James was important. Maybe Mary Lou had just been messing with him while she waited on the

Mexican to arrive. To think of that pale, slender body of hers in bed next to the broad, muscled Rojelio was unbearable. He jumped up to pick through her records, see could he find one he hadn't heard a thousand times already. Damn, didn't this woman know there was jazz in the world? What he needed right now was the Bird, or Coltrane, but all he could do was put the needle onto Otis Redding. This time, though, the music set him on edge, and right away he scratched the disc in his haste to get it off.

He could barely even see the furniture, though he believed he knew exactly where everything was. No moon tonight. Dark out there. He glided toward the window to crack the side of the shade and look out at the trees, but on the way he hit his shin so hard on an end table that he almost cried out. He rubbed at it, staring at shifting leaves whose slight movements were the only reason they stood out in the dark, contending with a rush of emotion that softened his throat and threatened to flood his eyes.

A rustling sound came from the outside. Soft, couldn't hardly even hear it, just enough to start the adrenaline that had run through his body so often since Freeman he could predict its route, even as he couldn't seem to ever stop it. Just the wind, right? Or an animal maybe. How many times could a body go into this routine without damage?

He stood still to listen. A squeak, a rustle. A footstep on the front doorstep? He told himself it was just the drug, but fear pinched at him like a tight shoe he couldn't take off. Behind all this the gray-green blob and its sinister wires hovered in his mind, passing from his own hand to Nyame's, the reality that backed up every other thought.

The small sounds continued, here, there, at random until the sequence of noises suddenly made sense. The police were out there in the dark, quiet in their plan to block both doors and surround the house. Part of his brain watched and laughed at the rest, but he had to find out. He forced himself through the hall to the bedroom window and looked into the neighbors' backyards. The black shape of a shed loomed out from the fence—was there a human form hunkered down by its side?

Too quiet. They were waiting for him to make his move, so they could shoot him. Shoot to kill. But he'd take a pig or two with him, at least that much. Two long steps brought him to Mary Lou's closet where he bent low, parting the way through her skirts and dresses that hung there. Feeling foolish, he grabbed the .22 from its corner and ran through the hall to peek out again from behind the living room shade. No one at the front of the house; this time he was certain. He slid into the kitchen next and lifted the green frilly curtain. Only a cat, who strolled in majestic grace across the empty road. Absolute quiet in all directions. Just the drug. The drug, night rustles, animals, a breeze.

Maybe the weed was laced with something. He thought back to when he'd last smoked. Right before he'd slept with Mary Lou, and it'd loosened him up, helped pave the way. Same shit, too; it must be him who'd changed. Yet and still it was all he could do to make himself turn on the kitchen light. Sweat rolled down the back of his neck.

Ridiculous. Time to cut the damned drug. He pulled a beer out of the fridge, downed it, and made himself return the gun to its closet. Then he got out a full six pack, switched on the TV, and sat to drink in front of its flickering light. Slowly the image of police storming Joseph Street, the nightmare of Rojelio making love to Mary Lou, all of it was replaced by a blurry head and a quavering stomach. Halfway through the seventh beer he blacked out.

CHAPTER TWENTY

The two women left the office at the same time but drove in separate cars, pulling up by the kitchen door one behind the other. Except for the TV's glimmer, the living room was dark. They turned on the overhead light and stared down at a slack-jawed James, whose soft snores exhaled the odor of stale beer.

Mary Lou looked like she was holding her breath. About time for the reality of her lover's daily life to sink in, thought Carolyn; past time. True, he hadn't looked quite this bad before tonight, but then again he hadn't exactly been in good shape either, except when he was around the same Mary Lou who now stared at him as though the blinders were finally off her eyes.

They cajoled him to his feet and stood at each side in case he needed support as he wobbled down the hall.

"Got to thank you ladies," he slurred. "I need you, did y'all know that? Both you wonderful women, grateful too, beyond what you know."

For a terrible moment Carolyn expected him to cry, big fat maudlin tears like Mona's when she had too many, but he headed straight for the bed.

"James, you be sure and brush your teeth," snapped Mary Lou to keep him from landing there in all his clothes. "Use that Listerine in there, too."

Carolyn left the room, but she could still hear Mary Lou's critical voice guiding him through a bedtime ritual that would make him fit to sleep next to.

At ten the next morning Carolyn was dawdling at home, Mary Lou had already gone to the office, and James was still sleeping it off. Carolyn didn't mind. A rare moment of peace before the daily search for strikers. If she concentrated hard enough she could even have Mona here with her, rustling in the warm breeze that stirred the kitchen curtains, ushering Carolyn back through time.

A soft tap at the front door jolted her out of the reverie. She told herself only a salesman or a Jehovah's Witness would be there in the bright light of a sunny weekday morning when just the housewives were home. She decided to sit it out, but a second rap, more insistent, convinced her she had to answer. The police. It could always be the police. They would come whenever they wanted to.

She held her breath, afraid to peek around the shade, and opened up to find a couple her own age, pale urban types, and definitely not in uniform. The woman drew her attention first. Dark hair pulled straight back, strong features accentuated by long purple and black beaded earrings, broad shoulders, and a large body. She stood a little in front of the man, who was shorter, his red hair at unruly angles despite the close cut, his jutting eyebrows a source of nervous energy even as he stood still.

"Carolyn?" The woman took the lead and stepped forward with her hand out. Both wore jeans and T-shirts, her outfit topped with a bright red wind breaker, his with a jean jacket so worn it must be his favorite. "We're here to see James. May we come in?"

A quick handshake completed, they both moved past her before she quite said they could, and behind them she glimpsed men on the street clustered around a beat-up car. Bewildered, she shut the door. These two did not look like they were from the Valley, and if they were cops they were incredibly well disguised. Still, the people outside could be backup, and she had just let in the first wave of an undercover squad.

"Who are you?" she asked.

"I'm Donna," the woman said. "And this is Bob. Friends of Quincy's."

"Yes!" Carolyn exclaimed. She pumped the hand Bob held out. "We've been waiting for you!"

"Sorry we just pushed on in," he said as he matched her enthusiasm with a quick hug and a clap on the back. "Better to get off the street so no one has time to notice much."

"Oh God, that's okay. I can't believe it! You're here!"

Bob moved to the phonograph and put on the record closest to hand. Bolivian music, with a flute thin enough that he had to turn the volume as high as it would go. Carolyn was so grateful for his immediate attention to security that she wanted to embrace him all over again, but Donna's no-nonsense attitude indicated that business was at hand.

"Where is he?" she asked.

"Still asleep." Carolyn moved toward the hall. "Hold on a sec. I'll wake him up."

"Depressed?" This woman didn't fool around.

"A little," Carolyn admitted.

"I'm not surprised. Well, we've brought him things that will cheer him up."

Donna flashed a smile that was gone as fast as it came, and Bob turned from his examination of the titles on Mary Lou's bookshelves to give Carolyn a cloak-and-dagger wink.

Laughing, she flew through the bathroom to get him. Good thing she had insisted on her morning off, good thing Mary Lou was up and gone, good thing Carolyn had folded up the living room couch, good thing these people had come at last. She banged on James's closed door.

She had to open up and go right in there before his furry voice finally crept out from the lavender mound.

"What's up?" He sounded disoriented. "Where I got to go right now?"

An odor of dried sweat and stale beer hung over the airless room.

"They're here!" She yanked a curtain aside.

"Who you talkin' about?" He sat up in alarm, trying to shake his stupor. Troubled and harsh, his face was that of a man twenty years older.

"Donna and Bob," she told him. "Friends of Quincy's."

"Donna and Bob *who?*"

"They didn't give last names. They must be from the underground. They wanted to get inside right away. And they've brought you something."

"Black folks or white?"

"White."

"Can't be right," he stated, crestfallen. "Quincy would send some bloods. How do you know they're for real?"

"God, James, it's not like I can ask for identification, you know. But who else would come in here using Quincy's name?"

"Quincy would've given them proof," he said.

"And they have stuff to show you," she answered. "Come on, get dressed. They're waiting."

He seemed unable to register all this, unwilling to move.

"What if they're pigs?" Still in the bed, he rubbed at his bloodshot eyes, ran a hand over stubble on his jaw just to show, she supposed, that he was determined to take his own sweet time.

"James, they had Quincy's name." If they were cops then Quincy was either caught or a cop himself, and the whole thing was blown anyhow.

"They're dressed in jeans," she continued. "They're by themselves." She pushed away her own prick of uncertainty about the guys by the car.

"I gotta go to the head," James said. He unfolded himself in a laborious fashion and stood beside the bed.

"Come on, James. Shower and shave. We'll wait for you. Things are going to change now, you'll see."

"Sick of honkies," he muttered to himself as he shambled toward the bathroom. "Need to get back to my own."

Carolyn returned to the living room. They all heard a retching sound and then the toilet flush.

"He's a little hung over." Carolyn decided she might as well tell the truth. She sat in the armchair. Donna settled on the couch, tucking her long longs up under her.

"Hey, no rush. Quite a collection of books here. I've always wanted to know more about this farmworker shit." Bob thumbed through *Chavez*, a thick hardback biography of Cesar with a yellow paper cover.

"He's in pretty bad shape, huh?" Donna's gaze bored right into Carolyn.

"It's gotten worse," Carolyn admitted. She sure hoped she could trust these two. "He's had to sit around by himself all day and night because Mary Lou got me to work on the march, and—"

"Who's Mary Lou?" Bob was the type who could read and talk at the same time.

"She's in charge of the Union here, and she's planning this huge march against Colonia winery—"

"The Farm Workers Union, huh? Far out."

"You're staying at the home of a UFW organizer? Isn't that dangerous?" They both spoke at once.

"Well, I don't know . . . I mean, I guess it is, a little. But there was nowhere else to go. And when we got here, it was pretty quiet." Carolyn couldn't begin to explain it all in this yellow morning sun, so different from the stormy night when they arrived at this place with nowhere else to go.

"It's turned out a lot longer than we expected." She went on anyhow. "Now that this march is building up, yeah, I think it's risky."

"I'll say," Donna observed drily.

"What's the plan for the march?" asked Bob, his eyes darting behind their wire frames. Coughs emanated from the bathroom; the shower came on.

"It starts from Delano," said Carolyn. "Picks up hundreds, maybe thousands as they go along, then thousands, hopefully millions, come down from the Bay Area." Bob smiled. Donna did not.

"And on the last day," Carolyn finished, "everyone collides in Empire, where Colonia has its main offices."

"Collide and collude, huh?" said Bob. "In the center of Colonia's kingdom itself. Cesar knows how to build. That's the kind of stuff he learned from Saul Alinsky. Hot damn, I'd like to see that last day!" His eyes danced like the leaves out the window behind him, waving in the bright, brisk breeze.

"He's got to be gone by then." Donna stayed focused. "Does this Mary Lou know who he is?"

"Sure she does," Carolyn answered. "I couldn't lie to such a close friend; she'd see right through it. But they're sleeping together now, so maybe it's all right."

The words slid into the middle of the floor like mercury from a broken thermometer and lay there, all in one silver ball. God, what was the matter with her? She must really be feeling the pressure to spill out all over the place like this. She buried her face in her hands, yet nothing could be taken back. Bob continued to read but inclined his head to be sure to catch what whatever Donna would say next.

"You mean they're in a relationship?" Donna changed the language to something they could talk about.

Miserable, Carolyn nodded.

"Does that make any sense?" Donna asked. "Under the circumstances, I mean?"

Carolyn did what was expected, and shook her head.

"It'll be harder for him to leave." Donna continued. "And it gives this Mary Lou, whoever she is, all sorts of power, doesn't it?"

Like a marionette, Carolyn nodded again. In the pause, the shower stopped.

"Not such a surprise, though." Bob snapped the book shut. "We've got each other, Don. Otherwise, it would be a hell of a lonely life, you've got to admit."

Of course. They were a couple. Carolyn felt a stab of envy. Bob worked at catching Donna's eye, almost made her smile, and then he changed the subject.

"So why will this march make Colonia sign with the UFW?" He turned back to Carolyn. "What's the leverage?"

"Bad publicity," she answered. "Strengthen the boycott."

"They're the biggest winery around, aren't they?" Bob asked. "Why can't they just wait it out?"

Donna shifted on her couch cushion, marking time, waiting for James.

"Colonia has to crack sometime," Carolyn said. The bathroom sink faucet was on again. How many times could he wash, for God's sake?

"Anyhow, it's a way of making something big happen," she continued. "So the people around here don't give up."

"How involved with each other are they?" asked Donna. "Is it just a casual thing?"

Carolyn began to resent this woman for being so personal. Irrational, she knew, since she was the one who brought the subject up. But she liked Bob much better. Talking politics felt safe.

"They both know it can't be anything else," she answered dutifully. "But it's gotten intense."

"Is she safe?" asked Donna. "This Mary Lou? Will she go to the pigs?"

"No. She won't turn him in."

"Not even if he hurts her feelings?"

"I don't think so."

"How about you? What's your relationship with James?"

"Just an old friend." But Carolyn's face flushed. How could James not be out here yet? The whole morning was going by.

"Is he going to be able to leave her?" Donna kept at it. This woman had her nerve. Still, she felt helpless in Donna's grip.

"He'll have to," Carolyn answered. "Everyone and their brother is about to arrive here. One guy's only job will be to get the press out, so reporters will be around here too. It seems like we've waited forever for you guys."

"These things take time," Donna said.

"And even now, the plan is not complete," Bob added. "We wouldn't want to give the wrong idea. But we've got a good start."

Carolyn frowned. She had begun to believe James would soon be on his way, maybe even by nightfall.

"God, I hope he's gonna get through all this," Donna sighed.

"I'll bet he's got a mother hen already, Don," Bob chuckled. "Maybe even two of them."

Donna smiled at last, then leaned back on the worn couch and closed her eyes. Carolyn answered more questions from Bob about the UFW while the sunlight danced on the window and they waited for James.

When at last he stepped into the living room he was washed, shaved, and dressed for the street. Donna and Carolyn got up at once, and Bob strode forward. He reached into his jacket pocket for a letter, which he pressed into James's palm as they shook hands. James read it over twice while the other three stood clustered around him. At the end he folded the paper with care and slipped the envelope into the inside pocket of his sports jacket.

"I guess you're cool. Quincy says so, and Q would know." Even to himself James must have sounded far away.

"You thought we'd be black," Donna murmured. He acknowledged it with a curt nod.

"But they're here, James," Carolyn said. "Now things will go forward." She moved toward him, wanting to lay her hand on his arm, just a touch, a gesture of comfort, but he waved her off.

"That's exactly what's hard," Donna said. "You've settled in. When things change, it's back to being on the run." Her calm, brown eyes searched his, and then she took the time to sit down again.

Carolyn rushed to the kitchen for a chair, but by the time she wrestled it back into the living room, the tableau was set. James had taken the armchair, Bob was still pacing by the bookshelf, and there was an empty place by Donna on the couch. Just as well. She didn't want to sit there anyhow. This way she could keep track of what was going on.

"We know about this process," Donna was saying. "You get someplace and you're scared. You have to make the best of it, though, so like a dog run to ground, you shake your butt and lie down."

James leaned forward, hands on his knees, listening to every word, nodding his head. She had him down cold.

"You start to feel ordinary again, human almost," Donna continued. "Then all at once you have to be up and gone."

"When's that gonna happen?" James muttered. They acted as if they hadn't heard the question.

"So, speaking of settling," said Bob, on the move now toward Donna. "Don't you do that in here too long, m'love. Let's get to a place where we can have the full discussion."

"It's never quite comfortable to talk in a house," he explained, lips curved in a habitual half-smile. "We always feel safer in a public place, where we know it can't be bugged." A hand at her elbow, he was already moving with Donna toward the door.

James and Carolyn had no choice but to follow. On the front stoop he panicked, turned back, then came out again wearing his shades, all while she fumbled in her purse for car keys. Already the other two were down by the nondescript white Dodge parked in front of the house.

"Why don't you take your own car?" Bob issued quiet directions in his friendly fashion. "Pick a place where we won't be too conspicuous. We'll be right behind you."

Carolyn and James went around the corner to get the Volvo from its usual place near the kitchen door.

"And where might that be?" asked Carolyn, giggling. "Where the four of us won't be conspicuous?" He snorted along with her. For one brief moment they were in exactly the same space of excitement laced with fear.

"Maybe we should have come out in separate pairs," he mumbled to her as they picked their way through the ruts to the car.

"They seem to know what they want," she said.

She started the motor and pulled back around the corner. The group of men around the broken-down car didn't look up at all, which reassured her at first, but in the next instant seemed suspicious. She tried to ignore them and drove straight ahead. Donna and Bob pulled out from the curb behind them.

"It can't be Jovita's," Carolyn said to James. "We might see someone I know. What do you think?"

James shrugged. Of course. He hadn't exactly been around. He didn't even know what the choices were. Both cars turned right, then right again, then left at last, on the way to the intersection at Highway 99. Throughout all this they were the only moving vehicles in sight.

"How about J's, on the highway before Emerald?" Carolyn asked James. He shrugged again.

"It's definitely where the straight folks go." Carolyn babbled on like she always did whenever she was nervous. "I don't know how we'll fit in, but at least none of the Union people go there."

Huge trucks were lumbering by on their long green light as usual, when a sudden honk made them start in fear. A thin, dark guy waved as he turned his pickup left off 99 and into the Union lot on the other side of the highway. Carolyn tried to smile as she waved back, hoping James would have the sense to sit still and not slide down and disappear like he started to.

"It's Ramón, damn it," she said, patting at his knee. He took the hint and froze in place. "But I know what; I'll just tell him I had to take you to a doctor in Fresno. I have to remember, though. I'll write myself a note. He's the type to wonder, for sure."

At last the light changed, and she had to decide for all of them. She turned left onto the highway, headed south toward Fresno.

"Are they still there?" he asked, not turning to look.

"Oh God, I forgot to even check." She adjusted the rearview mirror. "They're right behind us. I can't believe they've finally gotten here, can you?"

He didn't answer, and she managed to be quiet for the few minutes it took to get to the turnoff for J's.

They met in the middle of the parking lot, and everyone but James grinned with the small success of having arrived. With a sudden gesture of female intimacy, Donna put an arm around Carolyn's shoulder as they started toward the entrance.

"You should see the way Bob travels by car," she said in a light tone. "He gets me to do the driving so he can read. He's got a whole shelf of books across the backseat. Great company, I'm telling you."

"How's the weather in these parts?" Bob asked, as the men strolled behind.

"Cold," James said. "More than you'd expect."

Bob reached around Donna to push open one side of the double glass door, and the four of them entered the restaurant looking as though they had known each other for years.

—∿—

They slid onto the orange plastic of the window booth farthest in back. The only other customers were two men at the counter.

The waitress, dressed in starched yellow and orange that rustled as she walked, bustled around them with large, shiny menus and glasses of water. She asked if they wanted coffee and finally retreated when they said yes.

"Sorry to drag you out of the house so quick, you might not have been ready for that." Donna began at once, directing her words right at James. "After you go for a long time without being caught, you're just positive it's because you always follow your own rules. I hope you don't mind."

"Naw, it's cool." He kept his voice flat. He was not going to show anything to these people until he knew they were for real.

"I'm glad you were home on the first try," she said.

"Yeah, it's not too hard to catch me at the house." He managed a tight wry smile.

The waitress returned with coffee. Bob beamed a polite thank you, which she liked. James dumped in his sugar and cream, stirred, sipped, and exhaled in a small sigh of pleasure.

"We brought you gifts," Donna continued.

She reached into her large purse and slid a small, flat package wrapped in white tissue and tied with midnight-blue yarn across the table to James.

He would never have guessed this for an opening move. His heart swollen with a foolish gratitude, he reached for the present. The other three watched as he uncovered *Jump Bad*, a slender anthology of poetry edited by Gwendolyn Brooks, the wonderful Afro-American poet that was old enough to be everybody's grandma.

Jump Bad. The two words were such an apt description of what his life had come to be that he had to smile. In the middle of the book was a folded strip of African cloth, hand woven in an intricate pattern of orange, yellow, and red.

"These were sent by your brothers and sisters in the Black Liberation Army," Donna was saying. "They made a special trip to find us, to make sure the package would get to you."

"It's Kente cloth, from Ghana," murmured James, as if to himself. "Comes from the Ashanti tribe, where Nyame got his name."

He opened the book at random to something called "Incidental Pieces to a Walk: For Conrad." Strange title. Everyone was quiet while he read it to himself:

they
say
you
went
abroad
some
say
you'll
stay
a sister
swears
she
saw
a
shadow
another
swears
a
whisper

a
brother
swears
he
heard
a
step
I
swear
nothing
at all

Someone named James Cunningham wrote it, and he'd never even heard of the brother who'd managed to name James Sweet's invisibility as if he owned it. Everyone was waiting for a reaction, but James was overcome. He sat there, sipping at his coffee and rubbing the bright cloth between his fingers.

"I know you're disappointed." It was Donna again, as if she understood full well that he could not say one word right now. "But if blacks came here to meet with you, the group would be way too conspicuous. You can bet that waitress would wonder."

That's it, white girl, he thought, resentful in an instant. Rap it on down. Hey, by what you say *I'm* too conspicuous, right here as we speak. Why do white folks think they know exactly how things are for us and proceed to tell us all about it?

But he knew, too, that Quincy must have agreed with her. He had to rely on Donna now, and she was trying to be his friend. It was just he hated always being the only black person around.

"Not that we're blaming anyone." Donna held up a hand to forestall Carolyn's explanation about why they had chosen such a place as this. "You did what you had to do. And once you got here, there was no easy way to move on. We know that. But I want you to understand, you're not forgotten."

James nodded.

"You've been depressed," she said.

She stated it as a fact, and he nodded again. He had no truck with instant psychoanalysis, but this woman who pulled things out of her purse like Santa Claus told the truth.

"But what you don't know is a whole lot of people out there view you as a hero, under any version of what happened that day."

"I wish I believed that." At last James looked up.

"You will," she answered. "It'll take time to build a new self-image, a knowledge that you're not an ordinary criminal, that you're a good person, full of courage. That is, if you ever appreciated that about yourself in the first place."

"Nyame died," James said. "Right after I was there."

"Just imagine what we went through after the townhouse explosion," Donna answered. "As responsible political people, we had to look at the fact that our inexperience and clumsiness had caused the deaths of three of our closest comrades. But we faced it head on. We talked it out."

"I'm never gonna get over that fact," Bob said.

"When you're truly safe," Donna continued, "with people around to help you, you can feel your way through it. But not now. Now you've done just what you had to. Kept everything in, waited. And you're going to have to do more of it. But one of these days you'll arrive at where you're going, and you'll have a life again."

"The worst thing in the world is isolation, man, and that's what you've had out here," Bob pitched in.

He offered his merry smile up at the waitress, who approached with the coffee. After she poured refills and turned away, he hailed her back for more cream. As she took the dispenser back toward the counter, the door opened and two highway patrolmen walked in, heavy with their sticks and guns.

"Look who's coming to dinner," said Donna softly. "But don't turn around."

"What's happening?" asked James.

"Pigs. They're standing right by the register, checking out the menu. Don't worry. They're not even noticing us."

The waitress greeted the policemen by name, and came back to the rear booth with the creamer full. Bob thanked her, poured from it into his coffee, clanking his spoon energetically.

"Does Colonia own the land right out there?" he asked Carolyn. He waved at the vineyards that stretched beyond the window.

"Probably," she answered. "Seems as if everything around here is theirs."

James concentrated on refolding the tissue around the book, as if clinging to his precious gifts might keep his fingers from trembling like they always did when the fear kicked in.

"But should we talk about this right now?" Carolyn was asking Bob in a whisper. "It's not like the UFW is a popular topic in places like this."

"They can't hear what we're saying," Donna said. "Just act normal. It's more suspicious if they walk in and all at once everything's quiet."

"What portion of the domestic wine market does Colonia control?" Bob continued his diversionary interrogation. He seemed to have an absolute hunger for information.

"Seventy-five, eighty percent," Carolyn recited what she'd been told last summer.

"Moral pressure will never do it, then. It'll have to show in the profit margin."

"That's where the boycott comes in," Carolyn said.

"A whole lot of people are going to have to change their buying habits. Could it be Cesar Chavez has bitten off more than he can chew?"

"He has a way of surprising people. And when they don't win right off, he's the type who never goes away."

James took it all in, surprising himself by feeling pretty calm.

"The pigs have their takeout coffee, they've paid the waitress, and they're about to leave," Donna said. "I think we can get back to business."

"Plus, it's always worth having the fight," Bob finished off Carolyn's point. "For its own sake. This will all add up someday."

"Let's just wait 'til they're all the way out of here," James said. "Okay?"

The other three nodded, and all four sipped their coffee at once, conscious as it happened that it might look odd, but afraid to change in the middle. The door slipped open and the police were gone.

"Now. Man does not live by gifts alone." Bob's sunny laugh surged over them like fresh air.

Donna rummaged in her purse again and extracted a plain white unsealed envelope. She gave it to Bob, who held it aloft, grinned, and handed it on to James. He tore it open and unfolded a document so stiff it could have been parchment. It was a certified birth certificate.

"Robert Johnson, born October 10, 1946, Walter Combs State Hospital, Macon, Georgia." James read out his new identity, then looked up with the corners of his lips twitching. "Not so bad. There's a famous blues man goes by that name."

"Far out," said Bob. "Don't give us the credit, though, 'cause this name is by total chance."

"How'd you get this thing?" James asked.

"You go to the death records and find someone who was born far away who would be right around your age," Donna explained. "Then you use that name and write to the place of birth. Make sure he was born far away from where he died so you don't happen to run into a clerk who knows the guy is dead. Tell them you lost your birth certificate, and ask them to send a copy. It takes time, but it works."

James examined the second item from the envelope, a social security card in the same name. He smiled for real now, his heart beating fast.

"Then you take the certificate," she continued. "You find the right people and get a social security card made. Can you begin to see why this took us a month?"

"You know, though, Don," said Bob. "Next time let's make up a reason and write for the birth certificate without the lie that the person's still alive. A sister or brother, maybe, who wants to complete the family records. Because what if they get a computer that does a cross-check, even between states?"

"We'll try it," she agreed. "Sounds like it's safer."

James put the documents back in their envelope with care and slipped it into his inside pocket by Quincy's letter.

"*And*—we've still got more." Donna foraged in her magic purse yet another time. With a flourish she drew out a different envelope, and held it up.

"Ta-da! We've got money!"

She passed it over to James, who hefted its thickness, then fitted it into the breast pocket on the other side of his jacket. When he looked up he had his big smile, the grin that showed the gap between his teeth.

"So what's next?" asked Bob. He fingered the check and waved away the waitress as she approached with more coffee.

"Well, what you've done means a lot to me, and don't think I'm not grateful." James chose his words carefully. "But has anyone talked more about where I'm gonna end up?"

"We're working on it," said Donna. "We're still waiting to hear from the Cubans. We know from other situations, they take their time on stuff like this. Now you can take the steps to get your passport, though. They'll want to see a passport before they issue their visa, if they say yes."

"And they will say yes," Bob chimed in with his usual optimism. "They let in the ones they view as potential political prisoners. Especially people of color."

"Lord save me if it works in my favor for once." James laughed. "I'll likely die of surprise."

"How much time will it take?" asked Carolyn. "That's what he doesn't have much of. The march is going to come right up on us."

"You just move on before then," said Bob, and Donna nodded her agreement.

"You hear us, James?" she said. "Now you've got money and some paper, but you'll need more. Get started on a driver's license, then the passport if there's time. You can go to a courthouse, if there's no town big enough around here to have a federal building. You'll need picture ID in addition to the birth certificate, so you have to wait until they mail you the license. And things take longer than you expect. So if you have to, you just put off the passport until you're at your next place."

The instructions stopped, and James sat there. Nothing hard to understand, but to set out and do it was another thing. First off, to tell the truth, unless the Cubans came through fast, he had no more idea where he'd go next than he did on the day they got here. Second, when he did leave, he'd have money and papers, yeah, but this time he'd be alone. For real.

"I know what." Donna's definite voice cut into his gloom. "Why can't James come with us?" James looked up as though a lifesaving device had been cast his way.

"We gotta go to New York in a week, Don," Bob said.

"I know, but we're just hanging out until then," Donna answered. "It doesn't solve where he goes next, but at least it gets him out of here for a while."

"We've got this place lined up in Tahoe, some rich person's summer home," Bob explained. "Just the two of us right now, but there's room for one more. You could join us there until we have to leave. That way we'll have some time to talk it all through."

"In fact, you should get a learner's permit up there, in Robert Johnson's name," said Donna. "Then you can apply for the license here when you get back. We've found it means fewer questions if you have the permit, because it's weird enough that someone your age hasn't driven before. Otherwise you'd have to say you lost an old out-of-state license, and that's too risky, because they might check. As it is, you better tell them you've been in New York City or out of the country for the last fifteen years, and that's why you never needed to drive. Those are the only good reasons we've ever been able to think of."

Girl's mind was like a damned linear jigsaw puzzle. Each piece fit with what came before and after. Everyone else, himself included he was sure, looked a little confused.

"So you get your permit in Tahoe and come back here to take the driving test. That way you don't have to go back to the same DMV office twice. Then you've got what you need for the passport. And if you have to leave in the middle, at least you'll be able to drive. You could even get a secondhand car. There's bucks in there." She nodded toward his pocket that contained the money.

James felt in both pockets and touched all the envelopes.

"What do you think, man?" He looked at Bob. "This idea of me coming okay with you?"

"Sure it is."

"Carolyn?"

"It's a good idea, James. You need to get away."

She meant away from Mary Lou, he knew, and she sounded relieved. "Then when you come back," she added, "there's still some time before the march."

To say goodbye to Mary Lou. He winced, then eased ice water down his throat. Everyone watched while he tried to make himself decide to do what clearly made the most sense, which was to wean himself off of Mary Lou and leave with these people he had never seen before. Maybe he could even trust them, and all the talk that was bound to occur might possibly get him somewhere.

"If I go, will you stay for the week?" He had to make sure Carolyn didn't disappear back to the Bay Area.

"Sure. I'll be here."

"There's only one thing. It's just for the week. You can't come back East with us." Donna wanted everything clear.

"I don't want to join up with you anyhow," James was quick to answer. He had no desire to be in some honky radical group; there were black people in Cuba. It was supposed to actually be more fair down there, even if he did have to learn Spanish. His heart soared with hope. Equality and socialism, that was all he'd ever wished for. And somewhere in this lifetime to feel safe again.

"It's settled then. Let's get out of here." Bob went to the register to pay the check.

"How will he get back?" Carolyn asked Donna.

"We'll put him on the Greyhound."

"The Greyhound? You've got to be kidding."

"It's safer than you'd think. The cops can't watch every station in California for this long. He won't be recognized if he's careful."

"'Swim like a fish in the sea of the people,' just like Mao said," was Bob's cheerful contribution as he returned to shepherd them outside.

While Carolyn got out her key to unlock the car door, James looked at his book again.

Talkin
to people everyday
Black, they are
I know them
we talk the same ways
believe, I am told, similar dreams.

The words marched right on down the page, in the middle of some way longer poem. There were black people out there somewhere who had known these poems would speak to his life, and they had made sure this book got to him. Some day he would be among them again, even if it was in Cuba. Lord willin', as his auntie would say. He clutched the slim book to his chest as if it were the only thing that could save him.

CHAPTER TWENTY-ONE

"He left?" It was four in the afternoon by the time Carolyn delivered the news, and Mary Lou sounded desolate. "Why'd he do that?"

Carolyn had just come into the UFW office, and since Mary Lou was the only one there, she told her right away.

"Donna and Bob are cool, Mary Lou." Carolyn kept speaking as her friend rose from her desk and came over to stand right next to her. "They can help him onto the next stage."

"When's he coming back?" Mary Lou sounded desperate.

"Ten days from now," Carolyn said. "But then he'll have to go again. You used to want him to leave, remember?"

"Jeez, we had that fight," Mary Lou muttered to herself. "He must still be mad at me. And then Rojelio walked right in the door like that."

"And that's another thing that's changed." Carolyn kept at it. "You used to want Cesar to send Rojelio back from the boycott, remember?"

"I still do," she replied automatically. "I need the help."

"Yeah, but that wasn't the only reason."

Why was she taunting Mary Lou like this? As if things weren't painful enough already.

The door across the cavernous space opened and Rojelio walked in, like they had conjured him up. The women had been so intent on their conversation they hadn't even heard his car pull into the lot. Here's one who never changes, thought Carolyn, and she liked him for that. Dressed in his usual jeans and work shirt, set off by the most basic UFW button, black eagle on red, his face unlined and unguarded, Rojelio had the perpetual look of a kid who has just invented a new game. He and Bob would have a lot in common, except, of course, that they could never meet. Excited, Rojelio stood between the two women and talked fast.

"You know Pacheco, with the restaurant in Emerald? The one from Michoacan?"

"Yeah, when the strike began he used his life savings to open that place," Mary Lou answered, working hard at composure. "I eat there every time I go to town, but he never lets me pay. How's he gonna make a living that way?"

"Well, Pacheco says he'll make lunch for everyone when the march comes through Allen. That way we eat on the road and we won't lose time, since those are the days we have to cover so many miles. *And—*" He gave each of them an affectionate squeeze around the waist.

"—he's promised to house twenty-five marchers. He's got family around here, so he says he can take that many all three days. *¡Si se puede!*" His grin widened, if that were possible.

Mary Lou moved back to the lists on her desk.

"This march might even come off," she said without looking at him.

"So let's celebrate," he countered. "Let's close up and go to El Bucanero for a drink." He held up his hand to forestall any objections. "You'll come too, won't you Carolyn?" He pulled down the Venetian blinds they used when the office was closed.

"It's so early," Mary Lou protested, but she began to gather her things.

"And we've already accomplished more than we usually do when we work 'til nine," he answered.

"Someone will see us in that bar. It's right in the middle of downtown Allen."

"So what if they do? *La gente* likes its leaders to be human, *m'hija.*"

"The people," thought Carolyn. She liked the way Rojelio threw in Spanish phrases, ones she could understand. "My little daughter." Term of affection. God, Rojelio being here right now must be complicated for Mary Lou.

He ushered both women out of the office and locked the door. A sudden pile of clouds moving in from the west was so low it already seemed dark. Carolyn shivered in her thin sweater. She should have brought her coat but it had been sunny, even when James had folded himself into the backseat behind Donna and Bob and taken his small suitcase she thrust in after him.

"Let me drive separately," Carolyn said to Rojelio and Mary Lou. "I still have to go out with Ramón to get strikers tonight." She started up her car and headed through the intersection with Highway 99 for the fourth time already that day.

Large drops began to spatter on her windshield as she negotiated the potholes on Allen's main street. She turned on the wipers, rubbed at the film inside the windshield with her bare hand, then settled back, relieved that for once, with James gone, all she had to do was take care of herself.

Who were Donna and Bob, anyhow? She sensed that they were important, but she liked them anyway. Bernardine Dohrn and Billy Ayers, the most famous leaders of the Weather Underground? Today was exciting, the way it had been when she first helped James. With people like this in charge, maybe the Movement would get somewhere. Maybe America would change, and she would have been part of it all.

The rain fell thick and hard by the time she entered the tiny bar, its interior lit by a lurid sign that switched between Pabst Blue Ribbon letters in red white and blue, then back to a lake again. The shifting colors played across the forms of Rojelio and Mary Lou, huddled already at a small table in the corner, a bottle of Cuervo Gold, three shot glasses, and three tumblers of ice water before them.

Rojelio poured the drinks, and the tequila's amber slid right in with the rest of the iridescent hues. As her eyes adjusted to the dark, her nose to the sour-sweet odor of beer and cigarette smoke, Carolyn felt happy to be in here.

"*¡Que viva la Unión!*" Rojelio offered it as a toast and raised his jigger.

"*¡Que viva!*" answered the women softly, in unison. Mary Lou took a small sip, and Carolyn downed half her shot.

"*¡Abajo con Colonia!*" was Rojelio's next sally. He took his liquor all in one gulp.

"*¡Abajo!*" said the women, and Carolyn drained the tiny glass. The liquor spread through her veins and capillaries and relaxed her limbs at once. The outside world and its weighty matters dissolved into the everlasting progression of colored lights.

Que viva Donna and Bob, she thought. *Que viva* James! She poured herself a tad more and silently raised her glass to the other three, driving north on 99 through this gathering storm even as she sat here.

Mary Lou took one more tiny sip, grimaced, and set her shot glass down to reach for her ice water.

"What's the matter, *m'hija?*" Rojelio leaned toward her solicitously. "You don't like the taste?"

"It doesn't sit right. Maybe I'm catching a cold."

"Hope it's not the stomach flu," Carolyn trilled. "Can't afford that with the march coming up, right?"

She giggled and Rojelio smiled.

"Just a cold, Carolyn." Mary Lou asserted her control over the matter.

Rojelio poured another jigger for Carolyn and himself, and Carolyn settled down to sipping. She listened to them chat on about the strike, the boycott, the march, the usual. She had handed James over to people who were safe. Rojelio was here, and more were coming to help Mary Lou. Why did she have to stay here now? Yeah so she had promised James, but why? Because she didn't have a life at home since Mona had died, that was why. Because all there was back there was grief.

A solitary drinker sat at the bar, and with his thin, straight back and cowboy hat he reminded Carolyn of Ramón. She glanced at her watch. Fifteen minutes until she had to meet him. Could she talk to strikers in this shape? Sure, why not? Ramón could do the driving. She could even try her little wrap-up speech in Spanish for once; the liquor would loosen her tongue.

A Mexican love song cried out from the jukebox at the side of the room, and the tantalizing scent of meat and refried beans wafted in from the tiny kitchen behind the bar. Rojelio was almost through with his second shot, so she hurried to catch up. Mona had prided herself on being able to drink any man under the table; could her only daughter do less? He refilled their glasses and, leaning toward Mary Lou as if the two of them were alone, urged more on her without success.

Their heads bent close, the bar colors marching across their faces, Carolyn noticed, as she always had, what a nice-looking couple they made. Rojelio was wonderful—straightforward, hardworking, handsome, all of that. Maybe not as quick verbally as Mary Lou, but so what, you can't have everything. Not that Carolyn herself had given up trying, but then again, with so little romantic action in her own life, she had to smile at this pathetic notion.

It would make everyone's existence easier if these two could just get it on again. Hard as it was to leave this warm and cozy bar, what they needed was time to themselves. She downed her shot glass one last time and stood up. A little unsteady, maybe even three sheets to the wind as her mother would have called it, but no one seemed to notice.

"Time to meet Ramón," she enunciated carefully.

"*Buen suerte*," said Rojelio, without the slightest inclination to get up himself. "Good luck, Carolyn. Get those strikers in line for us, will you?"

"Oh, I forgot," said Mary Lou. "Lupe called. She can't go tonight. Her father's sick, and her mother's at work."

"So what else is new? Lupe's punking out, Mary Lou. Ramón and I have done it alone for the whole past week."

"She's out looking for a boyfriend," Rojelio joked. "Doesn't want her little sister to get ahead of her."

"I doubt that," said Mary Lou. "As if Chuey Vargas ever did Patsy one bit of good."

"Chuey Vargas is a lowlife," said Rojelio. "But hey, check it out, most of us *chicanos* are not like him at all. Look at my father, my brothers—"

"Jeez," Mary Lou agreed. "Compared to the Okies, Mexican families are straight out of Ozzie and Harriet."

Could her friend be a just a teeny bit tipsy herself, wondered Carolyn?

"*Poco Indio* in comparison, that's all, just a little darker." They both laughed. The two of them hardly noticed as Carolyn made her way toward the door.

It's going to work, she thought as she negotiated through sheets of rain falling in the pitch dark. Rojelio's going to ask her to be with him again, and she'll see the sense in it. It might hurt James a little, but he'll have to know it's better. He'll be on his way, I'll have done my bit for him and the history books, and maybe even I'll have a life of my own one of these days. Things may not be easy, but they do work out.

She covered her head as much as she could with the back of her crewneck sweater, clutched her arms to her chest in a useless effort to stay dry, and picked her way over the streaming sidewalk and through the muddy hole in the street by her car. By the time she was behind the wheel, she was thoroughly wet and cold.

The red of Ramón's pickup was the only spot of color in the bleak-looking UFW parking lot. As Carolyn pulled up, he snapped on the interior light and jumped out to open her car door. They both held his jacket over their two heads and ran toward the darkened office.

"Lupe can't come," she yelled over the storm as they splashed through puddles.

"Again," he said. "And today she promised me."

"But we'll go anyway, right?" So cold it was an effort to keep her teeth from chattering, Carolyn hoped he would say they could skip it for once.

"*Cierto*," was his reply. "Of course we must go."

"I just need my files," she said. She reached into her purse. "Damn it, the key! I forgot to get it from Mary Lou."

"And it's locked?" Ramón rattled at the doorknob. "Yes, *claro*. You don't have another key?"

"I don't have another key," she echoed. There had been no need. Mary Lou was always here. Except tonight.

"Who else has one?"

"Rojelio must."

"And where is he?"

"They're both at El Bucanero. We've been drinking tequila."

She saw his look of surprise. Maybe he thought she never touched alcohol.

"I'm getting soaked," she wailed.

"Come back to the truck," he offered at once. Still using his jacket as a shield, he hurried them both over to the pickup, where the cab still glowed from its overhead bulb like a cave lit by a kerosene lamp. He opened her door and she clambered up, glad to settle onto the familiar high seat.

"You're shivering," he said, and he arranged his jacket over her shoulders. When he turned on the motor for heat, mariachi music from his radio station blared out loud. Chagrined, he leaned past her to switch it off, but she stopped him. The way the horn and guitar bounced off each other always made her feel as though someone, somewhere, was happy.

Ramón assessed the situation.

"*Pues*, let's go to El Bucanero then. It's not that far."

But by the time they got there, Rojelio's car was gone, and when they swung by Joseph Street, it wasn't there either.

"I'm freezing," she said.

"Let's stop," he suggested. "You can change clothes."

"No!"

He gave her a strange look, but she couldn't have him go into the Joseph Street house. Though James was gone, some of his things were still around, and Ramón might ask where he was. Damn, and of course he had seen them this morning when they drove out to J's, and she hadn't given him the story yet about the trip to the doctor. But then James should be here tonight, shouldn't he? Unless he had to stay at the hospital or something. Too much to think about all at once.

"I mean," she stammered, "we should get going, or we'll never get anything done."

"I'll tell you what," he offered. "I have my notes at the motel. Even without your list maybe we can still remember where to go. And you can get warm there while I figure it out."

She nodded, relieved, leaned back on the vinyl seat, closed her eyes, and ran her tongue around a mouth suddenly gone dry from the alcohol's aftermath. Just as the pickup's motion began to soothe her, they were across the intersection and past the Hillside Motel's vacancy sign, so red it flashed beneath her lids. They stopped at the row of rooms on the far end.

Again they used his jacket for protection against the downpour. He took her elbow to guide her under the sheltered walkway. Her father used to do the same years ago when they went to restaurants together after the divorce.

His room was behind a pillar that concealed an ice machine, and when he opened the door, it triggered an automatic television tuned to a Spanish quiz show. Confused, she stopped at the threshold of the tiny place. From behind her he moved with decision into the cramped space between the two double beds. He snapped off the TV, motioned for her to sit in the only armchair, and got her a thin, white hand towel from the bathroom so she could dry off. Through the insubstantial wall to the next room she heard shrieks of joy as cash prizes were won.

"Do you want something to drink, Carolyn? I have soda." He picked up a small transistor radio from the nightstand beside the bed, tuned it to the mariachi music, and leaned around her to put it by her chair. She nodded yes, so he retrieved the cardboard bucket from the bathroom and went to get ice.

"Coke or 7up?" His voice drifted back into the room, almost lost against the truck gears that ground down before the highway light.

"7up, thank you." She heard the thunk of the can as it fell, and realized he had bought her one from a machine. He came back in the room, filled a motel glass with ice, poured the clear fizzy liquid, and handed it to her with a small ceremonious bow.

She was so thirsty she just about drank the whole thing while she watched him rummage in a suitcase. First he came up with a warm bottle of *Buena Noche*, the Mexican Christmas beer, which he pried open with a folding knife he drew from his pocket. He took a solid swig. She wished he would offer her some, but he didn't. Next he pulled out his black plastic zippered case, from which he extracted a bent manila folder. He moved the desk chair with its green cracked seat near to her so he could show her the contents.

"I don't know," he said, as he glanced over sparse notes on a sheet of lined paper. "Not so easy to tell where to go next." He turned his snapping black eyes onto hers and almost smiled.

"Already you have finished your soda."

"I needed it," she confessed.

"You were celebrating?"

"Yes. Well, you see, I'm hoping Mary Lou and Rojelio will get back together, because . . ." She stopped in horror. It would have been so easy to talk about Rojelio's small victory with food and lodging for the march, though she sensed Ramón wouldn't have thought it enough to justify tequila in the afternoon. But instead she had been about to mention James. God, she must still be drunk.

"I mean, well. You see, it's my mother's birthday."

At once she felt ashamed. Tell no lies, except about your mother.

"Did Rojelio teach you *Las Mañanitas* so you could call your mother and sing to her?" He gave a gentle smile.

"My mother isn't alive, Ramón. She died four months ago."

"So soon. So recent." He murmured his sympathy. "You must still miss her."

"I miss her very much. Very, very much." She would weep if this went on. "You don't have another beer, do you? I love that kind. You don't find it everywhere."

"*Cierto.* Of course."

He got a second one out, opened it, and brought her a new glass from the bathroom. She liked this man's manners. Her father always got out a glass when he drank beer with Mona. "Fancy, like in New York." That's what Mona would say every time he did it for her.

She drank deeply. Might as well continue the evening the way it had started. Even close to tears she felt lighter, happier than she had in months.

"So now I understand. You have seemed at times so *desolada*—how do you say it in English?"

"Desolate. Sad." Again the grief threatened to overwhelm her, but she did not want to cry. It was raining like crazy; they would never find the strikers' houses without the information that was locked in the office. It had been so long since she had just talked to someone without a crisis going on.

"So what about your family?" she asked. "How many kids do you have?"

"Three. Two little ones and a baby." A note of reverence entered his voice. "Everyone is safe, in Coachella."

Coachella. Where the first luscious table grapes of the season were harvested. Rojelio once told her this when a farmworker delivered a case of Coachella's green perlettes to the office, nestled in their tissue paper like precious stones. Plus the mountains, he had described sheer mountains that rose straight out of the desert there.

"And you, *Carolina?*" Ramón drained his bottle and leaned forward to put it on the table between them. "Do you have a boyfriend? Are you married?"

"Not now. I was married once."

"You remind me of a lamb I saw once," he said. "A small lamb who couldn't find its mother, who needed refuge from the cold."

She almost chuckled because it was corny, but instead she sobbed out loud, despite herself. She allowed his thin, strong arms to lift her onto her feet, and he kissed her cheeks where they were damp with tears, as if to share her sorrow.

"You need to be under covers," he murmured. "Warm. In bed."

It was true, she told herself. Her legs, her shoulders, everything was still wet and cold where her clothes stuck flat against her body.

She was not the type to be involved with another woman's man, let alone one who was married and had kids, yet she hesitated only long enough to grab at her glass and gulp down the rest of her beer. After that she thought only of his rough, calloused hands as they urged her with a gentle tenderness to let herself be comforted by the animal touch.

Together they got her out of her soaked jeans and sweater and underneath the thin blanket and spread, between sheets worn smooth with use. When she lay back on the pillow and saw the built-in "Magic Fingers" massage machine, she had to laugh. Ramón smiled too, but labored nonetheless to dig out a quarter out from his jeans. He shoved the coin in. For a moment nothing happened. Then the bed emitted a dull roar and began a soft back-and-forth motion that to her surprise was soothing.

He bent over her and lifted the remaining articles of clothing from her body with a fastidious delicacy, accompanied by quiet exclamations in Spanish. She reclined into an unaccustomed passivity and let herself be treated with care. Eyes closed, she allowed herself only a glance as his thin, sinewy body emerged from his clothes, and he was there beside her before she remembered something which, even in this fog of alcohol, grief, and pleasure, she could not let herself ignore.

"We can't," she gasped and tried to turn away.

"¿Como no? Why not, Carolyn?" His inky eyes fastened on her.

"I have no protection," she stammered, uncertain how to word this so he would understand but not find her crass.

"Ah, but you forget about me."

He reached for his trousers folded over the back of his chair, extracted a tooled leather wallet, and brought out a slim, shiny packet. Again she shut her eyes while he sat on the side of the bed to apply the contents and get another quarter into the machine, all with the same unhurried calm. Whatever came next, she thought, she would be well taken care of.

She soaked up the affection of his caresses like moss expanding in water. Eyes closed, it was his hands, those warm, rough palms that defined her contours, the shape of her pleasure. Her conscience about his family hovered above them like a gnat that pricked but was easily swatted away. His hands were her guidance; his hands were her salvation. The rest was an awkward series of thrusts and groans, and she even managed to come, but barely. She loved those hands, she loved him, she loved the unexpected turn the night had taken.

They separated and she lay spooned in his arms, her soft flesh spread to fill the gaps left by his slender angles. He was thinner than she, though muscular, and not too much taller. She stared at his hands, one under her shoulder at rest near her breast, the other first on her hip bone, then up to cut off what had become an endless rhythm of Spanish radio ads, then cupping her pelvic rim again. Her last awareness was of the wet splash of constant rain outside the steamed-up window, and then she was asleep, curled against him like a child.

She woke up right at dawn, free for once of the first flash of grief she had come to take as ordinary since her mother's death before it dissolved into the events of the day. In her doze she savored an uncommon physical peace. But when she looked at Ramón, pulled away from her in his sleep, his closest shoulder tattooed in a teal and rose eagle, talons spread, she knew that they were still strangers.

She crept out of bed, gathered up her clothes, and tiptoed into the bathroom where she ran hot water over a threadbare washcloth, wiped her legs off, and dried with a towel. As she got dressed and combed her hair in front of the mirror, she felt more familiar to herself. While she sat on the toilet she read the signs—"Please Don't Use These Towels on your Car, Truck, or Other Machinery." "Please Don't Take Towels—Higher Motel Costs for You." She had never been in a place quite like this before.

Fully dressed, she slipped back into the room. He still breathed deeply. Worried every second about the noise, she picked up her purse, opened the door only to jump at the rumble of the ice machine as it dropped its cubes, and pressed the knob shut with a soft click.

High clouds formed a slate dome over the fresh-washed expanse of the highway and its adjoining fields. She hummed to herself as she made her way down the cement driveway and onto the highway's access road, then walked the long block to the stoplight that marked the same old intersection of 99 and the town of Allen. So familiar and everything she knew out here so close by the Hillside, or the Punjuabi motel as everyone called it, yet her body, dwarfed before the bulk of the trucks stopped at the light, felt brand new.

She crossed, the lone pedestrian, and on the other side she passed two Mexican boys who looked like teenagers. Lunch boxes and thermoses that dangled from thick blackened fingers made it clear they were on their way to work. Early. It couldn't be later than 6:30 a.m. She wanted to smile, but they stared at her with what she interpreted as dislike, so she looked at the ground. What were they thinking—that only a woman with loose morals would be out at this early hour? Annoyed, she had to remind herself that it didn't matter. She was free to walk whenever and wherever she wanted.

When she got to her car, the only vehicle in the muddy UFW parking lot, she was relieved to be out of there before anyone else noticed her.

At Joseph Street she worked the unfamiliar door at the front of the house to get in without waking anyone. Everything was quiet. She put water on for coffee and couldn't resist looking, even though it was none of her business. She tiptoed down the hall to the bedroom and peeked inside the cracked door.

There was Mary Lou, a long, thin shape in the double bed. Alone.

CHAPTER TWENTY-TWO

Carolyn stands near the wall to avoid the wind while she waits for James to arrive on the Greyhound in Carleton. It's ten-thirty a.m. on Thursday, March the fifth, and the bus was supposed to have been there at ten. Not only is she worried about that, but today they have to go straight to Emerald get James's driver's license without being discovered, followed, or busted. Then they have to figure out how to get him the hell away from here when marchers step onto the highway from Delano next Monday, March the ninth. The line won't get to Allen until ten days later, but still.

The return of James. Back to the picking and choosing which lies need to be told to which people and keeping track of it all. The thing about this habit of lying is that it's not all that difficult. No wonder so many people make up stuff for their own benefit. Most of the time they must get away with it.

She's told Ramón she'll be late for their ongoing project of getting the strikers to commit to the march because of "personal business." They were lying together in their damp and rumbled motel sheets when she said it. They had learned how to make her come that time. She'd climbed up on top of him, then moved around like crazy to make it happen. He seemed fine, even happy with it. They turned back over and he came too, of course. So it was good.

Yet even after intimacy he didn't press for any detail. He never does, unless it's about the strikers. That's a good thing, she tells herself, but it bothers her anyhow. Those black eyes of his. So expressive when he's inside her. So impenetrable, like obsidian, after it's over.

The minute their clothes are on he's back to that courtesy of his that makes her jumpy. By that point she, who usually can't shut up even when she should, doesn't really have anything to say either.

She hasn't even used her excuse about why he saw her in the car with James the day Donna and Bob came. That particular untruth isn't worth the attention it would draw. Does he care at all where she is when she's not with him?

The bus lumbers into its port and suddenly James is there, long and lanky and black and conspicuous in the middle of a file of weary passengers. He has his sunglasses on as always. He looks different, better. His shirt is pressed, his pants creased, his hair's been cut, but most of all, his forehead has lost that scrunched-up worried look. She's swept by a rush of affection. The old Charles, the one who got her to grow up. But not hers now, she reminds herself. As if he ever was.

"Hey, girl? What's happenin'?" He doesn't quite stop when he approaches, so any gesture of physical affection is out of the question. Just as well. "You look good. Like things calmed down with me gone."

"And you the same." She falls in with his step. "You changed your hair. Shorter yet."

Wind flurries swirl dirt at them as they walk across a vacant lot to the Volvo. He heaves his suitcase into the backseat, and moments later they're on the highway headed south.

"Got this haircut where the brothers hang out." James smiles his gap-tooth grin. "We found the place in Sacramento, on the way up to Tahoe? Even a guy with a do-rag, gettin' his conk in place for Saturday night. He must not have heard it yet, that on behalf of us all, Malcolm gave up that hair-straightening shit years ago. There's still black folks in the big ol' world out there, Curly. That was nice to see."

They pass an orchard of young peach trees, blown almost horizontal by the sharp wind. James stares out the window. He seems rested, peaceful even, in contrast to the weather. Distant, with the cutting wind so near.

"Did you have a good time with the two of them?" Carolyn asks.

"Hunh? Who, Donna and Bob?" he says. "Oh, they were quite cool, I must say. Brought me up to speed."

"Donna told me you got your passport photos."

The two women had spoken pay phone to pay phone this morning, per the detailed plan they had made before they and James even took off, and it worked like a charm.

"Yep," James says. "I've faced the camera and lived to tell the tale."

Both are quiet. The car purrs along through sudden calm outside.

"And the learner's permit?" Carolyn asks. "Was that hard?"

"Passed the written test on the very first try," he answers cheerfully.

"Could there be any doubt?"

"I like your attitude, Curls." He pauses. "How's Ms. Mary Louise doing?"

Damn. Doesn't take long enough for that question to come.

"Working hard, as always," Carolyn says. "Rojelio's been a big help." She watches to see if this deflates him. Not enough.

"They been puttin' in those long hours together then?" He tries to keep a light tone. The wind picks up again, to the point where she can feel it trying to move the car into the next lane.

Carolyn nods yes, and his forehead falls into that line between his brows. He doesn't ask anything more. Maybe he's come to his senses and knows this thing with Mary Lou is crazy. Maybe he's realized he has to work on being less concerned.

"So, we've got the plan straight?" she asks him as they roll past the first exit to Emerald.

"Temporary license 'til they send the one with the picture at the PO box. Then we have that, the photos, the birth certificate, and we apply for the passport."

As he recites all this he stares at the walnut trees flashing by, stately and still even in the wind.

"But if it all takes too long?" Carolyn wants his attention. "You can leave town before the license comes. I'll send it to you and you get the passport somewhere else."

"Sure thing, Curls." He agrees almost too fast, and she wonders if he heard her right.

"So, the DMV again," he says. "Should I wear a tie?"

"Why not? You're supposed to be from New York, right? They're more formal back East."

He reaches behind them, clicks the suitcase open to get at the striped neckpiece, and puts it on, bending the rearview mirror to see the knot.

"Lookin' good, James Sweet. Lookin' fine."

He smiles when he hears her repeat his own talismanic words from six weeks ago.

"Want to drive?" she offers next. "Get used to the car?"

She pulls into a highway rest stop and hands him the keys. The wind scuds at their backs as they switch sides and in the next instant tears at them head on. The skirt she's borrowed from Mary Lou is cut so full that it just about ends up around her waist.

He looks as though being behind the wheel is pure joy. Smooth with the gears, he's back up to highway speed in no time. Maybe this is the first time he's driven since Freeman Penitentiary. Freedom.

They pass J's Diner, shoot through flat-bottomed almond orchards leafed out in a newborn green, then past heaps of crushed hulls, stockpiled for feed under roofs that stand on two-story poles.

"You know where the Emerald DMV is?" he asks her.

Of course she knows. Hasn't she already gone over every detail with Donna, studied her map of Emerald, worried a lot? Hasn't he counted on her for this?

"By the post office," she tells him. "How do you want to handle the logistics?"

"Why don't you check the place out for me so I know what to expect when I go in? Drop me off somewhere, then pick me back up and I'll take the car. I've got my permit, so I'm not a 'Violator of the Law'"—this last in his best preacher cadence. "And then I'll go in and take the driving test. Simple as that."

Off the highway, he slows down and rolls down his window to look out at Emerald.

"Big-time city all of a sudden," he observes, pulling to a stop near a tiny corner park that swirls with blowing trash. Shacks line an unpaved side alley in a neighborhood even more tumbledown than the one around Joseph Street. School-aged girls with braids laugh into the breeze and dance on down the road.

"Check it out," he says. "My folks all around us, and it's not even Fresno or Sacramento."

On a broken bench sits an old black man dressed in farm clothes, huddled against the wind.

"So poor, though." Carolyn sighs.

"Poor?" he says. "That's nothin' new. It does look worse than most of Oakland, though," he adds, affable enough. "But a good place for me to wait, don't you think? Twenty minutes. That should give you enough time."

His eyes follow the kids and he looks right at home in the exact place where she has no thought but sadness. Too late she realizes how beautiful the children are. It must be hard to be in a category that half the white people hate and the other half feel sorry for.

The wind cuts through her again as she makes her way back to the driver's seat. James, hunched into his jacket, hands in his pockets, already looks cold, older, more like the guy next to him on the bench. She remembers her dream where he was all bundled up, riding down the road, waiting to be caught.

She drives off and soon finds the low, green structure that houses Emerald's DMV. She climbs out of the car clutching at her billowing skirt. She could've worn her own serviceable suit, but she loves this green silky outfit of Mary Lou's, the matching top with its scoop neck decorated by blue crosshatch stitches.

She sees four middle-aged men watching her from in front of the building as she crosses the street. Plainclothes cops who know somehow that she picked up James?

Eyes downcast so all she can look at is their polyester pant legs, she hurries by. One of them has on white buckle shoes. Aren't white shoes supposed to be for the summer? Whenever she leaves the Union enclave out here in this Valley, she feels as if she's in a foreign country.

On an impulse she stops short, snaps her fingers as though she's forgotten something, changes directions, and heads up the broad stairs to the post office next door so they won't see her go into the DMV. Not that this exactly makes sense, but she needs a minute out of their view to figure out what kind of threat they pose.

Once inside there is another steeper staircase that leads to the stamp windows, and by the time she gets to the top of all this she is panting for breath.

She watches people go by, on their way to get stamps. She's got to get into the DMV, even if the men are still there. If they're cops, James is already caught. He has to get his license, and if it's not here, it's all the way to Fresno. She's been waiting long enough to have bought her own stamps; it won't look strange now when she goes out and into the DMV.

She turns to go back down, and the wanted posters on the wall behind her come into full view. It won't include James. Her eyes race through the line of pictures.

But he is there, the last one tacked up at the end of the row. She clutches at the banister like she needs it to hold her up.

"WANTED BY THE FBI," in large black letters. Then "Interstate flight, first degree murder, conspiracy, felony firearm," in smaller but still in bold print. "CHARLES BROWN" underneath the photograph, different font but just as large. "Caution—Armed and Dangerous."

That horrible mug shot, the one from the newspaper with a side view added. The type who butchers people. Not the face of the man back on the bench, she tells herself. This doesn't even look like James. Except when he's depressed.

A young woman clacks by, high heels scraping on the steps. A man's sneakers slap past her, stop, then return.

"You okay, miss?" he asks. He's come back out of concern. Stupid of her. He'll remember, damn it.

"I'm fine," she murmurs, without looking up. "Just waiting for someone."

She makes a show of examining her watch and fakes impatience, embarrassment at being stood up. But it's all too late; he's bounded off. She finds that she has to stare at the thing all over again. Her friend. Mary Lou's lover. Charles Brown, now James Sweet. Soon to be Robert Johnson. Armed and dangerous.

Ten minutes left and she hasn't even gotten into the right building yet. Plus, in a second Mr. Do Good will've bought his stamps and she'll still be here when he comes back by. She squares her shoulders and sets off down the stairs at a brisk pace.

The men are still at the bottom of the wide, flat steps. The wind still tosses at her skirt. She knows she looks nervous and still they stare, saying nothing.

She holds her breath, crosses at the corner, and comes back down the block to the actual DMV entrance. The glass door gives way at her push and she's almost blown into the building. Once there, clumsy and uncertain, she can't quite grasp why she and James decided she should come at all. It's a DMV like any other.

She waits in line under the "Information" sign to ask about procedure. Turn in your permit at the desk to the right, over to the red line on the floor to get your picture taken, out to the parking lot for the driving test. Temporary license at the end of it all, permanent one with the picture to be mailed out who knows when. In the Bay Area sometimes it took weeks to get the permanent license. She and Donna and Bob would have to set a limit for James to leave Allen with or without it.

Anyone watching would wonder why she goes out now instead of beginning the process, but of course she has to get back to him. She hurries to the corner, and damned if the foursome doesn't *still* loiter by the steps. The wind has died down so she doesn't have to hold her skirt. For the first time she looks at their faces, and at once they begin to talk.

"Hey, honey, you married?" This from the one with white shoes, no less. "Got a boyfriend?"

Carolyn never knows what to say even in normal circumstances. And these guys must be in their forties, for God's sake. If she answers, will they remember her more or less than if she walks right by?

"Not anymore," she murmurs, watching him strain his neck toward her to hear. "He's the one who just didn't show up."

"Awww," they chorus on cue.

"Come on over here, then."

"Comfort is on the way."

"I can make you feel better than he ever would."

The usual idiots. She finds herself relieved and even smiling, so next she sticks her nose in the air and parades on past them. Nothing nefarious about these guys.

Back at the car, she gets in and drives around three extra blocks just to make sure she's right and these guys aren't tailing her, though exactly how you can tell one way or the other she's never quite sure. She turns a bunch of times and sees no consistent car, so she heads back to the postage-stamp park. James waits alone on the bench, right where she left him.

"The worst thing is," her words tumble out. "Your poster is there." He gets in and she drives off at once.

He turns on the heater and rubs his hands, blowing on them, waiting for what comes next.

"A wanted poster, with your picture. 'Armed and Dangerous.'"

"Where?" he asks, intent now. "Right there in the DMV?"

"Post office, across the street." She decides the four men were just coming on to her, and she won't mention them at all. Wait and see if they're still there. The poster is enough bad news.

She turns onto a stately tree-lined avenue, spacious high school and sports fields on one side, commodious homes on the other. Bare branches rub and sway in the brisk breeze.

"Folks don't mess around out here," James observes. "The brothers don't have shit in the poorest damned neighborhood I ever did see, and four blocks later it's a place where the Rockefellers could live. What's there to do about it?"

"About what?" Carolyn asks, confused. She hates this wind. It makes her instincts scrape together, wood on bald wood like the branches, until she doesn't know what's dangerous and what's safe.

"The poster," James says. "It's not in the DMV, so it's not like people are gonna be lookin' right at it when they see me."

"But they could have stopped to buy their stamps," Carolyn says. "They could have seen the picture just before they see you."

"What's our choice?" he asks.

"Go to Fresno. Do it there."

"Don't you think they have their own post office?" he points out. "Could be even more dangerous in a big city."

"So it doesn't scare you?" she asks.

The houses give way to the stores downtown. These towns out here look like they're straight out of the 1950s. Nothing has changed since McCarthy, Carolyn thinks. They were getting close to where she had parked before.

"I'm always scared." James gives out a bitter laugh. "The way I see it, Curls? It's time to get this done."

If he can, she can. She forces herself to be composed, explains the procedure over the next two blocks, and parks the car.

The men, thank God, are gone.

"See that restaurant over there?" He points across the street to a nondescript cafe she hadn't even noticed before. "Wait for me. When I get back from the driving test I'll meet you."

They both climb out of the car and stand there, awkward, aware that they make a strange-looking pair out here.

"You know your birth date and stuff, right?"

"Girl, I got Robert Johnson *memorized*." He grins and raises a fist clenched by his chest that only she can see. "Power to the people," he whispers.

"Good luck." She squeezes his arm, and they walk in opposite directions.

—◊◊—

James heads straight to the first line, not looking at anyone though he knows exactly where each person is. Not too many, though, and no one is staring at him. When he gets to the window he pushes his permit across the counter toward a white woman with faded-out red hair and tired eyes. She takes it without even looking up. Fine. Be like that. Better that way anyhow.

"This your current address?" she asks him.

"No, ma'am," he says. "I got the permit where I was on vacation." He's rehearsed that one.

"Then you'll have to fill this out." She shoves a form toward him. "After that, come back to the front of the line."

He obeys her instructions, puts on the post office box they've rented in Emerald, and takes the slip she gives him for the picture line. She still hasn't even glanced at his face.

His turn at the camera comes, and a man with a narrow face and gray hair tells him to step up to the shoe marks and take off his dark glasses.

It'd already happened once when he got passport photos with Donna, and he feels stripped again, but he has no choice. Shades in his right hand, he looks straight at the red dot. After the flash he gets them back on before he can even see again.

The photograph, the hardest part, and it's over already. He knows two clerks' faces by heart, and neither has so much as glanced at him. Smooth as fine wine. Better yet, Panama Red.

Back in the Volvo he settles into the driver's seat and waits. Birds chatter high in a row of palms that remind him of the ones in front of his mother's house. At home in Leimert Park they would be sparrows, the nondescript brown ones he never could find in that bird book she always had lying around. He closes his eyes, enjoying their song.

The DMV. Today it seems efficient. Like when you arrive at the concentration camp and they lead you to the shower real fast, then hand you the soap and turn on the gas. He smiles. He could just hear Carolyn saying that.

The passenger door opens and a fat middle-aged man settles his bulk onto the seat. He's so close that James has no choice but to inspect all the broken veins that march over his cheeks, turning from red to purple as they arrive at the top of his bulbous nose. White man, of course. Lordy, as his Auntie would say. What terrible skin they have sometimes.

"Mr. Robert Johnson, correct?" Drill sergeant type.

"Yes, sir." Answer in kind.

"You ready, son?" Man sounds like a cracker.

"Yes, sir." No reason why Robert Johnson from Macon, Georgia, wouldn't say "sir" over and over, for safety's sake.

He lets the clutch out easy as pie, and they're on their way. He remembers to slow down to fifteen mph when they pass a school crosswalk, and the man scribbles on the clipboard that rests on the soft flesh of his pot belly. Chalk one up for Robert.

"Right at the next corner there," he says. "So how old are you, young man?"

Just his luck to pull the type who liked to interrogate. The personal question moves his body along on its familiar march through fear.

"Twenty-eight." Born in October, Robert Johnson's birthday hasn't arrived yet, fool. "Um. I mean twenty-seven."

"This your first license?" the man asks.

"Yes, sir," James answers. He executes the right turn, heart pounding like it might jump right out of his chest.

"Why haven't you had one before?"

"Lived in New York City after I was thirteen, sir. You take your life in your hands when you drive an automobile up there."

One more "sir" and he'd just about puke, but good to make common cause with the Southerner, and sure enough, the guy compresses his lips into a line about a yard wide that's supposed to pass for a smile.

"Just go on up there six more blocks and turn left," he orders. "You said you do what kind of work?"

James has said nothing of the sort, and why does this fool ask so many questions and he can almost hear the "boy" at the end of every one of them? Sweat pops out on his forehead.

"I'm in between jobs right now," he answers. He hears the birds clacking away again, but he stays focused, eyes straight ahead.

"What'd you do before?"

"I worked in a store."

"That what you did up there in New York City? Now you turn left at this here next block, okay?"

"Yes, sir." Yet another "sir," and he wishes he could cut his tongue out. But he guides Carolyn's Volvo right where that ofay sucker tells him to. Always have been a good driver, he tells himself. He'll do fine, just so long as that's the only thing being tested out here.

"Fixin' on settlin' down in these parts?" This man is never going to run out of questions. "Turn right at the corner."

"No sir, I'm not." Catch me dead, motherfucker, before I'd live in that sorry slum with the raggedy park bench. His mouth dry as a bone, he turns right.

"Where you gonna live, then?"

"Might head on down to Fresno."

Could all this be normal? In the days and nights since Freeman the cause of his terror had never been right next to him before. He wonders if fear has an odor, realizes yes, then prays the man wouldn't know to pick up on it.

"See that driveway on the left? That's where you'll do your turnaround."

"Yes, sir." Against his will, James says it again.

"Have your family down there in Fresno then?"

"My mother and my aunt live in East Fresno." The black part of town, he gets that part right. But how could he be so dumb as to say mother and aunt? If the man knew to look for Charles Brown, he'd listen for just that fact.

"No sisters and brothers?" Relentless.

"Oh yeah, I've got plenty. Scattered all over the country." All right 'til that "scattered" part. Too big a word for a colored boy.

"Now go on up there and parallel park. Use that space on the curb to the right."

James strains at the steering wheel. No power steering, and Carolyn's Volvo is heavy. Good. Gives him a reason to sweat.

"You been to school?" Oh Lordy. What does this fool want as an answer to this question?

"Yeah." James grunts with the effort and hits the curb. Scribble, scribble. Perspiration rolls down his ribs and soaks into his shirt.

"Try it again. Where'd you go to school?"

"Brooklyn High." He hopes there is one.

James pulls back out to start over, and pauses. He has to get one thing done, even if they're gonna arrest him in five minutes. Park this motherfuckin' car.

"College?"

"Never did get there." That would make the redneck feel better. The car slides into the place, thank God. Scribble scribble.

"Okay now, time to head back. Where'd this here foreign car come from, anyhow?"

"Belongs to a friend of mine," James says. "They make them in Sweden."

At last the guy is quiet as they cruise toward the DMV parking lot. No wind at all now. Everything looks hot, wilted, even though it's only March. He'd wanted this guy to shut up a minute ago, but by the third stop sign the silence is eerie. He turns into the DMV driveway, listening so hard for the inner workings of the examiner's mind he believes he can hear each tread of every tire. Why doesn't the motherfucker have anything to say now; why so quiet after all this time?

He pulls into a place at the far end of the parking lot, bumps the front wheel to the cement block guard with a soft expert touch, and switches off the motor. A white-crowned sparrow hops up onto a shrub branch right in front of him.

Now he's about to know. If the guy pulls out a police badge, he'll cut and run. Take his chances down that alley, between the buildings, stop the traffic on the next street, honking mixed with the sound of bullets, wild and crazy to the end.

While James concentrates on not moving a muscle, the man scrawls one last thing on his board, then hands him a thin, yellow piece of paper. A crisp slam of the car's door, and his tormentor is gone.

James examines the slip. Small black letters march across the front: "Temporary Driver's License." He gets out and waves in the direction of Carolyn's restaurant, then does a little jig, the skimpy paper held aloft like a flag won in war.

Carolyn rushes over, meets him on the sidewalk, and hugs him, which he allows even though it's foolish out here in the open. Mary Lou would never do that. Without a word they know he'll be the one to drive them home, and when they approach the entrance to 99, he guns the Volvo up the ramp and shoots out onto the highway's smooth pavement.

"Robert Johnson," he whoops. "Ready to roll!" He pumps a clenched fist out of the open window.

A hawk rises from a bare tree in the middle of a plowed field, angles toward the highway and away, its tail a flash of rufous against the gray sky. The wind has died yet again, this time leaving a solid bank of charcoal clouds massed on the horizon. The Volvo skims the road through air so still it feels like empty space.

"'Ain't gonna let nobody turn me around,'" James sings as he drives. "'Turn me around, turn me around . . .'" He belts the civil rights song out as if nothing has changed since those days of innocence.

"You're crazy!" Carolyn shouts at him, smiling. "A speeding ticket could still mess you up, James. For real."

"Robert Johnson can drive, and whenever he wants to, he'll be gone, whoosh, into the night!" James laughs as he weaves easily around lumbering semis and smaller cars, then slows down at once. It starts to drizzle.

"'Gonna keep on a'talkin', keep on a'walkin', walkin' 'til I get to Freedom Land." He gulps a breath, ready to start from the top again.

"Let's celebrate," Carolyn suggests. "Let's stop somewhere. Let's have a drink."

"Sure. Name the place, Curls." Mood he was in, he'd go anywhere. Fuck the Man and all his rules. Robert Johnson lived, and if he wanted to he could drive fast, he could be out in public with a white woman. Robert Johnson *lived.*

"You know what, James? Let's just go to Fresno." Carolyn was working on a plan. "Lay low for a few days. Hang out. Have fun."

"What about Mary Lou?" he asks. Can't have fun around here without my Mary Louise, he almost tells Carolyn.

"She's busy," Carolyn states.

"Naw, you can't leave, Carolyn." James says. "You got to do that striker work. You got to help her with that march of hers."

The red-tailed hawk is all the way to the horizon now, its broad circles leading far, far away. Rain begins a light tap steadily at the car roof. Time to get to Joseph Street. To Mary Lou.

"The march is not as important as keeping you safe," Carolyn insists.

"I'll be all right. I'm gonna get out of town soon, Curls, I promise you that, and I'll know the right time, too." He even pats her hand.

"Tell you what, though," he adds. "Let's go to a liquor store instead. That way Mary Lou—"

"She won't be home 'til late."

"—can have some. Whenever she gets there."

Water coats the windshield. No birds in the air now. Everyone has to find shelter.

"She goes to house meetings every single night at this point," Carolyn is saying. "She asks people to invite their friends and gets them to promise food and housing for the marchers. That's all she's thinking about these days."

"This weather must worry her to death," he comments. "It could really mess her march up from the get-go."

He wipes at the fogged-up windshield with his sleeve and settles the Volvo way below the limit. The wipers click away. Got to replace those blades. Stripes of water in arcs instead of clean glass. Need to see clearly now. He hums as they splash along. Nobody Knows the Trouble I've Seen.

"How many times you been out of the country, Curly?" he asks after awhile.

"God, let's see—Ghana with the Experiment in International Living after my first year in college."

"Ghana. Damn. That must have been nice."

"It was. Nkrumah was in power, so everyone was into socialism. They made us all work on building a community center. Old men with plumb lines, women breaking up little rocks with hammers for the cement."

"Where else?" he asks.

"Well, the next summer I went to Italy with my boyfriend. Then once I went to Israel with my friend Rachel after my marriage broke up. We stayed on a kibbutz and visited her aunt in Jerusalem. That was the only time I ever traveled with another woman. Plus I went to Mexico two years ago with a boyfriend. It was over so quick with him I'm embarrassed to add that trip to the list. How about you? Where all have you been?"

"Well, let me see now. There was that trip out to Westwood, when I went to UCLA." He chuckles, low.

"No, I'm serious."

"Hey girl, that was farther than you think. Whole other country for me at the time."

"But you traveled South, didn't you, during the civil rights years?"

"Naw, I knew enough about the South from when I was a kid. Stayed busy with CORE demonstrations in LA and then when the Panthers got bad I went on up to Oakland to check them out."

"Well, you're going to like it out of this country, James. Not everyone has America's limitations."

"What if you had to leave home for good, Curls?"

"That would be hard," she admits, and then she has to add detail. "Every once in a while, I'd be way out there and homesick and I'd realize that I really am an American, even though there's a lot I hate about this country. It's what I'm used to."

After that it's actually quiet until that first stoplight north of Mexico, as Carolyn tells him when they get there. He turns off into Allen and pulls in front of the liquor store on the town's tiny main street, drenched and deserted except for the one godforsaken little bar. Carolyn runs in to buy Tecate and tequila.

When they arrive at Joseph Street it's still pouring, just like the first time. The musty smell of wet wool greets them. Only mid-afternoon, nowhere near dark yet, but Mary Lou's blue coat is here, spread out to dry over the backs of two kitchen chairs.

James puts down the brown paper bag and watches carefully while Carolyn decides to retreat, listens as she announces her intent as always—that she'll change out of Mary Lou's city clothes and go back out to find Ramón and some strikers. All this stretched-out time, as she well knows, he can think of only one thing.

He tiptoes into the bedroom and sure enough, there she is. Mary Louise, her own fine self miraculously asleep on her bed. Under the spread, but not the sheets. Still dressed except with her wet shoes off. He sets down the suitcase that contains just about every material possession he has in the world and contemplates the reclining shape of the woman he loves. Who just might even love him back. The rain on the roof makes such a steady sound that it could always have been there.

"Hey, girl," he whispers, afraid of what might happen next, but desiring nothing else. "Hey, Mary Louise." He snaps on the small bedside lamp, and its shade glows like a warm little fire.

—⚊—

She drifts to the surface of her feverish dream, where the water level in the canal is rising, slow and steady, as if someone has unlocked the dam. Rojelio floats by, and Jensen is there, his truck roaring through the water and straight at her. She can't swim. She'll breathe in water. She'll drown. She feels so sick that she doesn't have the energy to be terrified. Every muscle aches. She turns her pounding head and forces her eyes open.

James is sitting on the edge of her bed, waving a little slip of yellow paper in front of her face. James. She didn't even know if she would ever see him again.

"What're you doing home so early?" he is asking her. "I'm back," he is telling her. "I got my license! I've been missing you."

She rubs her eyes and takes the document, then reaches for her Parliaments and lights one, so happy to find him here that her first instinct is she shouldn't let it show.

"Why aren't you at the office?" he asks. "You're always at the office. The march is about to start. What are you doing here?"

"I have a fever," she croaks. "And I keep feeling like I could throw up. Even Rojelio said I should go home." The first thing out of her mouth and it's definitely the wrong way to start. James's eyes glisten; he looks down and away.

"We like each other, *m'hija*," Rojelio had said to her after Carolyn left El Bucanero that night. "We work well together. It doesn't happen that often. Let's try again."

She'd been waiting for these exact words, and she'd believed she'd say yes. But when it'd been the time to nod her head, she shook it no instead. She'd been doing that ever since Carolyn brought this man to Joseph Street.

This man. When he left she refused to think about him, spent all her time worrying about the march. Now that he's sitting next to her right here on this bed all she wants is those beautiful brown eyes of his back on her face, which is so hot it must look bright red to him.

"We're not doing anything, me and Rojelio," she tells him.

"Well, then. Well, well, well." He chuckles a little, deep in his throat, and she smiles at him. "What can I get you, Ms. Mary Louise? You want a cool washcloth for your forehead? That was my mama's remedy for a fever."

"Sure," she tells him. "I'll take anything." She has to close her eyes again, just for this minute. She hears the water run, the cloth being wrung out, his footsteps coming back to her. She loves his smooth palm, cupping her forehead to test its heat, his elegant long fingers arranging the washcloth with its cool relief.

When she dares to look, his exquisite face with its broad nose and thick fluted lips floats above her, hovers attentively in the darkening room, and it's all she can focus on. Now that he's back she understands how much she has missed him. She worries already about what it'll be like when he leaves again.

"What about the rain?" she asks him, turning to what she knows best. "What if it doesn't stop? This march has got to leave from Delano on Monday. Everything else depends on that."

"We were thinking about that too, Curls and me . . ." He stops midsentence and reaches for her hand. One set of fingers interlocks with hers; his other cool palm strokes her arm, raising every tiny hair as it moves softly over her hot flesh. Not Curls and me, his gaze tells her. You, Mary Louise. You and me. It's as if he has spoken the words.

"Couldn't you postpone the march for a few days?" he is asking her. He understands what to talk about with her.

"Call off the press?" Her eyes are closed again. Sweet darkness, sweet touch. "Get the boycott offices to switch the publicity at the last minute? Can't be done."

"Well then, the weather will just have to clear up by Monday." His voice is low and lilting. "The people will walk no matter what. Through rain and wind and sleet and snow, and the press will come and the stories will flow." She doesn't look, but she knows he's smiling.

"They won't march," she tells him. "No one in their right mind would come out in this mess, including the press." It doesn't matter what she's saying; she has to smile too.

His hand leaves her body to reach the cigarette on the night table and snuff it out, then moves back to her neck and onto her cheek. They both hear the door slam. Carolyn leaving, to go find Ramón. Mary Lou opens her eyes enough to squint at the yellow slip still in her left hand, the side of her body he is not touching, not yet.

"What is this thing anyhow?" she asks him. He is still looking at her face and he will not look away. Embarrassed, expanded below the waist, wet and yearning, again she closes her eyes. She shifts. She wants to move herself toward him, she needs to.

"A driver's license," he whispers, staying still. Except for those fingers, twining, untwining, twining again. Except for that hand, touching her cheek, her shoulder, the length of her arm. "Robert Johnson's got wheels."

"That's good," she tells him, dropping the permit onto the far side of the bed. "I'm glad."

James reaches over her to reclaim the paper, and folds it back in his wallet. She knows this careful gesture about the next stage to come means he'll leave her when the time comes. He'll have to. Right now the time is ticking inexorably toward that moment.

Next he moves to put his body along the length of hers. His side of the bed. He takes the cloth off her forehead and kisses her.

"You could get sick," she murmurs. "I bet I'm catching."

"I'm glad you worry about me, Mary Louise," he mumbles. "Truly. That way I can leave it up to you."

Tongues slide inside mouths, clothes are shed by him then taken off her, skin is smooth and cool, blessedly cool, against skin, fingers rove lightly on delicate tissue, legs push urgently on legs and next he is inside her, which she has wanted already for a long long time and she is lost, she is disappearing, she is sweaty and moaning and gasping for breath. She is there for him after a time she cannot measure, and he for her the moment after.

More than taking anything, she is thinking as she lies there with him still blanketing her, he has gathered himself up and offered it to her as a gift, and she has done the same. He extricates his long limbs from hers, turns her on her side, and cradles her from behind.

How is it possible for them to be apart after all this, she wonders with a sinking heart, but now she has to sleep.

He must have dozed too, because by the next time he stirs against her it's pitch dark outside.

"Don't you need fluids?" he asks. "How about something to drink?" He's up on hands and knees, then off the bed and into his pants, while she can hardly move. She does, though, when he offers her lavender robe and helps her into it, leads her shaky self into the kitchen. He sits her down at her own Formica table and she looks at him from a hundred miles away.

"Orange juice?" he asks, looking in the fridge. But she hasn't had time to shop.

"Ice water is all."

She watches as he pops a beer and unscrews the cap on the tequila, all in slow motion.

"What'd I tell you, Mary Louise," he blurts as he pries the metal tray out of the ice-bound freezer. "The power of the people is greater than the Man's technology, just like Huey Newton said. We proved it today. We went on down there past all the pigs, past all the posters, and Robert Johnson got himself a *license*."

He gives the tray a sharp crack on the counter and cubes skitter over the surface, into the sink, onto the floor.

"What posters?" Mary Lou picks at the word.

"Oh, just pictures of yours truly on the post office wall." He's bent over, words muffled, getting the cold squares up in his hand. "Murder one, that's all." He throws them into the sink with a distant clatter.

"You mean a wanted poster?" He nods, sits down beside her, and swirls the ice in both the glasses. She covers his nervous fingers with her own warm hand. The tableau is in focus now, and she is calm. She likes being sick. A whole new personality. She knows he needs her.

"So what happens next?" she asks, not wanting to hear the answer.

"They'll mail the permanent license from Sacramento to the PO box," he tells her.

He pours two inches of liquor over his ice, water over hers, then lifts his glass. Mary Lou does the same.

"To friends," he says. Their glasses click and then he's on his feet, standing next to the window, searching the night with his eyes.

He bows, once to herself, again toward the kitchen door where Carolyn left, and finally to the north, where he's been with Donna and Bob, then downs his tequila in one gulp and chases it with the beer.

"We don't have much time, Mary Louise," he says, coming back to put his hand at the crook where her neck meets her shoulder. The touch makes her adjust and hollow out, to make just the right space. A shiver runs down her spine.

"I'm going to have to leave soon," he is telling her. "Very soon."

"I know that." She means it to sound firm, but her voice rasps and tears well up in her eyes.

"Come with me. We can live together in Cuba. You can teach me Spanish." He's sitting back down now, smiling at her, but he looks sad.

"I don't see how—" she starts.

"No, you're right," he says before she can add anything. "It wouldn't be fair to you."

"Maybe I want to come." Now she has to argue with him, to make sure he doesn't leave her behind. A wave of nausea sweeps through her.

"I would like that," he says, his forefinger tilting her chin so she can't do anything but look into his eyes. "More than you can possibly imagine."

It's so still they hear the ice cracking in the glasses.

"James, when you leave—"

"I might never be able to come back."

"And if I went—"

"I don't know if that would be true for you. You're not the one they're looking for."

"But I would be helping you get away."

"You've already done that," he reminds her. In a state of mind and body where she's foreign to herself she finds this funny, and giggles. The rain is soft against the roof, then more insistent, then soft again at once. Perhaps she can stay this way forever, alone with him in her small, warm kitchen, dark outside, quiet rain falling, time out of mind.

"Maybe we could ask a lawyer," he suggests. "Maybe Carolyn can find one to talk to, to see exactly what it would mean for you."

"Will they take you in Cuba?" Now she wants detail.

"I'm waiting to find that out."

"Will they take me?"

"Haven't even broached that one yet."

"To have to leave and never come back," she murmurs. She hasn't let herself think this through before. When you're sick, things are different, closer to the bone. They move closer together, not touching anymore.

"Well, I'm not gone yet." As if he has to assure her.

"No." She gives out a hoarse laugh that ends in a cough. "You just got here."

He takes her hand.

"Time for you to get back into bed, Mary Louise," he says.

"Come with me," she begs him in a voice she doesn't recognize. She wants nothing else but this.

"Where else would I go?" he asks. "Where you are is home for me now."

He picks up the glasses, clicks off the kitchen light, takes her arm, and guides them both back to their bed.

CHAPTER TWENTY-THREE

Ten days later, James was still here, and she was still driving him around like a fool, Carolyn thought. Of course he could use the permit, but they had both realized it was too risky. All he needed was to be stopped out here as Robert Johnson, and that could happen way too easily what with him being black.

The license had come a week and a day after he took the driving test, nestled in the Emerald post office box just like it was supposed to be. The only piece of mail ever sent there. She should've made sure there were other items sent to that box rented for just this purpose so the official envelope wouldn't be so conspicuous. Too late now.

So today they had already applied for Robert Johnson's passport, and it was in and out of the Fresno Federal Building like a charm. No wanted posters, he'd told her. No trembling when they took his picture. No problem at all, he'd assured her. Except for the fact that it was now seven whole days since the march had started out of Delano.

It was time for Robert Johnson to go. Leave town. Hide somewhere else until the passport came, then get out of the whole damned country.

But here he was, James Sweet, sitting right beside her in the Volvo, quiet as they watched the white clouds scud across the bright blue sky, and a hundred times more easy-going than he was on that first day. Must be all those hours with Mary Lou in the bedroom, while she was "sick."

"It could be a time just like this," Carolyn said.

"What do you mean by that?" he asked her even though he had to know.

"Everything's cool, the passport is on its way. The sun is out; the trees are in bloom. It'll be a day like this. You'll have almost forgotten, you'll be off your guard."

She looked over at him. She didn't have the heart for the next sentence about his getting caught.

All at once they saw it—a thin line of people across the highway, dwarfed by the vast fling of the Valley, inching its way north through the mud and the refuse at the side of the road. UFW flags, brazen in red and black, stood horizontal in the brisk breeze. A line of cars wiped it all from view, but then the walkers reappeared, heroic. Despite all the logistical problems, despite the rumors that Silveira and his thugs were going to intimidate anyone from showing up, the march was wending its way north toward Empire.

"*¡Que Viva!*" she shouted out the window, pressing on her horn.

"*¡Que Viva!*" A hundred fists shot into the air.

Unable to slow down with cars right behind them, they passed the whole thing in an instant.

"How many do you think there were?" she asked James. Goose bumps prickled her spine.

"Got to be at least a couple hundred." He craned his head back to see it again. "Not bad this far from Empire. Mary Louise is one fine organizer."

"This isn't her section," she reminded him. "It's out of Fresno, Aurelio's turf."

"And the whole thing was the headline in Fresno," he stated. "I saw the paper at the Federal Building, comparing it to that pilgrimage in '64. She'll be feeling good about that."

"James, why not take off now?" she pleaded with him. "Everything you need to do here is finished. It's the right time to say goodbye to Mary Lou, while her march unfolds. I could even lend you my car."

"Where would I go?" he asked.

"Anywhere. Far from here. Chicago, maybe." Carolyn picked the city where she had gone to college. "There's a huge black community there where you could wait for word from Donna and Bob. All it takes is you call when you get there and give a phone number in code, get a new post office box, and—"

"No one's come around," he muttered. They passed a cement truck, its double tank revolving. "I don't see where it's that different from before."

"No different, when the march will bring in cops from every county, reporters from the Bay Area, and lead them right through the center of Allen?"

"They won't come to Joseph Street, Carolyn, and you know I don't plan to attend the event."

His voice was so soft she could barely hear him. She remembered this from way back. The quieter he got, the more he wouldn't change his mind. She decided to shut up, and after awhile he settled back and closed his eyes to catch the sun's warmth on his face. She inched into the faster lane. God he was stubborn.

"And it rained," he intoned. "Forty days and forty nights, but when the rain ceased, the world was beautiful, and life began anew."

"You missed your calling," Carolyn said with a smile.

"Just what my auntie always told me. 'Ch—James, you're cut out to do the Lord's work, so don't you even think to stray from His path.'" He paused. "If we'd stayed down South I might've even gone into the church for real. She'd have loved that. My mama too."

"Must be hard not to be able to see your family."

"Early on it was worse. Now they're getting distant."

Carolyn wished she could say the same. Mona's voice was with her all the time. Agitated, worried, anxious about the risk with James, but then again angry with her too, whenever she considered leaving the rash couple to their fate. Desertion, after all, would be a dereliction of duty. Didn't Mona sacrifice everything, her daughter's need for attention, even her marriage, to see her work against McCarthy through to the end?

But if James got caught in Allen, all three of them would pay heavy dues. Did he even think about that? Great. In jail she would finally have the time to figure out her relationship with her dead mother, once and for all. Dead. The word was so stark.

When they arrived at Joseph Street, James put on coffee, made tuna sandwiches for each of them, and squared his newspapers at the table, prepared to settle into his afternoon alone. Carolyn wolfed down her food and gathered up her lists for yet another round of finding strikers.

Maybe Ramón would go with her, but most likely it would be Lupe instead. These days she only caught a glimpse of him now and then, racing in and out with Rojelio at the endless meetings on lining up food, microphones, speakers, housing, halls, churches. Intense, determined, mouth set in a line, eyes as hard as ebony, especially whenever the subject of Silveira and his gang of goons came up, Ramón wasn't exactly the nonviolent type, it seemed to Carolyn, though of course she'd never seen him with a weapon or anything like that. He sure was ready to focus on anything that was necessary, except for the two of them.

Each time they had sex it was a little better, so it couldn't be that. How many occasions? Five, to be exact. Okay, so they weren't going to be together for the rest of their life, but shouldn't all that mean she could count on his friendship at least? This, like everything else, seemed way out of her control.

She put all the papers in a manila folder and got her clipboard. Mary Lou used to have Rojelio, nicest of them all, she mused, right nearby every single day, and now she could care less. She, Carolyn, was always looking for Ramón, although since he was married the two of them would never get anywhere even if she did find him. James and Mary Lou, at great risk, found each other every single minute they could. Was it love or lust with them? What a mess.

—⁂—

James didn't dare say goodbye as Carolyn banged out of the house. She was irritated today, to say the least, and with good cause. But when Mary Lou walked in the kitchen door fifteen minutes later he put down his reading at once. Now here was something.

"Whatchou doin' here so early in the afternoon?" He took her in his arms and kissed her, which she barely tolerated.

"I could get used to this," he told her. "I could get used to this."

"I just got back from Sanger," she said.

She kicked off her shoes, padded through to Carolyn's living room, and curled into the one chair with the wide arms and the deep lap. She looked pale and exhausted.

"What's in Sanger?" he asked.

"The union clinic," she answered. There was a pause. "I had to get medical supplies for when the march comes through."

She stared at him as if she had never seen him before. She was so intent, it felt as if she were tracing his features with a pen. Sometimes he did not know what was going on between them at all. On his end all he was sure of was need. He didn't have his mama, his brother, his auntie, not a single friend, but he did have Mary Lou. She was his only life raft on a huge unknown ocean. All he wanted was to cling to her, and the only way he knew how was physical.

As for her, at times he was certain she was in love with him, and at other times he didn't even know whether she liked him. Today it seemed like both extremes were there at once. Yet gazing right at this woman was like examining a precious stone, new sides at every angle. He realized, as he had before, that he would take Mary Louise with him wherever he went, if only she would let him.

"So guess what we saw," he said when he couldn't stand the scrutiny any more. "We were drivin' back from Fresno, and—"

"Oh yeah, how'd the passport thing go?" she remembered to ask.

"Smooth as silk. Ought to arrive in the mail in ten days, two weeks at the most."

"And after that you'll really have to leave, won't you?"

This sounded like a challenge. In this living room it was completely quiet. He couldn't even hear the kitchen clock, and nothing from the outside.

"Well, that might be the right time," he started, not sure which way she wanted him to go. "Then again I still haven't heard from Donna and Bob, which means they haven't heard from the Cubans. Doesn't make too much sense to pull out of here until I know where I'm goin' now, does it?"

She gave out a little yawn at all that, leaned back in the chair, and closed her eyes like she could care less.

"But here is what I am trying to say, Mary Louise. We saw the march."

"You did?" That news made her sit up straight. "How big was it?"

"We went by so fast it was hard to tell."

"Not that many, then."

"But with the flags and all, the sun finally out, the whole thing looked fine, it truly did. Now that the rain's really gone, more will come."

"What time? Where was it?"

"Just north of Fresno. Eleven, eleven thirty."

"They were late. Aurelio said they'd start at eight."

"Hey now, with all the mud, he's lucky he got the operation on the road at all. What I'm telling you is that your march was downright beautiful. Like you."

He leaned over to kiss her again, but she pulled away. Then she moved back to meet his lips as if she was gonna get into it, and then, all of a sudden, there was someone at the front door.

No knock, no sound, a person peering around to look through a gap in the curtains. This didn't happen here; everyone Mary Lou knew came to the kitchen. He tried a quick retreat to the bedroom, but the door opened and a woman with waist-long black hair walked right in like she lived there. Had they been stupid and left it unlocked?

"Jeez, Carmen, you scared me half to death." Mary Lou's hand was at her heart.

"You gave me a key last summer, remember? No one knew if you were back yet, but they need you at the office."

Carmen stepped right up to James and proffered a slim, brown hand.

"I don't believe we've met," she said.

A pulse jumped in his neck, out of control. He would always be afraid of strangers from now on. He managed to shake Carmen's hand, then found it difficult not to get caught in her green-eyed gaze. Her beauty was like a cold wave surging into every corner of the room.

"This is James, Carolyn's friend from the city." Mary Lou spoke so slowly it were if she was underwater. "The one with hepatitis. You must have heard."

Her curtain of hair undulated as she put down the Guatemalan bag that matched her jacket on Carolyn's sofa bed, then glided into the kitchen. Dumbly, they both followed her. As if the place belonged to her, she rummaged for beer, found the usual Tecates, and brought them to the table.

"Did you get those supplies, Mary Lou?" she asked.

"What? Yeah, sure. Dr. Dan had the first-aid kits all made up." Mary Lou shook her head no to the offer of beer.

"Aurelio called the office," Carmen said. "This march is big. Over two hundred this morning, and at least a hundred more joined during the day. They're just about to stop for the night."

"That's great!" Mary Lou said. James murmured his assent.

"Cesar told me to report directly to him about the size of the march, every day," Carmen continued. "He's going to like this. If the weather holds, by Saturday morning in Empire you'll have thousands."

She popped the lid off her own can and slid another across the table to James.

"No thanks," he told her. "Got to excuse myself. Doctor said not to drink, and I need my rest."

He sounded foolish, but he knew his role. With a gentle click he closed the hall door behind himself, then stayed right there to listen in on them.

"Your friend is cute," said Carmen.

"Carolyn's friend," corrected Mary Lou. She was running water in the kitchen sink.

"Where's he from?"

"LA. Carolyn's known him for years."

"Is he as nice as he looks?"

"I guess so. He's got hepatitis, so he keeps to himself. He's real contagious."

"Lucky for me I'm the healthy type. I never catch things." The water stopped. An aimless cricket sounded outside, early in the day and out of season both.

This foxy lady was dangerous, thought James. About as likely to respect Carolyn's territory as the real animal would be to lay off a chicken coop. Too bad there was no way Mary Lou could claim him as hers. Carmen just might respect that.

"Tell you what," Carmen was saying. "Let's get shit done at the office, and later I told Hank and Rojelio we would eat dinner with them. Jovita's, seven thirty."

"So Hank finally got here?"

"Came in at eleven and already he's got two new phone lines in at the office. One to call out from and the other for reporters to call in. I'm not quite used to the wheelchair yet, but he seems to be."

"What a shame about his accident," Mary Lou said. "God, can you imagine getting hit by one of those trucks? Everyone's worst nightmare out here."

The women were rustling around, maybe getting a snack together.

"His own fault," Carmen said. "Apparently he was drunk."

"Yeah, but it was after a fight with his wife. Could happen to anyone."

"Not to me," said Carmen.

Surely not, thought James. The second time in two minutes that the lady with the long black hair claimed immunity. Too perfect for any faults. The worst kind.

Mary Lou went to get her coat, and James waylaid her in the bedroom.

"Who is that woman?" he whispered, hulking over her.

"Friend of the Chavez family. Hard worker."

"Does she always take over like that?"

"Yeah. She does." Mary Lou moved away as if she wanted nothing to do with him.

"She's scary." He followed her over to the closet. "Who else has a key to this place?"

"I can't remember. I gave some out last summer." She seemed to think nothing of it, but this was startling news.

"I'll take her to the office," Mary Lou was telling him. "By the time we're through there, she'll have so much to do she'll forget all about you."

This was said all business, yet the next second Mary Lou sagged against him in a new way.

"Dang, James." She laid her head along his chest and closed her eyes. "I haven't ever been this tired before."

"Get Carmen out of here," he told her, even as he untangled a strand of her fine blonde hair. This was too crazy. Carolyn was right. He had to go, and soon. Yet even now he could feel his need for Mary Lou tug at his body.

"And get that key back from her," he added. "Please!"

Mary Lou nodded and went back in the kitchen. He just about held his breath until he heard the two women leave, then expelled it all in a rush.

The march was making it more crowded around here, but hadn't Mary Lou promised to keep people away from Joseph Street? He could leave, sure, by himself, go thousands of miles from home, brood on the circumstances, and wait it out alone. But if they just made it through this march, maybe he could convince his own Mary Louise to come on out there with him. Of course she should say no, he had less than nothing to offer her, but then again, she just might say yes. Stranger things had happened. He went back to his newspapers to calm himself down.

—⚇—

Two hours later Carolyn came flying through the kitchen door, up-set, agitated, worried, every word for scared she could think of. Calm down, she told herself.

"You've got to leave, James, right now," she said to him. "There's about to be a meeting here, in this house!"

"What?" She had gotten his attention, for sure.

"The leaders came to the office after the march was over for the day. Then Jack Marsh limps all around the place and eventually says 'We gotta have a meeting and it's gonna be at your house, Mary Lou, 'cause after four days walking I need to soak my goddamned feet!'"

"What's wrong with where he's staying?" James asked.

"He's on someone's couch, James. This union is completely cheapskate, remember? And Jack is not the kind of guy gives you a choice."

"Mary Lou has got to say no!"

"I was right there, I heard the whole thing. She couldn't think of any way to turn him down."

James looked completely immobilized.

"They're coming right after dinner, any minute now," she said to him. "Take my car. Get out of here!"

"Where should I go?"

"Anyplace but here."

"When should I come back?"

"You shouldn't."

"But you'll need your car."

Of course he would reach for the one thing she didn't have an answer for, just to prolong his time with Mary Lou. With just about every UFW leader but Cesar Chavez on the way to this house, he looked panicked, like he was about to drown. And he still couldn't make himself leave. But Carolyn did need her car tomorrow. And he hadn't packed. They hadn't figured out how they would stay in contact, settled on any of the endless details that always took forever.

"Stay away until at least eleven," she said. Relief spread over his face. "When you get back, remember to check if any cars are parked here except Mary Lou's and mine. I'll make sure all your stuff is out of sight."

"No," he said. "They know I'm here. But take everything out of Mary Lou's bedroom and put your own things back in there."

Carolyn flushed, yet of course he was right. It wouldn't do for anyone to realize who was sharing Mary Lou's bed.

"Okay, okay," she said, in a panic. "But get going. They could be here anytime."

"What will you say if they ask where I am?"

"We'll come up with something. Just go!"

He put on old tennis shoes and a sweater under his sports jacket, and fled.

An hour later Mary Lou had stoked up water on the stove in her largest pot and filled the teapot, too. Steam fogged the windows, and the Joseph Street kitchen seemed like a boat at sea. It turned out all the leaders from the other offices wanted to soak their feet. Carolyn stood in the doorway, chuckling at the sight they made in Mary Lou's living room.

Aurelio, a beefy young guy with black hair matted into damp curls on his sweaty forehead, tried to settle his bulk onto one of the narrow kitchen chairs, wincing as Mary Lou poured hot water from her teapot into the dishpan at his feet.

"*¡Ayi, chinga la madre!*"

"Want me to stop?"

"Oh no," he said between gritted teeth. "No no, not at all." He exhaled and grinned. "The more pain the faster the cure, *¿qué no?*"

Teófilo, small, wiry, and twenty years older, sporting an elaborate mustache he loved to touch, sat in a wheelchair that was too large for him, a dishtowel spread over his knees. When Mary Lou approached with her teapot he stopped examining a lobster-red foot, took a blue and white bandanna from around his neck, and draped it over his head.

"*Venga, m'hija.*" Transformed into an old woman, he winked and crooked a finger at her, then pointed to his own pot, not yet full.

"*Dámelo, dámelo mas.* Lay it on me, baby, more, more. Oooh, that feels so good!"

Everyone laughed out loud at his accented hippie English. Except for Jack Marsh, a pale man of indeterminate age whose homely creased face made him hard to forget. Barely able to move his flabby body on his swollen bandaged feet, he was irritated and paced in slow, elongated circles behind the others.

"You should sit down, Jack," said Mary Lou as he hobbled toward the sofa. "You look like you've walked enough for one day."

"I sat plenty at Jovita's," he growled.

They both reached simultaneously for Mary Lou's Parliaments on the coffee table, then courtesy won out. She made it clear he could have one, he tapped it out for her first, lit it, and watched her take a drag. After he had fired up his own, he resumed his restless limping walk.

"Let's get the show on the road," he grumbled. Mary Lou got up to empty an ashtray.

"How about Hank?" she asked.

"He's tired," said Jack. "Let him sleep."

"Must be hard on him," said Carolyn.

"Nah, he's in his element," said Jack. "Probably happier here feeding his line to reporters than he's been ever since he ran into that semi." The other three nodded in agreement.

"Okay now," Marsh continued. "We're gonna start the rallies tomorrow after dinner and every night after that, work up the pitch for Saturday. We've got ours arranged for Emerald, but the next one's gonna have to be in Carleton, and Cesar wants a press conference there. So you gotta set it up between dinner and the program, Mary Lou, six thirty or seven on Thursday, and be ready to answer the questions."

"I can't do it. You guys will have to handle things. I have a house meeting."

"Well cancel the goddamned thing!" Marsh bellowed.

Teófilo and Aurelio exchanged covert smiles and sat back to watch the fireworks.

"Listen to me, Jack Marsh," Mary Lou said. "You can boss people around in Delano, but this is Allen. Carleton's right north of here, in case you forgot that. You don't give the orders in my territory." She stopped to take a breath.

"Ramón arranged the meeting with the Portuguese strikers," she continued. "They're on the 'no' list, 'cause they're scared. Maybe I can change their minds. You know how important Cesar thinks house meetings are. You don't just back out 'cause there's something else to do."

Carolyn heard it all from her doorway. Ramón should have told her about this plan; she was the one in charge of the strikers. The Portuguese workers who said no were hopeless; they would take up Mary Lou's whole Thursday night and still not come out on Saturday.

"You have to change the plans," Jack shouted at Mary Lou. "If you're the leader here, then goddamn it, you gotta handle the press! Where the hell is your head nowadays, anyhow? You even got some guy staying here in this house who doesn't do shit for the Union. That's no way to show leadership!"

Carolyn thought she saw both Aurelio and Teófilo nod at this, as though it had been discussed beforehand.

"Look, Jack," Mary Lou spoke through clenched teeth. "Cesar's the only one who can tell me what to do."

"So I'll get Cesar to tell you. I'll call him up." Jack nodded in the direction of the phone but made no move except to light another cigarette off his first one.

Suddenly Hank swung in from the hall to the bedroom, powerful forearms resting on the metal crutches needed to support his shrunken legs. A dapper gray beard couldn't cover the lines of pain that framed his light blue watery eyes, and he looked older than everyone else in the room.

"How about wheelin' my cart over for me, Teófilo," he said. "For some reason I ain't got too much energy tonight."

Hank's way of talking was even more white bread than Jack's, thought Carolyn. She wondered how Aurelio and Teófilo felt about there being so much anglo leadership in this Union. Teófilo jumped right up, ashamed to be caught in comfort he didn't deserve, and hurried the chair across the room, saying he was sorry.

"Don't you worry about a thing. Everyone should try it out once in a while, see how nice it is not to have to walk." The weak joke made, Hank eased himself into the wheelchair with a quiet sigh.

"So I was just lyin' in there readin' my newspaper 'cause I had trouble sleepin', and then I hear all this fuss out here. What's the big problem?"

Teófilo dried his feet and started to get back into his thin socks and scuffed black shoes. Aurelio felt around for his own beat-up tennis shoes that lay behind his chair. Jack continued to pace and puff on his cigarette. No one answered Hank's question.

Suddenly the room seemed damp without warmth, and everything smelled like old socks.

"How come you're not soaking your feet?" Hank asked Jack, nodding toward one of the foot pans.

"'Cause I don't feel like it, and I got to ride tomorrow anyhow in that van we got set up for water and first aid. The doc says it's worse than blisters, and I shouldn't walk for a couple of days."

"He can't walk," Teófilo commented to Mary Lou softly in Spanish. "But he walks all the time."

"Now why can't we compromise this thing?" asked Hank. "Any reason not to have that press conference the morning after, when the march starts up? Get all the flags there, have a guy with a collar say mass. He can tell how the Colonia brothers will never squeeze through the eye of that needle the way they're goin', remind everyone the meek shall inherit the earth. The press'll eat it up."

Carolyn was sure Teófilo and Aurelio would look offended at this cavalier way of talking about a priest, but both had shifted into an impassive mode she couldn't read at all.

"Mary Lou, honey," Hank asked her. "Could you just find me that little pillow I left on your bed? I need it for my chair here."

"I'll get it," said Carolyn. She had just noticed that her own photograph of Mona, placed right where she could check it every night before she dropped off to sleep, was still on the little table by the couch. She started toward the group of men to snatch up this evidence of who slept where, thought better of it, then retreated to the bedroom, listing in her mind where she had put everything else. By the time she got the pillow and reappeared to tuck it behind Hank's back, the conversation had switched to the program for the Carleton rally.

After fifteen more minutes of who was going to do what, with the press conference issue still unresolved as far as Carolyn could tell, Hank stated that he was ready to go. He leaned on his crutches, pillow tucked under his arm, while Aurelio folded up the wheelchair and took it out to load into the trunk of the car.

"Mary Lou." He waited to speak until the other men were outside. "Didn't I hear tell you had someone staying in this place with you?"

"You mean Carolyn?" Mary Lou asked.

It seemed so ridiculous for Mary Lou to say that with her right here in the room that Carolyn wanted to giggle and cry both.

"No, a third person," pressed Hank. "A man. Negro man, I believe."

"Oh yeah. James," Mary Lou said. "He's Carolyn's friend. He's been sick, so he's resting here."

Carolyn cleared her throat, trying to work some moisture into her dry mouth so she could answer questions if she had to.

"James what?" Hank asked Mary Lou.

"James Sweet."

"And where is this James Sweet this evening?"

"He went out. Said he wanted to get some fresh air, he'd been cooped up too long."

Hank nodded good night, got down the kitchen steps and into the car with a personal struggle that seemed to take forever. Jack kicked the motor into life, and all four of them were around the corner and gone.

The women had worried over the whole evening in detail and were just starting to calm down when another automobile pulled up to the curb outside the Joseph Street kitchen.

Carolyn went to the window expecting James, but it was Rojelio, who took the two stairs in a bound, gave a sharp rap at the door, and then recoiled when it opened to both women at once.

"What in the world are you doing here?" asked Mary Lou.

Her certainty that he wasn't expected also told him he wasn't welcome. Carolyn remembered last summer when the ongoing crisis of the strike meant that anyone and everyone came over to Joseph Street whenever they wanted to. She could see that this hurt.

"And why weren't you at the meeting, anyhow?" Mary Lou asked him.

"You're mad that I've come and mad that I missed the meeting, both at once," he answered. "You're not making much sense these days, Mary Lou."

"Well?" she demanded. "What happened?"

"The women came to the office to sew the flags, remember? But only one brought a sewing machine, so I kept the others busy cutting out striker badges for Saturday. Then I closed up the office. Is that okay with you?"

Impatient, Mary Lou strode to the thermostat in the living room and snapped the heat on.

"All right, it's fine," she said.

"The women were worried. It's Silveira. They're scared their men are going to get hurt. They say *la placa* won't do anything."

"When we get to Empire there's gonna be all sorts of Bay Area types there," Mary Lou answered.

"The police know they'll be scrutinized from outside the Valley," Carolyn added. "That ought to keep them on their good behavior. We hope."

"I can't think of anything to do about it tonight," Mary Lou finished up. "I've got to get some sleep."

"Not so easy in the Muñoz living room," Rojelio said. "I have to wait 'til everyone else has gone to bed."

He had never been one to complain before, Carolyn thought. Then again, he always had his own place to sleep last summer, and it had been here with Mary Lou.

"Ramón told me," Mary Lou said. "He suggested you should move into the Punjabi, stay with him. Cesar says it's okay; the Union will spring for the motel from now on."

Ramón again. Busy man. Talked to everyone but her, Carolyn realized, even about the fact that apparently Rojelio would occupy her half of his double bed from now on.

"Yeah, well that's news to me," Rojelio was saying. "Good. I'll take my things there tomorrow."

He came into the kitchen and sat down at the familiar table looking pained, as though he remembered every single meal he had eaten at it. Carolyn wished she could offer him a beer, but they both wanted him out of there before James returned.

"Listen to me, Mary Lou," he said. "Just now I was coming out of the office, late at night, you know? Well Jensen glides up behind me in his huge black Buick, so quiet I didn't even hear him."

"Jensen?" she asked. "What was Jensen doing there?"

"That's what I'm telling you. He said we're on the news too much, that we have to cancel the march, and this was a warning. That's what he called it, a warning."

"What does he mean?" Carolyn asked.

"I don't know," he answered. "I'm worried it's connected to the Silveira thing. Maybe we should call Cesar tomorrow."

"Nah. Jensen said something like that to me once, too." Mary Lou yawned and got to her feet. "I told Jack about it and he said ignore it. It's late. I need sleep." She left the kitchen and went toward her room.

Rojelio's face burned with humiliation at the rude dismissal.

"That's not like her," Carolyn said, surprised. "She knows it's serious, she's just beat. She's been sick."

"Where's your friend?" Rojelio worked hard to conceal his emotion. "The black man."

She couldn't believe it. Jack mentioned James, Hank asked about him, and here it was all over again.

"James?" She knew she sounded stupid.

Now surely even James would agree that it was time to leave. She would insist that they make their plan as soon as he walked in the door. He should stay somewhere else, starting tonight.

"Yeah, James," Rojelio said. "Has he gone back home or what?"

"No, he's still around."

"What's he doing here? Why doesn't he help out?"

"He's sick, and he's weak. He sleeps all the time, like right at this moment he's already down for the count, in the living room."

So now something different was coming out of her mouth to Rojelio than Mary Lou had said to Hank. All the little lies to aid the main falsehood, proliferating out of control.

"Yeah. Well, it's late. I guess we all need sleep."

Rojelio's voice was laced with sarcasm as he parroted the household line he had already heard twice, but at least he left, brakes squealing as he rounded the corner onto Eighth Street. Carolyn realized then that the light was still on in that very living room where she had claimed James was asleep. Okay, okay, so the next time she spoke to Rojelio she would have to squeeze in the fact that James liked a light burning at night. Awkward, but she would find a way.

"Tell no lies, claim no easy victories." The last half was no problem, she realized, but the first part was impossible.

CHAPTER TWENTY-FOUR

Mary Lou was sitting on her green living room couch. She ran a palm over its brushy texture for comfort. She had bought this fancy sofa at Goodwill for cheap. She loved it. Just like the chair that faced her, with its arms wide enough to hold a coffee cup and book. She loved them both.

"I thought you were going to bed?" Carolyn asked, barreling into the living room.

"I could never sleep with all this going on." Mary Lou waved a hand as if to take in the whole house, then stared at her poster with the old couple facing forward, eternal in their plea to boycott Colonia wine.

"I told Rojelio that James was down for the night in here," Carolyn said. "And then I realized the light was still on."

Mary Lou didn't want to answer. Why was Carolyn always focused on tiny details when far more was at stake?

"I'm worried he'll know I'm lying."

"Rojelio might sympathize with James, even if he figured it all out," Mary Lou said after a pause. "Rojelio's militant. People don't know that, but he is." To herself she sounded like a tired old woman.

"When do I get to fold out my bed?" Carolyn demanded. "It's cold in here. Why did you turn off the heat?" She strode over to the thermostat on the wall and snapped its plastic lever to the top. The pilot light ripped on with a shudder. Mary Lou's heating bill had skyrocketed with these two here. The Union paid for the house and the cost was sure to be noticed. Still, she could not move, let alone argue. The heat felt good.

"Rojelio is like a puppy that's been kicked," Carolyn said. "How could you act so mean to him? He's gonna get pissed. It's dangerous!"

"I'm practical, Carolyn," Mary Lou told her. "I had to get him out of here. But I am not hard-hearted."

Carolyn looked angry, but who had gotten Mary Lou into this mess anyhow? The woman with the dark curly hair who was glaring at her, that's who.

Mary Lou punched at the couch cushion aimlessly.

"Don't you say a word to Rojelio," she warned Carolyn. "You've got a way of blurting things out."

"Are you crazy? Who's been the careful one around here?"

"Rojelio's Mexican," Mary Lou continued. "If he finds out about me and James, his pride will be involved. That'll be a whole other story."

"So now all Mexican men are alike? Think about it, Mary Lou. Too many people are asking questions. You have got to make James leave!"

Mary Lou's eyes filled with tears that Carolyn—stripping off jeans and getting into T-shirt and flannel pajama bottoms—either didn't see or didn't care about.

"I'm doing the best I can with a difficult situation here, Carolyn," Mary Lou said, wiping her cheeks with the backs of both hands.

"You used to tell me and James that this was not safe," Carolyn answered. "Now the march is all around us and you've changed your mind?"

Mary Lou's stomach began the familiar queasy flips, eddies swirling backward. She was not the type to show how upset she was to others, but now she was barely able to contain herself. Did Carolyn care about her at all?

"No one's stopped at the house for a long time," Mary Lou muttered.

"Until today," said Carolyn. "When it's been Hank, Jack, Aurelio, Teófilo, Rojelio—"

"And Carmen," Mary Lou added. "I get the point."

"Carmen came too?" Carolyn sat down at the other end of the couch and put her face in her hands.

Mary Lou rubbed her eyes. "Yeah, I'm worried about James staying in this house. But I'm even more worried about what happens when James leaves."

"And what about the marchers?" Carolyn said. "They're coming through Allen in two days! Doesn't it look weird that we don't let anyone stay here when everyone has to double up in all the other houses?"

"I haven't thought about that yet."

Mary Lou was aware of herself hiding behind her own long hair. Taffy-colored—that's what the adults called it when she was little. Taffy that swirled in browns and blondes and whites between her and everything else when she wanted it to. She shook her head so she could watch the ends of it dance. She had never tried an illegal drug in her life, but she felt like she was high on something.

"We have got to get him out of here," Carolyn kept saying like a broken record.

"Have you seen Patsy lately?"

"No, why? Is she digging around about James too?"

"She's gotten big. No way to hide it now."

"Is she staying out of public? Is she ashamed of it?" Carolyn was distracted from the subject of James needing to leave. Good.

"Hell no, why should she be?" Good old wholesome Mary Lou never swore, so the one four-letter word got her friend's attention. "It's on Chuey Vargas's head, not Patsy's," she added weakly. "She'll take good care of that child."

The two women heard a car turn around the corner from Fourth Avenue. The thick maroon living room curtains were drawn tight and kept out the glare of the passing headlights. It didn't stop; it wasn't James. And it didn't slow down; it wasn't Rojelio. Or Silveira. Or Jensen. Or the cops.

"Do they even know where James will end up yet?" Mary Lou asked. "How about this Quincy guy? Has he figured anything out?"

Carolyn's face was like a cartoon in slow motion as she prepared another explanation for why everything took so long, then registered shock at the tears streaming down her friend's cheeks.

"I'm pregnant," Mary Lou told her. "I got a test in Sanger today."

"I cannot believe this!"

Mary Lou's nausea returned in force. Her stomach writhing like a fish sliding over rocks, she dug an old tissue out of her jeans and held it over her mouth to stave off an intense need to retch.

Carolyn was on her feet, striding back and forth in front of the couch. "If it's just missing your period, I've read that stress alone is enough to make that happen."

"Carolyn, I got a test. They give you the results the same day."

Mary Lou yanked saltines she'd saved from Jovita's out of her jacket pocket, fingers shaking so hard she had a difficult time pulling the red cellophane strip, and stuffed one between dry lips.

Carolyn watched it all.

"Didn't you use birth control?" she demanded.

"No."

The tiny syllable lay there.

"And why not, if I might ask?"

"I never got pregnant with Rojelio." Even when I wanted to, thought Mary Lou for the thousandth time. Even when I tried.

"But Mary Lou! That could have been because of him!" Carolyn actually shook a finger in her face.

Mary Lou knew all this. She didn't have to be lectured like she was still in school. She sat with her head down, afraid to move. The sense that she would vomit subsided.

Why in the world hadn't she used anything? She just didn't think. She was out of the habit. She wanted a baby. She couldn't speak. All she could do was run her hand over that rough raised pattern of her couch, again and again.

"What are you going to do?" Carolyn shifted gears.

"I don't know."

Carolyn stopped pacing and plopped down in the big chair. She laid her head back and draped her arms over its broad sides. Now the room was too warm, but Mary Lou still lacked the energy to do anything about it. "This is awful," Carolyn said. "What a mess!"

"Babies aren't awful," Mary Lou whispered. Maybe she was talking to herself instead of aloud, since Carolyn didn't react. Mary Lou counted the paisley swirls in her cushion. "A baby's not awful, is it? A baby's a gift."

"Have you told James?"

"No."

"Are you going to?"

"I don't know."

Carolyn's questions were like bullets from a machine gun. Mary Lou twirled a piece of hair, then chewed on it. "Do you think he could live out here? Once the march is over?" She lifted her head to see Carolyn's reaction.

"Just work in the Foster Chicken sheds, raise his little family?" Carolyn's blue eyes focused on her target. "You aren't thinking straight, Mary Louise. Sooner or later he'll be recognized. If it hasn't happened already, that is."

"Then why can't he go for a little while and then come back? After things calm down a little."

"Yeah, sure. After ten years or so."

"So maybe I should go with him?"

"Bring up a baby on the run, underground? In Cuba maybe, or Prague? Leave everything you know, and worry for the rest of your life—the baby's life—about being caught? People have done it, I guess, but it doesn't seem your style."

Mary Lou gulped a couple of deep breaths and ate another cracker. Enough of this lecture from Ms. Rationality, who sounded like she never made mistakes. Two could play this game.

"Then again, Carolyn, who'd have ever guessed that your style was to sleep with a married man?"

Sure enough, when Carolyn spoke again, it was in a voice soft with chagrin.

"Who told you that?"

"Haven't you ever read women's magazines? Don't you realize that office romances are never secret?"

"Who else knows about it?"

"Anyone whose eyes are open. Anyone smart enough to look. You're always trying to find Ramón, Carolyn."

"But you haven't heard about it from someone else?"

"Nah, and I won't. I know his wife, and people aren't gonna talk to me about it 'cause it'd put me in a bad position with Catalina. That's why these guys can have whole second families for cripes sake. Everyone lets the first wife pretend she doesn't know a thing. It's how it works, don't you know that?"

For a moment the room was completely still. Mary Lou listened for what was missing. The soft tick of the clock in the kitchen, where the women spent most of their time.

"I try to find Ramón?" From her seat in the corner, palms clasping the wooden ends on both arms of her spacious chair, Carolyn talked to herself as much as Mary Lou. "And he tries not to be found. God, poor Catalina."

"Not necessarily, Carolyn. She's got the kids. Poor you, might be more like it."

"And poor you."

"Not to mention Ja—"

"And poor James."

They laughed at the way their voices came in together. Sappy, like the violins in an orchestra. Then once they started they couldn't stop and they howled until both their faces shone wet with tears, mucous, hysteria. Why blame the other when each of them had done everything possible to screw up her own life?

—⚏—

Only Mary Lou's car was there, and it was three in the morning. Lights were still on in all the rooms. James pulled up cautiously.

He turned the ignition off and waited while Carolyn's Volvo shook and coughed and finally died down.

"That car is sick," he said when he found them both at the kitchen door. "That automobile has a disease. Hepatitis, I believe."

"Dang, James, it's late!" Mary Lou actually sounded worried about him.

"We've been concerned," Carolyn chimed in. "About you. About everything. Where were you?"

The three of them stood in the middle of the small room. The clock on the wall ticked the lateness of the hour. He warmed his hands in the heat from the furnace vent. Above the table the same old poster shone in the fluorescent glare with its Spanish slogan underneath. The lady farmworker bent over the seedling. The land belonged to her because she worked it, thought James. His life belonged to him because he insisted it was his.

"Hey now, you two," he said with a smile. "Didn't I have to get out of here in one hot second so you all could have your meeting, and now you're telling me I stayed away too long?"

"God, that seems like a year ago already," Carolyn said.

They settled into their usual places around the chrome-bound table. The room was warm; the counters were clean; the dishes lay in their rubber rack. This was what he'd remember after he left, he told himself. The way they fit so well together in this kitchen. Everywhere else they each had their own turf, even if his was only one side of Mary Lou's bed and the space between it and the wall. But this kitchen was where they lived as family.

"I went up into those Sierra foothills," he told them. "Once I got out of this house it felt so good to drive. That car of yours just hummed around those curves, Curls, and I was all alone on the road. I pulled up in a place I thought I knew from one time right after I got the license. I wanted to see how all that springtime green looked under the light of the full moon."

He watched Mary Lou get up and go over to the window to pick at the crisp frill that lined her gauzy curtain, not solid enough, not heavy like the living room curtains. What if the cops drove by, he wondered for the thousandth time. What if they saw him through the window that was just about even with his eyes? As always, he set that fear aside.

"It was completely bright outside," he continued. "But it was that moonlight sort of a thing where if you put your foot down without thinking you'd find your ankle twisted in a gopher hole. Which is exactly what I did—but I was okay."

Carolyn looked alarmed.

"After that I slowed down," he said to her.

"Walking step by step like that made me realize everything was just downright beautiful up there. No walls around me, no visitors to find me, no need to listen and jump at every tiny little sound."

"Did you trespass?" Carolyn asked.

"Sure did, Curls, sure did."

"Isn't that dangerous?" she admonished him. "Maybe I'm up-tight, but couldn't you have figured out something else? Driven to Fresno maybe, gone to a movie?"

"Since when is it so difficult to get yourself in between a couple of strands of barbed wire?" James asked her. "And who's gonna be way out there with a shotgun in the middle of the night? You know, I heard the more you walk in the dark the better your night vision is, and after tonight I believe that's true."

"What in the world are you talking about?" Mary Lou asked, staring at her curtain. She sounded impatient and amused at once.

"For once I had a clear head," he said. "I realized life didn't get much better than this, even back when I was legal. I walked and I thought, and I talked to myself I'm sure. Eventually I came to some hard truths."

He lit a cigarette, offered it to Mary Lou, and when she shook her head, still not looking at him, he took it for himself.

"I turned a corner around a hill and I found a waterfall," he continued. "It was like a long ribbon made of silver silk. There was actually a rock so I could walk in behind it and see the moon through the spray. I hunkered down there. Didn't move a muscle for a long time. By the time I got up, my knees were stiff, but I knew more. I had become wiser, I swear."

James took a deep drag off his cigarette, held his breath and stared at the burning tip, then expelled the smoke in a rush.

"You know how I've always said that motherfucker Kwesi set me up, but not Nyame? Not my man, he wouldn't do such a thing, right? He was too pure, too good. Well, Nyame must have known the plan. Shit, he must have made the plan."

He wasn't even looking at the women anymore. He didn't care what they thought, because finally he knew what *he* thought. He stubbed the half-smoked butt out with three quick jabs.

"'Use whatever money you need to get the plastique,' he must have said to Kwesi. 'Though don't tell any of those white liberals who gave you the money, mind you, don't even think to bring one of them into this. Pay off a pig or two, then get me a brother. Find me the sucker who will do whatever you say. Hand him a briefcase right before he comes in. Make sure he's embarrassed to look through it with you there. Get me some poor little black-ass fool to bring in what I need to blow my way out of this place.'"

His left calf cramped suddenly, as if he was on his haunches behind the waterfall again. Rubbing at it, trying not to cry out in distress, James got up and limped around the women to empty his ashtray.

"And that sucker was me," he sighed as the pain ebbed. "The original true believer, perfect for the setup."

Carefully he washed and dried the ashtray, his back to the women so they wouldn't see his face.

"It might not have been that way," Carolyn said. "Nyame might have just told Kwesi to get the plastique in however he could, and left the details to him."

"Yeah, that's possible," answered James. "But you know what? You pick a motherfucker like Kwesi for a tiny little detail like smuggling a bomb in, and maybe you've got to take responsibility for how he goes about getting it done."

Back at the table he set the ashtray down and leaned over, his elbows on the old green Formica to massage his forehead with his fingertips, his temple bones with his thumbs.

When he lifted his head, Mary Lou was still at her curtain frill, the sound raspy as she rubbed it between her fingers. He felt desolate. His whole life gone, wasted, just like that.

"For all I know," he muttered, "I can't even trust Donna and Bob."

"Quincy sent them," said Carolyn. "You trust him, right?"

"Yeah." James managed a small smile. "Q's my friend."

"Besides, Donna and Bob didn't ask you for anything. They just helped you."

"Dang, James," Mary Lou finally spoke up. "You sound so sad now, but you bounded in here like a puppy dog. You seemed happy. How come?"

"'Tell no lies,'" as Curly here says. "Figure out the truth. Makes you feel better, I guess." James sighed and continued his story.

"So after all that I keep on walking and almost bump right into these cows I hadn't seen. I scared them as much as they scared me, I guess. One had an udder so big she could hardly drag it around, but she still crashed off through the underbrush. That's how it's felt to leave the Bay area. Running, dragging along my whole entire life."

He lifted up Mary Lou's cigarettes to ask her permission. She nodded and he started the whole cigarette ritual all over again.

"By this time I'm on a clear path up to the top of the highest hill around, and my eyes are so adjusted I can see everything. There are rocks by the side, perfect flat ones that fit right into my palm. I picked out a scraggly little tree and decided that was Kwesi. The longer I threw those stones at Kwesi, the better my aim got, and by the end I just about stripped the bark off clean. Then I chose a bigger one and set to work on Nyame, the Great Man himself. I pounded on that tree with every stone I could find. First I scared out some birds, then I broke off all the lower branches. Finally I heaved something boulder sized that splintered the whole damned trunk. It felt good. It felt very good."

James stubbed out the cigarette after one deep drag. He was tired of hurting his own lungs.

"When I got up on top of that mountain I'd been climbing," he told them, "I sat myself down cross-legged, like an Indian guru, or maybe one of them *orisha* voodoo gods. I felt smart enough to get over on Nyame and that whole Ashanti tribe of his. It wasn't easy being out in the middle of the night all by myself, but when I made it to the top of that mountain, I'm tellin' you, I was ready to testify. I just sat there in that high windy place and I stared at this valley that was spread out before me like a magic silver carpet, and I knew I could do it."

"Do what?" Carolyn asked, on cue. The women's faces shone up at him.

"I could go out there all on my own and be all right," he told them. "Once I understood how alone I was from the get-go, alone on that day at Freeman and alone since that day at Freeman, then I saw that I've already been alone. I *know* how to be alone."

He paused and looked straight into Carolyn's blue eyes, determined to ignore the way that Mary Lou was shifting in her seat.

"Let's make that plan for how to get me out of here, Curls. First thing in the morning, okay?"

"Got to do strikers in the morning," Carolyn replied, staring down at the table. "I'm not sure how long that will take."

Damn. Wasn't this what Carolyn had been bugging him to do ever since he came back on the Greyhound? Why wouldn't this be the most important thing? Why wouldn't she set everything else aside?

As for the lovely Ms. Mary Louise, she wouldn't even meet his eye. But he'd expected her to be upset. He'd try and talk her into joining up with him somewhere down the road.

"I'll start over wherever I am, that's all." If he just kept on talking they would have to understand. "But this time I'll pick my people better. No heroes, no Jimmy Cliff, *You Can Get It If You Really Want It.* No Huey Newton. 'The sky's the limit.' 'Off the pigs.' Just people I can trust, like you two ladies.

"Here, let me read you something." He got up and headed toward the bedroom. "Where'd you put my suitcase?"

Carolyn pointed at the coat closet. He found the Kente cloth strip and hung it around his neck. Next he took the poetry book Donna and Bob had brought for him, ran a hand over its blue cloth cover, then went straight for one of its dog-eared pages and read:

"goin' ta be cleaner,
Hunh
"goin' ta be stronger
Hunh
"goin' ta be wiser
Hunh
"goin' ta be quick ta be quicker
Hunh
"goin' ta be."

The women said nothing. Must be the grunts, the call and response. They didn't know what to make of all that.

"Cat named Don L. Lee wrote it," he told them. "He called it 'Black Political Prisoners/on the Inside and Outside.' He closed the book and then another line came up at him from memory just as it had looked, the black letters alone on their own white page:

"My main man/change yr name like the wind."

Mary Lou, after a panicked glance at Carolyn, rushed for the bathroom, pulled up the toilet seat, and wretched, out of control. She threw up until there was no more left, then sat on the old brown linoleum staring at the porcelain knobs on the toilet base, hiccupping softly through quiet tears. She stayed right there for the longest time, legs folded and scissored at the knees, cheek against the closed toilet lid to hold herself up.

No one came. Didn't either of them care? She examined the grime in the cracks around the toilet bottom and at the edges of the wall. She had tried so hard to get at the dirt when she scrubbed this floor; she'd even used a toothbrush. And it never had worked. She was so tired, so spent that she couldn't imagine ever doing that again. Yet she had to summon the energy to get up off this floor. She had to tell James.

She dragged herself to her feet, flushed the toilet one last time, and washed her face and hands over and over in the sink's warm tap water until she believed she could get into bed without the nausea coming back. She cracked the door to the bedroom.

In the dark, over on his far side of her bed, turned to the wall, James was a still shape, breathing evenly in his slumber. All of a sudden sleep was all she wanted. She was more exhausted this moment than she had ever been before in her life. She could not put herself or anyone else through one more thing. She had to sleep too.

—〰—

Left alone in the kitchen, Carolyn felt relieved to be alone. They would find each other. They did it every night. She was sick and tired of both of them. It wasn't fair, she knew, but she just could not stand this whole situation, getting more hopeless by the minute. James was going to get caught. Or Mary Lou was going to do something stupid, and then James would get caught. And when James got caught, they would get her too. Accessory after the fact—for way too long by now.

She sat still and waited for the coast to be clear. She did not want to run into either of them, not in the hall, not in the bathroom, not anywhere. Her mind darted everywhere, worrying. Not a single clear plan about any of it would jell. Just a jumble, until her being settled into pure emotion. Sorrow about Mona, fear about James. She could have heard a quiet sob or two, which might have been one of them. Or both, if they were talking yet. Everyone had plenty of cause to cry. Maybe it was her own sound. She was so tired that she couldn't be certain of anything.

Finally she remembered to look at the clock. Four in the morning. Enough. She tiptoed down the empty hall and brushed her teeth in the empty bathroom. Ears alert against her will, she worried about noise from the bedroom. None, thank God. She folded out her very own sofa bed, got the thin sheets and wool blankets from the shelf of the coat closet, smoothed them with the palm of her hand, and inserted herself between the covers, grateful for sleep.

—⚇—

Finally the Joseph Street house was dark. Outside, the total quiet of the last part of night prevailed. The neighborhood dogs, large and small, lay curled into still, silent shapes, their yaps and growls and barks spent. The early spring's warm air forecast the brutal San Joaquin Valley summer to come, yet not a single cricket sounded to foretell the premature turn of season. No car moved stealthily through the deserted streets; no eye searched for anyone; no ear was cocked.

Jerry Jensen, clad in royal blue satin pajamas, lay in a king-size bed surrounded by the eleven rooms of his spread-out single-story compound in the suburbs of Empire where there was still plenty of land. His firm-bodied blonde beauty, twenty years younger, was in a quiet pile as far away from him as she could get. Before he drifted off, he realized to his surprise that he missed his first wife. He had been the one to leave her suddenly once the kids were grown, and yet his life still seemed to travel along a predetermined track. The Colonia brothers, with their combination of generosity and threats for disloyalty, had made sure of that.

Too late to change anything now. Never look back. Farmworkers in their place, him in his, and he was sure as hell glad it wasn't the other way around. After he figured all this out in a rare bout of introspection, he slept like an angel with a child's quiet breaths.

Silveira, awake in his shack out by the labor camp, mouth dry and head pounding, molded himself around the comfort of his fat wife. He had hurt no one, he told himself yet again, and his family had eaten better since that night he shot his gun off at the camp. Best of all, with his payoff he'd gotten six bottles of *Herradura Reposado,* the most expensive tequila he could find. He'd finished the last one off that very night and fallen into bed early, hoping for a sound sleep. He sighed and swallowed and worried about his headache and thought he should get up for water and didn't, then slipped back into a restless doze once more.

Those who had marched for the day, soothed by their hosts' showers that helped erase the long miles of highway exhaust and litter, slept the sound slumber of bodies worked hard.

In Emerald, down Highway 99, the next day's cooks for the marchers' meals had the necessary piles of bags packed with food, raised from donations, ready in their kitchens. The women slept at ease, confident of their expertise. They would rise early, assemble lunches to be handed out in the park at the morning meeting, and meet after that at the Carleton Church of our Lady of Sorrows, where the marchers would be by the next evening, to prepare dinner for hundreds.

Aurelio and Teófilo lay on the floor on opposite sides of the table in Enrique Vargas's small dining area, the only place in the house where there weren't already family members on couches, bunk beds, double beds, and sofas. Piles of blankets served as pallets for their cotton sleeping bags. Aurelio snored loudly. Teófilo slept on his side, knees pulled up, undisturbed.

Jack Marsh was with the Martinez family. After Amelia finally stopped her talk about the next Mexican revolution, he'd scrunched up his thick body to fit onto their living room couch that did not fold out. No matter which way he turned, he felt as if he were about to fall onto the floor, but at last he gave it all up and fell asleep.

Hank, his metal crutches tilted against the mattress in easy reach, snoozed peacefully in Patsy Muñoz's comfortable bed under her flowered coverlet, while Patsy, exiled to her sister's, slept on the lower bunk with her five-year-old nephew, his tiny arm thrown over the increasing mound of her stomach. Carmen, hair spread in a dark fan on the pillow, breathed deeply, untroubled by the middle-aged rasp from Lupe Muñoz, who lay in her own bedroom as close to the far edge of her own double bed as she could.

Rojelio was in tangled blankets on the fold-out couch in the Muñoz living room. By the time he got there it was too late to move his stuff over to Ramón's motel. He would do it tomorrow, though; he needed the privacy of a single room shared with a quiet man who would not require him to socialize. His sheets were damp from a feverish sweat, but now at last he slept, eyes darting beneath his lids in an agitated dream.

Ramón, breaths deep and even, was flat on his back at the Punjabi motel, arms and legs splayed, sound asleep, oblivious to Carolyn's absence in the undisturbed half of their bed.

Minute sounds of pre-dawn movements began outside the Joseph Street house. A possum's nails scratched against the macadam as it shuffled across Fourth Avenue. A branch in the high tree, still bare of leaves, creaked in a sudden warm breeze by the kitchen door. A robin's single note rose and dropped, then rose again. Night gave way to the pallid light before dawn. The time for sleep was almost over.

CHAPTER TWENTY-FIVE

James woke up to a note taped to the bathroom mirror that said Mary Lou and Carolyn were already off to the seven a.m. meeting. You'd think Carolyn would have stayed back, or gotten him up to plan his departure. He went to the bedroom to look out the window. Both cars gone. They could have left him one in case he had to leave the house.

The bright sun of high morning streamed into the bathroom's small window. He shaved, then staggered out to the kitchen for his coffee and spread every section of the previous day's *Fresno Bee* on the table.

The lady with the long dark hair came back. He looked up to find her peering at him through one of the cracks between Mary Lou's frilly curtains, her VW Rabbit parked in the empty rutted place by the kitchen door. Not even a knock. Eleven a.m. on the kitchen clock.

He cracked the door against a surprising chilly breeze, his tongue gone dumb like a schoolboy's.

"Carmen," she said. "Remember me?"

"You're hard to forget," he answered, then worried that this was way too friendly. This time she wore skintight jeans with a bright yellow blouse made of a shiny material that picked up the yellow in her Guatemalan handbag.

"Uh, may I help you?" he asked.

"It's cold out here," she said. "You could start by inviting me in."

"Mary Lou isn't here," he told her. "Neither is Carolyn."

"Yes, I know that." She spoke as if she were talking to a child. He watched the harsh glare of sunlight dance off her straight black hair. "I know they're not here. They left early, to go to Hank's meeting. He's had them every single morning since he came."

"So—" James stammered. So then, he wanted to ask, what are you doing here?

The fast wind raced through the high bare branches of the towering oaks with an ominous sound. Carolyn wouldn't stay away long, he told himself. She'd be back soon to help him get out of here.

"So I came to see you." Carmen smiled up at him. "Are you going to let me in or not?"

He held the door wide and watched her walk by. Her hair swayed over her butt with the same smooth rhythm that moved her legs. His body betrayed him with an automatic animal response.

His auntie would've called her a Jezebel, and as usual, his auntie would have been correct. Hadn't he just taught himself the world was full of people who could not be trusted?

"As for me," Carmen told him. "I like to catch people by surprise."

He stood there in his wrinkled jeans and plain white T-shirt with his mouth hanging open, not sure what to do. She laughed, then set her purse down on the kitchen table and sat where he'd been in front of his own open newspaper, shameless.

"Now what about the next step?" she asked. "May I please have something to drink?"

She smiled like she was handing her smooth face to him on a damned platter. He stared for a second, fascinated in a horrible way. Then he turned his back to her and, aware of his body under her gaze, crossed the room to open the refrigerator.

"What's your pleasure, Carmen whatever-your-last-name-is? Beer? Orange juice? Coke?"

"Coke would be great. And it's Gutierrez." She rolled her r's like an expert, which of course she was, then watched him get out the can, fill a glass with ice, and bring it all over to her.

She snapped off the top and poured. James willed himself to be calm. He decided his physical excitement did not show and leaned on the counter by the sink, facing her but not close by. He crossed his arms and watched the dark liquid fizz over the cubes.

"There's a press conference at the UFW office right about now," she said. She glanced at her watch. "After that's over they'll shut the office, and we'll all march for the afternoon. It's a fantastic way to spend a sunny day. Want to come?" She grinned at him again.

"Not me, I've been too sick for that," he said.

"Looks like you're on the mend to me." He could have sworn she was about to wink. Who did this woman think she was, Mata Hari? She was so extreme that it made him want to laugh out loud. But then she'd ask why and he'd have to justify himself, and she'd take off and run with whatever he said.

"What sickness did you say you had?" she asked.

"I don't believe we spoke about it." Against his will, he sparred with her.

"That's true, James, or do you like to be called Jim?"

He did not answer. This whole conversation was dangerous, but he couldn't exactly tell a friend of Mary Lou's just to get out of the house.

"But Mary Lou told me what you had," she continued. "Hepatitis I believe it was." She pronounced the word with a titter, to demonstrate what a light little disease it was, he supposed.

"Did you have jaundice and everything?" she asked.

She twisted up out of her chair and reached toward his face, as if to pull down his eyelid to see if the white was yellow. He put up a hand to stop her and her arm fell to the table, but she had managed to get close enough that he could smell her perfume. His mind raced through the scents of the women he'd known—Rosetta's body oils, Mary Lou's natural earthy odor, cheap perfume on a cheap lady he'd met at a club one time. But this Carmen wore a fragrance on her. Something expensive.

Carmen Gutierrez, my eye. She had the black hair and the bronze skin, but she was true Wasp on the inside, one who would take on whatever ladder presented itself and sleep her way to the top.

"I was yellow all over at first," he found himself saying. "Now I'm just tired all the time. The doctors say recovery is slow and you have to be careful because you can get a relapse otherwise. And, of course, they do reiterate that it's definitely catching."

Formal. Methodical. That was the way to speak to this woman. He moved even farther away to resume his lean, this time against the wall in the corner by the door.

"So, Carolyn brought you out here." Carmen lifted her glass to her lips. "Have you known her long?"

"We've been friends for a while."

"Is she the one?" Here she was, messing with his head again.

"What one?" he asked her back, acting the fool.

"Is Carolyn your girlfriend?"

"Do we know each other well enough to discuss all this?" he parried. Outside the wind blew the low grass across the street almost level to the ground. A car eased around the corner onto Joseph Street. No markings, nothing special.

"How about Mary Lou?" Carmen was not going to give up. "Is she the one?"

"Naw," he said. "We just met."

"So you don't actually have a girlfriend, then?"

"I don't think I answered that one way or the other."

She lapsed into a friendly silence, interspersed with thoughtful sips from her coke. He took a deep breath to relax his shoulders and waited to see what she'd do next.

All at once she was on her feet and through the door to the living room. He followed. To his relief Carolyn had been her usual neat self and folded up her bed, put her clothes away. Carmen plopped herself down on the couch and picked up Carolyn's silver-framed photo of her mother to examine it.

"Anyhow, what about you?" he asked to distract her from asking who that was in the picture and ascertaining that Carolyn slept in here instead of himself. "What made you come out here to work on the march?"

"I wouldn't know what else to do with myself." She twirled a tendril of hair while she spoke. "I've been around this Union all my life. And the town of Allen, small as it may be, sure does beat La Paz. You do know what La Paz is, don't you?"

"That's the Union headquarters," he answered. Mary Lou had described La Paz once, an ex-tuberculosis sanatorium with high-ceilings and damp rooms. "Down south near Bakersfield. In the Tehachapi mountains."

His mind had taken control; he was alert but no longer aroused. He glanced outside. The trees were still, the grass stood straight. He could afford to be affable.

"This march comes right through Allen tomorrow, doesn't it?" he asked her. "Don't you have stuff to do?"

"I was curious about you," Carmen answered. "So I decided to come and see for myself."

She got up off the couch and began to fool around with the record player.

"I'm on a break from school," she continued. "Don't I get at least one morning of vacation?" Otis Redding came on, the side that started with the "Feh Feh Feh" song.

"So now you know all there is to know," he said.

"No I don't," she said. "You haven't told me anything. Want to dance?"

"You shouldn't dance with me," he told her. "You could get sick."

"I'll take the chance." She took his hand.

If he had a choice he couldn't figure out how to exercise it. He tried to hold her at a distance, but of course she moved in close. Graceful and aware of it, she followed his fanciest step, the one he thought of as a latin rhythm, without so much as one tromped-on toe. At the small of her back her lustrous hair lay under his palm. He got hard again, and he knew she felt it. Her body brushed against his, expert at making this happen. When the song was finally over they stood there, still close.

Otis swung into *Try a Little Tenderness.* She tilted her head up at him, ready to move in on a true slow dance.

This was the last thing he wanted, he told himself. One woman at a time; he had always been that way. Even one was too many in this little situation of his, but Mary Lou was special. He would get somewhere safe and send for her, see if she would come. The woman here with him now was not his friend.

"Well now, Carmen Gutierrez," he said. He pronounced it "Guteares" on purpose and went right past her to close the thick maroon curtains on all three windows. Carolyn always left them open. What was the matter with her? If someone walked by and wanted to, they could see right into the room.

"I don't mean to disappoint you," he continued, turning back to Carmen. "But I have to get my afternoon rest right now."

Her eyes narrowed. The girl was not used to being turned down.

"You do that, Mr. James Sweet," she said. "I've got to go myself. I told Jack I'd check in with the Empire Junior College MECHA students who are supposed to turn some people out for the rally tonight." And as fast as she got here, Carmen picked up that Guatemalan handbag of hers and was gone the same way she came in, through the kitchen and out the door.

He stood at the window to watch her snappy red car round the corner from Fourth Avenue. He switched to the living room, cracked the curtain, and made sure she went all the way down the block and turned right to get back to the highway.

"Thank the Lord," as his auntie would've said. And then she would have followed up with something literal, like "He will save my black ass in a pinch."

Well, will He or won't He? He had so far, James supposed. He rubbed at the back of his neck and found it wet with sweat.

He had to leave Allen. And Chicago would be just fine; it made sense. As soon as Carolyn got back they'd make their plan. No reason, in fact, not to start right now. He returned to the kitchen, picked up the phone, dialed information for American Airlines in Fresno, and then hung up before it rang. It was probably long distance, and if the pigs ever tracked him here they could get the call off the bill and figure out what city he'd gone to. It would be better for Carolyn to drive out and do it from a pay phone.

Carolyn. Was she testing him? Since he had told her last night he could go it alone, was she requiring that right away? No. She wouldn't do that to him. He settled down in the kitchen to wait for her. It felt like this was what he'd been doing for most of his life, waiting here for one of the women. Or both.

He must have dozed with his head down on the table, because when the door opened, the kitchen clock said it was 3:50 p.m. and the light from a lowering sun was coming in the window from the west.

He wanted Carolyn, but it was Mary Lou. She switched on the long fluorescent bulb between the cabinets and the walls took on a harsh white glow. He rubbed his eyes. A pinkish-brown color spread over her cheeks like a mask. She looked very tired.

"I wish you could've been there today, James," she said, trying to sound excited. "You would have loved it."

She headed straight past him to the living room and flopped into the stuffed chair. He followed her. All the curtains still drawn, the room was reassuringly dark.

"When the march got around all the houses," Mary Lou continued, eyes closed, "doors flew open and kids came running out with the family's old UFW flag someone had dug out of the closet. Black eagle on red, everywhere you looked."

"Masses in action," he muttered like an automaton. "Where's Carolyn, Mary Lou? I need her help."

"She told me I had to talk to you," Mary Lou said.

"Isn't the march coming right through here tomorrow?" he asked. "I have got to get out of this place. Carolyn's always said that. Why isn't she here?"

"Everything smells about ten times stronger than usual," she said, as if that answered all his questions.

He wondered if Carmen's scent could still be on him, but that had been hours ago and they had barely touched. Mary Lou looked upset, like she might cry.

"What's wrong?" he asked her. He came around to the front of the chair and tilted her chin up so she would look at him. "Are you sick? Did you pick up that flu again?"

"No. I'm pregnant."

The words tore through the room like a blaze close to the ground, eating up the space between them. He moved back as though he had been burned.

"Say what?" He braced to hear it again. Her face was wavy, as if seen through heat.

"I wasn't going to tell you," she said. "Not ever. You didn't have to find out about this. But Carolyn said that wouldn't be fair. I couldn't make her change her mind, so I figured she must be right."

"How do you know?" His mind struggled with the basic fact. "How do you know that, Mary Lou?"

"I got a test."

"Get another one."

"I gave myself one at home too. Last week."

"You can't do this to me!"

"Do it to you?" Mary Lou stood up, her face a pale blotch. "You think I did this on purpose, James? You think I did it to get at you?"

He paced into the kitchen to kick at the stainless steel table leg. His skin felt so hot he could burn up. The wind had risen again to howl around the corners of the house as the sun slid down into the dark of night.

He returned to the living room to stand in front of her.

"Didn't you use anything?" he asked, his voice rising. "Mary Louise! Didn't you use any goddamned thing?"

She looked scared, and he had to move away again. He settled for standing at the front door so he could back off even further if it got any worse.

"You think we're all niggers!" He never used that word, and now it came tumbling out of his mouth. "You think we just put our children into the world like we haven't got anything more to do with it after that? Is that what you think, Mary Louise? Is that what you want from me?"

She stared at him, stunned.

"Did you ask how we were going to make sure this didn't happen?" She held her ground. "Did I miss something, James?"

No, he had not asked; in fact, he hadn't even wondered. In a situation already several steps past impossible, James Sweet had not given one single thought to precautions, just like the lady said. Like Kwesi's betrayal, the event was on top of him before he'd dreamed up its possibility. It never came to mind that the ordinary was the same as ever. He had just assumed that this woman, who had faced Silveira out at the labor camp and stood him off, would handle things.

Charles Brown—now there had been a man who could take care of business, who would call the shots if the woman hadn't or didn't want to. But Mary Lou didn't even know that self-assured soon-to-be-law-student. Charles Brown. A long-gone stranger, even to himself. His anger ebbed, leaving him limp and discouraged.

James sat down on the scratchy green couch, his head in his hands. Mary Lou, a palm on her abdomen, went back to her chair, re-curled her legs under her body, and fidgeted to get comfortable. The sound of the wind came from the outside in small, uncontrolled spurts.

"You can't do this to me," he muttered. He could still remember his mother's harsh and bitter cry when she realized his daddy wasn't coming back, his own shock at seeing her like that, and the tears that streamed down his little brother's face.

"I cannot leave this place and go off alone with a baby coming." He rubbed at his eyes with his fists. "Damn it, Mary Louise, if there's one thing I've sworn to myself, it's that I would never run off on a baby of mine!"

The wind gave out a fitful sigh and stopped. No dogs, no cars, nothing at all.

Again Mary Lou got herself out of the chair, this time to come to the sofa and sit next to him. Why was this woman always closest at hand when he was so utterly desperate? She started to place her palm on his knee, but he shrank from her touch and folded into himself with his hands clenched between his legs.

The wind started up again with a low whine. The wind. All day and all night with this horrible wind.

"I mean, look, James," Mary Lou said in a miserable voice. "If you want me to, I might. You know. End the pregnancy."

If there was one thing James understood about Mary Louise Gilman, the one who had a fit of happiness when she got to hold that Martinez baby the very first night he was here, the one who just about thought abortion was a mortal sin, it was that she did not mean a single word of what she had just said.

Elbows on his knees, hands over his eyes, he sat listening to the wind for he didn't know how long. He heard a choking sound from her and then she just about ran into the bathroom. Even when she had flushed the toilet and returned, he didn't lift his head.

"I won't do it," he muttered into his palms.

"You won't do what?" she asked. "You won't stay with me?"

He straightened out and stared ahead.

"I won't be that black man you've always heard about. Get a woman pregnant and disappear. No."

"You don't want me to get rid of it?" Now she sounded just a little bit pleased about this mess.

"Naw," he muttered. "I wouldn't ask you for that."

She touched his arm but still he wouldn't look at her. He took her hand like they were both made of singed twigs and led her toward the kitchen where he could get cigarettes and beer. He popped the top off a Tecate and took a long pull, lit a Marlboro, and dragged the smoke into his lungs. He sank into his usual chair at the Formica table, and she took her own place, perched at the edge of her seat.

"Is everything all normal?" he asked. He glanced at her. "With the baby, I mean?"

"Nothing seems normal to me." But her thin lips curved into a tiny smile. "So far so good. Except that I always feel sick to my stomach."

"So that's why you've been acting so odd." He sounded strange to himself, like he was discussing the weather.

They sat for some time in silence. He crushed out the butt, lit the next cigarette, and drank more beer; she didn't move at all.

"Now you seem calm," she said eventually.

"Girl, I got to act like I got it together, don't I?"

She reached across the Formica table to put her palm on his cheek and refused to notice that it made him flinch. Next she gathered his ashtray and bottle in one hand, took his hand with the other, and led them both back to the living room. She sat him down on the couch, then laid down on it with her head resting in his lap.

"So then you feel okay right now?" he asked. He wanted to stroke her hair but he didn't.

"No. I'm nauseous." She closed her eyes. "But I'm sort of used to it."

"That's how it's supposed to be, isn't it?"

"You're asking me?" She laughed. "I've never been pregnant before."

"And how about pregnant by me?"

"Never before by you, either."

He smiled a bit, and dared to place a tentative hand over her flat belly. She laughed again and moved it up past her waist.

"Don't be silly," she said. "You can't feel anything yet. It's just at the beginning."

His fingers traveled to cup lightly at her breast, which made her stir, to brush over her neck, her lips. Eyes closed, hair fallen away to show a face that looked happy, his Mary Louise was beautiful. They had a baby from their love. Maybe it was just that simple.

"Well now you are," he whispered with his lips brushing her ear. "You're pregnant by me, Ms. Mary Louise."

"Do you want a boy or a girl?" she asked without opening her eyes.

"Mama, I'll take whichever you deliver."

"If it's a boy, it could be Charles or James or Robert, and still be named after its dad."

Her quiet joke, at the core of what was real, made him smile.

"If it's a girl, we could name it Pearl," he said, stroking her arm. "After my granny, on my daddy's side of the family. She died just before he and my mother began to decide they couldn't get along, right after Ronnie came."

"Pearl has a nice sound to it," she said, nestling into his touch.

The wind had died down. Not a sound out there.

"What was your grandmother's name?" he asked her.

"Ginger. Now I ask you, where did that come from back there in Oklahoma? Ginger Rogers? Ginger snaps?"

"Not so bad," he whispered. He touched her lower lip with his index finger. "Maybe that's where you got that spicy taste of yours."

A car cruised by, and they both tensed up. The Allen police maybe, on their evening patrol.

"What else did Carolyn say?" he asked. "Besides that you had to tell me?"

"Not much. She wasn't exactly pleased."

"I have got to get out of this place, Mary Louise."

"When?"

"As soon as I can. Chicago. Come with me."

He'd have to send word to Donna and Bob. They would need two Cuban visas instead of one. Maybe even three, given how long everything took. There had been talk about going through Prague instead of Mexico City. This whole thing would mean another long wait. Would he ever feel safe again?

"You have to leave now?" Mary Lou asked. "Even before it's born?"

"Especially before it's born. The sooner the better."

He wanted her to look at him, but her eyes stayed closed.

He gazed at the thick weave of the drawn curtain. Behind that was the dark of the night, the endless hills, the quicksilver moon, and his waterfall. What if they came for him? What if she had to climb out a window and run? How was she going to do that with a big belly?

"You have got to be ready to quit this country, Mary Lou," he said. "Do you understand that? Can you leave all this behind?"

"All what?" She sounded as if she was about to fall asleep.

"The San Joaquin Valley," he said. He squeezed her cheek just enough to get her to look at him. "The Union. Your life."

"Heck, yeah," she said, gazing at his face. "I can leave. Everything seems like a danged mirage right now anyhow."

She closed her eyes again, and her body jumped in that strange way that happens before a person drops off.

He thought about the next steps, but practical answers eluded him. Where in Chicago? The most segregated damned city in the North from what he'd heard. They were bound to draw notice. And the money wouldn't stretch that far with two people. How could they hold out if it took this much time all over again to get a new visa?

"After the march, maybe," was the last thing she muttered. "We can go when the march is over."

Wait for the answers anywhere but here, Carolyn would say. If she bothered to stop by, that was. He frowned and reached for his cigarettes. If he left without Mary Lou she might never come. She could hook back up with her Mexican boyfriend. Rojelio as father to James's own flesh and blood? No. He wouldn't go alone. He wanted his baby.

He woke Mary Lou enough to walk her into the bedroom and tuck the covers around her. Then he heated a leftover taco he found in the refrigerator, ate it standing up, and left a note asking for Carolyn's car keys. He could not just sit around Joseph Street tomorrow and hope no one stopped by while the march went through town. He would head to the country and have his own march, a solitary one. And whenever Carolyn chose to appear, he would tell her they had to come up with a whole new plan. She would think he was crazy.

He tiptoed into the bedroom, shut the door, and lay down next to Mary Lou, all his clothes on but his shoes. Outside, dogs yapped. There was a chorus of crickets and frogs. And even though he had dozed all afternoon, he was bone tired and collapsed into sleep.

CHAPTER TWENTY-SIX

Carolyn worried about James all day long. It started at the morning meeting, with her and Mary Lou acting like things were normal. James and Mary Lou had to have time to react to the news, she told herself. She would wait until they had had the chance to talk.

She worried again in the afternoon while she marched next to Carmen, the wind tearing at both their clothes. Everyone was there except for Mary Lou, so she must have been with James. He should go to Chicago, and Mary Lou should get an abortion. That was what ought to happen.

By three thirty she couldn't stand it anymore. She felt bad for leaving the march before it stopped for the night, but she had to get back to James. So she took a ride back to Allen with Rebecca Flores, who had come out to look but said she wasn't well enough to join in. Rebecca did not seem to feel guilty. Carolyn always felt guilty. Mona and her incessant politics had made her this way. She was sick of it.

She trudged over the gravel parking lot, head down to avert the gusty wind, on her way into the office to get the striker files. She would take them to Joseph Street, work on them there.

She heard a vehicle crunch to a stop, saw his cowboy boot descend from the cab, and looked up, heart bouncing.

"*¡Hola Carolina!*" Ramón's thin face was wreathed in smiles; his black eyes danced at her as if they had just been together instead of not seeing each other for days.

"*Hola Ramón.*" She couldn't help but laugh back. "Where've you been?" she asked.

"I had to go to La Paz. Cesar wanted representatives of all three marches to plan the final day. Rojelio sent me."

"Three marches?"

"*Si, tres.* Ours, of course. Another one is coming down from Stockton. The third is from the Bay Area. It will have thousands."

It was the first she had heard of all this, but she didn't care. It passed for an explanation of why she hadn't been able to find him anywhere.

"What are you doing now?" he asked her, holding the office door open.

"Getting ready for tomorrow. The strikers' lists have to be organized for the final push."

The large room was empty except for Amelia Martinez at the corner desk.

"Let's do it together," Ramón suggested. "But not here. I get tired of this place."

A moment later they reemerged, arms full of folders and accordion files. The sun was low in the sky. The wind raced across the vineyards, challenging the tiny furls of new leaves to come out and play.

"We can take all this stuff over to the Punjabi motel," Ramón was saying. "There's a shower there. You can get refreshed. You left some clothes the last time, remember? I washed them, *como no?* Why not?"

Why not indeed? She could taste the grit from the highway's wind in her mouth, feel it in the folds of her clothes. She accepted at once.

Two hours later they still lay curled together, weary and content between thin, clean sheets redolent with the yeasty scent of fresh lovemaking. The wind was down and they were calm. Ramón kissed the tip of her nose, put his pants on, scrounged for a quarter, and started the Magic Massage machine. Carolyn giggled as she watched her jiggling breasts. He left the room and returned with drinks from the dispenser, Coke for himself and a 7up for her. He knew what she liked.

"*Vienen, Carolina,*" he said, serious suddenly.

"*¿Quien?*" When she was relaxed like this she could answer in Spanish. She studied the angles of his face.

"*La esposa. Los niños.*" Not *my* wife, *my* children, she thought, but *the* wife and children. Was that what the grammar required for some reason? The meaning washed over her and she sat up, grabbed her fresh T-shirt, and threw it over her head.

"I always knew they would be here," she stammered, although she had known no such thing. Her face burned as she struggled to fit her arms into the sleeves. "They'll want to go to the march, of course. When do they arrive?"

"Tomorrow." The three short syllables expanded the distance between them.

She scooped up the rest of her clean clothes and headed for the bathroom. She managed to close the door gently, then flipped down the toilet seat and sat on its cold, hard surface, tears in her eyes.

Don't be foolish, she told herself. She didn't care for him that much anyhow. She ran the water as hot as it would go and washed him off her. Then she dressed, pulled her brush through her hair, smashed her dirty underwear down into her purse, and emerged.

"So this is the last time then, right?" Arms folded, she flung the words at him as if he had deceived her.

"*Me parese que sí . . .*" he answered.

"Speak in English," she commanded. "I've got to get this straight. Let's see, you disappear without saying anything. Next you come back and act like you're glad to see me. And now you tell me this!"

"I am glad to see you. I was glad." His voice trailed off. "I guess I wanted to—"

"You wanted to have sex. That's what you wanted!"

"—to say goodbye."

"To have sex, you mean. Why don't you admit it?"

"Isn't that the good way?"

"Good way for what exactly?"

"To say goodbye?"

He stood there, calm, his black eyes focused right on her. Could it really be so easy for him? This was the deal, she knew that. But she was going to miss him.

"*¿Hola? ¿Ramón? ¿Estás aquí?*" A man's voice came from out on the concrete walkway in front of the door.'

"*¿Eres tu, Rojelio?*"

"*Si. Con mi equipaje. ¿Puedo entrar?*"

"Rojelio's brought his suitcase," he told her. "He's going to stay here, remember?"

Of course she remembered. Of course this whole thing of theirs was just a little bit of time out. Of course these had always been the terms. Of course. She was an idiot.

"Should I open the door?" Ramón asked her in a low voice.

"What do I care?" Carolyn said. "I'm leaving."

"Who'll have the lists?" Ever diligent, he remembered the task at hand.

"You keep them," she told him. "Get them organized for us both."

Thank God she had brought her biggest purse. She stuffed everything down as far as it would go and put her hairbrush in on top. Barely enough space, but nothing would show. As Rojelio came in the room, she swept right past him.

"Deputy Sage," he was saying. "Now he tells us we don't get the permit for the route we want in Allen."

Not her problem, she decided.

"Gotta go," she tossed back over her shoulder as she ducked under the second-story supports to get to the parking lot. "There's a whole other bunch of things to get done before tomorrow. See you guys later."

She catapulted away from the motel, out into the pitch dark. They had come in Ramón's truck, of course, so she had to trudge down the access road and cross the highway at the stoplight to get back to the UFW parking lot where she had left her car. The wind was up again, rushing at her body so hard she had to curl into it to make headway. All the lights were on in the office, and there were several other automobiles at random angles in the gravel as though they had arrived in a hurry. She got into her own Volvo and started the motor, hoping she hadn't been seen. She headed for Joseph Street.

Though it wasn't past nine, the whole house was dark. She flipped on the fluorescent kitchen light and read James's note to the faint buzz of its white glow. Make sure he had the car keys for tomorrow. All right, the man had the sense to know he had to get out and away the day the march came through Allen. But not another word. He should be up and waiting to go over the details if his plan was to leave right away—shouldn't he?

She scrounged in the fridge for food, banged pots on the stove to heat up day-old rice and beans, clanked utensils to cut up a small salad. Still no sound from the bedroom hallway. She thought while she ate. She should wake him up. She could drive him out of town, at least get to Fresno. But she was exhausted and sick of it all. It was his situation, damn it, and he just asked for the keys. So she'd give him the keys.

She dropped them on the table, went into the living room, unfolded the couch, and settled in. She expected to be unhappy. She thought she wouldn't be able to sleep. But when she tried to read Nero Wolfe, the letters crowded on the page and blurred before her eyes.

When she heard him leave the next morning, she experienced her usual guilt, yet she did not get up. She fell back asleep, but by six fifteen Mary Lou was insistent. Once the seven a.m. meeting had been established they could not be late, she scolded, and certainly not today.

There was light to the east. The sky was clear and the air was calm.

"The weather is going to be okay for this danged march," Mary Lou said as Carolyn bent to get into the passenger side of her car. "No rain, no wind. It's perfect."

"Did you tell him yet?" Carolyn asked as soon as they pulled away from the curb.

"You said I had to, so I did," Mary Lou answered with a contented smile. "And you were right."

"So did you make any decisions?" All these questions should not be necessary. Mary Lou should just describe what happened, damn it.

"Yeah, we got it all figured out." With only a cardigan sweater on for warmth, Mary Lou fooled with the knob to turn on the heat.

"But you heard him leave this morning, right?" she asked. Carolyn nodded.

"So where'd he go, anyhow?" Mary Lou asked again.

"Shit, I don't know if you don't know," Carolyn answered. "Back to his waterfall? Not far enough, but he'll stay away today. He knows he has to do that."

"And what was his reaction?" Carolyn asked while Mary Lou turned around on Fourth Avenue.

"First he tried to blame it on me. Then he got real sad. He told me that I should come with him."

The two women were silent. The heater kicked in.

"With the baby, of course," Mary Lou added, her hands gripping the steering wheel. She had a spot of color in her cheeks. She hadn't locked herself in the bathroom this morning, Carolyn realized. Mary Lou slipped through the highway intersection with a green light, quiet again, forcing her to ask the obvious.

"What are you two going to do, for God's sake?" Carolyn knew her tone showed how annoyed she was.

Mary Lou pulled the car into the Union lot and parked it. The next thing the two women knew, all the organizers were crunching over the gravel and going into the office together. No chance to talk now. Carolyn felt a surge of anger at James and Mary Lou.

Inside, the men pulled out folding chairs and put them in a circle; everyone settled. Mary Lou called the meeting to order, pencil poised at the top of her list.

"Sleeping arrangements. Rojelio?"

"Last night we took care of three hundred," he said. "Fresno found the rest. Tonight it's all ours. We've got places for four hundred at least."

He looked around the group from under his dark brows, serious, annoyed almost, intent on the effort of the day. Too strange, thought Carolyn, to be here planning the tiny details of this march while James's safety slipped further and further out of reach.

"We need more," Mary Lou told him, all business. "Can you work on it this afternoon?" He nodded yes.

"We'll have five hundred marchers by the end of today," Jack said.

"So five fifty," Mary Lou said to Rojelio. "You've got the whole day to drum up new space before the people get to the church for dinner. You can march for a while in the morning, after the park, and then Carmen can help you. Where is she, anyhow?"

"She had to go to Fresno," Rojelio said.

"What in the world is she down there for?" Mary Lou asked. "Today's the day we need everyone here!"

Hank's low, slow voice cut in, mellow though his face looked haggard in the early morning light. "I sent her there. Had to get some info straight to the *Fresno Bee*, and I promised a hand delivery. Oughtn't to take her long."

"Well, Lupe then," Mary Lou said.

"I need someone," Ramón called over from the side of the room. He was checking their lists for the first time in days. "We still haven't found all the strikers."

Carolyn wouldn't look at him, but she knew those black eyes were searching her face, snapping at her to take these lists back from him and get the work done. He didn't dare ask her directly, though. Good.

"Sorry, Lupe's gotta help Rojelio," Mary Lou said. "At least 'til Carmen gets back. Ramón, you stick with Aurelio and Teófilo, bang on doors, get people out for this march. Carolyn, you work on the strikers."

Of course, thought Carolyn, I'm the one stuck in the office. Me and Hank and his wheelchair. The women get marginalized, Mona had always told her, and then she would add that, still, people had to put things aside when work had to get done. So of course Carolyn would do that. She'd be Mona's daughter to the end.

"How about clipboards?" Mary Lou asked Ramón. "That way you can make a list of people who have floor space. In your bottom drawer, Carolyn. Dang, Carmen was going to stay on top of Teresa, make sure she had the food under control. Now it's five-fifty she has to cook for."

"Tell Teresa to get to Pacheco and all the other food donors," Rojelio suggested. "More of everything. Rice and beans especially. Stretch the meat."

"And salsa," Ramón quietly interjected.

"What about Silveira?" Teófilo asked.

"What about him?" Aurelio answered. "I told you. He's harmless."

"I heard he'd be out there," Teófilo said. "With his thugs."

"Thugs?" Jack Marsh put in his two cents. "The guys he drinks with? They're drunks, that's all." Aurelio laughed.

"Yeah, well, I'm the only one here who's seen him in action," Mary Lou said. "When he shot up the camp, remember?"

"I heard about that." Hank's soft drawl cut in. "Let's get Manuel Chavez and his boys out there, just to be safe. Ramón, you go out to Mendota and take care of that. Then you can go back to your door-knocking, after Manny knows he has to show up."

"What about Jensen?" Jack Marsh called out.

"Nah, *rata blanca* won't be a problem," Rojelio said. "He'll sit this one out in that fancy office of his. Count on Sage and the cops to do his bidding for him."

"Let's go," Mary Lou said. "The marchers will be at the park by now. We've got to start out with *la gente*. Give it an hour, then get to your jobs. Today's the day."

"*Si se puede*," Rojelio said quietly.

Yes it can be done, thought Carolyn. For *la gente*, the people. Today she would work for *la gente*. It was the least she could do.

"*¡Si se puede!*" Everyone delivered the reply in unison. The meeting was over as quickly as it had begun.

—⚏—

The march got to Allen's city limit at two thirty, an hour and a half late. Carolyn hustled everyone working there over to the highway shoulder by the stoplight, to form a welcoming group. The march in Allen. For once an event more important than anything in the office.

Hank had done his press job well. There was a guy they knew from the *Fresno Bee*, a writer for Empire's Chicano student newspaper, *El Grito*, and best of all, the labor reporter from the *Los Angeles Times*. Hank himself was missing, but no one expected him to handle all this by wheelchair. Carmen had finally showed, dressed in matching corduroy pants and jacket, looking fresh and devoted at once.

Everyone yelled when they saw the group waiting for them on the highway shoulder.

"*¡Que viva la Union!*"

"*¡Que viva!*"

"*¡Que viva Cesar Chavez!*"

"*¡Que viva!*"

The cheers rolled like cannon balls between the approaching groups. The men at the beginning of the line each had a sign stapled onto a strong wooden pole. Along with Manuel Chavez, Ramón was at their lead. Carolyn watched him, amazed at how little she knew this sinewy, determined man. She could see no trace of the delicacy he had shown her in his motel room. Now he looked foreign almost, indigenous and fierce.

The welcome committee and the front of the line collided, and everyone stopped. After greetings, slaps on the back, and hugs among the women, many of the marchers sat at once on the grass at the side of the road.

Just as the *Times* reporter cornered Mary Lou and began his questions, Jack Marsh leaned out of the medical van.

"Get your rear end over here, Mary Lou," he yelled.

"I'm busy," she called back.

"We got to talk. Now."

"Who said he gave the orders?" Mary Lou grumbled to Rojelio.

"*Pues*, it doesn't hurt to know what he wants, Mary Louise," Rojelio said. "Don't let the people see you argue with him."

Quiet and sweet, smooth and friendly, Rojelio won out, and Mary Lou went over to talk with Jack. Rojelio accompanied the *Times* man to the truck where they were ladling water into paper cups. Carolyn went along, thirsty too.

"So how many on the march?" asked the reporter, a white guy in solid khaki clothing.

"Over six hundred by now," Rojelio answered. "And this is just one of three marches, you know."

"Really? What does that mean?"

Rojelio described each march, and the guy wrote down every word. Rojelio would be the UFW spokesman in the *LA Times*. Yet Mary Lou had done all the groundwork before he even got there.

Carolyn crossed back to Mary Lou and Jack.

"The cops are fucking with us," Jack was informing Mary Lou, who looked as though the exhaust from his van might make her throw up.

"They made us take a detour to avoid a ditch," he said. "They told us we couldn't cross it, and then the goddamned thing was dry as a witch's tit! That's why we're late."

"How far extra did you have to walk?" Mary Lou motioned for the other leaders to gather close and listen in.

"At least three miles. We had to move the line real fast, just to have a chance to make it to the goddamn church tonight. People even jogged part way, for chrissakes. Now they're dog-tired, with four miles still to go."

Carmen, Mary Lou, Rojelio, and Jack clustered to decide how to handle this. Carolyn, suddenly tired of the inner group, dropped away to walk down the long row.

Hundreds of people all around her, and what she couldn't get over was what they wore on their feet. Cheap tennis shoes, dusty old work boots, worthless fake leather sandals strapped onto the women's toes and ankles. No one had the proper equipment for a long hike. It was a miracle they had made it this far. At least the weather had held. Sunshine, crisp and clean, with a few puffy clouds in the sky.

Those who had found space in the soft green grass sank into it. The marchers looked tired. Some lay back, faces to the afternoon sun, to rest. Others opened bags to find bits of food. A group took off for Jovita's to see if she still had soft drinks. Many more stood and milled around.

"Carolyn, Carolyn!" A person all bundled into several layers of clothing hurried over to greet her. "*Cómo estás?* What are you doing here? I thought you'd be drinking your coffee in Berkeley by now."

She peered under a huge straw hat covered with Union buttons to find quick dark eyes set deep in the brown wrinkles of an old woman's face. Elena, Rojelio's mother, who lived in La Paz. A UFW activist as long as anyone could remember, everyone knew Elena. Last summer she and Carolyn had stayed up in the UFW office until one in the morning talking about Carolyn's life as Elena tried to convince her to come out to the Valley and work full time for the UFW.

Rojelio's mom. Envy shot through her. In that one long conversation she had told Elena more about herself than her own mother ever did know.

"I didn't know you'd be here," said Carolyn, leaning under the hat to kiss Elena's cheek.

"*Como no?* Why wouldn't I come with all this going on?" Elena's wrinkles crinkled into a warm smile.

"Have you seen Rojelio yet?" Carolyn asked.

"Rojelio I see all the time. But you, you're so much more unusual. How are you, Carolyn?" The old woman's dark brown eyes stared right into her own.

Such a simple question. How was she doing, anyhow? Elena, warm, solicitous, and so poor she wore someone else's tennis shoes with holes cut out to make room for her toes, wanted to know.

"Not so bad," Carolyn answered. "It's been a hard time."

"Yes," Elena said. "Your mother passed."

"But I'm getting better now."

"Did you think I wouldn't come?" Elena chattered on. "After the *Peregrinación* in '66, this one is *nada*. Only about half as far. But Rojelio tells me you have a friend," she was saying now with a wink. "*Negrito, si,* but what's wrong with that? A nice *joven,* good-looking *también,* according to my son, and I'm glad for you, Carolyn. There's such a thing as being too long alone, you know. We'll get an invitation from you someday soon, no? For wedding bells?"

She poked at Carolyn's ribs with her small red and black flag, and laughed.

Carolyn had tried to shrug everything else off for the day, the crowd, the sun, and the chartreuse new spring grass by the side of the road, but now it all closed back in. The grass was just weeds, full of highway trash, and James would be caught if he stayed. It was only a question of when.

All at once the red-banded monitors urged everyone to their feet. People hauled themselves up and were brushing each other off when angry shouts broke out nearby, where the leaders were. The line surged forward. The monitors urged it back and everyone stood still, silent as they craned to watch. A phalanx of highway patrol and local police had materialized from a side dirt road to stand on the highway shoulder, where they blocked the path of the march.

The marchers parted as the men with the poles, Carolyn in their wake, moved forward quickly to join the group at the head.

"Goddamned highway patrol." Jack clambered down from his van. "Now they decide to appear."

"Allen's finest over there, the ones in riot gear." Mary Lou nodded at a group of three cops dressed in black, young and nervous, hands on their sticks.

"And *mira,*" said Rojelio. "Our old friend Deputy Sage, but with new toys. Maybe Jensen provided them, *quizás?* Who knows?"

Two county sheriffs with Sage carried portable movie cameras that hummed away as they filmed the encounter.

"Jensen," Aurelio said. "We saw him on that last side street before we stopped the group. Just sitting there in his fancy car."

"Are you sure it was him?" Mary Lou asked, surprised. "Yeah, the white guy with the crew cut," Teófilo said.

"Big car. Had to be him."

"Yeah, it was Jensen," Jack chimed in.

How would they know? Carolyn wondered. They weren't from around here.

Teófilo took the arm of a tall, thin kid with a red arm band and huge brown eyes and whispered in his ear. The boy nodded and began the chant.

"*¡El pueblo, unido!*" he shouted in a voice that projected from his slim frame as if he had a microphone. "*¡Jamás será vencido!*" He punctuated each word with an upward jab of his fist.

"*¡El pueblo! ¡Unido! ¡Jamás será vencido!*" The black eagle on the boy's red arm band flew in the air in time with the chant, which the whole crowd took up at once. The boy's long black hair bounced off his shoulders as he jumped straight up, fist raised, with each phrase.

"'The people, united. Will never be defeated.'" Carolyn had heard this chant before in the Mission District of San Francisco during a protest about American foreign policy. Then it was alternated with Effay Emmay Ellay Ennay. FMLN—the left-wing party in El Salvador. If the Movement groups in Latin America got together with the Chicanos in the US there would be no stopping them. Was this what it was like for Mona in the thirties?

"*Es loco* that one from South America," Elena said, still at her side. "They call him *chapulín*. The grasshopper. He does this *todo el tiempo*. Every day since the march started."

The young man strode back and forth along the line, his upraised arm beating time for the chant. Waves of sound assaulted the motionless police ranks. Sage and his group did not move. They were outnumbered.

After the tenth time through, Aurelio extended his hands palms down, and the yell shrank to a soft but steady background.

Teófilo spoke to the nearest policeman, who managed to refer him to the one in charge with a curt nod. The knot of leaders moved over to Deputy Sage.

"What's the problem, Sage?" Mary Lou asked him.

"Where's your permit, Mary Lou?" Sage demanded. "You know you need a permit!"

"*Yo lo tengo, placa mía,*" said Teófilo. The marchers laughed at the slang word for policeman. Sage didn't understand a word and frowned.

"I have *el permiso*, right here," Teófilo assured him.

He got a worn packet of papers out of his back pants pocket and began a laborious search for the correct one. The long moment he took to find it surged with the sibilance of the chant. A steady stream of highway traffic swished by, faces gaping for an instant but the vehicles not stopping. Eventually Teófilo waved the Allen permit in the officer's face.

Sage grabbed it, read every word on both sides, and handed it back. The crowd shifted and the deputy stood there, arms folded, until the Union people had to ask all over again.

"So what in the world's the problem here?" Mary Lou repeated, her face as pale as the permit.

"It says you go straight through town without a halt. No rallies, no meetings, no nothin'."

"Which is just what we plan to do," said Mary Lou. "You have your spies; you know exactly where we plan to end up. The Carleton Catholic Church, and it's outside the town limit. We don't have time to stop before that, Deputy Sage, because of your little detour. So if you'll step aside, we'll be on our way."

"You were stopped when we got here," he growled. "No stops means what it says. You got to keep moving."

"Oh come on, Sage!" Jack's gritty voice matched his. "The people had to catch their breath after your goddamned extra mileage, and now you're the one holding us up. You got room in your lockup for all six hundred of us? And how's that gonna look for your boss Colonia, anyhow?"

The chant had stopped. It was so still Carolyn could hear the *Times* reporter's pen scratch at his pad.

"Listen, Mary Lou, you know I don't like no back talk." Sage's face turned bright red with the effort it took to ignore Jack. "You people just follow my instructions, okay?"

"And just what are your instructions, officer?" Teófilo asked mildly, as if Sage hadn't given them twice already.

"Move right on through this town," Sage asserted once again. "No streets your permit doesn't cover."

Jack handed Teófilo a bullhorn.

"These *placas* welcome us to Allen, the home of the *campesinos* who harvest the grape of Colonia for the wine of the world. They are grateful. That is why this deputy says that we must march directly across the town without stopping. And because we are polite people, we are going to act in accord with his request. Especially since we are in a hurry anyhow."

The people laughed again.

"And if I have to go to the bathroom?" This from a middle-aged man near the front, accompanied by guffaws among his friends.

"You must run into the gas station, then back out," Teófilo informed him. "No stops. Not even to button up your pants." The crowd roared.

Teófilo turned back to Deputy Sage and said in English, "We are ready, officer, as soon as you are."

At Sage's signal the police rows opened and the leaders set out at a dog trot. The crowd surged to keep up, and the police backed off before the peaceful onslaught. The monitors molded the group into a file of four abreast and urged everybody to maintain the pace. Highway patrol, sheriffs, and Allen police alike had to break into a jog to keep up. One of the sheriffs with a movie camera sprinted to follow and film it all.

Carolyn, heart pounding in a potent mix of fear and excitement, ran in the line, overweight women and middle-aged men huffing and puffing all around her. She too was quickly out of breath and, although she had sneakers on, her feet hurt. She wanted to stop.

This was absurd. Yet she was close enough to hear the guns and batons and mace on the sheriffs' belts bounce with their heavy steps. She remembered exactly where she had left off in the work, but she would not go back to that office. She would not let the *police*, accent on the first syllable as James would have it, scare her away. No. She would stay on the march.

Chapulín, knees and arms high like a drum major's, pranced up and down the row, urging the chant, the endless chant. Crazy, but effective. The line streamed into the intersection and broadened out as everyone slowed to a walk and expanded to fill the wider space. All the trucks on the highway had to wait, and the police could do nothing about it. This one and only traffic light on the main artery of the San Joaquin Valley between Empire and Mexico—the one that meant Allen, home of the Colonia farmworkers—turned from red to green and back again, over and over, while six hundred people surged like a mighty river, like an army of escaped slaves, across the road to the wider side to continue their journey north.

CHAPTER TWENTY-SEVEN

In the lead, with the UFW office across an empty lot to the left and the small town of Allen spread out on the right, Mary Lou and Jack ran side by side, breathing hard.

"Could have been worse," Mary Lou gasped, so winded she could barely get the words out. "Sage was outnumbered. He couldn't do anything."

"Glad the reporters were here," Jack answered. He was limping, and they both had to stop. Teófilo and Aurelio sprinted past, followed by the line.

"I'll do the press conference," she said, panting. A sudden wave of cramps took her over. Like her period, only worse, the pain belonged to a realm she hadn't known about before. She crossed her arms over her stomach and rocked her upper body. It was all she could do not to cry out.

"What changed your mind?" Jack asked. Bent over, tugging at bandages to cover raw, peeled skin, he noticed nothing. When she didn't answer he decided to lecture her.

"The march is so big that all we have to do is announce the rally and word will spread," he said. "We don't need small meetings anymore."

"I'll cancel the house meeting," she groaned. A miscarriage wouldn't be so bad, she supposed, tears in her eyes.

"Just what I wanted to hear," Jack told her. He had gotten his way. He didn't care why. He straightened out and decided he could walk again, though now they would never catch up.

"Look at that march," he said, gesturing toward the intersection. "We've taken over the highway and there ain't nothin' Old Smokey can do about it."

Hundreds of people, now past the light, had settled into a determined brisk walk, and formed a continuous and steady stream up the narrow side of the highway. The Highway Patrol, spread out on their motorcycles, roared between the marchers and oncoming traffic. The Allen police still stood at the blocked intersection, soon to be left behind.

"You should stop and get back in the van," she told him from between gritted teeth. "We need you to last all the way. I'll go with you."

She would not continue to march. She wanted this baby. She had heard that there was a long black car with tinted glass back when they first got to Allen. A resident told her it glided off down a side street as the march arrived in town. Was that Jensen? No way to tell, but Colonia had to be here somewhere. Yet she wanted this baby. Even more than she wanted to defy Jerry Jensen.

The line passed the two of them by as they waited together at the edge of a ditch for the medical van. Where was James? She needed James.

The van arrived and took them back to the office. Jack settled in to rest on the cot that had been set up for Hank, who was busy at the telephone. By the time Mary Lou got in her car, the cramps had subsided a little and the highway intersection was clear. If she squinted, she could still see the flags in the rear of the line on the left of the highway. The marchers were making good time. She headed home.

At Joseph Street, Carolyn's car was missing and James was nowhere to be seen. Mary Lou fell onto her bed, pulled the lavender cover over her from the side, and slept as if she had blacked out.

When she woke up, the bedroom was in the shade of the late afternoon and the cramps were gone. The house was totally quiet.

She got up and walked slowly to the bathroom. No nausea either. She hadn't thrown up all day. No blood; that was the best thing.

She splashed water on her face, gathered her purse, car keys, and a jacket, and let herself out the kitchen door. A disc of dark orange, the sun was near the horizon after a day of perfect weather. She settled into the car, determined at least to make it to the rally.

On the way up the highway, getting close to the Carleton church, the march was stretched ragged and tired looking. Still, the marchers cheered when she honked her horn. "The people, united, will never be defeated!"

She parked, walked up the church's broad steps, and surveyed its cavernous meeting hall filled with long tables and rows of benches and folding chairs. The women had established their serving line. A meal cooked for over six hundred people, and everything ready before a single guest arrived. Huge pans of hot and savory *carnitas* were next to baskets of warm, fresh tortillas. Rubber tubs, some filled with salad and others with beans and rice, stood alongside bowls of salsa.

A little boy with arms, legs, eyes, hair, everything bouncing in excitement, yelled from the doorway—"*¡esta aquí, la marcha esta aquí!*" The matron at the head of the line stared down at the child from wrinkles massed under salt and pepper hair and said, "*Estamos listos.* We are ready."

Mary Lou helped the kid swing open the large doors at the front to a mauve twilight, and the tide of marchers poured in. Exhaustion gave way to a burst of energy with the prospect of food and rest, and laughter and chatter swelled into the far corners of the room. The people lined up and the women, Mary Lou included, ladled up food onto light plastic plates as fast as they could, still finding time to salute people by name, exchange news of their families, pass them on with a joke or a compliment.

Eventually quiet set in as everyone unwrapped plastic forks from thin paper napkins and ate. Of the leaders, Ramón was closest by, herding Catalina, her baby and their two chubby kids to their places, sitting them down, putting full plates before them. The family, reunited. Mary Lou glanced around for Carolyn and found her sitting a few tables away, her back to them.

Ramón's children were breathtaking—the beauty of black eyes and brown skin. Would that be what her baby would look like? But their hair was straight as a board, not frizzy like James's. What would happen with the combination of her straight blonde hair and his spongy mat? What if the child had wide lips and an African nose? Her mother would have a conniption, and a lot of the farmworkers wouldn't like it either. None of it mattered, though. She and James would be in Cuba. Lots of black people there, and Castro said they were equal. Besides, the child could still look Mexican. Lots of Mexicans had African hair.

She watched Ramón get the little ones settled and hover around the group, protector of his clan. Rojelio tapped her on the shoulder and caught her by surprise.

"It'll be a long night, Mary Louise," he was saying. "Hank is saving places. Let's eat before the program begins."

He pointed to two empty seats across from Carolyn, between Hank and Carmen. They served themselves food and went over. Hungry for the first time in days, Mary Lou listened to Hank's detailed description of his press conferences and ate everything on her plate.

"Pacheco, with the restaurant in Emerald?" Rojelio spoke as he finished up his food. "He wants us at his place for breakfast tomorrow, before the march. He says it would be an honor to have the Allen office staff there."

"Holy cow, it'll have to be early," Hank said.

"Six a.m." Rojelio's toothpick, set at a rakish angle, bobbed.

"I'm barely making it through as it is," Mary Lou said in a low tone.

"Pacheco's one of our best," he told her. "You always have more energy than you think, *m'hija*."

"Glad I'm not part of the leadership," Carolyn said. "I'd rather sleep the extra hour."

"He said to bring you for sure," Rojelio answered. Carolyn groaned but looked pleased.

"Don't you think it singles us out?" Carmen asked. "Doesn't it make the leadership seem too important?"

"Carmen, honey," Hank said. "Sometimes you analyze things too much." He put down his napkin and gave a satisfied belch.

"I think we should go," Rojelio said. "Otherwise Pacheco feels bad, and the story will get around. Why should the supporters do what we ask if we won't make ourselves accessible to them?"

Everyone looked to Mary Lou for the final decision.

"Okay, we'll be there," she said. "Pacheco's a great cook. Why turn down good food?" Everyone laughed, happy at the prospect, and Carolyn nodded to show she would join in.

Marchers got up for refills, and the women began to dole out the extra food to supporters as they arrived for the rally. Whole families circulated between tables. Dishes clattered over the din of voices. Children ran in all directions, but the older people looked tired. Today had been the longest stretch so far.

"*Vámonos, pues.*" Rojelio pushed his chair back, threw away his toothpick, and got up. "Ramón's trying to hook up the microphone. Let's get going."

They all started toward the stage as a group, until Jack waylaid Mary Lou to talk to the press. Carmen stuck to her like glue as camera flashes went off in little pops.

"So the women get to be spokespeople at last," Carolyn said and stopped with them. "This I've got to hear."

"How will this march affect Colonia's stance toward the UFW?" asked the *Times* reporter.

Pregnant and about to disappear underground with a black militant fugitive, Mary Lou found that she could still focus on what needed to be said.

"The march brings attention to the cause, worldwide, from all of you," she answered.

"*La causa,*" Carmen said, and nodded her agreement.

"And it reinforces the Colonia Wine boycott, our main economic tool," Mary Lou added. The reporter scribbled away.

"Isn't that boycott illegal?" asked the guy from the *Bee*.

"Secondary boycotts are only illegal under the National Labor Relations Act," Mary Lou said. "Farmworkers don't have the protections of federal law, so they don't have those limitations either."

That stopped him cold, and she turned to the student from *El Grito* to make sure he got his chance.

"The kids from *La Raza* say Cesar Chavez is wrong because he helps the INS get undocumented workers out of the fields," he said, eyes intense. "Isn't that morally unjust for our people?"

Carmen stepped in to handle this one.

"The growers ship the illegals up here from Mexico to break our strikes," she snapped. "They're *esquiroles*, scabs. If we let the scabs break the strike, no one will have a union on either side of the border."

With that she swept on past the reporters to get to the podium, Mary Lou and Carolyn following in her wake.

"That's a pretty easy answer to a complicated issue, isn't it?" Carolyn whispered to Mary Lou.

"It's a true answer," Mary Lou asserted, glad that Carmen had been at hand. "You can't be all complicated when you're talking to the press, Carolyn."

Rojelio reached down to help each woman up onto the raised stage. Next he directed the people to push tables to the sides and set out rows of benches and chairs. Ramón tapped the microphone to test it. The older marchers sat and settled, and someone began the rhythmic clap that was part of any UFW gathering. Slow at first, a little faster, faster again, sharper, louder, and soon the room filled with waves of sound that put an end to side talk.

People scurried to move the rest of the tables, and once the younger generation sat down, all the young males and a lot of the girls added their feet, pounding the floor as hard as they could. Marchers, strikers, community people from every Mexican town around, a student group from Empire State College wearing T-shirts that read "Royal Chicano Air Force," Anglo boycotters and supporters, even some of the journalists—the huge crowd stomped and clapped and cheered.

"*¡Que viva la huelga!*" Ramón yelled into the microphone. "Long live the strike!"

"*¡Que viva!*" The people flung it back at the stage.

"*¡Que viva el boicoteo!*"

"*¡Que viva!*"

The *Times* reporter at the foot of the stage looked puzzled.

"The boycott," Mary Lou yelled.

"Down with Colonia*! ¡Abajo con Colonia!*"

"*¡Abajo!*" The word was like a thunderclap.

"Too bad Jensen can't be here," Rojelio called to Mary Lou as he tugged to get Ramón's microphone cord out from under the onlookers' feet. "All this would scare that little worm to death."

"*¡Gusanito!*" Mary Lou yelled back, laughing. *Gusanos*, the worms who left Cuba for Florida. And Jensen? A little worm, a scrawny one.

She wondered again if that was Jensen, biding his time hidden behind the dark glass of the big car. That's what worms did, hide in the dark. But today the Movement was strong; in Cuba the Movement had a whole country. When she and James ever got there they would find out what it was like to live in a world without *gusanos*.

¡Que viva la Unión! One person stood, and everyone else rose to join him, fatigue and sore feet forgotten.

¡Que viva!

¡Que viva Cesar Chavez!

¡Que viva!

Next Teófilo, up on the stage with Ramón, led the clapping all over again to a continuous explosion of breakneck sound. Finally he put his hands out, palms down, and everyone was quiet.

"The march has been long and difficult," he said. Aurelio demonstrated by limping, his crusty unlaced work shoes flapping with each step. He was exaggerating, but not much. The crowd burst into laughter.

"And yet we still march. Women march, old people march, children march," continued Teófilo. "They made you walk extra miles today, but not one of you complained. They cannot defeat us when you act that way. And after all that, we took over the stoplight and brought all of Highway 99 to a halt!" He alternated Spanish with English in phrases that overlapped but did not exactly repeat.

Next he launched into an announcement that Cesar Chavez had scheduled a vigil for the next morning at the Carleton courthouse to protest the unforeseen detour imposed by the Allen police, furnishing the time and location and instructions to all to be there.

From her place on the stage Mary Lou watched Rojelio, back down on the floor below, moving the microphone cord to the side so it wouldn't get stepped on. He got Ramón's kids to help him, leaning down to speak face to face with the girl, touching the boy on his head, leading them both to their places on the long cord, where, with somber faces intent on the task, they lifted their part so others would pass it over their own heads to the corner where the stage met the floor.

"Cesar has also instructed me to tell you—" Teófilo spoke on. "Tomorrow, the Union's legal department will file an action against the police—"

The people were on their feet again to cheer for their Union's president, who always knew what to do. After that, to the ever-present clap, Teófilo turned the microphone over to Mary Lou. She consulted the list in her hand and introduced Carlos, an irrigator from a unionized Napa winery, whose hulk dwarfed the guitar in his hand. People laughed and shouted jokes as he lumbered up to the stage. He swung into "*Huelga General,*" and hundreds of people belted out the chorus together:

"*Viva la Huelga en los files;*
Viva la Causa en historia;
La Raza llena de gloria;
¡La Victoria va cumplir!"

"What does it mean?" the *Times* reporter called over to Mary Lou.

"'Long live the strike in the fields,'" She yelled back. "'Long live the Cause in history. The Race rises in glory. Victory will be accomplished.' It's from the 1910 Revolution in Mexico."

The guy stared at her like she was crazy, but that was what the words said.

After the song, Mary Lou brought up a young, long-haired Anglo sent from the Bay Area's secondary march, three hundred strong and growing. In passable Spanish he explained that it seemed the hippies from San Francisco just could not walk in a straight single-file line. The farmworkers would have to show them what Union discipline meant when they all came together tomorrow night. The crowd loved it. They stamped and cheered, but no chant broke out.

The rally began to wind down. Mary Lou consulted her notes. All the speeches were done, except for assigning sleeping quarters, which was Rojelio's job, and saying goodnight. But one more introduction, the final stage of what had been a huge task.

"Carolyn Weintraub!" she yelled into the growing hubbub. She saw her friend snap to attention.

"Carolyn is back with us after last summer's strike." She continued with her strident voice until the farmworkers, always polite, managed to quiet down.

"We have told her she has to find every single Colonia striker to march with Cesar on Saturday. Carolyn needs your help."

Carolyn felt in her pockets for her notes, looking as though she had forgotten all about this. She clutched the sheet of paper she had found, let herself be hoisted to the stage, took the microphone, and cleared her throat.

"*Dispénseme, por favor,*" she managed to get out.

That was when Mary Lou saw James. He was way in the back, leaning onto the side of the wide doorway, barely visible in a shaded area. Still, there he was, holding his left hand out down at waist level, to get her attention. He must have seen her start with surprise, because in the next instant she couldn't find him at all. But he had been there.

"*Ustedes me han dado buen acento,*" Carolyn went on with her careful apology for her poor Spanish. "*Pero yo se que no tengo ni vocabulario ni gramática, entonces, ayúdame, por favor.*"

Mary Lou gave the striker list to Rojelio.

"Tell Carolyn to introduce the strikers who are here," she told him.

"Where are you going?" he demanded.

"I've got to leave. I don't feel well."

She clambered down from the stage and made her way through the crowd toward the entrance to the room, where the apparition had appeared. The crowd was thinner in the back; people were already leaving if they knew where they were going to sleep. He had been at the left side of the huge doors used to close off the church from the outside steps. She stepped out of the doorway into the cold night air.

James emerged from where he was standing in the dark behind the heavy opened door and came toward her from behind. He touched her shoulder, then turned back at once. She followed him toward the hidden space. Slowly, quietly, so they wouldn't attract any notice from the families walking by just a few feet away. When they were concealed together she moved into his arms, her alarm at the danger overcome by the wave of her own desire.

He backed off from her at once.

"It's bad enough that I'm here at all," he said in a low voice.

"Why did you come, then?" she whispered, smiling.

"I had to. I needed to see you."

"I felt the same. I even went home in the middle of the day."

"I told you I'd be gone for the day. But now I'm back. Next time we leave together."

More and more people passed nearby, eager to leave once they had Rojelio's sleeping assignments. No one seemed to notice anything.

"I was watching," James told her. "I saw Rojelio with those kids."

"Those were Ramón's children," she told him. "This is our baby."

All at once Carolyn was there, grabbing at them both. "I cannot believe you two are doing this," she hissed. Rojelio's voice droned on, amplified by loudspeakers so that it seemed to be everywhere.

"This is so dangerous! Give me your car keys, Mary Lou. I'll bring your car back. Get out of here, both of you!"

Dodging and moving fast, laughing under their breath like kids caught outside school, Mary Lou and James did what she said. Of course Carolyn would spot him, thought Mary Lou, as they got in the front seat of the Volvo and took off. She knew him so well. It didn't mean anyone else had seen him.

Fifteen minutes later the two of them were sitting together at the Joseph Street kitchen table. The chrome band of the table's edge seemed to glow because they both were the type to keep things so clean, Mary Lou supposed, and because by tacit agreement, neither one had turned on a light. The night was totally quiet, to the point where when James got up to put on water for coffee, Mary Lou felt that he was making a lot of noise. She was getting to be like him, she realized. On the alert all the time.

"I'm glad you came out there," she told him when he sat back down. "I don't care what Carolyn says."

"So, you're coming with me?" he asked her.

"We have to get things figured out," she said.

"You and Rojelio were sitting together. Right next to each other."

"We're the leaders of the march, James. We were all at the same table."

She stroked his forearm where it lay on the green Formica.

"I got these cramps," she told them. "They're gone now. But James. What if I have a miscarriage?"

"You won't," he said. "We're going to have this baby, that's all."

He went to the cupboard for saltines, put some on a saucer, laid it down on the table before her, and returned to his chair.

"I wasn't sick to my stomach at all today," she said. "Just pain. But now I could make love. I swear we could."

Her fingers sought out his and intertwined them.

"Let's wait," James said. He disengaged, but stayed close enough to touch the back of her hand. "You had pain today. It's crazy, but let's keep this baby, Mary Lou."

An hour later, they were still talking, sitting in the dark and making their plans in low voices when Carolyn came in, alone.

"It's done," she announced, collapsing onto the third chair at the table. "The march made it all the way through Allen. I'm exhausted!"

"The strikers got up there?" Mary Lou asked.

"They were all on the stage. A bunch of people came to me with new information, like there's time to follow up before tomorrow. Then Rojelio led everyone in *Des Colores*, and after that, believe me, every single marcher in there just wanted to get to where they could go to sleep. The whole place was empty in ten minutes. Then there was cleanup." Carolyn paused.

"Someone said they saw Silveira outside the church tonight," she continued in a low voice. "He was with his friends, standing on the side, watching everyone go in."

"He's trying to scare people," Mary Lou said. "He won't do anything near that church. His type just acts bad late at night, not in public."

"They do their damage in the dark," Carolyn agreed.

"Speaking of which," said James. "I sort of like it here in the dark."

"Me too," Mary Lou agreed.

"I heard about another thing," she told Carolyn. "A big black car, driving away from the march. It might have been Jensen."

"Now Jensen will do his damage in the daytime," Carolyn said. "But not when he's outnumbered."

All three of them laughed softly. James poured coffee into three cups and set out sugar and cream.

"Do you think anyone noticed?" Mary Lou murmured. James tried to look as if he didn't care.

"I hope not," Carolyn said. "There was a lot going on. But please. Do not do that again!"

They were three ghostly contours in the sifted moonlight that came from the outside; Mary Lou couldn't even see either of the others clearly. The ticking of the kitchen clock was the only sound.

"When are you leaving, James?" Carolyn asked him.

"We're going together," he told her.

"So you're going to do this," Carolyn said to Mary Lou. "You're going to live this way."

"I like the dark," she answered. Her fingers closed over James's hand where it lay on the table. "The underground will be okay."

"Why don't you go first, James?" Carolyn turned back to him. A dog barked on the next block. "Mary Lou can meet you in Chicago."

"I don't want to leave her alone here," he answered.

With Rojelio, Mary Lou thought. He wanted her and the baby for himself. He would take care of them. They would leave together after the march.

"You two are something else." Carolyn got up to empty the cups and wipe down the table. "You have to be out of this house, James, day and night, okay? Until the people leave to go home after Empire on Saturday."

"You can come with us, Carolyn," Mary Lou said and laughed. "*Los Tres.*"

"Yeah, Curls, the three of us." Even James was smiling.

"Three for the road," Carolyn mused. "Sounds like the last call at a bar."

Not a chance that Carolyn was coming, Mary Lou realized. In fact, for the first time since it all began, her friend was not put out by the fact that she and James were together. James had started being jealous, but Carolyn had stopped.

Carolyn rose to stretch, then got a scratch pad and pen off the counter by the phone. She warned them both, and switched on the fluorescent light. The three faces sprang out in the white glare.

"Come on, let's work on the details," she said. "We've got to get the two of you somewhere safe. You have a passport, right, Mary Lou?"

"You kidding?" Mary Lou laughed. "LA and the Bay Area's the farthest I've ever gotten from the San Joaquin Valley."

"It's not really a joke, you know," Carolyn said, shaking her head. "The Cubans give permission ahead of time when they want to, but they still require the actual passport before they'll issue a visa."

"So I'll get a passport. Then they'll give me the visa, right?"

"Don't be naive, Mary Louise. This will mean everything takes longer. You'll probably have to wait in Prague, not in Mexico City. Mexico might be too close for that long of a time."

Mary Lou shivered and moved closer to James, who lifted an arm and draped it over her shoulder.

"You know what to do, don't you?" she asked Carolyn. "You'll tell me how to get the documents I need?"

"Got it memorized."

"Good. I still think it'll be easier than working for this Union." This got a small smile from James.

"We'll have to call Donna and Bob." Carolyn started the list. A second dog began to yap. "Tell them the news; get them to let the Cubans know."

"I could try it tomorrow," James said. "I can find a pay phone, say Fresno?"

"Don't forget the code," Carolyn reminded him. "One number up, both for phone and addresses."

"And times of the day, too, right?"

"That's right. For everything."

Mary Lou sat and drank her coffee and looked at them, one after the other and both together. James, of course, was handsome, was sexy, was hers. And Carolyn, curly head bent over to concentrate on her list, Carolyn was her friend again. Carolyn would help them. Mary Lou was about to leave everything she knew to stay with James, and three days from now, after this march was over, she would be serious as all get out. For this moment, though, she thought of the baby and allowed herself to smile again.

CHAPTER TWENTY-EIGHT

The next morning, lulled by her car's smooth motion on the highway going south, Mary Lou stared out at the brightening horizon formed by the high shelf of distant mountains to the east, then dozed while Carolyn drove them both down to Pacheco's restaurant for breakfast before the march.

The next thing she knew, the car was in the poor side of town, bumping over rutted streets. Always the poor side of town with this Union. She looked out the window at the tiny houses with their no-sidewalk yards. Junk in just about every yard. Still, most places had a bright color somewhere, whether a painted door or plastic flowers on the porch, and a few looked totally nice.

Carolyn came near the corner of a street with stores, and they saw "Michoacan Restaurant" lit up far ahead in red and white neon.

"Yesterday I thought I was losing the baby," Mary Lou told her all at once. "I had cramps that bad."

"Oh no." Carolyn's hand flew to her mouth. She slowed right away to soften the jounces. "Did it hurt bad?"

"After all, wouldn't a miscarriage be the simplest solution?" Mary Lou asked.

"Oh I don't know. I like decisions," Carolyn said. "How about this morning? How do you feel?"

"Better. I haven't even touched my saltines." Still, she fingered the cellophane packet in her purse just to be sure it was still there.

"Any blood?" Carolyn asked. She was guiding the car carefully now and the ride was smooth. "I've heard if there's blood you have to go to bed and stay there."

"Not a drop," Mary Lou assured her.

"You want the baby." Carolyn looked straight at Mary Lou. "And you're in love with him, right? He's making it past the march so far. Maybe I was wrong. Maybe you should have it."

Carolyn? Ms. Practicality herself? Saying she ought to have the baby and be with James?

"Maybe I should get an abortion."

Mary Lou never thought she'd hear her mother's daughter say such a thing. Ever since these two arrived in Allen she had no idea what would come out of her own mouth from one minute to the next. She didn't like it.

An old jalopy passed on the left, driver honking, people waving, but it was still dark enough that they couldn't tell who it was.

"An abortion could be arranged," Carolyn said in a neutral tone. "It's legal. It's safe. Not like it used to be."

"Does it hurt?"

"I've never had one, but I've heard it's easy." Carolyn paused. "Physically, that is. Psychologically, who knows?"

"What would you do?"

"Have an abortion. But that's me."

"Have an abortion." Mary Lou turned each word over with care. "The march is over, and James moves on. You leave. Rojelio's back on the boycott, everyone else is gone—"

"I'd stay until it's done," Carolyn assured her. "Or we could do it in the Bay Area. You come to my place. No one would know you there."

They had reached the Michoacan's parking lot, already half full. Lights spilled from the restaurant's windows and open door out into the clear morning. More cars and pickups were arriving; each carried people they knew. They were about to be caught in the day's full tide of events. After she turned the motor off, Carolyn gave Mary Lou a clumsy pat on her knee.

"Today you get that march up to Empire," Carolyn said. "Tomorrow you go to the largest demonstration this Valley has ever seen. The next day it's over, and we'll have time to figure this out. I'll help you. I promise."

"So don't throw up," Mary Lou instructed herself as she opened the car door. The cold air felt like being doused with a chilled white wine. "Don't double over in pain. Try to act normal."

"And don't fall asleep." Carolyn smiled. "At least not while people are looking."

Together they walked into the Michoacan. Hank, in his wheelchair, was stationed by the door.

"Rojelio and Carmen aren't going to make it down here this morning," he told the two women.

"Why not?" Carolyn asked.

"Rojelio was the one who set up the plan," Mary Lou observed.

"I sent them up to Empire to be at the Colonia office, first thing when it opened," Hank said. "I want them to protest the fact that Jensen has been hanging around intimidating people."

"You shouldn't have bothered," Mary Lou said, annoyed. "Jensen's not doing anything but snoop around like Colonia always does. We're not even sure it was him. We need Rojelio at the vigil. He's good to get the people started."

"Well it's done," Hank said. He turned his back and wheeled his chair around and into the restaurant.

"Bunch of bossy men in this Union," Mary Lou observed. "That's one thing I like about James. He doesn't boss me around."

"Not that he's in a position to," Carolyn pointed out. "But you're right. It's not the way he is."

The warm air of the restaurant, redolent with coffee and food, was like coming home. Pacheco himself greeted them by name, dancing around like a ballerina despite his paunch. He sat them both down at a huge table in the middle of the room, among all the people talking fast as they drank their coffee. Right away his daughter served the women two huge bowls of *menudo*.

"Can you stand this stuff?" Carolyn whispered, pointing to the soup.

"Oh sure. *Menudo*'s good for what ails you." Mary Lou took her first spoonful, then more. The pungent liquid cleared her sinuses and now she felt perfect, for the first time in days.

Carolyn thanked Pacheco's daughter at least three times over, once for the soup, next for the basket of hot handmade tortillas wrapped in a clean cloth, and finally just for smiling, as far as Mary Lou could figure out, all the while postponing her first taste. Then she had to add diced onions and oregano, and squeeze lemon over it all like she'd seen the others do. Finally she took a sip, and everyone cheered.

"How do you like it, Carolyn?" Pacheco shouted at her from the other end of the table. "Tripe soup with hominy. Cure *para los crudos*—how do you say it?"

"Hangovers," yelled Aurelio, his broad brown face bright with perspiration.

"It's okay, or no?" Pacheco asked in front of everyone.

"*Amigos y amigas*," Carolyn announced. "*Me gusta mucho el menudo, este gabacha.*"

Everyone roared and Carolyn beamed. She had used the slang for gringo and made it a compliment to boot.

Pacheco greeted every guest and soon the place was filled. The man was happy, Mary Lou thought watching him, yet he was not going to make a penny out of this. Quite the opposite, in fact. James would love it if he were here. If only the world were like this Union when it was on the move.

By six forty-five Pacheco had poured his last cup of coffee and they were all back outside under a new sky, clear and calm, white to the east and a deepening blue overhead.

By seven fifteen everyone had driven with the rising sun up the highway to the Carleton courthouse. The crowd seemed small and sleepy. Now that she felt herself again, Mary Lou worried that not enough people would show up for this last day of walking.

The priest, dressed in ordinary clothes except for his collar, stood with bowed head at the top of the courthouse stairs that were jammed with silent people. Sparrows chirped as they hopped over the ground.

"Do we have a permit for this, Mary Lou?" Jack Marsh strolled behind her and managed a whisper that sounded like a cop.

"Heck no, you old goat. They won't dare move on us while we pray, and if they do? We'll fill up that jail of theirs and more." They both grinned.

The quiet of the vigil took hold. A mild breeze riffled the red flags and banners, and the sun, already strong, warmed Mary Lou's neck and the back of her bowed head. Each bird's trill sounded out like a small clear bell over the hushed shuffle of new arrivals. When she left the country with James, it'd be the Union scenes like this that she would miss. She thought of the warmth of his body in bed. Even pregnant she still wanted this man inside her. How crazy was that?

A murmured prayer ended the silence. The marchers formed their line and began to pull out. Deputies dotted the town street outside the park, enough to make the group wait for the traffic lights. The more here, Mary Lou thought as she watched the crowd swell, the fewer driving by Joseph Street. He was probably up and gone anyhow, just to be safe. But the march was already past Allen, and James hadn't been caught.

Carmen strolled up to Hank, as if she were arriving at a fete in her honor instead of getting there so late she had missed the whole morning event. Rojelio was right behind her. People greeted him, but he barely responded. Hank stopped his wheelchair, the crowd moving around it like water separating for the rocks, to talk with them both.

Mary Lou started toward the group to find out what had happened at the Colonia office. It was so early that usually no one would even have been there yet, she realized. But maybe today Colonia would be on full alert because of the march. Before she could reach them, Hank wheeled quickly toward the front of the line with Carmen, and Rojelio dog trotted to the back.

Suddenly everyone was talking at once. The last day of the march had begun.

—◊◊◊—

The women were already gone to Pacheco's breakfast when Carmen rapped at the kitchen door so hard the door rattled in its frame. It was still dark outside, but James, dressed and almost ready to leave, could see enough from the hall ceiling light to move around in all four rooms of the house. He grabbed Carolyn's car keys from the Formica table and his tennis shoes off the floor, then headed for the front door, the place where Carmen wasn't. He looked through the crack of the drape at the side of the window to make sure the way was clear. Rojelio was there, ready for him.

James ran to the bedroom, quiet in his socks. He was pulling the window up, anticipating his path through the backyards, when Rojelio tore by the corner of the house and saw him.

They stared at each other through the cheap window's wavy glass pane, Rojelio panting from his sprint around the house, James holding his breath. James felt the chill of the pre-dawn air, and took in the unblinking eye of a planet near the line of the eastern horizon. He imagined himself squeezing out the window, jumping down from the sill, slipping in the damp morning grass, gaining purchase, and dodging through the yards with their dug-up troughs filled with rusted junk. He could outdistance the stocky Mexican, even in his stocking feet, especially in the dark pre-morning night.

Yet in the same instant he knew that the long-planned escape route was futile. Where would he hide? In the vineyards filled with bare wires that didn't even reach his waist? The orchards with the flat ground and wide-open rows? Past all that to the Colonia vats, the guard house with barbed wire on top of its chain-link fence?

Rojelio stood fast, shaking his head to warn him not to even try it. The knocks at the kitchen door came even louder now.

He walked back there, shoes still in his hand. If the women hadn't left the door locked he wouldn't have had the dignity of looking like he chose whatever happened next, since by now Carmen was trying the handle, rattling it back and forth. Just answer the motherfuckin' door, he told himself.

He turned the knob, heard its button pop out, and found himself face to face with Carmen, who walked right in. Once again he stared at her long black hair as it swung over her jeans. She called for Rojelio to come to where they were, then waited, cool as frost.

James tried to be natural; he even pulled on his tennis shoes, but as he bent over to tie the laces, Rojelio bounded up the kitchen steps in one leap. He crowded into the kitchen, then cut around James and headed for the bedroom, where he rustled around for a minute and came back out, face bright red. The .22 was crooked in his arm, the box of ammunition in his hand.

Of course, thought James, Rojelio had lived here. He knew where the piece was, where it had its own corner of the closet. And now he understood, in one hot second of recognition, that James and Mary Lou were a couple. Their clothes were hung together in that closet, right in front of the gun. James's own white shirt with the brown and green striped tie on the hanger's wire neck, right next to a yellow sundress he had never even seen Mary Lou wear.

"We know who you are, Charles." The words slid out of Carmen's mouth like separate drops of cooking oil onto a red-hot pan. Rojelio stared at them both, distressed.

"Who's Charles?" James asked. Dumb question, but it was all he could manage. He was calm though. Alert, ready to survive.

"Charles Brown," she was saying. "Conspiracy to commit murder. Four guards dead, plus Nyame Jones."

The fear of exactly this had dominated him time and again. Yet now that being caught was at hand, he felt removed, detached, as if he were up on the ceiling, alone and careful, watching what occurred below.

"You brought the plastique in," Carmen droned on. "Smuggled it past the guards so Nyame Jones could kill people. You'll be in jail for the rest of your life."

Carmen the Righteous, so certain that she was pure and he was evil. Well this wasn't the time to debate the fine points with her. This was the time to talk himself out of being caught.

"You two want coffee?" he asked like a fool.

"Hell no," Rojelio answered, still in the hall doorway.

"I was the one who recognized you," Carmen bragged, oblivious.

"You're full of shit," James told her, trying to ignore Rojelio, who was upset, very upset. His fingertips held the gun upright by its barrel tip, its stock resting easily on the floor. They were white with the effort of a motion that should have been simple.

"I wanted to be sure," Carmen continued, "so I came here to look at you. Really look at you."

"And you liked what you saw, if I remember correctly," he reminded her. Anything to distract Rojelio, who looked as though he had been stung by something vicious, something that hurt.

"Maybe," she conceded. "But that's not the point. I talked to Hank, and he said we should bring Rojelio into it."

Rojelio fumbled with the gun and broke it down in jerky movements to get a bullet in.

"Hey, man," James protested. "Now it's getting dangerous."

Rojelio said nothing but continued with his shaky fingers, bent to the task. James's daddy had taught him long ago. Use a shotgun when you hunt. You'll get your game, as long as it's close enough to see. That way your buddy, out of sight in the thick woods, won't get hurt. A solo .22 bullet would travel far and then penetrate whatever it hit.

The thoughts filed by in a clear quick succession, but it didn't mean James knew what to do. Only what not to do, which was to run. If he stood here the same thing might happen, but if he ran, he'd get shot for sure.

"We decided I should go to the *Bee* and look up the picture." Carmen kept up her monologue. "That was yesterday. Then we knew."

Rojelio finished up and pointed the thing right at James. So this was what it felt like right before you died. A detailed tableau with the past as the present, all before you. Everything distinct, waiting to be shattered.

"What is the matter with you, Rojelio?" Carmen cried out, finally aware. "This wasn't the plan!"

A long moment went by, James holding his breath, Carmen still, not even moving to stand up. Outside a cacophony of birds announced the dawn. In the midst of their clatter Rojelio lowered the rifle without a word, and went back to holding it upright, again balancing the barrel by the side of his leg.

Maybe Rojelio just could not shoot an unarmed man point blank, James thought. Maybe the danger of dying, right here and now at least, was over.

"You just have to leave," Carmen said to James. "Simple as that." Grim, she stared up at him from his own chair at the green Formica table.

All the effort to get here, all the trouble to stay, all the work to figure out how and when to leave, and it came down to simple as that. He ought to be relieved that Rojelio hadn't shot him, but he wasn't. He wanted to laugh, but he couldn't.

"What are you going to do?" he asked them both, his voice so quiet he could be discussing the weather.

"We're going to turn you in, motherfucker," Rojelio said.

"You better be gone when this march is over," Carmen explained. "Or we'll call the police."

"No," Rojelio said. "Now!"

"Now or later?" James asked. "Which is it?"

"You leave this house now or I'm calling the cops," Rojelio said.

"That's not what we said," Carmen was loud, strident. "That's not what we agreed to. Hank's not going to like it!"

"Tough shit," Rojelio responded. "This man comes here with Carolyn, puts everyone at risk, and then moves into Mary Lou's bedroom? I don't think he gets one motherfuckin' minute more to sit around here and ruin her life. He has to do it right now!"

"This isn't about you, Rojelio," Carmen said. "You can't get the cops in here while the march is going on. The UFW will get blamed for everything!"

Carmen was so intent on being right that she gave the whole game away. If they had just threatened him, James would have assumed they would carry out that threat right away. Now he understood that Hank wanted no fuss until after this march was over. Good thing the woman was the type to argue it all out in the open. If she and Hank got their way, he could leave after the march. With Mary Lou.

Rojelio was still the wild card, though. Was he being macho, James wondered. Would he really do it? If the leadership didn't want him to?

"You had the nerve to show your face at the rally," Rojelio spit out at him. "We already had the plan, but that's what made us decide to find you this morning, *pendejo!*"

"I saw you playing with some kids," James said to him. "There was a baby there, too."

"What are you talking about?" Rojelio asked.

"Whose kids were they? Yours?"

"I don't have no kids."

"But you want them someday, right? If you had a kid, would you run out on it? Just like that?"

"What does that have to do with anything?"

"You have your nerve come to the church like that!" Carmen stood up, right up in James's face "Don't you know what it would have done to the Union if someone had recognized you?"

Rojelio could shoot him in the very next moment for all James knew, but all at once he could not tolerate this woman in his kitchen for one more instant. He turned on his heel and went to the living room, where he sat on the couch to lace his shoes. He'd get these shoes on and look decent if it was the last thing he ever did. The raucous bird chorus reached its highest pitch so far.

He glanced out the window. The sky was lemon-yellow above the eastern mountains, swelling with the light of the sun, whose flattened edge had turned to orange just above the horizon.

"Twelve hours," said Carmen, following right behind him. "We'll compromise. We'll give him twelve hours, no more." She said the last part over her shoulder to Rojelio, still rooted to his spot.

"Twelve hours or what?" James asked her.

"You get out of here in twelve hours," she said. "Or we'll turn you in."

Twelve hours. He ought to be relieved, but Mary Lou and Carolyn wouldn't even be home again in twelve hours. And they were marching. No way to reach them by telephone. He'd have to leave without talking to them, and after that he might never even meet his own child in this world.

"He said he'd turn me in right away," James pointed out, gesturing at Rojelio, right behind her now, face silhouetted against the poster that said the land belonged to those who worked it. Maybe Rojelio didn't mean it. Maybe he was too chicken-shit.

"I'm not giving him time!" Rojelio spoke as if he meant it. "Why should I?"

He moved so that he was right in front of James.

"I make my own decisions. I don't need Hank and I don't need her." He gestured with the gun, and Carmen flinched. "I don't care what in the hell your problem is, motherfucker. You leave when I say so. And I say now! Or I'll call the cops myself."

With that Rojelio turned and stalked straight out the front door, taking the gun with him.

Carmen had no choice but to follow. Rojelio jacked up the motor of their car, and then, wheels squealing as they careened around the corner to Joseph Street, they were gone. Not toward the highway. Toward the center of town. Where the police station was.

The sun had popped up, shining on a new day. The birds still sang. The trees' bare branches were absolutely still. Great weather for the march, James thought. But now his fear returned. The same old pattern of sweat on his forehead, breath shallow, heart pounding.

He sat down and bent over so his head was between his knees, full veins pulsing at both his temples.

Should he pack? Should he put both their things into suitcases, shopping bags, whatever he could find, get the stuff into the car, and call them when they got back here to the house tonight? But that would take time. And Mary Lou would never leave with him until the march was over, even if she did have his child in her belly. He could be in handcuffs in the next few minutes if Rojelio made good on his threat.

He fingered Carolyn's car keys in his pocket, then moved. Large steps took him into the bedroom where he got a sweater and jacket. He took the book—Donna and Bob's gift sent by people out there somewhere who cared for him—from the bottom of his suitcase. He checked its pages to make sure Robert Johnson's license was still tucked inside, then went out the kitchen door and climbed into Carolyn's Volvo. He stopped for a moment to look at the house. The old bare-limbed oak tree framed Mary Lou's familiar starched kitchen curtains. There was nothing more to do. He turned the ignition and headed due east.

CHAPTER TWENTY-NINE

Carolyn marched all morning. Mary Lou walked with her for miles, but finally, pale and tired, she dropped out to catch a ride in one of the cars that shuttled back and forth, feeding the march as though it had a life of its own. The leaders' phalanx expanded when Rojelio and Carmen arrived with Jack Henning, head of the California AFL-CIO, strolling with fanfare on this last day before Empire. Carolyn dropped behind, content to walk alone in a sea of friendly strangers.

At noon Pacheco fed her again, this time with tamales furnished from his truck to countless marchers clustered around four picnic tables made of cold, indestructible stone at a highway rest stop. Others sat on the dry brown grass to eat what they had brought with them, while everyone joined the bathroom line sooner or later. Then they started out again.

Her energy renewed, Carolyn trudged along by the side of the road, breathing car fumes and dodging trash. Into an effortless rhythm, she thought about her mother and James, then found herself matching an internal chant with the slow, even tempo of her steps. James and Mona, Mona and James. One had gotten her into all this, the other kept her here, and she couldn't have quite said which was which. She had stretched between them for weeks now, trying to please them both.

She always wanted to do right. To impress Mona would not only make a mother happy but solve the Cold War, so she read the weekly

National Guardian cover to cover in college, got herself arrested at a CORE demonstration during summer vacation, and led a hunger strike to protest the fact that the university ranked students for the Vietnam draft.

And to stick with James meant redress of discrimination as well as loyalty to a friend. So she harbored a fugitive, planned his escape and falsified documents, foiled wiretaps with codes, sabotaged listening bugs with loud music and conversations held outside. She knew all about the FBI, after all, from Mona herself.

With the strikers added to the list, she had worked hard out here. She had played her part.

As they neared Empire, its outskirts composed of small houses and shacks on rutted roads as if it were Allen writ large, more people spilled out of doors and school yards, packed station wagons and pickup beds, to join the march. They weren't all from the fields, but most of them, men and women both, had the plain clothes and calloused hands to show they had done their share of physical work. At last the growing crowd, buoyed with enthusiasm for the final push into neighborhoods of houses with front and back yards, clean streets and sidewalks, burst past the billboard that read "Welcome to Empire—Water, Wealth, Contentment, Health," into Colonia's own town.

Her section of the march, no beginning or end to the line in sight, stopped to wait for the ranks ahead to go up a rise and turn two and three abreast onto the sidewalk of a narrow bridge crowded with traffic. Red armbands ran back and forth to get everyone in double file, but like an overgrown puppy the multitude spilled into the street. After five o'clock now, drivers, eager to get home, leaned on their horns. Photographers jumped from the line to run down the slope and get the perfect picture of the marchers in silhouette against the late afternoon sky, where the sun cast the clouds on the horizon into striations of pink and gray. A hint of twilight, of dark blue calm, began to settle above the multitude.

On the old bridge, clotted with people and cars, Carolyn looked over the edge at the blackened cement pilings, then down the hill to where the marchers spilled into a broad avenue in a gush that ran from curb to curb. The crowd was quiet, as if to match the solemn beauty of the gathering evening. The bright red of bandannas, blouses, and shirts accented the procession as the people streamed from the end of the street onto the grassy fields of the Empire State College campus. Crimson flags and black eagles furled in the breeze over the darkening mass.

Her part of the crowd edged over the two-lane bridge at last, and Carolyn marched up the avenue with the rest. The throng surged forward with certainty and purpose. There was no way that Colonia would be able to ignore this march. There must be thousands here by now, maybe even ten thousand. Maybe more. The crowd was so large that it could sit in at Colonia's offices and demand negotiations. It could take over Empire's college and set up its own school. It could be an occupying army if it set up tents. Power to the People! That's what James would say. Mona would have called it direct democracy as she mellowed into what turned out to be the last years of her life.

Suddenly everyone drew to a halt. Straining to see what was ahead, Carolyn glimpsed telltale splashes of red rippling from flags along a mighty line that approached. A loud and raucous cheer rose from the ranks ahead of her, spreading back through her part of the line and beyond. Another march that looked as large as theirs had arrived.

The two fronts merged and mingled within the spacious grassy fields. Workers from the San Joaquin Valley met marchers from the Bay Area, with their backpacks and hiking shoes, tie-dyed shirts and miniskirts, beards and guitars. The people chattered, sang, chanted, and laughed as they walked together for the final mile.

An essential piece of the larger whole—that was her style, thought Carolyn. Invisible rather than being in the lead. It didn't matter if no one around her knew how many meetings she had sat through, lists she had pored over, evenings she had spent cornering the strikers, all in the midst of James's drama. She was entitled to be one with this huge event, which flowed in a swollen stream all around her. In this moment, at home in both the cultures around her, understanding for once that she had done her share, she was jubilant.

Thank you, Mona, she found herself mouthing, who had laced her milk with the memory of the downtrodden. Thank you, James, who had propelled her out of the dark whorls of grief. *Gracias a* Mona, who always urged her only child forward, taught her how to thrust herself into the unknown. Gratitude to James, who had led her back into the broader world of actions that mattered. And Mary Lou. Thank you, Mary Louise, for giving shelter, for making me work, and above all for being the one James had chosen. Each step that brought Carolyn closer to Empire also approached completion of the long detour with James. She was about to spring free.

She would gather the strikers tomorrow for the big day; she would meet with the pregnant couple the day after that, to plan their exit. Then at last she would drive back to Berkeley with a clear conscience to create a post-Mona, post-James life, all her own.

—⁂—

When James came back from wandering the hills at ten at night Mary Lou was already in bed, so sound asleep he could see her eyes working hard behind their lids. He called out her name and whispered at her to wake up, but she didn't. He wouldn't turn on the light. The police could arrive any minute. He shook her shoulder gently until she finally opened her eyes.

Before he got out one single word, her own garbled sentences tumbled at him: "Oh James, oh God, I had this worst dream, and it's still happening—" She lay her head on his chest, and at once it was damp with her tears.

"Mary Lou, I'm in trouble—" he tried to tell her, but she was caught in problems of her own.

"The baby was so strange, more like a little bird than a human being. It was tossed in a corner. It was tiny. I wasn't even sure it had a head. I put a dropper of milk in its pouch, and it came alive and looked at me. I changed it, but there weren't any clean diapers, so I had to rinse one out and I didn't know how to get it dry, and the baby's head was missing and then it rolled back, with real eyes and a sort of a smile. This thing was my responsibility, but I wasn't even sure what it was—"

She ended with a little wail so he held her, and by the time she stopped trembling she was asleep again. He stroked her fine blonde hair. How could he say it, in the middle of her nightmare? Get up, pack your stuff, we have to leave right now. We'll start out in a Chicago slum, we won't have much money, we don't know how long we'll have to wait or where we'll end up.

He laid Mary Lou back down on her bed, softly so as not to wake her again. All right then, he would tell Carolyn when she got here. She would say he had to go right away, she would be ready to help him, and this time he would let her. But he couldn't wait for her here in the house. He had to be outside where he could see the police if they came. He slipped out the kitchen door and went around to the back shed, where he huddled in its doorway under the clear, cold light of a moon just past full.

When he saw the headlights he crept to the corner of the house nearest her and waited until Carolyn, back at last, parked Mary Lou's car and turned the motor off, then called out to her.

"Carolyn."

"James? I can't see you," she answered. "Why are you out here like this?"

"Here," he whispered, stepping out of the shadows. "They told me they would turn me in." She came around to where he stood, arms held close, shivering uncontrollably.

"Who told you?" Her voice rose in alarm. "What happened?"

"Shhh." He laid a shaking hand on her wrist and tried not to have his teeth chatter. "Rojelio and Carmen. They came this morning."

"You're freezing. How long have you been out here?"

"Rojelio said he would call the police, Carolyn," he said. "I'm afraid."

The dogs began their yapping in the cold night air. The two of them stood stock still, nerves on edge.

"We have to go in, James," she said at last. She gestured at the neighbor's window, still lit. "It's almost midnight. We're too conspicuous out here."

She grabbed his hand, led him around to the Joseph Street kitchen door, and all of a sudden he was settled at their familiar kitchen table.

"Don't turn it on," he told her when she started for the light switch. She paid attention to that and came back to sit across from him in the dark.

"Now tell me," she asked. "Exactly what happened this morning?"

"They were going to give me until after the march," he said. "But Rojelio went into the bedroom for the gun."

"What gun?" Carolyn's eyebrows shot up in alarm.

"Mary Lou has a .22 rifle in there, in the closet," he said.

"How come you didn't tell me?"

"How come you didn't know?"

She had no answer for that. In all their political discussions Carolyn never had been able to acknowledge that someday the people might have to pick up the gun. So apparently she ignored guns altogether, and she hadn't even looked around.

He told her the rest of what had happened.

"I thought I'd get shot," he concluded. "I still don't know why I didn't."

"Did you tell him how you were set up?" she asked him. "Mary Lou said that Rojelio had politics, that maybe he'd care about what happened to you."

"I thought I would die," James repeated, shaking his head. He had warmed up, but his right knee was bouncing around, shaking as if it weren't even part of the rest of his body.

A car came around the corner of Joseph Street onto Fourth Avenue, its headlights sweeping into the darkened room, then out and beyond.

"We've got to get you out of here," Carolyn said. "Pack your stuff; I'll drive you to Fresno."

"But Mary Lou—"

"She'll be all right. The worst that's going to happen to her is a miscarriage. The worst for you—" She stopped.

"Stay in Fresno with me, Carolyn, just the night." He hated to beg, but this would be the last time. He had spent the day remembering his resolve to go it alone when he had to. But if they went too fast right here, he could find himself out there with no safe way to reach anyone.

"Help me get my ticket, figure out how to handle the first twenty-four hours in Chicago, make sure I don't lose contact with you and Donna and Bob. And Mary Lou."

"Have you told her?" Carolyn asked. "Where is she?"

"In her room, asleep. Did she tell you she's coming with me? She must've had someone drop her off while I was gone. Rojelio, probably. I don't even know what he said to her. I couldn't bring myself to wake her up, but how will she join me? I need you to help, and so does she."

He stopped talking, afraid.

"I'll help you, James," she assured him. "Mary Lou and I talked today. I'll help you both. We'll get this figured out."

Carolyn Weintraub. She had never let him down. He actually took her hand from across the table and kissed it.

"I'm supposed to meet Ramón at seven in the morning," she said, thinking out loud. "To turn the strikers out for the march."

He had nothing to answer to that except a silent squeeze of the hand that still lay in his.

"I've got to tell Ramón I won't be there," she mumbled. If he's not around I'll leave him a note at the Punjabi. It'll only take five minutes. You wait. Right here." Before he could answer she was out the kitchen door, headed for her car.

—⟋⟍—

James deserved her undivided attention, and she would give it to him, Carolyn told herself as she sped back to the highway intersection. She was the one with the lists. All she had to do was give them to Ramón. Then she would drive James out of Allen for the last time.

His pickup was in front of the ice machine, right where they left it that first night in the pouring rain. She couldn't knock on that door; what if Catalina answered? All right then, she would leave a note on his truck, stack the files in its metal bed. Nothing personal, just that something had come up and she had to leave.

She was scrambling through her purse to find a pen when someone tapped on her car. Rojelio, all serious, with that phony friendly boyish look. She rolled down her window.

"What are you doing here?" she asked, hating him.

"I stay here, remember?" he answered.

"Have you called the police, Rojelio?" she asked him. "You don't even know James. You want him to die?"

"He has to leave." Rojelio flinched at her aggressive tone, but he was ready to defend himself. "Your friend, is that what he is? He puts everything at risk."

"I never knew you were so cruel—"

"You better come in, Carolyn." His placating tone meant she was shouting.

"But Ramón—"

"He's not here."

"That's his truck."

"I lent him my car. To drive his *familia* out to where they're staying tonight. I have to get this food for tomorrow out of the back." He hauled a heavy box down from the truck bed, the last one in there.

"Have you called the police yet? I can't stay here if you've called the police. I'm taking him out of town."

"If I'd called the police you'd get stopped between here and Fresno," Rojelio said. He balanced the weight against the door, got it open, and wrestled the box into place on top of the others. "You'd be arrested as an accomplice. You're a fool, Carolyn."

She followed him inside so no one could hear them, then found herself staring down at the rumpled bed that took up half the remaining space. With Ramón gone the little room looked shabby, rundown, and small.

"I don't care how good a friend he is," Rojelio was saying. "You should never have brought a fugitive to Allen. It was a bad idea, damn it, for everyone! Think about it."

Think about it? She had done nothing else for months now. And only James was more at risk than she. Even Mary Lou could claim she didn't know who he was.

"Why didn't you turn him in yet?" she asked. "What are you waiting for?"

"He put both you women in danger," Rojelio continued as if he hadn't heard or didn't want to answer. "He didn't mind that, did he?"

"You think James wanted it that way? I'm one of his oldest friends. I made my own choices."

"And Mary Lou?"

"From the night we got here, we told her we'd leave if she wanted us to. She was the one who decided to let us stay." But Carolyn remembered how long and how often Mary Lou had been uncertain of what to do.

"At first she felt sorry for us, Rojelio," Carolyn told him. "Now she's changed. She wants to go with James."

"I don't believe you," Rojelio told her. "The Union always comes first for Mary Lou. What's she got with James that would replace this Union?" His brow was furrowed as if he was speaking to himself. Carolyn took a risk and attacked what he disliked about this situation the most.

"He didn't take her from you, Rojelio," she told him. "You weren't on the scene. She was unhappy."

"She's always unhappy," he said.

"You don't even know James. He's head and shoulders above your partner Carmen, I'll tell you that. And Hank, with all his orders. Not one of you understands what happened to him!"

He plumped up a pillow and sat on the bed, legs out, as if he owned it. She sat on the little hard chair by the small round table where she had gone over the strikers' lists more than once.

"Have you ever read Nyame Jones's book?" Carolyn's words tumbled out in a rush. "The one with the letters to his lawyer?"

"Yeah, so what?" Rojelio answered. "Everyone knows that book."

"Nyame made sense, though, didn't he?"

"He was all right."

"All he did was stand up for himself and they tried to keep him in prison forever. Put him in solitary in the so-called adjustment center, where you go crazy and smear your feces on the walls after you're there long enough. All over a few bucks at a gas station."

Rojelio said nothing to this. She decided on another tack.

"What if James was jammed in there?" she demanded. "What if he was set up?"

All in a second everything she had struggled so long to hide in a labyrinth of lies was out in the open, careening out of control. Like a fast train, she rattled straight ahead at a reckless speed.

"What if he didn't even know he had the plastique until Nyame Jones demanded that he turn it over. I don't know what I would have done, do you?"

She remembered something James had said to her once.

"The farmworkers aren't so damned different from black people as slaves, are they?" she asked him.

"That's not the point," Rojelio answered.

"So what is the point? That he and Mary Lou got involved? I didn't like that either, but what am I going to do? Turn James in so he can be in prison the rest of his life, make my friend Mary Lou miserable forever, just because I'm jealous?"

"Leave her out of it, Carolyn," Rojelio snapped.

"Doesn't it depend on which side you're on?" she asked. "If you turn him in, you're on the pigs' side, aren't you?"

"You know whose side I'm not on? His."

"But you're not on the prison's side, either. What do you think, Rojelio, is he really guilty of a crime? Should he have gone to the police and turned Nyame in? You wouldn't have done that. You know what the police are like if you're black or brown. You know what they would have done to Nyame, and probably James too for that matter. And anyhow what if the police set the whole thing up? They do that sort of thing. You know they do!"

She stopped, out of words for a second. She heard steps right outside the window, two people, probably on the way to their room.

"Nyame Jones," Carolyn repeated, her voice lower. "They had him in their total power but he never bowed to the man, right? Would you have helped him?"

"I don't know," Rojelio admitted. "What kind of help? It meant he died that day, right?"

"You think that was what James wanted? He was totally jammed in there. And maybe Nyame would rather die than be stuck in prison forever, doing the white man's bidding."

"Maybe so." Rojelio spoke so softly it could have been an apology. He was trying to think it through.

"Why didn't he tell me?" he asked suddenly. "Why did he send you here with this story?"

"James doesn't even know I'm talking to you," she said. "He doesn't want anyone to know what happened in there. He's just got to get out of the country. Think about how that feels."

The clunk of a soft drink can dropped through the vending machine outside, and the ice machine emitted the soft sound of cubes moving around.

"And what about Mary Louise?" Carolyn went on. "Shouldn't she be the one to decide? What makes you think you get to figure out what's going to happen with her life?" Rojelio winced as if he had been hit.

"Are you telling me the truth?" he asked. He had learned to whisper like the rest of them.

"Come on, Rojelio. Are you kidding? Why would I say all this if it wasn't true? Have you ever known me to lie?"

"Your whole time here you've been lying," he said, but he wouldn't look her in the face.

For a moment they were both silent. Carolyn could hear the constant hum of the highway traffic, as always when she was in this motel room. It reminded her of Ramón. Everything here reminded her of Ramón.

"She's pregnant, Rojelio," Carolyn said.

"Jesus Christ," Rojelio muttered, staring at her, stricken.

"So what about that, what about her baby?" Carolyn started in again. "Your Mary Louise. Just give them until the end of the march, like Hank said to. She needs you to do that."

Head down, face hidden, Rojelio combed his fingers through his hair, stammering to himself as if she weren't there.

"*Paciencia.* That's what Ramón told me—" he muttered.

Oh God, did Ramón know about James too? Carolyn could only do so much damage control.

"—that it was for the best." Rojelio went on. "I'm young and healthy. I'll find someone else, it won't take long. He said it would be here, not in that cold East. *Paciencia.* The right person will appear soon enough."

Ramón had told him all that? Quite a mouthful, more than he had ever said to her at one time. Ramón took care of people, it seemed, lots of people besides herself.

"What are you going to do, Rojelio?" she demanded. "I have to know." She heard a television and voices from the next room.

"Who's going to call the pigs in the middle of this march, anyhow?" he murmured, not looking at her. "Have the media find out that we have a fugitive hiding out, on the last day, when Cesar's here?"

"That's right," she said. "You shouldn't do that."

"But not for that *pendejo* son of a bitch!" he shouted. "For Cesar. And for Mary Lou."

Now that Carolyn had what she wanted, she had to get back to James. Still, she made Rojelio promise three more times to wait at least until after the march. When she finally left she was in such a hurry that she just about went up on the pavement getting around a corner on her way back to Joseph Street. She slowed down. All she needed now was to run into the Allen police car on its nightly round.

She was breathing hard when she got back. She felt as if she had run a long race.

James was still sitting alone in the darkened kitchen. She knocked softly, to scare him as little as possible, then told him that Rojelio had changed his mind at the hotel to keep the Union safe from bad publicity right now. She didn't see the need to emphasize that she had had to give up all the facts.

"So you can stay 'til the march is over," she said once her story was complete. "Maybe we'll even turn the light on again, what do you think?"

"You really believe it's safe?" he asked. Neither of them moved for the switch.

"Is anything safe?" she asked him back. He actually smiled at that.

"Maybe I don't even have to tell Mary Lou that they know," he mused after a moment's reflection. "I'm sure I'll know if any of them told her."

"They probably didn't," Carolyn said. "She left the march early; I was with her, and none of them walked with us. There's no rally tonight. She probably got a ride home from Rebecca Flores or someone like that."

"She needs her rest. Why go through all this now?"

"You can wait until tomorrow night," Carolyn agreed. She switched the fluorescent bulb on, and it crackled, then lit the room in a harsh glare. "Tell her after the march is over. Otherwise she'll just worry. And everyone will be together all day. Who knows what would be said? Who knows who'll hear it?"

"There's nothing to do right now anyhow," he muttered, as if it were an incantation.

"But then you'll both have to leave," she said. "Sunday. Just one more day."

"One more day," he repeated.

"You'll settle in somewhere," she said.

"You know me, Carolyn."

James paused to watch a car go by, then continued.

"When Ronnie was still at Dorsey High and I was at UCLA, remember? You met my mama and my auntie, that time we all three were playing poker when they got home from work. Remember how conventional they were, and all we wanted was to be cool?"

"You and Ronnie could dance." Carolyn laughed. "Remember the dirty bop?"

"The next year I wanted more," James continued. "Cool had to be sexy. Then came the Panthers and the Revolution. Change the world. Now you know what I want?"

"What's that, James?" Carolyn wished she could rest his head on her chest, comfort him as if he were a little kid. "What do you want?"

"To have a woman I'm crazy about and a kid or two. Doesn't matter where we are. That's all I need, just what everyone else has."

"We'll get you two out of here Sunday morning," she told him. "It'll work."

"And then we'll have a life?" he asked her. "Tell me I'll have a life out there, Carolyn."

"You'll have a life," she said. She patted his shoulder, an awkward gesture, but the best she could do. James put his head down on the table to rest, like a child in school.

CHAPTER THIRTY

Surprised she had slept at all, Carolyn woke up at six the next morning, right before the alarm was set to go off. She could hear James and Mary Lou talking while she was in the bathroom brushing her teeth, and still talking when she got out of the shower. Low, gentle voices—there was no reason to disturb them.

She drank a glass of stale orange juice from the carton in the fridge and grabbed her striker lists. James had the keys to her Volvo and Mary Lou would want her own car to get over to the march, so Carolyn decided to walk to the office. It wasn't that far and she would have the time to think. She left as quietly as she could, by the front door onto Joseph Street.

Rarely up at dawn, Carolyn appreciated its beauty for the second morning in a row. At six thirty the sky was black to the west and dark blue overhead. The eastern horizon presented a haze of bright white light. The only one out this early, her solitude was a comfort. When she came to the curve in Fourth Avenue where the cactus yard was located, its ramshackle Mexican look reminded her of what she liked about this Valley. *Como en México.*

She went over the evening before in her mind. James had promised before they went to bed that he would go to Fresno and buy his and Mary Lou's tickets to Chicago while the women were at the march. Tomorrow they would leave. She could go back home, whatever that would be like.

The sun came over the horizon behind her just as she turned west to the highway intersection. Its rays cast horizontal shafts of light that threw her own shape into a long drawn-out shadow that preceded her every step. It would be another day of fair weather.

Ramón's was the only vehicle in the parking lot. He was alone in the cab of his pickup waiting for her, as she had known he would be. This was the day to make sure the Colonia strikers came and marched together.

"*Hola, Carolina.*" He greeted her cautiously as he dismounted.

"*Hola, Ramón,*" she answered. "They better come like they told us they would."

"They'll be here," Ramón said as he followed her up to the office door. "Our hard work will pay off." He smiled, glad she wasn't going to make a fuss.

Carolyn struggled with the office door's old lock, aware of his breathing behind her.

"Your wife is well?" she asked. "And the children?"

"Yes, thank you." Ever polite, he reached around her, took the key by its tip without touching her hand, and worked at the door. He opened it with a little bow and waited while she went in.

"Catalina is happy to have arrived," he told her. "And the children are excited."

"I'm glad," she said, but actually they both seemed a bit sad.

"Good weather," he stated. "This Union is lucky, you know?"

"God, hasn't the sun been wonderful?" She sounded like an idiot. "Hard even to remember the way it rained last week," she trailed off.

They busied themselves pulling out striker badges and red flags from the storage cabinet. Their bodies in proximity, she hoped that he was hungry for her touch. His black eyes focused on her whenever she drew close, and she rewarded him with a smile of inordinate gratitude.

Three dusty cars weighted down with people pulled onto the gravel lot. The small, plump Señora Lopez was there, the one who had served her coffee and sponge cake the first night she had worked with Ramón. And Demetrio Lopez, her husband, with all his brothers, who greeted Ramón as if they had been *compañeros* in the struggle for years. Their wives and children were with them, all crowding into the office at once.

After that, strikers and their families appeared so fast she couldn't think straight, couldn't remember the names of even the ones she knew best, and certainly could not speak one word of Spanish.

The strikers stood around the cavernous office in family clusters, soaking in the sunlight that poured through the open door and windows, three or four generations in a group. Soft conversations in Spanish and Portuguese rose along with the steam from coffee out of thermoses. The office parking lot packed, newcomers left their vehicles in a row by the railroad tracks, like all the lines of cars and trucks that bordered the fields at harvest time.

Carolyn, dispensing badges and marking off names as fast as she could, kept track of Ramón. He was outside directing overflow traffic, then back, dispatching cars to pick up those who needed rides, bantering with the ladies who pressed him to accept coffee and fruit from their coolers. Everyone knew him. Everyone wanted to be near him on this great day.

A single man appeared before her, gnarled and bent, and gave his name as Benjamin Marquez.

"You're kidding!" she exclaimed. "You're the one person I had absolutely no information on. How did you find out about the march?"

Her English mystified the old guy, so she had a reason to signal Ramón to come over. He translated, and the man's reply tumbled out in such a rush that Carolyn couldn't catch a word.

"He says he heard on the radio, and right away he decided to come," Ramón told her. "He's had no work since the strike, so he moved to the coast. He figured if he couldn't eat, at least he would see the ocean. He started out two days ago, hitchhiked, slept by the side of the road, and here he is. On time, as he is proud to say."

By the time this speech was over, Benjamin Marquez had coffee in one hand, a fat cookie covered with red and green sugar in the other, and was surrounded by a gaggle of women who made such a to-do over him that he looked as if he might expire from happiness.

"*On'ta Manuel Silva y Francisco López?*" The question came to Ramón from a man Carolyn didn't know. She smiled, though, because the first word of the sentence was one only the Mexicans said. A contraction of *donde esta* that made people from other latino countries laugh at them.

"*No están aquí,*" Ramón replied. "*Porque no tienen huevos.*"

Carolyn laughed out loud. The veil had lifted, she could understand the Spanish again, and how could you not love a language where a man with no balls was one who didn't have eggs?

Lupe arrived, and she took Carolyn's place with the lists and badges. Carolyn and Ramón moved outside to organize the car caravan.

"*Los Gilbertos?*" Ramón directed a sharp question to the driver of a car that he had sent out ten minutes ago.

"*Dice que la mujer esta trabajando,*" came the reply. "*Dice que no sabia nada de este marcha.*"

"Just a work day like any other?" Carolyn repeated. "How can Señora Gilberto pretend there's no march? I talked to her myself. No way she could have forgotten all about it."

"This type is the most frightened," Ramón told her. "*Esclavos.* Like the black man used to be. They don't want to make the master angry."

Slaves and Mexicans, black and brown. Had Rojelio told Ramón about their conversation last night? He gave no other sign, so she certainly was not going to bring it up.

"So what do we do about these Gilbertos?" she asked.

"*Nada.* Cesar wanted a large group, and you got one. Plus, more said they would join us in Empire. But *ahora es cuando.* Time for everyone to be on the road."

Ahora es cuando. Now is when.

He barked out orders, and ten minutes later they were waving at the last pickup in the line of over a hundred vehicles, all filled with people as they swung onto Highway 99.

"Would you like to drive to Empire together?" Ramón accompanied his request with a small bow, and Carolyn nodded yes at once.

"Perhaps you will ride in my truck, but how will you return, then?" A tactful way to tell her he would be with his wife and family by the end of the day. She had to give him credit; he had never been dishonest.

"I'll come back with Mary Lou," she said.

"So there is no problem." He touched her elbow to help her onto the high seat, and a moment later, finally together again, they were on 99.

"I've liked being with you." She made herself say it. "You've helped me in a difficult time."

Her hand lay on the seat between them. He covered it with his, and her skin tingled from just the warmth of his hard palm. She watched his lips, where an affectionate smile played that she knew was for her.

She waited for a reply, but none came. He was so taciturn. This would never have worked, even if he had been available. Yet what a relief it was, sometimes, not to have words. Soothed by his touch and the tires' hum on smooth asphalt, she leaned her head against the back of the vinyl seat and closed her eyes.

"*Mira, Carolina.*" He tapped her shoulder. "Today we are in charge of the highway."

A Chevy so low it threatened to scrape the road—all chrome and electric blue, loaded with people, signs and flags—edged by them on the left. Next came a Volvo sedan with a "Boycott Colonia" sticker on the back bumper, and after that a dusty old Ford that trailed a red and black flag from its rear window. Carolyn and Ramón cheered and waved, and the occupants replied in kind. Bringing up the rear, held up by the Union cars in both lanes, was a Lincoln Continental with a Farm Bureau sticker in the window above the dashboard. Its driver was red in the face with wanting to get away from this mess, but he couldn't. Today the black eagle controlled the road.

—m—

Mary Lou woke up feeling rested although it was still pitch dark outside. No cramps, no nausea. Maybe this baby was gonna stay around after all. She felt as if she had slept forever. She had no memory of James coming to bed, but here he was, dozing next to her, his brow furrowed as if he never had been and never would be as young as he really was. He opened his eyes when she started to get up, and smiled.

"Your day," he said simply.

"Yeah, but it's still early," she said. "I don't have to go quite yet."

After she flushed the toilet, she came back to bed and burrowed under the covers, spooning her back against his warmth.

"We'll go to Chicago first," he told her. "Is that okay with you?"

"I don't know anyone in Chicago," she said.

"Better that way, right? No one will recognize you on the street and wonder about this black guy you're with."

This black guy. Father of her baby. She heard herself moan softly; she felt him grow hard against her backside. They lay together like that, listening to Carolyn's quiet movements in the nearby bathroom.

"I'll come with you, James." She spoke into her pillow, but she knew he heard her. "I'll pack when I get back from this march. I'll apply for a passport when we get to Chicago, and you can work on the visa. I've got a little savings account in Fresno; I'll get the money on Monday. We'll need it for the first and last month's rent, right?"

"Wouldn't hurt," he told her. "I have that money Donna and Bob brought, and they tell me there's more where that came from. We won't starve."

He said this like he meant it, like it was true.

She sighed. Who was there to say goodbye to? Her mother, her brother, and his wife? Her friends in the Union? Basilio, Lupe, Patricia, the Mendozas? She couldn't tell a single one of them where she was going, why she was going, who she was going with. All she had to do was pack.

Everything was quiet this morning. Not even any birds. She wondered why the birds were so loud one day and gone the next.

"I have to go to this march, though." She sat up again, determined.

"It's your day," James repeated. "Go on out there and have it, Mary Louise. I'll be waiting when you get back."

She opened one of the packets she kept by the bed and swallowed two soda crackers by habit, then showered and got into her pink flowered dress she'd ironed and set out a week ago, just to dare the rain to stop. She threw on a white cardigan and glanced at herself in profile. Skinny as a rail, no reason for anyone to guess.

—⚊⚊—

She had to park six blocks away just to get to where the morning rally was scheduled, in the same field where the marches had met the night before. People were massed so close together she was forced to constantly excuse herself and slip between them just to make her way forward. Thousands whom she had never seen before and never would see again. Long before she got near the front of the line, where people began to greet her by name, she knew this was the largest crowd she had ever seen. She walked for what felt like an hour and finally got to the beginning of the march.

"About time," Jack yelled, face red and chapped in the morning breeze. But he was smiling.

"Where've you been?" Teófilo asked with a grin.

Aurelio just pumped his fist.

First were the teenage boys whose job was to hold the main flags and banners steady in the furling wind: the *Virgen de Guadalupe*, beautiful lady embroidered in blue and gold, with her downcast gaze and folded hands; the Mexican national flag with its eagle on the cactus, snake in its mouth, green to the left, red to the right; the UFW flag with its blocky Aztec eagle, black in a white circle of hope against the red of shared sacrifice; the homemade Boycott Colonia banner, stitched in huge block letters of black fabric on red, stretched across the whole street.

Next came Cesar Chavez, diminutive despite being the most important person present. He wore plain black pants and a white Mexican shirt with a geometric Aztec line across the top front, embroidered in red and black. No hat, just his neatly cut straight black Indian hair. Handsome as always, but today he looked older than he sounded when they spoke on the phone. The serious leader, at the height of his power, had replaced the boyish mischief maker.

Cesar was at the center of a line composed of the Union's Executive Board, flanked by Dolores Huerta, beautiful no matter how many children she had, and Philip Veracruz, the slender Filipino leader with his craggy features and snow-white hair. Gilbert Padilla, tall and elegant; Pablo Espinoza, black-haired with a Zapata mustache; Mack Lyon, ebony-skinned organizer of the Caribbean migrants who harvested oranges in Florida; Marshall Ganz, thick features and thick hair, organizer of the Salinas lettuce workers; Jerry Cohen, unkempt and flamboyant, head attorney of the UFW's legal department.

The third rank was where she had found her place: herself and Teófilo in the center, flanked by Aurelio and Jack. Carmen and Rojelio—who pushed Hank's wheelchair—completed the line on the right. Carolyn and Ramón were stationed on the far left. Everyone was in place, waiting to start.

"We counted three hundred and fifty!" Carolyn yelled. She meant the strikers, of course. If her number was right, that meant they had gotten about two-thirds of them even in the winter when they had all scattered to survive. Not bad, especially considering that it all got done with James around. Mary Lou grinned like a kid when Carolyn came over to hand her the list of names.

Jerry Cohen walked back from his row to pound her shoulder and shake her hand.

"Damned good," he said to her. "I've got to hand it to you, Mary Lou. You really got the people out."

These were the first words he had ever directed right to her, though she had sat through his lengthy legal analyses at every meeting she attended in La Paz. You had to prove yourself to get noticed in this Union.

"The strikers are here," she pointed out.

Cesar turned around and smiled at her from his place in line. "As big as civil rights," he said, the people all around him straining to hear every word. "Just like the Vietnam demonstrations. There must be a quarter million people here."

He spoke softly, and then the little guy, crazy when he wanted you to feel he was in cahoots with you, lost twenty years all at once and winked at her. Or maybe she imagined it, because no one else seemed to notice. In the next instant he faced forward with that intent serious look, bent on capturing history.

Of course the police would call it a hundred thousand, but it didn't get better than this. Leave while things were at their best. They would make it to Cuba. Her Spanish would mean she could be a translator after the baby was born, or an English teacher. There was good medical care there, she had always heard from her leftist friends. And good schools. The baby would thrive.

A hush fell, and the line began a slow surge forward. Colonia was nowhere to be seen. No security guards like the ones always stationed at their fancy offices just a few blocks from here. No large black cars with shadowy figures like Jensen keeping their eye on things. Too much press, national and even international, thanks to Hank.

A few city police officers watched passively as the red-banded monitors herded the people along. Everyone was in a fine mood at the beginning of this balmy, breezy, sunny day. Traffic was thin since it was Saturday morning and everyone in town knew this was about to happen. But the cars that were there had to yield while the people who planted and harvested their food, and their legions of supporters, took their time and filed by.

This power, this being part of a tide that carved its own way, this was what she loved about being in this Union. This would be harder to leave than any one person. Today was her day. James had told her to enjoy it, and she would.

The moving current of people surged around a corner onto a broader street. She caught a glimpse of Silveira and his friends, huddled together in a sheepish small throng. They stood there, embarrassed, urged to join by passersby who didn't even know them, and then they entered the anonymous ranks and paraded with all the others to the front of Colonia's main office.

Mary Lou had to laugh. In the light of day with everyone here, Silveira didn't have the nerve to stay apart. And when Colonia sent its people to visit him in his shack at night, he would probably turn their way again. But for today he was theirs, for whatever it was worth.

The red-bands called the march to a halt, because the front ranks were at the end of the broad avenue that brought them face-to-face with Colonia Winery's national headquarters. Mary Lou looked up at the higher stories of aqua panels and sheeted glass. Rumor had it that the Colonia brothers had penthouse offices up there. She brought her gaze down to the street-level offices that lay beyond pure white low stucco walls. She had walked past the low wooden gate and then through the carved dark metal doors, now bolted, built into the main building to belie the impression of easy accessibility. They had admitted her to the inner atrium, the high open space with its tropical birds and plants that heralded the offices of the corporate big shots, including Jensen. Today not a single person was visible in any part of the building she could see.

The strikers' lives had been so damaged by this fight, yet behind her all she sensed was happiness at being this strong. Not a rock was thrown, not a mark made on the wealthy unblemished facade that had been purchased with the farmworkers' underpaid labor. When it counted most, this Union had discipline.

Add that to the number of people the UFW could turn out, whether to march for the day or the week or the whole freezing cold winter in front of a chain grocery store. Add all that up and the UFW simply could not lose. In fact the strikers had better lives already. Look at the pride on their faces.

The march turned right, skirted the Colonia building, eventually completed its two-mile route through the heart of Empire, and spilled onto the spacious grounds of Empire's city park. The site of the final rally, this was the largest in the whole San Joaquin Valley, for which the Colonia Brothers were forever claiming credit. Mary Lou scurried to help make sure everything was as it should be on the stage the La Paz people had built, and from up there she could see it all. The currents of people had widened into a lake that filled the broad grassy plain under spreading new-leafed oaks and elms, its calm surface ruffled everywhere while the people craned to see friends, sat, chatted, lay in the sun as they waited for those behind to find a place.

After Ramón and Rojelio tested the microphones, Juan Mehia and his group from Stockton finally made their official entrance, throwing hats in the air and ay-yi-yi-ing as though they'd been on a month-long cattle drive. With all this going, the program began, even as the relentless lines of marchers kept rolling in at the back.

The head of the LA boycott, *muy suave* with his movie star looks, came on stage. Mariachis filed in behind him, splendid musicians with their shining horns and tight black pants, white curlicue decorations on their jackets like frosting on a cake. The MC tapped the microphone, and at once the people were quiet.

"By being here," he said, "you have shown to America the face of the farmworker. The one who loads its tables with fruits, vegetables, and even its wine, the one ignored too long, the one none of us could live without!"

The people clapped wildly, apart at first, together in the Union rhythm, an ocean of sound at the end, with yells and whistles and shouts and cheers.

"The Colonia brothers"—the MC held up a hand to stop the boos and hisses—"the Colonia brothers, as you know, avoid publicity whenever they can. Yet today they have seen that we are here, and they are afraid to remain silent. Today they have decided to hold their own press conference, they are that frightened. They told the press, they actually said this: 'After Cesar's talk, that's when we want to talk to you.' And Cesar will speak, but only after all of you have found places. So Colonia waits until its workers, *la gente*, are seated."

Laughter trickled through the crowd.

He waved his hand and the mariachis broke into their music, loud and happy, just like the crowd. Next Joan Baez was handed up to the stage, beautiful dark hair gleaming in the sun, to sing *Gracias a la Vida, todo en español.* For once the English speakers had to remain uncertain.

Then Luis Valdez and his *Teatro Campesino* jumped up to enact the Colonia brothers as slave drivers, whips in one hand, brandy snifters in the other, with Luis and his wife as the heroic strikers who stood up to them and won the day.

After that, labor leaders and political figures no one listened to spoke anyway, and, an hour after it all began, it was time for Mary Lou.

She had no idea why, but she never was scared to speak to the people, even as she faced by far her largest crowd. It was the getting them all together that had frightened her. Once they were here in front of her, it was easy.

She greeted them in Spanish first, then Portuguese, and finally English, and just this was enough for the crowd to go wild. She read out the strikers' names and they stood one by one, then their families, until the group, showered with applause, assumed its rightful size.

"Today," she told them, "you have come here to confront the Colonia Winery. They have hurt you with their feudal ways and their starvation tactics, but you have shown great dignity. You have left their fancy places untouched, though you could have done them harm. Many of you have come from afar. Others have risked whatever new employment you have. Everyone has lost wages, time, and money. But by being here you have demonstrated to the Colonia brothers that you will not give up, that all these other people here stand in solidarity with you, that the boycott will continue to grow, and that the United Farm Workers Union will not rest until they negotiate a contract and meet your terms."

She stopped, overcome with emotion. The vast sea of upturned faces, with the individual strikers whom she knew so well, in front and craning to see her, represented all she held dear. If only *la gente* could always be like this. All here together and all united. History would be different. Each time this happened—and this time she was the one who had made it happen, with the others of course;

she would never give herself credit alone. But each time this happened, it was one step closer to the day when the workers would get their share.

"Your names may never be engraved in the history books or on the sides of buildings," she told them, her voice quavering. "But everyone here today knows that you are the heroes, the ones who make history. And for that we engrave you in our hearts. Forever."

She came off the stage to deafening applause. Everyone was smiling, laughing even. Her own face ached with smiling. Yes, she could leave now, she could go with James. The workers had made their point.

The small, dark man in the white shirt with the Aztec pattern walked to the center of the stage. Thousands of red flags waved as the crowd paid tribute to the Union's president. Cesar Chavez gesticulated madly for a movie camera to catch the dramatic sight. Silence fell, and everyone focused on the figure before them.

He spoke for a half hour on the history, economics and politics of Colonia's wine industry, but suddenly he was very specific and mentioned Silveira by name:

"A man as poor as the rest of us," he said. "A man who does not know how to manage his sorrow except with drinks. A man who is vulnerable to Colonia's bribes. Yet a man who today has been unable to resist the pull of his brothers and sisters, united in a justified cause.

"We want to tell this to you, Antonio Silveira," Cesar said next. "You are among us again."

Mary Lou was startled. Even she had not known Silveira's first name, and she was from around here. Cesar was from Delano. She believed in no such thing, but the man had magical powers. She wondered if he knew James was in Allen. Maybe he didn't care.

"We will forgive you," Cesar continued. "We have forgiven you. But if you threaten us again we will come after you with the full force of the law, and we will not rest until justice is done."

Next Cesar recounted the forced detour of the march in Allen, but all Mary Lou could think of was that Silveira's crazy shooting up the camp had led to her first night with James. The night she learned what lovemaking was. She was wet. She was waiting. She wanted him.

The crowd cheered as if the struggle was already won when Cesar told them that yesterday's *Wall Street Journal* article had reported a 10 percent drop in Colonia's sales, and it brought Mary Lou back. But Cesar ended on a different note.

"Brothers and sisters. *Lo que es necesario* to understand is this: *Hay mas tiempo que vida.* More time than we need to win this fight with Colonia. More time than we need to complete the farmworkers' struggle for dignity. More time than life. We will never give up. We will never give up."

And with that he was off the stage. Everyone applauded, of course, and Mary Lou did too. But his words unnerved her.

More time than life. What in the world did that mean? Life was what she had plenty of. Her life and James's and their child's, hardly more than a speck but already getting its share of attention.

And time? Always in short supply, now more than ever. Down to just the time it would require for her to close her bank account, apply for her passport, pack and leave with James. What would she take with her? Maybe it didn't matter. Her shape would change; she would need maternity clothes. Nothing would ever be the same again.

More time than life? No, *el contrario.* More life, much more, than time.

The rest of the program went by fast—speeches by more pompous politicos, another Teatro skit as funny as the first, more songs, and finally the inevitable lengthy thank yous. At last, the march was over. It took a full hour just for the crowd to pour out of the park, though people were ready to leave as quickly as they could. The flood receded. The tide had run its course.

The ones who had put it all together—Teófilo, Jack, Aurelio, Rojelio, Carmen, Carolyn, herself, the people from La Paz—took it apart. They rolled up the cords, stored the microphones, folded the chairs, dismantled the stage, and collected huge amounts of trash in large plastic bags until the twilight had shifted into a starless cloudy night and the work was finally done.

"Pacheco's," Teófilo yelled to the rest as they finished up. "Food, beer. *Todos juntos,* all together. Everyone come, *todo el mundo. Tenemos que* celebrate tonight! Who's got a car here?"

"I do," Mary Lou sang out. Her energy was back, the miscarriage threat was past, she was sure of it. If ever there was a day to be dog-tired, this was it, and instead she was ready for more. "I drove up by myself. Plenty of room!"

"You're crazy," Carolyn whispered fiercely. She took her friend's arm to steer her away from the group. "We've got to get back. There's a lot to do!"

"Pacheco's first," insisted Mary Lou. "It won't take that long. They'll think it's strange if I don't come."

With no car of her own and the group all around them, Carolyn didn't have a choice. The two women led the way, Aurelio and Teófilo at their heels.

The four of them piled into Mary Lou's car. She took the back roads to Emerald, and they sang every Union song any of them had ever known, the sound spilling out of the open windows and bursting like bubbles into the warm night air. Even the grapes, in bunches of green pebbles peeking out at last from the vineyards' dark branches, knew that it was finally spring. They sang all the way to Pacheco's restaurant, and once they got inside they sang some more.

CHAPTER THIRTY-ONE

Seated at the morning's same large table within the red glow of La Michoacan's neon sign, after two margaritas Carolyn found her lips circling the rim of the glass, stinging yet searching for more salt. The scene lurched agreeably before her eyes in a lewd pastiche.

Ramón and his family sat at a separate table in their own gloomy corner. A devoted family man, she told herself, but all she could visualize was the dark and slender nude, already a ghost of her past, perhaps even a figment of her imagination, on the bare sheet at the Punjabi motel. The tequila informed her that when she got back home she would not miss him.

At Carolyn's right were Aurelio and Teófilo, off on a jaunt of their own in an incomprehensible Spanish laced with what had to be raunchy jokes, given the frequency of their loud and exclusive guffaws.

On her left she was flanked by Hank and his lady-in-waiting Carmen, who had spent the last half hour raving in turns about the size of the march and the importance of its attendees. Hank was enjoying his drink with a fierce pleasure that bespoke his need to appreciate life from a wheelchair. Carmen gestured for Jack's attention across the table, but he was pressing the plain and simple Lupe Muñoz with various important things he wanted to tell her. Lupe, perhaps not so virginal after all, tittered at his every word. In a maudlin rush, Carolyn decided she felt sorry for Carmen, of all people.

Hank wasn't fit to be her companion, and anyway it was said he had a wife somewhere. Carmen. Beautiful and intelligent and always alone.

And then there were Mary Lou and Rojelio, who sat across from her at the same wide table. Mary Lou had drunk only iced tea, and she had not smoked a single cigarette, but her face was flushed, her eyes glistening and animated as she took in everyone else's conversation. As for Rojelio, he had lined up four empty shot glasses and was asking for a brand new saucer of lime wedges and salt to go alongside his fifth tequila, gold and glowing. Carolyn had never thought of Rojelio as unreliable when he drank, but she had never seen him do this before either.

He sucked his lime, salted his tongue, and belted the shot down, and then, in a surprisingly melodious tenor, led the table in a verse of a song Carolyn hadn't heard before:

> . . . *¡a luchar con valor y con tesson!*
> *Sin dar pasos par detras, todos unidos,*
> *¡Por luchar en contra del patron!*

"What does it mean?" she mouthed to Mary Lou.

"To struggle with valor and courage, no steps backward, against the boss," Mary Lou shouted while the rest went on to the chorus, more typical of UFW rhetoric.

> *Viva la cause por cual luchamos;*
> *Viva la huelga en el fil;*
> *Viva la Virgen de Guadalupe;*

(Here Rojelio's lead voice launched into a plaintive wail that made everyone laugh.)

> *¡Viva nuestra Union!*

When it was done Rojelio placed an elbow as far onto the table as it could reach and leaned on it so he could stare right into his eyes of his former *novia.*

Carolyn wasn't even certain that his lips moved, but nonetheless he was pleading, beseeching: How could you do this to me, Mary Louise? How could you?

All at once Mary Lou was willing to engage, and they talked. So low that whatever they said was under the general noise, but in a manner so intense that anyone with two brain cells to rub together, as Mona would have said, could tell it was important. Mary Lou shook her head emphatically to refuse whatever it was he was asking of her, then rose to go to the bathroom.

Carolyn followed, suddenly tired of all of this. She didn't even want to know what the conversation was, she told herself. She just wanted the whole drama to be over.

"We have to leave," she said to the back of the stall door. "James will be going crazy, Mary Lou. It's not fair to him to make him wait."

"They haven't brought the food yet," Mary Lou answered. "I need something in my stomach."

"Why is it taking so long?" Carolyn stifled her own impulse to feel sick to her stomach. She had to eat. She had to get sober. She had to think straight.

"Yeah, Pacheco, what's wrong?" Mary Lou called out from her hidden place. "All you've done is feed about forty of us this morning and two hundred and fifty at lunch. Why are you taking so danged long?"

"Please, Mary Lou," Carolyn begged. "I don't even have my own car. The minute we're done eating, drive me to Joseph Street. I need you to do that."

"Of course. We'll go as soon as we can." Mary Lou came out, washed her hands, and drew a brush through her long hair. "I promise."

"He'll be there." Carolyn reminded her. "He'll be waiting for us."

—⚂—

James sat at his usual place at the green Formica table, his suitcase packed and by the kitchen door, with the poetry book, wrapped in the orange and red Kente cloth, on top. "We could leave tonight, even."

He spoke first to Mary Lou, who ignored him as she sank into her own chair and laid her head on her arms on the table.

"Did anything else happen?" Carolyn asked. He could smell the alcohol and coffee on her breath. "Did anyone come by?"

"I was gone all day," he told her. "Didn't see or hear a thing."

Carolyn was pacing the length of the small room, from the window past her side of the table to the hall door and back again. He nodded at her. It was time to begin.

"Mary Lou," she said, her voice sharp. "We have to talk."

Mary Lou didn't raise her head, but she held up a finger to tell them she was listening. The street was quiet.

"We didn't want to tell you until the march was over." James hoped he sounded gentle.

"They know who James is," Carolyn told her.

That got her attention. She sat up straight.

"Who knows?" she asked. "Rojelio?"

"Yes," Carolyn said, taking the third seat at the table. "And Carmen. And Hank. They gave him until tomorrow to leave."

James told her the part where Carmen and Rojelio came to the house. Carolyn told her the part where she spoke with Rojelio at the Punjabi motel. Mary Lou asked no questions but listened to every word.

"That explains a lot," she said when they were done. "Like why someone was always missing when there was work to be done. Like how Rojelio was acting tonight."

"Which was how?" James asked.

"He got drunker than I've ever seen him," she said. "He said mean things." Pale as bleached cloth, she paused. The soft ticking of the kitchen clock was the only sound. One thirty a.m.

"Like he told me I never was that much fun anyhow."

Now James got up to pace. The man had his nerve to make Mary Lou unhappy. And she had her nerve to look this miserable. She was supposed to be through with him. James took up a can of cleanser and scrubbed hard at the already spotless kitchen sink.

"He finally knows you're breaking up," Carolyn said.

"Why didn't you tell me when this first happened?" Mary Lou asked them both.

"You were leading a march and maybe having a miscarriage at the same time," said Carolyn. "It seemed better to wait, just past this final day. Then you were determined about Pacheco's. I didn't want to go, remember?"

"We have to leave in the morning," James said, turning around to face the two of them. "Where's your suitcase, Mary Lou? I'll help you pack."

"The shed," she mumbled. "There are two. Cheapo ones, like cardboard. And they're not big enough for hardly anything."

He went out back into the chill, rooted around in the dark shed, and returned with the suitcases, which he set down in the middle of the kitchen floor, tops open to get the mildew odor out. Neither of the women had moved.

"I'm tired," Mary Lou murmured. "Can't I sleep? Can't we do it in the morning?"

"It's been a hell of a long day, James," Carolyn said, as if he ought to feel sorry for them.

"No kidding," he answered. "As for me, first I went to Fresno for the tickets and next into the hills, all day and into the night, waiting."

"Remember," Carolyn admonished, gesturing toward Mary Lou whose head was down on the table again. "She's pregnant."

"She told me that, remember?" he answered. "The flight's at eight fifteen a.m., in case anyone's interested. And I used the new ID Robert Johnson, for real. We're leaving, and man, it's time."

He stroked Mary Lou's hair.

"You want coffee?" he asked her. "I can put the water on."

"It's felt like a family," Mary Lou sighed, eyes closed. "The three of us. I got used to it."

Outside they could hear the usual crickets. Her little town of Allen was peaceful tonight, James thought. All the excitement over, everyone passed out by now. Everything normal. Except it wasn't. Rojelio, Carmen, and Hank, for instance. They were probably talking somewhere, waiting to pounce.

"We did okay." Carolyn rested her chin on a palm, upright, but barely.

"We'll have our own family," James said to Mary Lou. "And Carolyn can come and visit. But come on, Mary Louise. Let me help you pack."

"I'll stay here a day or two," Carolyn told Mary Lou. "I'll notify the landlord—"

"Get the deposit back," said Mary Lou. She sat back up. "I've certainly kept the place clean enough."

"Then you'll send me an address," said Carolyn. I need to be able to reach you.

"Using the code, of course," James reminded them.

"The code, the code." Mary Lou smiled as she spoke. "Our good luck charm."

"Like bread crumbs in the forest," Carolyn laughed.

"Seriously, though," he admonished them. "We've got to remember the rules. It's important."

"You know how I am, James," Carolyn said. "The day I know where you are I'll mail you money, whatever I can raise in Berkeley. Eventually there will be more from Donna and Bob. And I'll write and let you know how everything went at the office, Mary Lou."

"Who do you think will be in charge?" Mary Lou asked.

"It'll have to be Rojelio, won't it?" Carolyn answered. "He knows this scene."

James glanced out the kitchen window. Tonight the moon was adrift in a sea of thin serried clouds within a luminous circle of its own phosphorescent glow. A beautiful night sky. Good time for a new beginning.

"Probably you're right," Mary Lou was saying. "Or it could be Ramón. Ramón could lead this place; he'd be good at it."

"Would his whole family move up here?"

"Farmworkers move, Carolyn, that's their lifestyle. Jeez, though. What're you gonna tell people about why I left?"

"Word will get around." Carolyn paused. "I told Rojelio about the baby. I told him about Freeman too, James. That you were set up."

The other two stared at her.

"I mean, I had to," she stammered. "Well, I thought I had to. I thought it was the only way to talk him into more time."

"You put me at risk, Carolyn," James said. "You said I committed the crime."

"No wonder Rojelio was so furious," Mary Lou added, as shocked as he was. "I can't believe you said I was pregnant!"

"It worked, didn't it?" Carolyn pointed out. "He decided not to turn James in during the march."

"Hank wasn't going to let that happen anyway," Mary Lou told her.

"What makes you think Hank was in control?" James said. "Rojelio could do whatever he wanted to."

One of the yappers started up outside, then stopped. James got up to make sure no one was there. Now the moon was alone in the cold clear sky, the stars as hard as diamonds.

"Well, it's two in the morning, so nothing's going to happen right now," Carolyn said. "I don't think."

Mary Lou hid her face in her hands for a second, emerged with a wan smile.

"Tell them we went to New York, okay Carolyn? I've always wanted to live in New York."

"What will Cesar think?" Carolyn asked. "How much detail should I make up?"

"He won't be that interested," Mary Lou answered. "He'll replace me, that's all."

"It's that way, isn't it?" Carolyn said. "In all of politics."

"Ain't that the truth?" James echoed.

"I've liked it," Carolyn went on. "You take risks, you work hard, in every once in a while, like today, you realize you've got a winning cause. Then you come home to your friends."

Maybe she was still tipsy, he thought. She was usually so logical, and now one thought didn't have any connection to the next.

"We actually got used to each other," Mary Lou said.

"James's cooking got better," Carolyn added.

"Hey now," he responded. "I've always been good in the kitchen. My mama taught me—"

"His mama taught him—" Carolyn interrupted.

"And his auntie—" Mary Lou interjected.

"That you had to be nice to the ladies—"

"For them to be nice to you," the two women chorused.

"And they were *soo* right." Carolyn lay her head down on the cool, smooth green Formica and giggled. "And James was *sooo* nice, especially to his hostess, that she let him stay. In her bed."

Mary Lou laughed at this pronouncement to James's amazement.

"What was that saying of yours?" she asked Carolyn.

"Revolution in our lifetime?"

"No, that's James's. Your other one."

"'Tell no lies,'" Carolyn said.

"Hah!" Mary Lou snorted.

"'Claim no easy victories,'" James finished.

"We've had victories," Carolyn pointed out. "James hasn't been caught."

"Yet," he countered. "But I know one, for real. The march."

"We stayed friends," Carolyn said.

They managed to smile, but if it kept on like this, James was afraid the women would end up crying. "We still got to pack," he said.

"You do it," Mary Lou told him. "Just fill them up. I don't know what to take anyhow. Get all the bathroom stuff in there, though, okay? And leave room for my bedspread. I've got to sleep now. No other choice."

"What time should I set the alarm?" Carolyn asked. "I've got a headache."

"Five a.m.," James said.

"How about six?" Carolyn said. "Might be better to walk on last thing. Less opportunity for anyone to check you two over."

Mary Lou left while they nailed down the last details, and by the time he got into their room she was in bed and asleep. He moved about softly and packed her bags. The last time he looked out the window, the clouds had taken back the sky and both moon and stars were gone.

CHAPTER THIRTY-TWO

When the alarm went off at six a.m. in the pitch dark, James was dreaming of home. Outside their house with his brother Ronnie, little kids looking up from underneath at the thin palms, endlessly tall, that lined their mother's street. The next instant he was on his feet and in a hurry. He stepped around Mary Lou's suitcases, piled high with her stuff, to collect his own things, quiet to begin with but ready to make a racket if that was what it took to get her up. He pulled on the pants, shirt, and jacket he had laid out the night before. The same exact outfit he had arrived here in.

He hit the kitchen, splashed himself with water to get alert, and made up some coffee. All he had to do was shave, get dressed, and put bathroom stuff in his toilet kit. He was almost ready to go. She had to wake up, and it had to be now. She would be tired. He would need the energy for both of them. The three of them. From this time on.

He got his own suitcase from where it had been by the door and headed to the bathroom through the bedroom instead of going down the hall so he could wake her. And there she was, still in bed but eyes wide open, sitting up straight, working at the bedspread with her fingers, gathering it up and letting it go. She stared right at him and said it.

"I can't leave with you, James."

"And why is that, Mary Louise, if you don't mind telling me." His voice was rising. "Why the hell not?"

"I thought I could, but I can't."

"Is it that oh-so-fatherly Mexican boyfriend of yours?" He found himself yelling.

Carolyn appeared at the doorway in a rumpled T-shirt that came down to her knees, rubbing her eyes. Good. He needed her here to keep him sane.

"Is he your reason, Mary Louise? Tell me, would you, because if it is, then I can just hate you for it and get the fuck out of here, which is what I got to do!"

"No, it's not Rojelio," Mary Lou said in a barely audible voice. "It's because I'm pregnant."

Tears rolled down her pale cheeks, but she managed to sound defiant at the same time.

"I believe I know that fact!" James shouted. He hauled his suitcase onto the bed and started throwing all the things back in that he had taken out the night before.

"Then and still, it's good you repeat it," he added in a savage tone. "Otherwise maybe you'd manage to change your mind about that too. Maybe it isn't even true!"

"I remember the night you got here, James." Mary Lou stayed right where she was to talk to him. "I opened my mouth to tell you one thing, and the opposite came out. I hated it, and I did it more than once. But this isn't like that. I know what I have to do now."

"You say you're pregnant like I haven't even heard you, yet I've told you, Mary Louise. I am not the type to run off and leave an child behind!"

"It's not safe," she told him in a calm voice. "It's not safe for the baby."

Maybe if he had an hour or two, maybe if he begged her, maybe if he got Carolyn out of here and they managed to make love. Maybe that would convince her. He looked out the window. It was already getting light. It took at least an hour to get to Fresno. There wasn't any goddamned motherfuckin' time.

Carolyn shifted from one bare foot to the other, rubbed at the goose flesh on her arms, and then spoke up.

"You have got to get out of here, James."

Girl had said those exact same words to him so often, she sounded like a broken record. No arguing with her this time, though.

"Doesn't our baby need a daddy?" He appealed to Mary Louise.

"A daddy in hiding?" she asked. "We'll have to run to stay in front of the police, jump at every sound. And where's this father going to be? Cuba? Prague? Mexico? And even if we make it there safely, then it's live in a strange country with no friends. What kind of a life is that for our baby?"

That long, thin, straight hair of hers tangled like it would never come loose. She rapped it on down, looking straight at him the whole time. And him? He just stood there. If she did come with him, which she wasn't going do anyhow, but if she did come with him? She would hate him for it. There would be nothing but arguments. Rosetta all over again, and worse.

"I'll protect you and the baby both," he said dully.

"You'll want to," Mary Lou said. "But under the circumstances, you'll be lucky if you can protect yourself."

Mary Lou looked awful. Tears rolling down her cheeks, face crumpled like paper. And Carolyn, without half her clothes on, legs mottled and red, hopping back and forth to stay warm, nodding her head as if to say she had agreed to all this from the get-go. And him. Pissed off and miserable. The third fool.

The rising sun, above the horizon suddenly, shot light into the bedroom's east window. No clouds after all, no rain, nothing to conceal the fact that the time had come to fly right out of here. To spend time on all this was the one luxury he did not have. It was time. He had to leave. Alone.

Shoulders slumped in defeat, he closed his suitcase, picked it up, and walked out into the kitchen. He wanted to kiss Mary Lou one more time, but then again he knew he couldn't stand that.

So instead he would force coffee down his throat and do a last check in every room to make sure he had all his things. Next he and Carolyn would get in that Volvo just like they had so many times before, talk over the details, and roll right on down the road.

—ɷ—

By seven thirty a.m. Carolyn was driving James south on 99 to Fresno, exactly ten miles over the speed limit, and they were more than half-way to Fresno. The sun had risen, and the glare from the east was strong enough that she had to put her visor down and move it over to the side.

Sixty-five was risky, she was thinking, but then again there weren't many cops on the road this early. They needed the refund on Mary Lou's ticket, and the worst thing of all would be to miss that airplane. James hadn't objected, so she decided to leave the speedometer right where it was.

"She'll be all right," Carolyn told him. They had both heard Mary Lou retching at the toilet before they got out of Joseph Street. "She can come later, James. You get set up. Send for her and the baby. It's you I'm worried about."

He said nothing.

"You'll have to buy a winter coat first thing," she said.

"All right." His voice was dull.

"It'll be expensive," she added. "But I'd say get a good one."

She watched his curt nod from the corner of her eye. After this she might never see him again. Better that than visit him in jail or go to his funeral, she supposed. Their time together was diminishing, only a sliver left.

"Take a bus to the Loop; that's what they call the downtown. They have good stores there, and you should do it right away. Otherwise you're gonna look strange, plus you'll freeze."

She glanced at him sideways again. She knew he wasn't happy, but his traveling clothes were clean and pressed, he had on his dark glasses, and his face was set for the street. Chicago would suit him fine. Next she chided herself. He hadn't even left yet. It wasn't right to look forward to the relief.

"So this makes me like Patsy's boyfriend, right?" he asked all of a sudden. "What's his name?"

"You are not one bit like Chuey Vargas, James. He didn't want to be around Patsy, much less have her leave town with him. He finally claimed someone else was the father, which he knew was not true."

"What's the cat's real name?" James asked her. "Chewy is not a real name."

"Chuey is the nickname for Jesus. Jesus Vargas."

"Me and Chewy. The bubblegum twins." He cracked a smile, and she laughed, too loud. If he could keep it light, then she could do it too.

They pulled into the airport parking lot at 7:50, and he was out of the passenger side to get his suitcase from the back before she even turned off the motor. Walk slow, she told herself once they got under way. Don't act any more unusual than they already were. One black, one white, both nervous. One tall, one short, one suitcase bouncing from his hand between them. Look casual, inconspicuous, as if all this were the most natural thing in the world. It was the last time they would have to do this. Guilt stabbed at her. Last time for her, that is. James, if he was lucky, would have to do it forever.

Not James, Robert. Charles Brown had lasted for twenty-six years. Robert Johnson, hopefully, would make it at least that long. James, whom she and Mary Lou had gotten to know so well, was the short-lived one.

"The code, for any number you need to give me." She muttered the incantation as they entered the airport's sliding doors. "Get a post office box, find a pay telephone, send the address as a backup when you have one. Use the code."

"We've been over all this, Curls," he told her. "Got it down."

"Think they'll give you a refund for her ticket?" she asked.

"I'm gonna try. I need the money."

Once inside she didn't quite know what to say among strangers in the straight world. She stood apart, as though she weren't even acquainted with this man while he checked in, handed over his bag, and was told he would have to go to another office to get his money back. Probably never happen, she thought. Too risky to show that new identification before he left the country any more often than necessary.

Together they took the final walk to the gate where, between purple velveteen ropes, the boarding process was well under way. Everything had that impersonal metallic airport look, and she shivered in the air-conditioned cold. By the time they got up there, they were alone with the ticket taker; everyone else must already be in the plane. She had just formed the words to begin her goodbye when he gave her a hug so quick she wasn't even certain it happened, then turned on his heel, showed his ticket, and disappeared into the accordion tunnel. James Sweet was gone.

CHAPTER THIRTY-THREE

Mary Lou shaded her eyes against the hot sun and looked out over the land. The housing camp was gone, nothing left but packed-down dirt all the way down to where the leafy green rows of vineyards, loaded with bulbous fruit, hung limp in the intense summer heat.

Of course, wouldn't Jensen be just the type to come up with the plan to destroy the housing camp in retribution for the march? Serve the danged three-day eviction notices on April first, just ten days after the event? Never mind that these families had lived here ten or twenty years. Make sure each and every one of them got the point. You cross Colonia and you have got to go.

The Union lawyers got the workers and their families a thirty-day extension from the Fresno Superior Court. Dolores Huerta drove down from La Paz and gave a speech about how feudalism ought to be over by now, and how it would be better to be out from under Colonia's thumb. And then they all had to move out.

Most of the people found other housing nearby. Some ended up on the coast and others went back to Mexico. As for the camp itself, after it was vacant, the entire place had been torn down and hauled away within days.

She'd been so angry she couldn't stand to come out to see what the site looked like until now, in mid-July, almost four months after the march. Nothing left behind. Not even a corner of the cinder block the houses were made of. Just the full, leafy plane trees and the bark they shed onto the hard, dry ground.

She picked up a piece of that tough outer tree cover and worked hard at ripping it into shreds. Once, when they had the celebration last summer after the strikers got out of jail, the people had slaughtered a goat and served up stew right under this tree. Families with their kids underfoot everywhere stood around on the patchy grass, cooking, laughing, drinking beer. Someone put a *cumbia* on a record player and everyone danced, grandparents down to the five-year-olds, even her and Rojelio.

She never would forget Carolyn's face when Chuey Vargas told her that she was eating *cabrón* that day. He translated, then tossed in an explanation of *pinche cabrón* for good measure. "Asshole," he said it meant, but she thought of it as more like a fool. Just the word "goat" had been enough for Carolyn. She looked as if she was gonna be sick right then and there, and after Chuey left she hid her full plate behind the beer keg and never touched it again. Chuey Vargas. *Pinche cabrón.* But that tiny Manuel of Patsy's? So cute, so sweet.

She sat down with a small groan and leaned back on the tree's solid trunk, knees apart to brace the body. Not that she was tired. The women always said the middle trimester was the easiest, and so far she had more energy than ever. Only thing was, it was getting more difficult to move around.

She stared out at the vines. Row after row, their broad, dark green leaves shielded the powdered purplish clusters of hard grape that everyone would fight over two and a half months from now. Colonia would bring in its scabs for the harvest, and there'd be more people out on the picket line than ever. No one was giving up. *Mas tiempo que vida.* The boycott would bring them to their knees. Colonia had to be worried. She'd heard boycotts like this could become permanent, that eventually people changed their buying habits once and for all.

She put her hand on her belly. Things had been quiet since the march. The growing mound of her stomach had seemed unreal until, right in the middle of that one particular meeting with Lupe, the Mendozas, Basilio de la Cruz, Rebecca Flores, everyone talking about how to keep anything at all going on around here now that the action was over, the first tiny kick made her stomach jump. After that baby knocked on her insides, Mary Lou understood. She wasn't producing anything like fruit off a vine. It could only be a child.

Her baby would probably look black. Light-skinned, but with its father's flared nose, his soft deep lips. She hoped its hair would be crimped; she needed the baby to remind her of James.

She missed him. At first, when the hormones made her want it so much she'd end up rubbing against every door frame she could find when she was alone, it'd been the weight of him she missed, on her, over her, around her. But she'd moved on to a new stage, more difficult. Now she missed his company, his smile, the cadence of his voice.

She knew where he was, of course, through Carolyn. For a while he was in Prague, but it got too lonely for him there where hardly anyone spoke English. So he risked London. He was still there, waiting on the Cubans after all this time. She'd been the one to pick up his passport from the post office box and send it on to Berkeley. Just that much had about given her a conniption. So after that she decided. Direct contact was out of the question. James had other people to protect him, but no one else besides her could keep this baby safe. Still, she hungered for every bit of secondhand news about him.

Pearl. Or Robert if it was a boy, call him after his daddy's third and final name. She rubbed at the gold ring on her left hand. The farmworkers were polite, as she knew they would be, and no one dared to ask her to her face.

Rojelio spoke to her about it once before he left, at Jovita's. He found her there dawdling over coffee, slid onto the smooth red Naugahyde right next to her and started in, talking without thinking.

"How could you?" His voice was angry but his face was hurt.

"I fell in love with him, Rojelio." She kept herself real still, surprised that she could put it out there so simple like that.

"And us? We didn't mean anything to you?"

"We meant a lot. We were good friends."

"Friends!" He gave out a derisive snort. "You think that's all I cared about?"

"The rest of it was never quite right."

"For you, you mean."

"Yes. For me."

Her hand strayed to touch her stomach, inevitable these days, and he noticed what she did, as always.

"But he's gone now," Rojelio said.

"Yes."

"Will you join him?"

"No."

"Then why not come with me? Back to Detroit. With a baby on the way Cesar would make sure we got housing. We could even get married if you wanted."

Shocked, she stared at him.

"You'd raise a baby that wasn't yours?"

"Why not? No one would have to know."

She thought about what he was saying, got all the way to how much easier it would be for her and the baby, and knew in the next second that she couldn't do it.

"It wouldn't work, Rojelio. But thank you."

"You afraid the baby would look, you know, too dark? My skin is blacker than his was, *m'hija*."

"I know." She placed her hand over his. "You need someone else, Rojelio."

He'd gotten up then, even though Jovita had just brought him a hot full plate of cheese enchiladas and rice and beans, and left the restaurant as fast as he could. And now he was long gone, picketing stores in the Detroit heat, pressuring labor unions, back to the boycott.

Carmen at law school, Hank wherever he took that tired broken body when the excitement was over. Jack, Aurelio, Teófilo, each in their own area, giving out orders left and right. And herself, still in Allen, getting people ready to picket when the harvest began, but with a body shape that showed the world she hadn't always been alone, and never would be again.

She'd figured out what she would say when people finally did inquire. In fact, she'd already tried it on her own mother:

"The father? An old friend of mine. He did it as a favor, so I'd have my baby to raise. He lives out of the country."

Of course her mother's face had gone all sour, and that was without even knowing that the baby's father was black. Mexican was bad enough, though, so she'd said don't look to anyone in the family for help, but that'd been true for a long time anyway.

She would be the one to keep this child safe. If she wanted, she could accept Carolyn's offer and go on up to her place for the birth. It would be near the holidays. She and Carolyn shared a kitchen well, not so easy for two grown women. Her old friend had sounded downright cheerful last week on the phone, what with a new job at that hippie *Whole Earth Catalogue* magazine, and some guy she had met there as well.

Maybe after she had the baby, they could even stay on in Berkeley. She could work on the boycott or go back to teaching. Maybe Carolyn would be gone so much that her apartment would be big enough for all of them. Maybe James would come back someday, though for the life of her she could not imagine how that would come to be.

All three of them had been face to face with fear while they were out here together. Some of it was obvious—that James would be caught, that the march wouldn't come off. But what they had also been scared of was loneliness. And they'd had no choice but to look the panic right in the eye and just keep on going. Already two of them had come out happier than they'd been before this whole mess began. The one to worry about was James.

Not that his life was all bad. He'd made friends with a bunch of West Africans, and he got work painting houses when he could, hawked watches and transistor radios the rest of the time. Still and all, he was so far from home, so uncertain still where he would end up, and the money that people sent wasn't that much and wouldn't hold out forever. At least he wasn't dead or in jail. But James's life was the hardest, by far. Always had been and always would be, which was not one bit fair.

She leaned against the tree and closed her eyes. His face close by hers, that soft mat of hair, those big sensuous lips closed over hers. And then there would be the baby. Smooth skin, coffee and cream like its daddy's, all over a chubby little body, and all hers to kiss and hug and hold. She dozed, then startled awake when a familiar green and white pickup rolled up the circular drive that now led to nowhere.

Jensen leaned over to crank the passenger window down.

"You're trespassing, aren't you, Mary Lou?" he asked her.

"Well, well, well. If it isn't *la rata blanca* himself." Angry and dreamy at once, she didn't care what she called the man anymore.

"How can you live with yourself?" she went right on. "How can you decide to throw families out in the cold, Jensen?"

"I told you," he whined. "I warned you, and I warned Rojelio."

"So what, Jensen? You want me to give you a medal?"

Truth was, though, she had no legal right to be here now that the workers were gone, and she knew it. She hauled herself to her feet and started off at a slow but steady pace toward the property line. He drove along even with her, so close she could hear the static from his two-way radio.

"You should have laid off that march," he said.

"Why, so you could have a clear conscience? I bet for the rest of your life you're gonna dream about all the little kids who used to play right here."

"I don't make the rules any more than you do," he sputtered. "You people went on strike, damn it! That means war."

James might have said Jensen was right, the Revolution being no tea party and all. As for Carolyn, she probably would've found a reason to feel sorry for this worm. But all Mary Lou wanted right now was to speak her piece. She stepped onto the macadam of the public road and turned toward where her car was parked.

"I know, I know, you were just following orders," she told him. "That's what they said when they put the Jews in the ovens, Jensen. That's what they say when they napalm babies in Vietnam."

Did she really say all that? Was it even true that this farmworker situation was like two of the worst things she could think of in the history of the world? True enough, dang it! You couldn't treat people like *caca* all the time and still have everyone be polite while you pushed them around. She had finally told him how she really felt.

Jensen's red face twitched with emotion, and for the first time ever she understood he could be at least as angry as she was.

"What did you expect?" he yelled at her. "Cookies and milk? Tea and crumpets?"

"We expect all too little," she told him. "And we want everything you already have. But we'll get what we need. It may take us awhile longer, and lucky you, 'cause you get to stay comfortable while you try to keep us in line. But you know what? We won't give up. Not ever."

Jensen made a U-turn, gunned his motor, and peeled off. For a second she was breathless. She had made Jensen listen to her at last. The next thing was that the whole conversation struck her as funny, so she stuck her stomach even farther out than it already was, and she whooped into the hot, sullen air until there were so many tears she couldn't tell if she was laughing or crying.

Acknowledgments

There are two people without whose help this book would not have been published. One is my editor, Michael B. Kaye, whose unflagging encouragement enabled me to complete the task. The other is poet Kay Lindsay, whose literary friendship over the years and belief in me as a writer with vision, have sustained me. Finally, I would like to thank my husband, Walter Riley, who has always urged me to follow my heart in matters concerning this book.

Author Barbara Rhine is a lawyer, activist, grandmother, tennis player, and amateur pianist. She lives in Oakland, California. Read her blog on books and politics at barbararhine.wordpress.com. Click on "literature" for her novella *The Lowest Form of Animal Life,* published long ago.

CPSIA information can be obtained at www.ICGtesting.com
Printed in the USA
LVOW11s0102291014

410992LV00010B/1903/P